PRAXIS

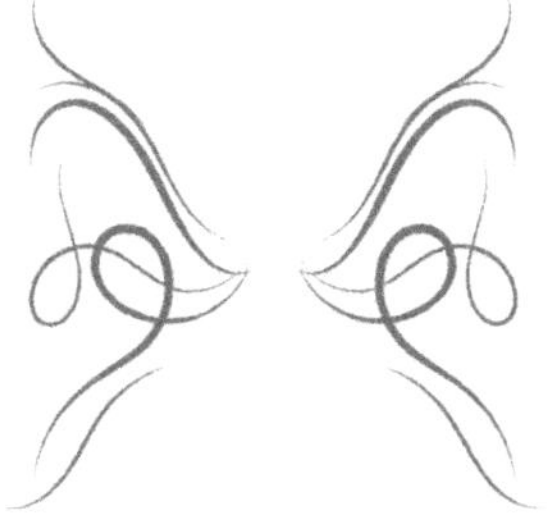

Also by C.A. Fox
PARADOX, Book One
PROPHECY, Book Two

PRAXIS

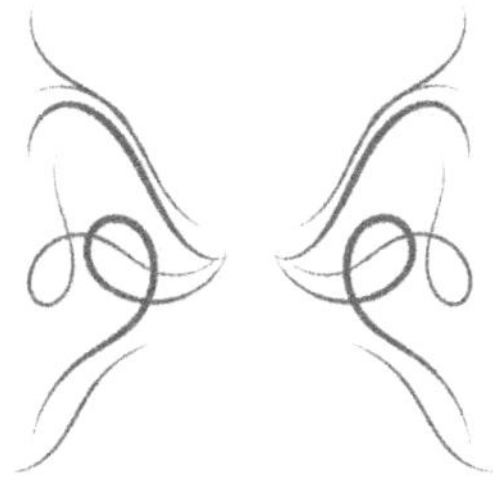

C.A. FOX

Book Three of the PARADOX Trilogy

Surrogate Press®

Published in the United States by
Surrogate Press®
an imprint of Faceted Press®
Surrogate Press, LLC
Park City, Utah

SurrogatePress.com

CAFoxbooks.com

ISBN: 978-1-964245-22-5

Library of Congress Control Number: 2025915213

Book Cover design by: Michelle Rayner, Cosmic Design
Interior design by: Katie Mullaly, Surrogate Press®

This is a work of fiction. Any resemblance to actual persons living or dead is simply coincidence.

For
Adrian and Willoughby

"We are here. We will work together for what purpose
seems to us right. We will work with calm, and with
tolerance and, please God, with saving laughter."
Dorothy Dunnett, *Checkmate*

THE KNOWNLANDS

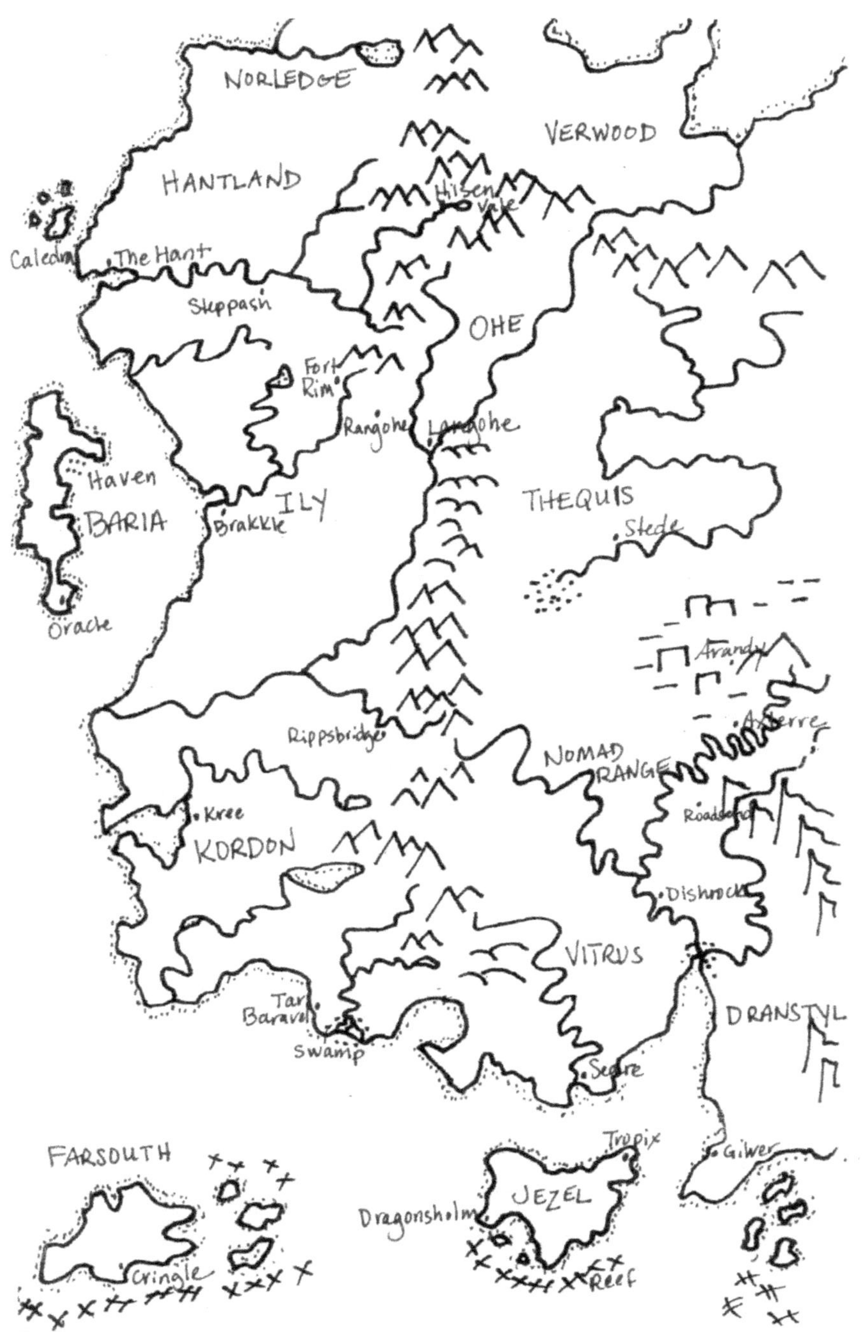

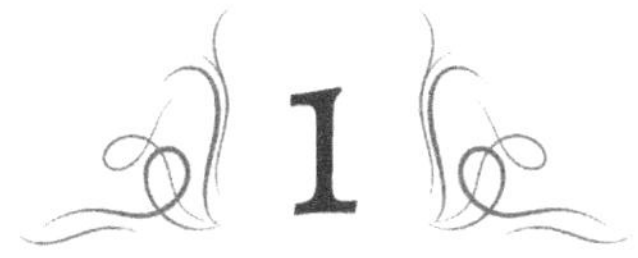

The flames roared to the ceiling, exploded through the red tiles of the roof, and climbed toward the hot sun.

"My lord!" screamed the librarian, writhing against the wall as the fire sucked the oxygen out of the room. "Highlord!"

Arms raised in the midst of the inferno, Dragon Highlord Raggar didn't hear anything but the flames of his own frustration. "Useless!" he shouted. "Dragon-blasted useless!"

"Highlord!" the librarian screamed again. Others were running now with buckets of water, but these puny splashes had no effect on the Highlord's magical fire.

The books and scrolls he'd been studying curled and whitened and rose as ash to the shimmering heat above Seare.

At last the librarian peeled herself away from the wall. She took a bucket from one of the others and aimed its water at the Highlord rather than at the flames.

"Highlord Raggar! Please stop!"

As suddenly as they'd begun, the flames were gone. A few wisps of smoke followed the greater plume now blowing away to the east.

The Highlord pushed trembling hands through his wet hair. "Goddess *damn* it."

"I am sorry our resources didn't satisfy you, Highlord," the librarian growled. "But those were ancient and valuable texts. Now I also have a roof to mend."

The Highlord's brown eyes swept up to the blue sky now visible through the smoking hole in the roof. "It won't matter," he said softly, in a voice rough with anguish. "It won't matter, your roofs, your precious, useless documents that tell us nothing we don't already know. It won't matter when the beasts come back."

"Look, Highlord, not everyone has achieved your level of learning. Our texts, our resources here are, or *were*, the most comprehensive in all the Desert Knownlands. We do not appreciate having them incinerated."

The Highlord flicked his magic and instantly his light silk robes dried. He frowned at the librarian. "Incinerated," he echoed. "How can you claim to have a comprehensive archive of information when you have nothing concrete about Axterre?"

"It's a myth, my lord. Myths aren't concrete."

"Goddess," Raggar swore. "So, nothing exists, or existed *ever*, unless you happen to believe in it?"

The librarian knew when her rhetoric was defeated. She gave the Highlord a very shallow obeisance. "May I escort you out, Highlord?"

"Don't bother."

Nevertheless, she followed the Highlord out of the ruined reading room, through the great hall, where other scholars stood in round-eyed silence as the most powerful Dragon Magician in the Knownlands swept past them.

At the far end of the room, just before the wide steps descended to the tall entry doors, the Highlord stopped and appeared to choke as he saw something at his feet. He said nothing but fled down the steps and ran from the building.

Those left behind watched as the Archive's fat and well-known cat jumped to a reading table and looked at the quiet crowd with sentient eyes. "He's right," the cat said distinctly. "Axterre isn't a myth."

The resulting pandemonium damaged the Searan Archive almost as much as the Highlord's angry fire.

"More wine, Raggar?" Raef Raegis refilled the Highlord's glass without waiting for an answer. Raef had been the Vitran Royal Dragon

Magician for longer than Raggar had been alive. In fact, it was Raef who had recognized the vast magical potential in the skinny street runner with the dirty face and quick hands. He had extracted him from the glass factory, taught him how to harness his Dragon force, and finally sent him to Dragonsholm for proper training.

Raef poured more wine into the cup before the Oracle's priest then his own glass. His wicker chair creaked as he resumed his seat. The breeze coming through the sheer curtain was hotter than the air here on the shady patio, but Raef didn't notice the heat of summer in Vitrus. His whole essence focused on the wildly fluctuating flow of Dragon force.

It was so unusual, so wrong, for Raggar's magic to waver like a guttering flame. One minute it was smooth, but weak, and Raggar had never been weak. Then it exploded like a wildfire consuming dry grass, annihilating everything in its path. Or it would, if Raggar didn't manage to hold on to it somehow. Raef, powerful as he was, knew he himself would not have had the discipline or force to subdue such wild vacillations.

The priest, Al-Sefir, sighed. "It may not comfort you, Highlord, but mystery lies at the heart of the goddess."

"Mystery?" Raggar said through gritted teeth. "It's *misery* that we will face if I cannot control the magic, if I lose my grip." His voice cracked, and he paused to drink off half his glass of wine. "If I lose my grip on the magic, every Dragon across the Knownlands will be unable to control his or her spells. Think of the horrible accidents! The infernos! The devastation.... It would be better if I were dead. Then the magic could lapse into its quiescent state as it does between Highlords. Maybe."

Raef saw the torment in Raggar's eyes, and his old heart hurt. "I know you will do what is best for the Dragon force, son. And I know you will not be rash in your decisions. But we cannot be sure the magic will be quiescent."

The Highlord ran the cool glass along his forehead. "No. We can't be sure of anything."

Al-Sefir pulled a small booklet from his gray robe. "Let's write down what we are sure of, Highlord. I have found that making a list can give coherence to situations that otherwise seem quite desperate."

"It will be a short list." Raggar sagged into his chair.

Raef made a temple of his bony fingers. "We know that the new Weaver accessed more power than has been available in centuries, perhaps millennia."

Al-Sefir's pencil scratched across a page. When it stopped, Raggar spoke: "We know that the dragons are returning to the Knownlands."

"We *know* this?" the priest asked carefully. "This list should be just what we are certain about."

"We know it," snapped Raggar. "The Oracle said as much, and I can feel them. You too, Dragon Raef. You can feel them, can't you?"

The old white head nodded. "I have felt the enhanced flow of Dragon force, the deeper current. I didn't know the source, but now it seems obvious."

"Dragons," Al-Sefir whispered. "Sweet goddess. We face a second dragon interregnum?"

"You can see why I'm concerned," Raggar snarled.

Al-Sefir took a deep breath. "Do we know when they're coming?"

Raggar shook his head. "I told you it would be a short list."

Al-Sefir looked bleakly at his booklet. "A more powerful Mystic. Dragons returning. Deeper Dragon force too. What else do we know?"

"Axterre," Raggar answered. "Axterre was not a myth. They worshiped something called the cat god. And the magicians there, or the Oracle, knew how to turn the dragons away."

"Cat god?" the priest snorted.

"Don't take that tone with me," Raggar growled. "This is also something we know. Cats are somehow related to dragons. Each one I see morphs into a small dragon. Some even spit fire. Lately, they've begun to talk to me."

"What do they say?" Al-Sefir kept his head down, writing.

"A bunch of drivel, usually." Raggar finished his wine. "But one in Dragonsholm told me to find the cat god. And a skinny old tomcat in an alley in Gilver called it the Cat God of Axterre."

"Axterre." Raef mused. "That's what you were searching for in the Searan Archive today?"

"Aye. But there was nothing there other than the poem. It's as if that one poem is supposed to encompass all the history, all the relevant knowledge anyone could ever require."

"Well, it is taught across the Knownlands," Raef said.

"But only to advanced scholars and some of the more conscientiously educated nobles," Raggar clarified. "They didn't even have a complete copy in Dranstyl."

"I'm afraid I don't know it," admitted Al-Sefir.

"Listen:" Raggar spoke:

> *"Far away to the south and east*
> *There the dragons come to feast,*
> *Confluence of sea and air:*
> *Cornerstone of old Axterre.*
>
> *Once the ocean lapped the wood*
> *An ancient henge sacred stood.*
> *Earthquake blocked the ocean's bay*
> *A river runs there to this day.*
>
> *On this site they built a tower,*
> *And from this root sprang the flower.*
> *A city broad and wide and fair*
> *Flourished in the sunshine there.*
>
> *Such wonders could their craft create*
> *That they were blinded to their fate.*
> *Denying goddess, moon and sun,*
> *They let their pride have full run.*

They lost their link with earth and beast
Exploited both at their feasts,
Ignored the fouling air and stream,
Lost in their self-centered dream.

Their dirty magic went astray
Explosions turned the night to day.
Acidic rain fell from the sky.
Those below prayed to die.

The boulevards ran with blood,
Tears and screams, a molten flood.
Buildings fell and fields flamed
'Till few were left, or so 'tis claimed.

With souls disfigured by their pride,
Flesh scorched and scarred they went to hide,
Snarling, gnashing, none that wept
To live like beasts upon the steppes."

The Highlord stopped and cleared his throat. "One version I found in the back of the library at Dragonsholm had a final stanza, scrawled in a different script. It's clearly not part of the Featherfetch poem, but it seems apropos to my search:

Is Axterre a myth or true?
Fear the cycle coming due.
Answers lost still are known
Engraved upon the Cornerstone."

"So, it's in ruins, Axterre, but not a myth." Al-Sefir said after a few moments of silence.

"One supposes." Raggar had pulled aside the curtain to stare across the heat-beaten rooftops of Seare. He spoke softly. "*Far away to the south and east*.... I can't use Dragon force. I dare not."

Raef slowly and rather painfully stood from his chair. He walked to the Highlord and put a hand on his sweaty shoulder. "You have the strength to do this, son."

Raggar smiled without humor. "Dragon Raef. I've lived more than half a century. No one has called me son in more than thirty years. And my strength is not reliable."

"Your magic is shaky, true," Raef said softly. "But that was not the strength I meant. Your soul, Raggar, must face this paradox."

Raggar choked. "What paradox?"

"You, who are the center of all Dragon force, you must work against the very source of your power if we are to avoid another dragon interregnum."

Al-Sefir watched the two Dragon Magicians and suddenly the air seemed to shiver. He felt the great peace of the holy mother and recognized the magical shove of the Oracle.

"I am adding a last item to our list," the priest said, the magic filling him with golden light. "We know that Raggar must find Axterre, but he does not have to go alone. In fact," Al-Sefir looked up. "In fact, a representative of the Oracle should go with him."

Both Dragon Magicians had felt the Oracle's magic, and they stared at the priest whose voice rang with the glory of his devotion: "I will go with you, Highlord Raggar, and together we will find Axterre."

Four men stood bound on the dock, their bodies chained to giant boulders. Behind them the water of Drix Harbor sparkled in the summer sun; before them an angry crowd of Barians jeered and cursed. Off to the side, a fifth man was bound and gagged and tightly held by three fierce guards.

Sealord Bryx V watched the crowd and judged his timing. He stepped forward as the breeze lifted his cloak and made him look even larger than he was. His voice carried across the crowd that fell silent to listen.

"Good people of Baria, for more than two thousand Risings, the Sharkins have held the Helm of Baria. We serve Baria willingly, with our lives and our blood, but to spill it, as these men did, is treason!"

The crowd roared.

Bryx nodded and raised his arms for silence. "They shall surely die, for drawing Sharkin blood. But these four will die quickly because we acknowledge that they, too, fell victim to a greater traitor. And now, Lord Admiral, when you are ready...." The sealord turned his round, pale Kordish eyes to his brother.

Standing quietly next to the Weaver, Jax had not expected to give the order for execution. He gave no sign of his surprise and stepped purposefully to the bound men.

"Mercy, milord," pleaded one of the men. "I've a motherless son."

"You should have thought of him when you were helping Dury chop off my finger."

"But please, sir—."

"Where is the child?"

"With the cobbler on Ayx."

Jax wanted to blame Bryx for these executions. When he'd put himself at the mercy of these men, he'd assumed the sealord would rescue him before anything truly terrible had happened. He should have known better than to trust Bryx to see the opportunity a speedy rescue offered him.

Now these men and Dury and their families would pay for Jax's miscalculation.

"I will see to your son," Jax said quietly to the condemned man. His eyes met Logil's. "We all made bad choices. I will pay wergild to each of your families."

He turned to the crowd and lifted his bandaged hand and his voice: "May the goddess care for your souls." His hand dropped and with it the boulders splashed into the water, dragging the men under. Bubbles of dying breath broke the surface of the water. The crowd stamped their feet, and the quay boomed and shook with their approval.

Jax returned to his place beside Klaris and the lords and ladies of the Floating Islands. The three guards now dragged the last man forward. The prisoner began to scream behind his gag.

The sealord's voice was louder. "This man, Dury Axyian, will suffer a traitor's death for inciting others to treason and for spilling royal Sharkin blood!"

"Feed the shark!" Cried a lone voice from the crowd. "Feed the shark!"

As the daughter of a royal house, Klaris de Farsouth understood the theoretical need for bloody spectacle as one means of keeping order, and she was grateful that treason and its horrible consequences were rare.

"Have you seen this before?" she asked Jax softly.

He just shook his head.

The crowd was now chanting: "The cage! The cage!" A system of pulleys and cranes towed a large cage through the clear water of the bay where guards in Royal Barian livery lashed it firmly to the quay. A dark figure swam within the metal bars, its black fin slicing the surface of the water with silent malevolence.

"First a finger," the sealord was saying almost casually. "Like the finger you took from Prince Jax." A knife flashed. A small bloody object sailed into the cage. With fearful speed, the shark rose and its teeth gleamed in the sun.

"Another!" Demanded the sealord.

The crowd was screaming, as crazed with bloodlust as the shark in the cage. Dury continued to bellow and squirm. His blood splattered the executioners, who continued to chop off fingers, then toes, then ears, and finally hands and feet. Each bit of flesh increased the frenzy of both the shark and the crowd.

Klaris glanced at Jax, who was looking at someone across the crowd. He turned and said something to one of his secretaries then caught Klaris's gaze upon him.

"You're not enjoying this?" she asked.

"I am," growled the Sealord. "Listen to the people! They're loving this and loving our rule."

"This isn't the kind of thing we want people to love," Jax snapped. "Dury was no hero, but he was provoked. And I came too close to a traitor's death myself."

"The difference," Klaris said distinctly, "is that you were not a traitor."

Jax took her hand in his bandaged one and lifted his chin to watch the end.

Dury's struggles had grown weaker, but he still whined.

"Feed him alive!" a voice demanded from the crowd. Others took up the chant: "Feed him alive!"

The sealord smiled. "See, little brother? They're a blood-thirsty lot."

Jax shook his head. "Enough!" he called. One of the guards applied her sharp knife to Dury's throat, and the others threw the now silent body into the water.

The shark took the bloody corpse into the depths.

Under the roar of the crowd, only Klaris heard Jax whisper, "Holy mother, forgive me."

Bryx stepped forward. He paused to let the cheering stop. "Death to any who would harm Baria!" He had to pause again as the crowd bellowed. "Now my loyal Barians, this unpleasant business is finished. I bid you a good Gather! To the fleet!"

The crowd on the quay disbursed like the traitor's blood into the sea. The nobles on the platform were giving the sealord the one-handed Barian salute, but Bryx had caught sight of the glittering sapphire ring on Klaris's finger. He lifted her hand. "Where did you get this?"

"Jax gave it to me, Sire."

"But it was our mother's."

She nodded. "I am honored."

"It was not his to give!" Bryx snapped.

The lords and ladies of the Floating Islands, like the sealord, recognized the great Sharkin Sapphire, worn by Barian Consorts for centuries. It was a gift of love and a commitment and had never been given without a hand-fasting. The nobles of Baria well knew that the goddess's *Rote and Rede* prohibited marriages between the powerful, so the Weaver could never be a royal consort.

Still, after four years serving under the land-loving Bryx, the Barian nobility was so relieved to have Jax Sharkin as lord admiral they'd grant him just about anything. Lord Fellix, who was the widower of Seaqueen Pyrriv and grandfather to Bryx and Jax, stepped forward. "Actually, Sealord, the ring does belong to Jax." He dropped to one knee. "You honor us, Weaver."

The sealord was not as generous. "There's no honor here." He turned away and was gone with a billow of Barian Blue silk.

"Thank you, Grandad," Jax helped Fellix to his feet. "My lords and ladies," Jax addressed the remaining nobles calmly. "We have a Gather to launch today, and the tide turns in a few short hours."

They bowed and went to prepare their ships.

Jax took Klaris's be-ringed hand, lifted it to his lips and kissed it. "How's that for being master of my destiny?"

"Your Highness," the secretary called Jax's attention away from Klaris's inviting lips. He turned to find a small boy with a bandage on his face and a ragged woman standing with his secretary. Klaris felt the child's Mystic and recognized that here was the boy who had been in that horrible bilge slum with the traitors who'd held Jax.

"Thyl." Jax addressed the woman. "I was surprised to see you here today."

"I wanted to see the end of Dury, milord," she whispered. "He had some good in him."

"I am sorry it ended this way," Jax said.

Thyl blinked at him with wary surprise. "Dury had a bad end coming for a long time." Her hand gently stroked her son's bandaged cheek.

Jax lifted the boy's chin and looked into his sea-blue islish eyes. "Tell me your name, lad."

"Vigo."

"My lord," prompted one of the secretaries with a gentle shove to the boy's shoulder.

"Vigo, milord."

Jax knelt so he could look into the boy's face. "A man doesn't choose his parents, Vigo. And he doesn't always choose what he will be, either: prince, or sailor, or magician. But he can choose *how* to be."

"How to be what?" the boy asked, and then remembered, "milord."

"How to be a good person. How to treat other people. Dury was smart, and you are, too. But Dury chose to be cruel, especially to the people who loved him. There's no excuse for that."

"He died," Vigo whispered, his eyes wide.

"He made bad choices, Vigo."

Tears were pouring down Thyl's face. Vigo looked up at her as he felt them drop on his head. He scratched at the bandage on his cheek.

"You could have drowned me too, milord." Thyl whispered.

"No!" Vigo threw his little arms around her legs.

"No," Jax agreed, standing. "You were Dury's victim long before he found me."

Thyl went to her knees, embracing her son.

Klaris bent towards the small boy. "The Mystic is thick in you, Vigo."

Feeling Klaris's power wash over him, Vigo smiled, then cupped a hand on his painful cheek. "Your magic is lovely, Weaver."

"So is yours. You mind your mother now, and you study with Wexalay, the Royal Mystic here, alright?"

"Can I stay with me mum?"

"Of course."

"Then I will," said the boy, taking his mother's hand.

Klaris watched the secretary escort Thyl and Vigo away. The Mystic weave shook, and she heard Jax talking to someone about wergild as if he was far away.

"Klaris?" He took her shoulders, alarmed at the glassy look in her eyes. "Klaris!"

She let the weave unravel, her eyes still on the retreating figure of the boy. When she spoke, her voice was soft with awe. "Vigo. He'll be Weaver someday."

Jax stood on the quarterdeck of the *Sharkin* and tried to let the roll of the great ship fill the grief and emptiness within him. He pulled a small shiny chunk of obsidian from his pocket. Klaris had found it that morning, deep in her satchel, and remembered holding it when she'd first left home to study at Sageham. Shyly, she'd slipped it into his hand a moment before the nobles gathered for the execution.

"It's a piece of Jezel," she told him softly. "And my heart."

He ran his fingers over the black stone, and she'd clasped her hands around his. "Careful, it's sharp."

"The stone or your heart?"

"Yes." She smiled, and he laughed.

The memory of that shared moment hurt now. So did his missing finger. He picked at the wrapping around the fourth finger of his right hand and stirred at the erotic memory of Klaris's magic working within him to reconnect the severed bone and vessels of his finger. He made a fist and winced. Once again, he wondered why Barian druids were so averse to using a little poppy extract to ease their patients' pain.

He opened and closed his fist, hoping the pain in his hand would eclipse the ache in his heart. Yet again, he glanced at the distant sail of the *Eagle*, flying away from him towards the north, towards Sageham. Another voyage without her. He dreaded the long weeks of nightmare-riven sleep that loomed until he'd see her again.

Goddess damned duty. Normally, he loved a Gather, loved the chance to renew old friendships and rivalries, relished the chance to sample some interesting Barian lovers and be sampled in return. Of course, the final yacht race would be exciting in the big wind and waves of this Gather, held as it was in the rougher ocean Back of Baria. But even that prospect couldn't lift his spirits today.

He had a duty to Baria as the lord admiral to be at this and every Gather now and as long as he lived. But all he wanted to do was to follow the Weaver, even though she'd lead him to face dragons. And then what? The nightmares had illuminated the hideous destruction of all that he loved.

But he loved Klaris, too, and he'd made that fact clear to everyone, despite the sealord's anger. He smiled, as a little of his heartache eased as he remembered the joy in her green eyes this morning. He'd follow her just about anywhere to see that look again.

He watched the *Eagle's* sail disappear over the horizon and dropped the piece of obsidian back into his pocket. Turning away from the empty sea, he took in the line of great ships following in the *Sharkin's* wake. The fleet of Helm, carrying all full sail through the blue summer sea was a sight to lift his heart. Nightmares be damned, but he'd spent those sleepless nights scrutinizing the ledgers from the fleet, and he'd managed to have a few ideas beyond what he wanted to do with his wonderful Klaris.

"Captain Blanx, summon the captains of the fleet, if you please."

"Aye, Admiral."

Jax watched signal flags fly up the halyards and listened to Blanx give the orders to hove to. He went below to his cabin, where he let his steward put him into a finer Barian Blue coat and fuss over his wind-mussed hair.

The fleet captains of Helm were the nobles most closely allied with the Sharkin family. Jax greeted each of them as they arrived. He'd known them all his life. His steward handed out glasses of fine Darkwood wine.

Jax stood with his back to the big stern windows, which illuminated his captains' faces, while leaving his own in some shadow.

He raised his glass. "My lords and ladies, a toast to Sealord Rax."

"Aye! Aye!"

Jax had expected a warm response to that. He smiled. "And to Sealord Bryx."

"Aye, the sealord." The voices were a little less warm, but only a little. After all, the nobles of Helm were Sharkins, too, and had benefited from centuries of close ties with the sealords and seaqueens. Almost all of them had attended pre-gather meetings like this with Sealord Rax. They would strategize and plan how to win the team regatta and discuss which alliances were proving fruitful or problematic and should be addressed at the Gather.

"Let's talk about the team regatta first," Jax began. After an hour of somewhat circular arguments about how to beat Port Jorel's team, captained by Jax's grandfather, a legendary sailor who should, they thought, be on the crew for Helm, Jax finally brought the discussion to his ideas for new markets.

"My ladies and lords. Whether or not Helm takes the team regatta this summer, we have three new trade markets opening to us. I want to decide today who among us is best poised to seize these opportunities." He pulled out pages of notes he'd made after reading the fleet manifests.

"First, I want those of you with galleons to refit them to hold sugar and horses. The Kordish and the Farsouthians have signed a trade treaty, but they need us for the shipping. I've written out the details. We want to get on this before the other fleets realize how easy and profitable this market will be.

"The next has to be done very quickly. Those of you with lighters will also make for Kree, where you'll load Darkwood wines coming down on my barges from Twistford. Take them to whatever markets you like."

"The Vitrans love to drink the chilled white wines," one of the captains noted.

"I want to start this as soon as possible, before the Kordish customs agents realize we've avoided them. Once they catch on, we'll have to share a portion of our profits with the Kordish royal treasury."

"May they be blinded by their fear of water!" Another captain raised her glass.

"And finally," Jax paused for a moment. It was one thing to scheme with a mentor like Admiral Hix or dream with Klaris, but he was about to put his most daring idea into words in a public forum for the first time. He looked at the faces before him. They were charged, inspired, enthusiastic, and a little relieved.

"Finally, the heaviest ships will sail north with me to Hanter Lake. We'll be taking on iron ore."

"We're trading with the trolls?" someone asked, frowning.

Jax's smile was unkind. "Yes, in fact."

"But Admiral, after all you went through...."

"Exactly. This venture may not make as much money right away as the other two, but eventually I think we'll handle all the shipping from the iron mines across the Knownlands. It will be heavy work, but with significant profit."

"But the trolls use slaves!"

"Not for much longer. I'm going to put a stop to slavery in the Hanter iron mines, and you're going to help me. We'll all profit from it, although I'm going to offer this idea to Rillt's fleet too. They have more heavy freighters than the other fleets, and I want us to have lots of support when we're in The Hant. We must assume that the trolls will capture any islish person they can lay their hands on."

The sun was touching the western waves when the *Sharkin* again came up into the wind to let the other captains jump down into their launches and return to their own ships. The excitement among them was palpable.

Captain Blanx considered the lord admiral out of the corner of his eye as the *Sharkin's* sails were reset and the ship plunged over the waves. He'd felt a profound sense of nostalgia for the days of Sealord Rax as he watched Jax handle the nobles. But over the course of the meeting, the sadness had faded as he and the others realized the scope of what the young lord admiral was proposing. "Helm's fleet stands to make millions, my lord, on any one of your plans."

"I hope so. You have the helm, Captain."

Blanx saw the famous Sharkin wolf grin flash, and then the admiral was disappearing down the companionway. The captain took a long slow breath of summer sea air. After all the prince had been through during the past four years, enslavement to the trolls, anonymity somewhere in the forgotten hinterlands, a close brush with a traitor's death in Kree, and a strange entanglement with the Weaver, you wouldn't think the lad would have had any time to spare a thought for Baria, its fleet, or its economy. But apparently, he had. Blanx did a quick calculation. The admiral couldn't have seen more than about fifty-six Risings, that would put him at about twenty-four the way Landish people counted age.

He paced to the other end of the quarterdeck and frowned until the lieutenant called a correcting order to a man in the rigging. A sail snapped tight.

It would be very good for Baria to have Prince Jax back. Very good indeed, even if he proved to be as miserable a sailor as his brother.

The Weaver watched the blue sparkles fly from the sapphire on her finger and wove the crystal light into the rainbow spray coming off the *Eagle*'s bow wave.

"That's beautiful," a sailor breathed.

Klaris, startled, looked away from the waves and noted that at least half the *Eagle*'s crew had lined the rail to watch the play of light and Mystic. Feeling exposed by the emotion she'd allowed into her weave, she turned away for the privacy of the quarterdeck. But even here she couldn't tear her gaze away from the sapphire. She wiggled her finger under its unfamiliar weight.

It echoed the increasingly familiar weight in her heart. The weight of loving Jax Sharkin. It was a wonderful thing that sent rivers of joy singing through her veins, but it also made her vulnerable in a way she'd never experienced. Her grief when he'd renounced her so that Bryx would make him lord admiral mingled with the torment of her nightmares. Last night she'd slept for the first time since Jax had been made lord admiral. She still felt giddy with knowledge that despite all this, Jax loved her. But, goddess, she prayed that those nightmares would not return now that they were headed in separate directions again.

Like the weight of his ring on her finger and the tickle of his magic within her weavings, she'd have to get used to the impact of Jax Sharkin on her heart, in her life, and all the entanglements that came with him. She mostly wanted him in her bed, but that seemed unlikely, and not just because they were hundreds of miles apart.

But if Jax had duties and promises, she certainly did, too. What would she find on Sageham? How would she marshal the Mystic to heal and rebuild? Could she find the answers to the dragon problem that the Oracle themselves seemed to have lost among the ruins of Caledra? She didn't have to sleep to find nightmares. Taking a bracing breath of air, the Weaver went to find another hour of sun salutations.

The cold water felt good on her face and her tear-swollen eyes. She rinsed her face again, tasting the salt of her grief. She groped for a towel and felt the lad place it in her hand.

"Thank you," she mumbled behind the cloth. With an exhausted sigh, she slumped into a chair before the small fire. "I feel absolutely empty."

"That's the purpose of the ritual." Lad Yob poured tea.

Klaris leaned to the fire, her elbows on her knees. This far north, evenings were chilly even at midsummer, and this long day had been full of emotional intensity, from the moment the summer sun rose to illuminate the great rock of Sageham Isle off the *Eagle's* bow, leaving her chilled inside and out. Returning to the font of Mystic for the first time as Weaver had almost overwhelmed her grip on the weave.

First, she'd been flooded with power, but that was almost immediately counteracted by the grief both magical and personal of seeing Castle Caledra as nothing but jagged rubble. Caledra had been her home for half her life. Its teachers, students and the lads and lasses who served them had been her family.

Old Father Mallix performed yet another ritual to honor the dead and Klaris, drenched with the grief and sorrow of the other magicians who surrounded her, did not stifle her tears.

Now, she huddled before the fire in the makeshift shelter the survivors had erected and let the peace of emptiness restore her.

She sipped the tea. "It looks like the lads and lasses will have a new castle built before winter."

"Aye." Lad Yob leaned against the windowsill, watching the Weaver. "The rock is giving itself easily."

"Then we'll need to assemble the magicians to finish it." Klaris looked up at him.

"Aye." His face was in the shadow, but she heard the reservation in his answer and knew where it came from.

"Yes, I probably won't be here."

"Your destiny pulls you in many ways," he said softly.

She rose and joined him at the window, looking out into the long summer evening. The new building rose smooth and symmetrical in contrast to the ruin that lay out of sight. She considered its lines and the magic that imbued them. "Is this how the old Castle looked when you built it?"

"How could I know that, Weaver?"

"Don't be coy with me, Lad Yob. There's almost nothing written about the lads and lasses, for good reason, I suppose. But I've noted a few things: I've never seen a baby Sagehamite. None of you ever seems to age."

Lad Yob's gray eyes met Klaris's green ones. "Oh, we age, Weaver." His voice was laden with sadness. "Our hearts age."

Klaris saw her own grief magnified by lifetimes of love and loss, and for the first time in her twenty-four years, she considered the costs of immortality. But this evening, her own losses were enough to bear, and she returned to the topic at hand.

"I saw that Rhella and Yan Chuan are already here," she said, referring to the two tower-tested Mystics who had returned to Sageham from their homes across the Knownlands to help train more magicians.

"More will come," Lad Yob promised. "They know that Mystic needs them now that the other tutors are gone."

Klaris spoke softly, still looking out the window. "And I'll be gone too, but goddess only knows where."

"You will return after you have dealt with the dragons."

"I wish I had your confidence."

"Weavers of old did it, Klaris," he used her name gently. "You have everything they had."

"I don't have their knowledge. I don't know what I'm supposed to *do*."

The gold and white cat jumped to the windowsill between them. "You can find out," it said.

"Where?"

"You must find the Cornerstone."

"Which cornerstone?"

The cat shivered and turned into a fat little dragon. "The right one, of course." It spread its leathery wings. "Open the window for me, Weaver."

"Gladly," Klaris growled. She slammed the sill down after the dragon disappeared into the deep twilight. "Cornerstone. First, I have to find the last of the Oracle's damned prophecy."

A clear summer sun sparkled on the dark ruin of Castle Caledra the next morning. Lad Yob and Professor Essen followed the Weaver through the piles of rubble. Great wooden beams stuck up in jagged shards, like broken bones protruding from ruined flesh.

"Here's the cornerstone, Weaver!" a lass called from a pile of rock.

Klaris knelt and brushed at the ancient stone, its magic speaking to her as plainly as the lass. She felt a great and ancient power, confidence, the hint of a challenge, and a veil of mystery. With a sad smile, Klaris remembered her first arrival at Castle Caledra and coming across its threshold as an impossibly young Dock and Portal acolyte. Then too, she'd felt the same deep power, the challenge and the mystery. Now, as master of the Mystic, the confidence was hers.

Words had been etched in the granite of the cornerstone, but lichen now filled the ancient fossae, obscuring a text that few could still read.

Klaris brushed at the stone and a small wash of Mystic cleared away the growth and dust.

"*Castle Caledra*," Essen read aloud. "What's this word? Reconstructed?"

"Yes," Klaris answered. "Listen: *Reconstructed post banishment, Second Millennium.*"

"Second Millennium,' Essen gasped. "That's three thousand years ago!"

Klaris, kneeling with her hands on the rock looked up at Lad Yob. "The earthquake. It's a precursor, isn't it?"

Essen watched the Lad nod. "Precursor to what?"

"To the return of the dragons." Klaris rose, brushing her hands on her skirt. "See what the rest says here?"

Essen squinted and read slowly:

"*By these signs you shall know,*

The time has come.... I can't understand the rest."

Klaris, her head cocked to one side gazed thoughtfully at the words. "I wonder if this is part of the prophecy too."

"What does it say?" Essen asked impatiently.

Klaris read the Ancient smoothly.

> *"By these signs you shall know,*
> *The time has come like long ago.*
> *Leathern wings fly from the east,*
> *Fire-breathing dragon beast."*

"Dragons," Essen swore, sweat beading on his brow.

"Look," she brushed at more of the rubble and the script continued:

> *"Is the cat god myth or true?*
> *Fear the cycle coming due!*
> *Answers lost still are known,*
> *Engraved upon the Cornerstone."*

The lad shook his head. "Not, however, on this cornerstone, apparently."

Klaris put her hands on her hips. "Damn! Damn! Damn! *Damn!*" Suddenly exhausted, she sat on the cornerstone and let the Mystic seep into her. She'd had another good night's sleep, so her fatigue on this lovely morning didn't make sense to her. With a deep breath, she pushed herself up. "Let's go look in the library."

"We moved all the books, Weaver," Essen said following her deeper into the ruins.

"Did any of them have a spark of Dragon force in them?"

"Dragon force? I don't think so."

"Then it should still be down here."

The worn stone steps curved down into what was now a roofless pit. Dust motes swirled in the sun. Smashed bookshelves lay in stacks. Essen watched Klaris stand amid the wreckage. Sunlight gilded her dark curls and shone on the tears, wet on her cheeks.

"Weaver?" Lad Yob spoke gently.

She shook her head and wiped her face with a sleeve. "I spent so much time in here." She turned and walked into the shadows. "It was over here, by the shelf with all the texts on water features." She moved to a spot on the wall. The bookshelves here hadn't fallen, but they now stood empty.

Essen and Lad Yob felt Klaris summon her Mystic. The wooden shelves slid away, revealing a small room, a study, its roof still sloping up to the sky. Two windows looked out to the north, their glass dark with dust and age. Soot had fallen from the flue and spilled from the grate, blackening what had been a bright nomad-woven carpet.

A glass lamp lay broken across a desk, but otherwise the room was tidy and showed no sign of having been harmed by the earthquake. Klaris put out a hand. Ancient warding magic flashed blue and orange into the bright day.

"Ouch!" Essen cried. "I feel Dragon force when you do that."

"Indeed." Klaris's voice was thoughtful and her eyes distant. After a moment she stepped back. "You know your history of Weavers, Professor."

"Naturally. I teach it, you know."

"Let's call the others. I'd like your backing when we undo these wards. Rhella and Yan Chuan can help too."

"But why? What is this place?" Essen demanded.

"Weaver Seldona's study."

"Weaver Seldona? But she lived...."

"A thousand years ago," Klaris's clear green eyes bore into Essen's brown. "And she died at the beginning of the dragon interregnum, trying to drive the beasts away."

"I'll go get the others." Essen dashed away, his footsteps clattering on the stone steps.

Klaris sat again. After a few moments she noticed that Lad Yob was wiping tears off his own face. She put out a hand to him.

"Seldona was so brave," he whispered.

"Did you help her, too?"

The lad turned his gray eyes to the sky. "I could not. None of us could. We didn't know.... You see, the Axterrans had solved the dragon problem for two thousand years. But Axterre had fallen. Then the cats began to talk. An earthquake shook the Verwood and wrecked the Nyad henge. A great wave destroyed Old Tropix. We, the lads and lassies, remembered, and we showed Seldona the cornerstone you saw this morning, so we knew they were coming."

"What did she do? Where did she go?"

"I don't know. Lassie Melrona went with her and perished. We supposed."

Klaris sat for a moment watching dust swirl silently. "You'll go with me, won't you Laddie?" She looked up at him suddenly, her green eyes vulnerable.

"Of course. That is my honor, and my destiny."

"I hope it's not your death as well," she whispered.

"Weaver!" Rhella led a troop of Mystics down the stairs. "What's this Essen says about Dragon force lurking within the very heart of Caledra?"

"Didn't you ever feel it?" Klaris stood slowly, wondering again why she felt like she needed a nap.

"Certainly not." Yan Chuan snapped. "This place should be free of the taint of Dragon force."

"Taint?"

"Because it hurts; it stings!"

"Is that the fault of the Dragon force, or our own reaction to it?" Klaris asked softly.

Rhella reached out to touch the wards. Again, they flared blue and orange. "Ouch!" she yelped.

Klaris raised her voice so all the gathered Mystics could hear her. "In our study and practice we usually focus on weaving the Mystic, but unweaving can be just as important."

"Weaver," Chuan interrupted. "The power in these wards is ancient and brittle. With all the Mystic you accessed with your mastery, you have more than enough strength to pop them open. As do I, and Rhella, and Essen."

"Perhaps," Klaris agreed. "But it is unusual for a spell to last so long beyond the spell-caster's death. Why do you think this one did?"

Chuan shrugged, but she could see calculation in his eyes. No one became tower-tested without developing a healthy sense of caution. Klaris felt one of the other students probe the weave with her Mystic.

"There's something else in there with the old Weaver's power," she said her voice dreamy. "Like two magics entwined. It's a different power." The student stepped back suddenly. "It stings," she gasped.

Klaris nodded. "When Weaver Seldona died, the Mystic must have shifted so that this study was hidden. The bookshelf probably slid here, and anyone who tried to move it would have felt the sting of Dragon force."

"But you knew it was here all along!" Essen said accusingly.

Klaris shrugged. "Yes. I felt the bit of Dragon force here. I assumed everyone did."

The heads shaking around her puzzled her. Once again something that had been so obvious to her had not been at all evident to her fellow Mystics.

"There's more to it than that," Klaris said, hiding her exasperation. "This isn't the kind of Dragon force people use. It's from the big beasts themselves."

"How can you tell?" asked Chuan.

"The force is entirely different. It throbs rather than flows. Also, it's lasted for a thousand years. Go ahead, probe it for yourselves."

Klaris watched as one by one the magicians carefully explored the warding. Many of them stung themselves.

"Now, if I simply slice this ward open," Klaris said finally. "The magic will fly free, whipping strands of power like a flail. The Mystic is so old that it probably won't harm us, but that bit of Dragon force is an unknown quantity. It's fresh and strong, so I assume the dragon who somehow put it here is still alive."

"What? But this warding is a thousand years old!"

Klaris shrugged, suddenly chilly in the summer sun. "A dragon lives forever..." she quoted softly.

"That's a fairy poem for children," chided one of the Foundation Firsts.

Klaris rounded on the man. "Given the staggering lack of serious dragon scholarship, I'll go with whatever source I can find."

A woman from the forests of Ily cleared her throat. "There's always truth in fairy stories. It just may not be what you expect."

"Truth often involves a paradox," Klaris whispered, quoting the Oracle. "Now then, let's unravel these wards." She opened her weave so the others could see how she picked at the strands of Mystic. Carefully she isolated the thin currents of Dragon force. This would be the tricky part.

She nodded to Rhella and Chuan who wove their Mystic into hers. Klaris pulled the Dragon force free from the rest of the weave and rolled it into a glowing orange ball, encased in her own power.

She snapped her fingers and a clear crystal appeared in her hand. With a deft flash, she forced the Dragon power into the crystal and locked it there. The clear stone throbbed from the orange fire within it.

Then she unwove the rest of the magic.

"Ahhhhhhh," a soft moan echoed off the half walls.

"What the goddess was that?" demanded Essen, looking fearfully into the shadows.

Klaris peered into the crystal. "I think we just released the spirit of Weaver Seldona, Professor."

"Now," Klaris slipped the dragon crystal into her pocket and stepped into Seldona's study. "Let's see if she left us any clues as to where she met this orange dragon."

The other Mystics backed away. "Do you want more help, Weaver?" Rhella asked reluctantly.

"We should move these scrolls and books," Klaris said, looking at the wall of bookshelves in the study. "But let me review them first." She turned to glance at Rhella and saw the fear and resistance in the faces around her. "Lad Yob will assist me," she said, dismissing them and their anxieties. She moved toward the books, her attention already focused on the remnants of Seldona's Mystic. The ancient chair creaked as she sat in it. With a wave of her hand, the glittering shards of glass from the broken lamp disappeared.

She sat there for a moment, analyzing the weave then she opened the book. It was a journal. Klaris cocked her head to one side as she read the early pages, interested to note that Seldona had chosen to keep her diary in what was now called Old Islish rather than in the more common Ancient that all Mystics still used to weave their spells.

A thousand years ago, it would have been called Nekkian. Like modern Islish, Nekkian had been the language of all the island peoples from Baria to Farsouth to Jezel. In those days the Empire of Nec united the islish people. In fact, Klaris's own royal family claimed descent from the Nekkian stewards of Farsouth. When the dragons finally flew away, the remnant of the Islish people on Jezel and

Farsouth formed their own separate and autonomous governments. Six hundred years later, when the Barians finally brought their Floating Islands home, they had been content to rule only themselves, anchored as far from the ruins of Nec as the island's geography allowed.

Klaris had mastered Old Nekkian even before she'd come to Caledra. Rapidly she flipped through the pages, following Seldona's archaic script with increasing fluency. There was a tragic complacency to the ancient Weaver's concerns for small magical issues, petty Mystic politics, and her own pride, given the terrible history that was soon to follow.

"She was Jezellian, Laddie. Did you know that?"

He glanced at her from the bookshelf where he'd been reading the titles.

"Not many Jezellians born with Mystic these days," she continued.

"Not now." Lad Yob agreed. "But in Seldona's time there were no people with Dragon force."

"Of course not." Klaris's eyes turned back to the pages of the book. The journal wasn't full. The writing stopped about halfway through the pages. As she neared the end, Klaris finally found something that set her heart pounding.

"Listen to this Laddie: *A curious half-isle called Darden Sharlquin arrived last night. He says he and I are supposed to banish the dragons that are coming. Unfortunately, he doesn't know how this is to be achieved. He thinks the nyads or the fairies must know. Xantha finds him oddly compelling and says the magic wants him, somehow.*" Klaris translated the Old Nekkian into Ancient.

"Xantha," Lad Yob repeated softly.

Klaris flipped back a few pages, paused, then went back further. "This Xantha was an impossibly young tower-tested magician, according to Seldona." Klaris glanced wryly at Lad Yob. "Seldona admits that Xantha has far more magic than she herself, but the Mystic wouldn't give her a Secret. So, when Seldona found her own

Secret, she went ahead and mastered the Mystic. Before that, Mystic had been without a Weaver for ten years."

Klaris stopped, her eyes focused on her own speculation. "Wasn't Xantha the Weaver after Seldona? She was the first Weaver during the dragon interregnum."

"Aye," the lad said heavily. "Xantha Cloverdale."

Klaris's eyes sharpened upon him, as Lad Yob went on.

"Xantha blamed Seldona for the dragon interregnum, you know. She blamed Seldona for not banishing them."

Klaris dropped her eyes to the last pages of the book and read a bit more. "Seldona sent this Darden Sharlquin away to find the answers. Once he'd gone, she discovered something in Caledra's vast library. She tried to scry for him but couldn't find him." Klaris looked up at Lad Yob. "Sweet goddess."

"The paradox who can't be found," he quoted softly.

Klaris dipped her nose back to the book. "Poor Seldona began to suffer from nightmares too."

Lad Yob brought a scroll from the shelf to the desk. "This might be what she'd found."

Klaris didn't need to read the scroll. The lines of the Oracle's prophecy were already etched into her memory, as clearly as they were written across the page before her now. But only the same three stanzas.

"So, Seldona had it too." Klaris leaned back in the chair. Lad Yob looked over her shoulder at the journal. "What language is this?" he asked suddenly.

"Old Islish."

"Nekkian," the Lad's voice was dark.

Klaris glanced her question up at him.

"Not one other Mystic on Sageham today could read that journal, Weaver. Only you."

Klaris sighed. "I've been given all the tools, haven't I?" It wasn't the first time she'd been the only one familiar with an ancient script or rare dialect. This was, however, the first time in years she could remember needing a nap.

She turned back to the journal and re-read Seldona's last recorded words:

"Clearly the dragons are returning and just as clearly the Weaver must perform a spell of banishment. I have combed the library here and found no information as to what that spell looks like. Belvon Starvale thinks the nyad magi may know what to do, but they are disorganized and devastated by the earthquake that shook the Verwood Henge to rubble during the last Rising.

Still, Darden also thought the nyads might hold knowledge about the banishment, so that is where I shall start. I hope I find him. The violent, erotic nightmares are leaving me sleepless and exhausted."

"The pattern is repeating itself," Lad Yob said.

"Yes. I'm exhausted, too." Klaris closed the book, releasing a small cloud of dust. "Hand me that scroll with the prophecy. I'll see if it holds anything else that might be useful, but then I'm going for a nap."

"The nightmares rob you of rest."

"Actually," she stood and stretched. "I haven't had the nightmare since...." She looked down at the sparkling ring. "Since Jax gave me this. But I'm dead tired this morning. Tired in my bones."

She took the scroll and sadly left the shattered library. In her small room, she settled into her bed and opened the scroll. She was asleep before she'd read the first paragraph.

The Dayfeast celebrations at Castle Caledra that year were necessarily small but undertaken with a kind of frenzied enthusiasm by Mystics and Sagehamites alike. Able at last to set aside the grief for their friends who had died in the earthquake, the survivors leapt into the Midsummer festivities with a desperation born of sorrow and fear for what a dragon-infested future would bring.

Klaris, still without her usual energy, watched from the edge of the shadows. She grieved for tall, reserved Istov who had perished in the earthquake. That thought led her to the deeper loss of Lellyn. As Father Mallix offered prayers to the death of the sun god, she saw that sacrifice in a new and far more personal light.

The bonfire rose, and couples disappeared into the twilight. Klaris sat on a rock and watched the firelight play in the sapphire depths in Jax's ring. Her body longed for him, longed for the taste of him, the feel of him on her, in her.

"Weaver?"

She looked up to find Mollen offering her a hand and a smile. "Come away with me, beautiful Klaris. Let's honor the god tonight."

Klaris rose. "No, thank you."

He bent his grey head to her. "It's Dayfeast, Weaver. Surely your Barian prince is honoring the god with some islish lass this night. You shouldn't deny yourself the same pleasure."

Klaris frowned. "Actually, I'm very tired." She turned and walked away from him, wishing it were as easy to leave the images he'd given her of Jax, laughing, dancing, and enjoying someone else this Dayfeast.

The deck of the *Sharkin* shook as a hundred islish feet pounded away in a Barian stomp-reel. In the heart of the dance, Jax was indeed laughing. When it ended, he shared a cold glass of seaspirit punch with Lady Zess. She ran her hands under his sweaty shirt, but he disentangled himself.

"Stop, my lady. I can't."

She leaned into him and licked his neck. "I bet you can, my lord."

He couldn't help his response to the soft, insistent pressure of her breasts and the seductive motions of her hips against him. She reached up and tangled her hands in his hair. He took her hands and pulled them down. "Zess, you are beautiful, but I'm not free."

"Who is?"

The fiddles began again. Shallyx came to Jax's rescue, dragging him into the dance and away from Zess. His nightmare had not returned, but his longing for Klaris was fiercely fanned by the seductive Dayfest music. So, he danced until he was so exhausted that no one, real or dream-borne, would rouse him once he fell into his solitary bed.

The Oracle sat in silence at a window overlooking the sea during the few hours of darkness at the summer solstice. Their senses thrummed with the power of thousands of Dayfest bonfires across the Knownlands and the passions buzzing in the flickering shadows. The grey eyes gazed at the twilight sky and noted two very clear pockets of withholding within the thrumming fabric of celebration. The creature shifted and grumbled.

And then, quite clearly, they heard the cry of a newborn baby. The sound reverberated and echoed off canyon walls. Relief flooded through the old body. "At last," they said. "At last."

A sequence of summer squalls raged through the fleet the day after the solstice, exacerbating a number of queasy stomachs. The lord admiral found that the wind and spray cleared his head and, rather to the chagrin of his coxswain and jolly boat crew, spent the day visiting the lords and ladies of the other Floating Islands on their own wing-ships. These crews were sometimes unpleasantly startled to see the lord admiral bearing down upon them from the dark bank of a squall, realizing that they had not quite cleaned up last night's mess.

Jax sat in Neben's cabin as the last squall drifted east and the long summer sunset poured golden light through the stern windows.

"Would you like to hold the baby?" Without waiting for an answer, Shallyx plopped the pudgy bundle into Jax's lap.

"Will you read the wind as well as your mother?" he asked the baby. She burbled and grabbed for the gold braid on Jax's jacket.

"She's grasping for an admiralty," Shallyx laughed, noting with some surprise the easy way Jax handled the baby. Where had he learned such skills?

Neben leaned back in his chair and propped his boots on his desk. "This has been a great Gather, Jax."

"I don't know if Koralixa or Janil agree," Shallyx said slyly.

Jax glanced up from the baby and raised an eyebrow.

Neben explained. "The fleet hasn't been so thoroughly reviewed since Rax died. Some of us have gotten a little lackadaisical."

"A little?" Jax's voice was hard. He settled the baby against his chest where she sat drooling happily. "I'm surprised how far the lords and ladies have let their ships deteriorate. Grandad's fleet and yours look good, but the fleets of Callisto, Phlyx, and Ayx are just slovenly."

Shallyx rose to pour more wine for Jax. "They need the motivation of approval, I guess."

"Perhaps the fear of another dragon interregnum will motivate them."

"I'm not sure about that," Neben said slowly. "People either don't believe the beasts are coming back, or they don't think they can do anything to prevent a catastrophe."

Jax shook his head. "They might be right, but that's not going to stop us from taking measures to secure our survival." He shifted the baby on his lap and removed a sealed parchment from his inner pocket.

"In fact, I've drawn up a list of precautions I want each fleet to instigate."

"In case the dragons come?" Neben broke the seal and scanned the list.

"*When* the dragons come."

Neben exchanged a glance with his wife. They'd both heard the command in Jax's voice.

"This isn't unreasonable." Neben handed the scroll to Shallyx. "But it will take some time and money we don't have."

Jax hid his exasperation. He was tired of Barian nobles complaining of poverty. Still, he had an answer ready. "I thought I'd share an opportunity I noticed during my years at The Hant." Jax briefly explained his plans for shipping Hantish iron. "This could be a lucrative new market when they stop using slave labor."

"And when will that be?" Neben asked.

"Soon."

"Interesting." Shallyx considered the smile on Jax's face and remembered their smuggling days. She pursed her lips and Jax could see her mind calculating tonnage and exchange rates.

Neben let his wife exercise her mathematical genius. "We're so glad you're back," he smiled at Jax.

"See if you feel that way after I beat you in the regatta tomorrow."

The baby chose that moment to spit up all over the lord admiral's dress jacket. Neben laughed. "She's defending Rillt already."

Klaris spent the week after Dayfest reviewing the teaching schedule, reading student exams, redrafting parts of the design for the new castle building, and overseeing a new library catalogue. This last resulted from a very frustrating afternoon spent trying to find a book she remembered about the nyad magi but couldn't locate amid the chaos of documents in the temporary shelter.

"You've just thrown everything in here willy-nilly!" She complained to Professor Essen.

"We were in a hurry to get things out of the Rising rain and snow, Weaver," Essen answered defensively.

"Yes, but since then?"

He shrugged. "No one has been studying much."

"What *have* you been doing?"

"It took us weeks to erect this shelter, and bury the dead, and then many of us felt compelled to go home for a while."

Klaris took a deep breath, remembering her own deep need to see her mother after Caledra had been destroyed. "Right. Let's get this place organized now. It will be easier when we're ready to move into the new building. And I must find that book on the magi."

Everyone on Sageham gathered in a loose circle in the shadows of the low-ceilinged shelter. Klaris took her usual place among Rhella and Yan Chuan. The circle was small, and Klaris's heart ached yet again for all those missing. She twisted the sapphire on her finger, dark and lightless in the dim space. A gold and white cat sauntered to the middle of the circle and sat, licking a paw.

"Weaver," Lad Yob bent to whisper in her ear. "Your place is in the center now."

Klaris closed her eyes. In every other gathering, ceremony, and meeting this week she had been working alongside the others, often led by the priest or those, like Professor Essen, who'd been here all along. This was the first formal Mystic Circle she'd attended since becoming Weaver, and she realized how intently the others were all looking at her and waiting.

She ran her senses along the thick pulse of the weave and stepped forward. For most of her life Klaris had stood on the perimeter of this Circle, and she knew the ritual. Bowing to the four cardinal directions she quoted the invocation in Ancient. The Mystic swelled and filled her with unlooked-for joy. "Oh my," she said. "I didn't expect this."

The lads and lasses applauded. Father Mallix raised his hands. "Blessings to Weaver Klaris!"

Klaris bent to pick up the cat.

"Thank you," she said finally. "I would like to tell you why I wanted to be Weaver.

"We all know that the Mystic Weave appears to be weakening. We don't know why the warp and weft seem thinner, but it is evident in the fact that fewer people are born with powerful Mystic, and it is manifested through the weaknesses in our own weavings. Too often in recent years, we've left shelters standing, or we've built without beauty and without respect for the resources we borrow.

"I hope, as Weaver, to restore not just our ability to work better, but also with the wisdom Mystics of old understood and revered.

"Those of us here, accepted by the Mystic to study its greatest lessons and powers, we must be the examples. We must manifest the reciprocity great Mystic demands."

"Hear, hear!" Yan Chuan cheered.

Klaris continued. "We will begin by returning the ruins of Castle Caledra to the rock of Sageham." She turned towards the door and made her way out of the temporary shelter. The others followed.

With the summer breeze blowing sea-scented air through her hair, Klaris opened her weave to the others. Together they gently and reverently returned the castle to the island. They felt the ground move slowly under their feet to accommodate the blocks of stone and veins of running water.

When it was done, the stony ground stood bare under the sun and the wind, circled by a low, storm-worn henge. The Sagehamites gathered around the fissured dolmens in small groups, patting the stones with their gray fingers.

"My heart breaks," Rhella said, through her tears. "And at the same time, it fills me with such reverence."

Yan Chuan, on his knees crossed his hands over his heart. "Holy mother," he whispered, "How blessed we are."

Professor Essen sat down on the one stone that remained of the ancient castle. He looked down at the words Klaris had found there just days ago. "This was my home," he sighed. With gentle insistence, he pulled the Mystic and added a new line of script to the ancient cornerstone: *Castle Caledra: Returned post-dragon 899.*

A few hours later, Klaris sat in the middle of the small boat and let Lad Yob take the tiller. This wasn't the first time she'd sailed one of

Sageham's coracles across the Barling Narrows. As usual, she felt the familiar emptiness that always came when she left Sageham, leaving the heart of the Mystic. Even the exertion of a rigorous hour of sun salutations had not entirely restored her from the effort of returning the old castle to its roots in the earth.

She thought about the bit of Dragon force imprisoned in a crystal carefully packed in her satchel. Capturing that had also been a feat of soul-wrenching magic.

The coracle rode up and over the waves, and she felt her soul similarly bounced and rocked by the demands of forces she neither understood nor controlled.

She had not considered all that she risked in attempting to change the way Mystic was managed. As so often in her past, Klaris had prepared, studied precedents, explored long skeins of possibilities, and parsed patterns both extant and theoretical. There were always surprises when she attempted to move an idea from theory to practice, but her preparation, her instincts, and maybe even luck had brought her success.

She shivered, not just from the wash of spray over the bow. As she'd read and re-read Seldona's journal and the crumbling document about the nyad magi, a niggling suspicion had begun to form in her mind. Her stomach rolled, not from the movement of the boat but from the bleak realization of what she and Jax faced.

She closed her eyes as another wave broke and splashed. Pulling up her hood, she huddled into herself. She had seen Jax demonstrate his own sense of duty often enough to know that he would step into whatever was required. The sapphire sparkled, wet in the sun and spray. Klaris was both grateful to have Jax with her on this journey and terrified that she might lose him as a result.

Jax's satisfaction with the way the *Sharkin* cut through the sea couldn't erase the hot ache in his hand. His finger had already cost five people their lives. He hoped it wouldn't cost him his. "You have the helm, Captain," he said and headed down to his cabin.

"Yes, Admiral." Captain Blanx and Lieutenant Warrix stood on the quarterdeck listening to a sailor call out the knots.

"By the goddess," Blanx said finally. "He was right."

Lieutenant Warrix's sea blue eyes surveyed the taut sails. The *Sharkin*, flying all the canvas she had, sped northward, leaving the dispersing ships of the Gather far behind.

Given the attention old Hix had lavished on the *Sharkin*, her trim and the set of her sails, Captain Blanx and most of the crew had hidden their skepticism this morning when the new lord admiral had asked for several labor intensive changes to the stowage below and the yardage above. Lieutenant Warrix, having grown up alongside the prince, knew that Jax's success in the Gather Regatta was not the anomaly that Captain Blanx and others assumed.

Warrix had quickly quelled the grumbling, reminding the crew of Jax's performance in the recent regatta. Half-islish though he was, Jax's handling of that boat in those heavy seas had been nothing short of genius. Even old Fellix couldn't beat him.

Now, seeing the effects of these adjustments as the wing-ship careened through the seas, Captain Blanx had to agree with the lieutenant. Jax Sharkin had coaxed two more knots out of her.

"Aye, he's damn good with the math too, sir." Warrix grinned. "But did you catch a look at his hand?"

"I did." Blanx answered in a grim tone. 'I noticed it seemed to be troubling him yesterday."

"Goddess damn the thoughtless bilge rats who harmed him," the lieutenant swore fervently.

"They've already paid their price," Blanx said, his eyes on the sails. "It's our damned druid who should be taking better care of him."

Jax rubbed his eyes. "Damn." The figures in the ledger open before him squirmed in their columns. Sweating, he shivered and bowed to the inevitable.

"Sentry!" he called.

"Milord?"

"Summon Father Plumly."

"Aye, sir."

Jax rose to find a glass of water and turned to look out the stern lights.

"My lord?" Father Plumly entered the cabin fastidiously, as if attending his lord admiral was somehow repellent to him.

Plumly had served on the *Sharkin* for as long as Jax could remember. Even as a small midshipman he had suffered the dislike of the ship's druid, but he had realized that Father Plumly treated everyone with the same indifferent cruelty.

"My hand is not healing."

Plumly's expression was smug, but he gestured for Jax to sit then unwrapped the bandage. The last layers stuck to the oozing wound underneath, but the druid just used more force to rip them away, tearing the crusted scabs.

He picked up the hand and twisted it toward the light from the windows.

Jax's head spun. "I'm getting a fever," he admitted.

Plumly's damp hand clamped on Jax's forehead. "Indeed, you are, sir."

Jax blinked at the swollen red line where the Barian priestess had stitched the finger back onto his hand. Having spent months assisting the druids in Hilsen Vale, Jax had seen wounds go septic. He knew the symptoms well enough, along with a couple of cures. The minimal options presenting themselves to him here were unpleasant.

"Priestess Ayslic should never have reattached it," Plumly announced, pulling the finger painfully.

Jax extracted his hand. "You're not helping. And that hurts."

"So sorry, my young lord," Plumly said patronizingly. "It has to come off."

"I need this finger," Jax snapped.

"Sure, it'll be handy when you're dead, my lord."

"Dragons," Jax swore, but there was defeat in his tone. "I had hoped that as druid to the lord admiral, you'd have other options."

"You may not have noticed, my lord, but all people bleed the same: sailor, lord or peasant."

"Do not presume to lecture me, Father."

The druid gave a small nod that did not hide his unkind smile. "I am merely reminding you that the goddess gives us many tools, but she requires us to follow her laws."

Jax pulled the Oracle's golden medallion from under his shirt and settled it pointedly on his chest. "It's possible that I am one of the goddess's tools myself. I will thank you to simply heal this damned hand."

"Damned indeed. The sepsis is already entering your blood. The finger must come off."

Jax took a deep breath. Why had Hix suffered this idiot for so many years? Jax had learned a great deal about healing from Marith and Doc, but even more, he'd seen how they solved medical problems, how they had cared deeply for each patient. Unlike them, Plumly had his standard solutions and memorized catechisms for problems both physical and spiritual and if these didn't work, it was somehow the sufferer's own fault.

Jax pulled the small wooden dragonpipe Doc had given him from his pocket. He blew the first notes of the First Tune. His finger was too stiff and swollen to be of use, so he tried to substitute either his middle or last finger. This didn't work well at all, and the First Tune became something else entirely, a tune of absences, and unfinished phrases.

"Are you going to play, my lord, or will you let me amputate?"

Jax curled his fingers painfully around the pipe. He considered the druid for a long moment. "Fine. You may take it."

He sat staring blankly at the dragonpipe while Plumly left to gather his instruments. The druid returned, followed by a nervous assistant and Jax's steward. They removed the papers from Jax's desk and set out towels, a basin, a knife.

Jax rose and let the steward take his jacket. "What's your antiseptic?"

"I wash all wounds in good, clean seawater."

"Which has worked so well for me," Jax growled.

Plumly shrugged. "If the goddess had wished you to keep that finger—."

"Spare me the sermon. I heard you the first ten times. Now, let's have some poppy."

"I have none."

"You're going to amputate without giving your patient any pain-killer?" Jax stared at him.

"I have a glass of seaspirit here, my lord," the assistant offered timorously.

"Seaspirit!" Jax turned to the assistant. "Go fetch the poppy."

"There is none on the ship." Plumly continued to adjust his instruments.

"Why not?"

"It is highly addictive."

"Not if—."

"Sit down, my lord. Let's get this over with."

Jax sat at his desk. "You know it is used all over the rest of the Knownlands."

Father Plumly pulled Jax's arm and laid the hand flat on the table. Even this move was painful, so Jax picked up the glass of sea-spirit and tossed it down.

"Hold still now." Plumly picked up the knife.

Jax closed his eyes.

Klaris wasn't going to be happy about this. Goddess damn Plumly and his stupid reliance on seawater to cure all ills. Over the course of the Gather, Jax had felt the finger grow hot and stiff. He'd asked the druid for a cure and even rifled through the man's collection of herbs and powders but found nothing that he recognized from Marith's pharmacopeia.

The knife cut slowly into the inflamed skin of his hand. Jax grit his teeth. Blood flowed wet onto his palm. The wound ached already. Plumly's mincing incision drew the pain out, lengthened it, heated it.

Jax gasped as Plumly leaned on the dull side of the knife and the bone broke with a slow crackle. Again, the blade cut into the throbbing flesh.

"Just whack it off!" Jax ordered through clenched teeth.

"It's coming," Plumly answered complacently. After a moment he spoke curtly to the steward. "Hold him still."

Jax glanced at the white-faced assistant. The knife continued its series of small, needle-like incisions. With a final tug, Plumly ripped the last of the stitches apart. The finger came away trailing uneven tails of skin, bone, and pus.

Jax leapt from his chair, swearing. The steward fell back. Jax shoved the druid to the floor and just barely stopped himself from kicking the man. "Get out of here, you bloody torturer!"

Plumly scrambled to his feet and ran. The assistant shrank against the cabin wall. He watched the lord admiral slump into the chair and lift his shaking hand to the light. Sweat soaked his silk shirt and blood had run onto his trousers. The steward poured more seaspirit and handed it to admiral.

Jax downed it. "This won't do," he admitted softly.

"My lord?"

"All these loose edges will get infected again. It's already dangerous."

The assistant came away from the wall and took the hand gently. "Shall I summon Father—?"

"No! That man shouldn't be permitted to treat a cadaver. This has to be cauterized."

The assistant druid left the great cabin, snuck behind Father Plumly, who was complaining about the lord admiral's lack of stoicism to an unsympathetic Lieutenant Warrix, and fetched the cauterizing equipment from the ship's dispensary. He returned to the admiral's cabin to find the prince had already used magic to create a small hot fire in the little brazier and the steward had gone to find a mop.

"I haven't cauterized anyone before," the assistant druid said.

Jax took a deep breath, thinking of Marith. "The trick is to be very sure and very quick. Don't dither the way Plumly does, that just causes more pain."

The druid put a small cauterizing iron into the white-hot coals. After a moment the iron was glowing red. Jax took a deep breath and shoved his sweaty hair off his forehead. "Now," he looked up, offering his hand to the assistant. "Firm and fast."

Jax bit back his howl of pain as the smell of his burning flesh filled the room.

The sentry's voice came through the door. "Captain Blanx, sir!"

"Enter," Jax's voice cracked.

Blanx blanched at the reek of burnt flesh and the sight of so much blood on the table, the floor, and the lord admiral himself.

"My lord?"

"The finger had gone septic," Jax bit tersely.

"My apologies for interrupting you, sir. But neither the *Fairy Fish* nor the *Leviathan* is able to keep up with us at this speed."

The other two ships were heavy galleons from Helm's fleet, hoping to profit from Hantish iron.

Jax flashed a wan wolf grin, but he didn't speak.

"I'm requesting permission to reduce sail, Admiral, to let the other ships keep up."

"Granted."

Captain Blanx bowed and left the room, shaking his head at the mess.

Jax let the assistant help him to his bed. When the hand was once again swathed in a clean white bandage, he cradled it to his chest.

"Here, sir."

Jax gulped the seaspirit and his head began to throb in time with his hand. He laid back on his pillows and felt the *Sharkin* slow her way over the rolling sea. He lay silent with the throbbing pain and watched his steward swab the floor.

"The shipments were spaced along the road, just as you described." Hix paused to sip more of Jax's fine wine. "We've taken seven loads and all the trolls with them. The *Eagle* isn't big enough to hold everything. I've already transferred some of the ore to the *Leviathan* along with half the trolls."

"I noticed you were low in the water." Jax fiddled with the bandage, trying to hide his disappointment that Hix's ship was full of trolls and trollish iron, but did not contain the one Farsouthian he'd been longing for. He turned to look out the stern lights. A summer rain fell in a straight curtain to the dark waters of Hanter Lake. The dim shapes of the two galleons loomed ghostly off the *Sharkin*'s stern.

"This rain will provide a good cover for us today," he said a little absently.

"Who is leading your crew?"

"Lieutenant Warrix."

"Ah. He'll do well." Hix poured himself more wine, thinking that good wine was definitely the upside to all the time Prince Jax had spent away from his Barian tutors while fostering among his Kordish relatives.

"Warrix was in my Captaincy class," Jax noted. "How many trolls do we have now?"

"Seventy-five."

Jax leaned back in his chair and smiled. "And so far, none of them have been prepared for your attack?"

Hix shook his head almost sadly. "No. You'd think they'd expect the teamsters to return to The Hant, but...." He shrugged.

Jax went to the window to watch the rain. "They ship a wagon-load each day, and it takes each wagon three days to get to Southant and two days to make the return. That means it would be six days before they'd miss the first group you took."

"Aye. We took them a week ago."

"The shipping master at Southant will have gotten suspicious by now too," Jax continued. "She'll have been wondering where her shipments are, and she'll send a fast rider to find out."

"So, warn Lieutenant Warrix to be ready for some resistance."

"Aye." Jax pulled his oiled cloak from a peg, swung it around his shoulders and left the cabin.

Hix settled back in his chair and poured the last of the wine into his glass.

Two days later, the cool summer rain long gone, Admiral Hix and Captain Blanx stood sweating side by side on the *Sharkin's* quarterdeck and watched the four small boats detach themselves from the pines along the shore.

"He's got them," Hix squinted into the distance.

"Aye, Admiral." Blanx focused his spyglass on the boats. "Good thing he took your jolly boat because he's got at least twenty trolls this time."

"Let me see!" Hix snatched the glass away from Captain Blanx. He watched for a moment then snapped the glass shut with a satisfied smile. "He's clever, our Jax."

"Too clever sometimes," Blanx muttered. "We're worried about his hand."

Hix looked surprised. "He told me it was healing fine now that he took the finger off again."

"No thanks to Father Plumly."

"A body heals or it don't." Hix shrugged, his eye caught by the signal flags running up the *Eagle*'s halyards. "Here's some news to please our lord admiral. The Weaver just boarded the *Eagle*."

Captain Blanx gave a series of orders to hoist up the panicked trolls and then the load of iron ore they'd been taking to Southant.

Jax climbed easily onto the deck to the piping of whistles and salutes from his crew. He joined his officers and Hix to watch the trolls brought aboard. Tall and thick, the trolls stood glowering in an uneasy mob on the foredeck. Barian sailors prodded the bound trolls with cutlasses and phrases of broken Landish. More sailors tied the trolls' ankles together.

"Goddess damn you thieving isles!" shouted a fe-troll. Sweeps of crimson decorated her cheeks and embellished her lips.

Jax addressed the trolls in his perfect Landish. "I am Jax Sharkin, and the goddess did condemn me to serve as a slave for four years. But since she saw fit to let me survive that experience, I am working to stop trollish use of slave labor in the mines."

"What does that have to do with us?" asked the fe-troll.

At this moment, the *Sharkin's* blocks and tackle hoisted a heavy crate of iron ore up from the small boat and settled it into the ship's hold.

"I'm confiscating your ore to pay wages to your slaves."

"Thievery!" shouted another troll.

"And you," Jax continued. "I'm going to trade each of you for at least two mine slaves."

The trolls looked uneasily at each other. "There are over a hundred slaves at the mines, and, what, twenty of us?"

"You'll find a few of your friends when we take you below," Jax said gently. Another crate of iron ore came up from the small boat.

"So, it's you. You're the one robbing our shipments?" The fe-troll frowned.

"It is I. Now, you will go below. You will be fed, but you will not see the sun again until the mines redeem you. If they redeem you."

The trolls growled. Some swore and fought. Others wailed. All of this resulted in a tangled mess of trollish limbs and a lot of noise. The Barians understood little of their admiral's Landish speech, but they'd seen the same reaction from the previous groups of trolls and knew they'd settle down in a moment and go quietly terrified to join their fellows chained below.

Jax turned away from the terror in their orange eyes. Remembering his own fear of the mine tunnels, he sympathized with the trolls more than he wanted. He took a deep breath and lifted his head. He walked frowning to the starboard rail. Hix jumped down into his jolly boat and headed back to the *Eagle* off the *Sharkin's* port beam. Meanwhile the *Sharkin's* crew lashed their own small boats in their places and Captain Blanx shouted orders to take the ship into the deeper water in the middle of the lake.

Jax's attention was focused on the horizon to the east. The sun hot on his shoulders, he squinted into the distance, looking for the haze he feared. There it was. Damn.

Jax had well learned the weather on Hanter Lake during the years he'd sailed and rowed the iron ferry two and three times a day across the lake as a slave. The first time he'd been hit by one of the fierce summer squalls he had nearly lost the boat. He'd barely dropped the sail in time before the gale hit them like something solid. Only the heavy load of iron ore in the bottom of the boat had kept the ferry from capsizing.

After that, Jax had kept a wary eye out and learned to recognize and fear the scent of sage and pine that the gale blew off the

Hantish steppes. The scent on the breeze now. It stuck in the back of his throat. He was turning to call Captain Blanx when he felt the familiar tingle of Klaris's magic.

She appeared on the deck with a great wash of magic. The trolls gaped; Barians applauded. Jax's heart soared. Focused on those green eyes, he didn't see the fe-troll launch herself toward him.

Jax opened his arms to Klaris and found himself embraced by the fe-troll. With the momentum of her rush, they crashed back against the starboard rail and went over into the blood-warm water of the lake.

"Hove to! Hove to!" Blanx shouted.

Klaris's vision had cleared and focused on Jax just in time to see the troll sweep him overboard. She rushed to the broken rail. Already the *Sharkin* had sailed a hundred yards away from the splashing bubbles in the blue-black water of the lake. Two sailors leapt off the ship and swam back towards the thrashing, while Lieutenant Warrix yelled at the frantic crew to get a boat launched.

Hix, standing in the stern of his own jolly boat, frowned back at the *Sharkin*. He could hear the shouts but not words. Should he go back to help?

"Weaver just appeared up there," his coxswain noted. "I got a bit of o'the Mystic, and I felt her use it."

Hix didn't think that the arrival of the Weaver would cause the type of near panic he'd heard in those shouts, but he knew he had to let young Jax handle his own situations.

"Carry on, then," he said to his crew and turned to face the *Eagle*.

Gripping the broken rail with white knuckles, Klaris reached her magic out to Jax, but as usual found nothing. "Damn it!"

Lad Yob stood next to her. "The swimmers will get him," he offered weakly.

"Get the rest of those damned trolls below!" Blanx bellowed.

Splashing and shouting sparkled the waves where Jax had gone in. The launch flew across the water. Lieutenant Warrix, standing at the stern, could see the swimmers wrestling with what appeared to be some kind of beast.

The troll's great strength pinned Jax's arms and no amount of kicking could dislodge her. The swimming Barians couldn't pry her free either.

Jax realized that they'd both sink if he stopped swimming. He took a last deep breath and relaxed. They sank together like an anchor.

Air bubbled from the troll and streamed upward. At last, her arms loosened. He pulled his legs up between them and kicked himself free of her, losing much of his own air. He pushed off the troll's shoulders towards the surface, but as he rose, she grabbed his leg.

The last of his breath escaped him then, and he sank with the troll.

It took all Warrix's self-discipline to stay in the launch and not jump in to help. The water grew quiet as the two swimmers dove down after Jax. It took too long, but finally they broke the surface, Jax limp in their arms. Something heavy still pulled him down, making it difficult for the swimmers to keep his head above the waves.

"The troll has a death grip on him!" gasped one of the swimmers. "Give me a knife!"

Warrix pulled the cutlass from his belt and handed it down.

The swimmer dove again, while sailors in the boat tried to pull Jax over the gunwale. A plume of orange blood rose through the water, and finally the lord admiral was free. They hauled him inelegantly into the boat.

"He's not breathing." The nearest rower pounded on Jax's back.

The swimmers climbed aboard, dripping. Jax coughed and then vomited sulfuric lake water.

"That's good, my lord!" the sailor pounded again. "Get the water out."

"Row for the ship!" Warrix ordered. "Sharply now!"

"They've got him," Lad Yob said on deck of the *Sharkin*.

The launch began to move across the water, but Klaris didn't wait. She reached out her hand and pulled the air. Jax rose from the floor of the boat and flew across the waves to arrive with a gentle thump on the *Sharkin*. Klaris knelt next to him. Sailors came running to help.

He coughed, gasping for air. "Blanx!"

"Hush, Jax. Let's get you below." Klaris pushed the hair back from his face.

"In a minute. Get me Captain Blanx." A fit of coughing doubled him over.

Father Plumly pushed his way through the crowd of sailors. He pounded on Jax's back, prompting a lot more painful coughing. "This won't do your hand any good." The druid noted the blood soaking through the wet bandage.

"Good clean seawater?" Jax snapped raggedly. "Get me Blanx, NOW!"

"I'm here, my lord," Blanx said. He bent to better hear the admiral's hoarse whisper.

"We're about to get a gale out of the east." Jax reached up to grab the captain's sleeve. "Furl every sail; batten every hatch; drop a sea anchor."

Blanx kept his face neutral. He knew without looking that the wind still blew from the west, although it had been dropping all day. He looked at the admiral's wild eyes and feared that perhaps the near drowning had made him delirious. The air was calm, the sky clear. Nothing seemed to warrant Jax's orders. "My lord—."

"Now!" Jax said through clenched teeth. "We're going to get knocked down in maybe five minutes."

Blanx put down his doubts, stood and shouted orders. Crews swarmed up the ratlines and the hawse hole smoked as a sea anchor plunged into the waves.

Father Plumly and his assistant hoisted Jax to his feet. Jax coughed until he gagged, but he clung desperately to consciousness.

"Gently, Father!" Klaris snapped.

Jax's eyes followed the workings of his crew and turned to the other ships. He turned back to Blanx. "Signal the fleet to do the same."

As Blanx watched the pennants race up the halyard, he saw that Hix was already furling the *Eagle's* sails and realized that the old admiral had a better understanding and a deeper respect for Jax's seamanship than any other Barian. The two galleons acknowledged the signal, but Blanx could see their crews weren't moving very quickly.

Plumly, his assistant, and Klaris had Jax to the companionway now. Before he went below, Jax took one last look to the east. He cleared his throat and raised his voice. "Hold tightly now, Sharkins! Hold tightly."

"Be quiet, my lord!" Plumly shook more coughing out of him and dragged him below. Once in the cabin, Plumly dropped him to the floor. "Let's get the wet things off before we put him in bed."

Jax shivered uncontrollably as the druids stripped off his wet clothes. Plumly ripped the bandage off Jax's hand. Blood dripped into the pool of seawater on the floor.

Klaris frowned as she realized that the finger was gone. "Sweet goddess, Jax. Can't you keep yourself in one piece for more than a week at a time?"

Jax looked at her angry green eyes and choked. Laughter bubbled up from his heart. "I'm so glad to see you."

"I don't think this is funny." Klaris frowned. She leaned over to take his hand. "What happened?"

"Infection."

"Not funny at all."

The druid pushed him back on his bed and pulled a blanket over his legs and hips.

Klaris bent to pull the covers up further.

Plumly was twisting the hand. "The cauterization you attempted was inadequate. I'll have to redo it."

"Not yet," Jax breathed. They didn't seem to hear him.

"He's shivering," Klaris noted.

"We'll warm him up." Plumly smiled pleasantly, digging through his bag of supplies, drawing out the cauterizing iron.

"Hold on," Jax coughed.

With a crash the gale hit the ship and heeled her over until the spars touched the waves. Klaris fell onto Jax's berth. He held her to his chest. Breathing hurt, but she felt so good.

"Will we capsize?" she whispered.

"Haven't we already?"

Klaris was pressing the breath out of him, but he didn't let her go.

Fired by the longing in his sea blue eyes, she kissed him. He closed his eyes as her warm lips touched his.

Klaris lifted her head and blinked. "He's passed out."

"Better for him." The answer was sour. "He won't feel the pain as I cauterize the wound."

It seemed a long time before the ship righted itself. The cabin rattled as the gale thrust the *Sharkin* through the waves. A crackling crash was followed by shouts in the bow and water dripped in where the wind forced it through the wooden seams.

"Sweet goddess, this *is* a gale," mumbled the druid's assistant as he carefully managed the small brazier.

The ship rolled again, and two crystal glasses came loose from their holders, crashing to the deck in a spray of sharp shards. Despite the awkward angles of the deck and the uneven movement of the ship, Plumly picked up the red-hot iron and stumbled to the bed. He grabbed Jax's hand, searing the limp knuckles before setting the iron against the bloody stump.

Jax awoke howling. "Dragons!"

Klaris held his shoulders.

"Stop!" Jax shouted. "That's enough. You'll cause more damage." He choked on the acrid smoke and coughed until he was dizzy.

The admiral's shouting brought both the steward and the sentry into the cabin. Plumy finally removed the iron, ripping away a patch of blackened skin. Blood flowed again. Jax pulled his hand to his chest, swearing around his desperate breaths.

Lad Yob stepped away from the wall. His gray face tinged with green at the uneven movement of the ship. "Allow me, my lord," he said, gently taking Jax's hand. Deftly he wrapped the clean bandages over the bloody mess.

"Poppy?" Jax croaked, almost begging.

"Have this," the assistant druid held out a glass of seaspirit.

Jax swallowed a large gulp, which made him choke and cough until blackness closed around him and took him down almost as effectively as any narcotic.

"You best let him go," Plumly said, pulling on Klaris's shoulder to move her away from the bed. He looked straight into Klaris's eyes, leaving no doubt that he considered that kiss blasphemous.

Klaris smiled sweetly. "Have you ever been in love, Father?"

"Yes, child. I've been in love."

"It is a gift of the goddess, isn't it?"

"It is, except when it's prohibited."

"In which case it would be a curse rather than a blessing?" Klaris's voice was soft. Lad Yob smiled slyly.

"I suppose." Plumly wiped his hands on a towel.

"Even a condemnation?"

"Yes!"

Klaris eyes smirked, but her face remained sweet. "But the goddess doesn't damn us and doesn't ask for sacrifice. Surely, she wouldn't let us fall into a prohibited love."

Plumly stared at her, aware that she'd trapped him. He turned away, tossing his tools into his bag. "Justify it if you like, Weaver. But don't go lightly down that road. Now, move aside so I can listen to his lungs."

He placed his ear on Jax's chest. After a few moments, he rose. "We'll have to watch that he doesn't get pneumonia. There's a lot of wet in his lungs still."

Klaris stared down at Jax. "Pneumonia. You must heal him, Father. And quickly."

Plumly snorted. "So you can pursue your unholy lust?"

Klaris shook her head. "No, Father. So he can banish dragons."

Plumly moved through the familiar poses of the sun salutation but found no peace in them this morning. The Weaver had joined him on the foredeck with three sailors as the sun rose to shine on the dark water, littered with flotsam of tree trunks, and leaves and dust from yesterday's gale. How could she move through these poses with such grace and devotion, while pursuing an illicit affair with the lord admiral? It was hypocritical, wrong, no matter how she twisted the goddess' logic to suit her own fancy.

Breakfast did nothing to improve his mood. Old Admiral Hix and Captain Blanx both cornered him, demanding to know how the lord admiral fared, and with no comforting answer, Plumly had felt their displeasure.

Grimly he banged into the lord admiral's dark cabin, startling his assistant out of the chair where he'd been dozing. "Let's get some light in here." He ripped the curtains back from the stern lights.

Jax coughed, rustled in the bed, coughed again.

Plumly bent over him. "Is he coughing up blood?"

"No," the assistant answered. "He's slept pretty quietly all the last watch."

The druid bent to listen to Jax's lungs. "Get the tisane," he said absently to his assistant. "And some seawater."

"Seawater."

Even in a whisper, Plumly heard the contempt in the lord admiral's voice.

"It will do," the druid snapped.

"Other things would do better." Jax slowly pushed himself up to sit, coughing as he moved.

"Cough it up," Plumly encouraged. "Clear those lungs."

Jax coughed until his head spun.

The assistant returned with a steaming cup of tea. "How do you feel this morning, my lord?" he asked with a smile.

"Splendid," Jax whispered, wrinkling his nose at the tea. "Spiderwort and henbane."

"Yes." Father Plumly didn't hide his surprise that the prince would recognize the herbs in the tea.

"If you put some mint in, it's a little less nasty." Jax sipped it and frowned at the foul taste.

"I suppose...."

Jax considered the druid over the rim of his cup. "Why are you a druid, Plumly?"

"Because the goddess called me. My lord. You would do well to listen to her also."

Jax finished the tea and set aside the cup. "Send Captain Blanx my compliments and ask him to attend me."

"Admiral Hix is here, too." Plumly dawdled. He was not happy being treated as a steward.

"Ah." Jax paused for a moment and gently cleared his throat. "Better send the steward to get me dressed first then."

"You're not getting dressed today," the druid snapped. "Not for a few days."

"I like the sound of that." Klaris came in, her smile openly suggestive.

Jax's voice was a little rough as he answered her smile. "Maybe you can use your magic on me again, like when you reattached my finger. That felt so...good."

"Good?" Klaris remembered the fire in Jax after she'd used the Mystic to realign bone and blood vessels.

"Magic can't heal," Plumly snorted. "Not even yours, Weaver."

"I didn't actually heal him," she clarified. "I just moved things into place."

"Moved me," Jax mumbled, reaching his good hand out to her. "Yes, you did."

"Sweet goddess!" Plumly groused as Klaris bent to kiss Jax. "Have you no respect?"

Klaris didn't look at the druid. She raised her head and sat on the edge of the bed. "I have plenty of respect, Father."

Plumly pushed between them. "Excuse me. I need to check the wound."

With his usual roughness, Plumly unwrapped the bandage around Jax's hand and pulled away the scab.

"Goddess," Jax whispered, as blood oozed onto his already stained sheets.

"Give me the seawater," Plumly held out a hand to his assistant.

"I think you should look at it first," the assistant said carefully. "It ain't the usual stuff."

All of them turned to look at the murky water in the assistant's bowl. "The lake's full of dirt and weeds and whatnot from the gale," he explained.

"It'll do." Father Plumly dipped a cloth into the water and moved to wipe Jax's wound with it.

"No!" Klaris snapped, as Jax drew back, shaking his head.

"It won't hurt," the druid said, his hard fingers digging into Jax's shoulder.

"Everything you do hurts!" Jax protested. "Stand away, Father."

"No. The wound must be washed. This is what we have to wash it with."

"Sentry!" Jax called. "Remove the druid from my cabin."

"My lord?"

"Don't be ridiculous." Father Plumly tried to make his voice soothing, but with little success.

"Get him out of here," Jax coughed. "And do not admit him again!"

The sentry looked confused. "Come along, Father. The lord admiral don't want you now."

"I don't want Father Plumly ever again," Jax bit.

"Fine!" Plumly shouted as he left the cabin. "Give the goddess my greetings then, as you'll surely be seeing her soon without my help!"

"Sooner with his help, I think." Jax coughed violently.

"Here, my lord." The assistant moved toward the bed. "Let me help you." He moved pillows gently and once Jax was settled, peered at the wound. "Plumly is right. It should be washed."

"Not with that foul lake water."

"No, sir."

"Don't you have some bee balm or feverfew?" Jax asked.

The assistant shook his head. "Plumly doesn't trust that stuff."

Jax ran his left hand over his face. "Is there a druid on the *Eagle*? Good. Go see what he or she has for antiseptic. In fact, get the *Eagle's* druid over here."

"Aye, my lord. Let's just wrap this up again."

Jax submitted to the assistant who moved with much more care than Plumly.

"I'm hungry," he muttered. "That tisane is just water and herbs."

"But, my lord—."

"Yes, I know. Next time you make it add some mint for me."

"Aye, sir. I'll fetch you some broth."

"And smoked oysters."

"Alright, sir."

The assistant left as Jax's steward came in bearing a clean white shirt like a flag. "My lord, Captain Blanx and Admiral Hix await your pleasure."

Jax pushed himself up and slanted a smirk at Klaris. "I can't see everyone wearing nothing but a bandage."

Klaris sat in the chair by the large stern windows and listened to Hix and Blanx discuss the damage caused by the gale. The *Leviathan* had been tardy in taking in its sails and had lost a mast. The other ships' captains were summoned and arrived with Jax's breakfast. Klaris watched him as the Barians discussed their options for repairs.

"I don't know how you knew that squall was coming," Blanx said finally.

"I spent two years on this lake, Captain. Back and forth two or three times a day."

"But that blow just came out of nowhere." The *Leviathan*'s captain shook her head.

"About sank me the first time, too." Jax coughed. "I'd have given you more warning, but that damn troll decided to take us for a swim. Still, you were slow to heed my signals."

"It won't happen again, my lord," the *Leviathan*'s captain squirmed.

The conversation then moved on to review the details of Jax's plan to negotiate with the trolls at the iron mines.

"We have one less troll to trade," Hix noted.

"We'll make do with what we have," Jax decided. "There isn't room in the holds for more of them. Besides, they'll be harder to surprise now, harder to take."

Hix rose. "Good! I want the unhappy creatures out of my ship."

"Aye. Make a course for The Hant." Jax coughed.

"We can fetch The Hant by tomorrow, my lord," Blanx noted. "You may need more time to regain your strength."

"I'll manage."

"Must the lord admiral negotiate this deal with the trolls?" Klaris asked.

"I think so, Weaver." Blanx stood with Hix. "No one else speaks Landish well enough to explain our terms clearly."

The Barians flourished the one-handed Barian salute and left the cabin. Klaris considered the closed door for a moment before turning to Jax. She opened her mouth to excoriate him but stopped at the drawn look on his face.

"I know,' he said softly. "I'm not fit to deal with the trolls. I'm sorry, Klaris." A seizure of coughing doubled him up.

She held her tongue, aware that patience was required and knowing how little she had.

Jax caught his breath finally and sat back against the pillows. "Tell me what you learned in Sageham."

"Heartbreak. So many dead; so much lost. I don't know who will teach the higher levels now. The other tower-tested Mystics are there to help, but....” She paused, took a deep breath and wiped at her tears. “Professor Lellyn was a mother to me.”

Jax reached out his good hand and pulled Klaris toward him. She joined him on his bed and let him wrap an arm around her.

“We found that bit of Dragon force that I remembered,” Klaris went on finally. “It was in a warding around Weaver Seldona’s study.”

“Who was she?”

“Seldona was the Weaver a thousand years ago.” Klaris continued, telling Jax of what she’d read in Seldona’s journal and found in her archives.

“It’s a pattern,” she finished. “And it’s repeating now: the earthquake, the tidal wave, the paradox who can’t be found.”

“Darden Sharlquin?” he repeated the name.

She nodded.

“That’s the archaic form of Sharkin.”

“An ancestor of yours, then.”

“Maybe.”

“Seldona was Jezellian.”

Jax had slipped down in his bed in an effort to open his lungs. “Where to now?”

“To the fairy queen, first. If she can’t help, then we seek the nyad magi.”

The sentry’s voice came through the door: “Father Oshel from the *Eagle*, my lord!”

Father Oshel and Plumly’s assistant moved to the bed. Klaris rose and stood back while they unwrapped Jax’s hand and washed the wound with something.

“Sweet goddess,” Oshel breathed. “This is butchery.”

The assistant grimaced. “Plumly ain’t gentle.”

The druid swabbed the stump with an ointment that clearly stung, but Jax apparently approved despite the pain. “I am so sorry, my lord.”

Jax turned away from the stinging and looked to Klaris. "We should go to Hilsen Vale and get Florin," he said, trying to keep the pain out of his voice.

"Florin?"

"Florin Starrish. She'll know where to find fairies."

Klaris leaned forward and took Jax's undamaged hand. "We are running out of time. The cat said the dragons will return at Darkfest."

"Dragons?" Oshel gasped. "Real dragons?"

"We'll have to be careful with the fairies then," Jax answered, ignoring the druid. "You know how they mess with time."

Klaris looked into Jax's eyes. She saw the distraction there as he tried to ignore what the druids were doing to him, but it was time to finally voice what her instinct was saying: "We'll talk to the fairy queen and maybe the nyads, but I think I know where we have to go."

"Where?"

"Axterre."

The breath went out of him. Of all the goddess-forsaken places in the Knownlands, the haunted ruins of Axterre had to be the worst. Far to the east, far from the sea, the ruins lay miles, both figurative and literal, from the home he had just rediscovered. "That's an evil place, Klaris."

Her heart clenched at the bleakness in Jax's voice. He coughed again and she thought he looked somehow defeated.

"It's just a hunch," she said, leaning toward him. "That book we found in Kree came from Axterre, even though it was incomplete. And the Axterran Oracles did know how to banish the dragons, once."

He reached up and cupped her face with his good hand. "Let me settle up with the trolls, then we'll go."

"You're not going anywhere, my lord!" protested Father Oshel. "Your lungs need time to clear."

"Give me your brews and tonics then, Father, because I'm going to face the trolls tomorrow."

The druid shook his head. Klaris stood up, those uncharacteristic tears gathering again. Jax saw them.

"What I'd really like is some duckweed tea," he said. "Weaver, would you kindly alert my steward?"

Klaris collected herself and left the cabin. When she had gone, Jax slumped back in his pillows and gazed with unseeing eyes out the window.

When the assistant druid followed Father Oshel out of the cabin a little later, he noticed that Jax hadn't touched the tea he'd requested. With all that Prince Jax had been through and all that he'd survived, this Axterre must be a grim place indeed, if it would worry him so now.

orrel felt her magic two days before he met Halla Felstar.
He'd left Hilsen Vale after Dayfest, driven away by his increasing discontent. His broken heart just wouldn't heal. In fact, it seemed to be festering. Florin was busy with her trekking business and Marith and Doc were happily training Dylith to be a druid. He seemed to be the only one who couldn't adjust to being home.

He kept thinking of Lexyl, far away in the distant desert, surrounded by rock and sky, and terribly vulnerable if the dragons did return, as the Weaver feared. He felt the changes in the Dragon force and finally, unable to find peace in the high clear air of the Vale, he decided to seek the nyad magi.

He followed thin tracks among the treeless peaks of the Ledden Rises. Eventually the mountains subsided to a rolling land covered with the ancient elm and oak of the Verwood. Here there was no path, but like all nyads, Borrel could understand the slow breathy voice of the trees. This led him to the dim causeway that came up from the passes through Ily. He hadn't gone far up this road when he found a trace of Dragon force in the cold ashes of a small campsite. His own magic resonated with this residual power in a way he hadn't felt since his days with Dragon Cyril in Kordon. Whoever had huddled at this fire was possessed of more Dragon force than anyone Borrel had ever met.

The next day he found the remains of her campsite at midday and realized that although the other magician was on horseback, he was making better time on foot. This didn't surprise him.

Acclimatized to the altitude of Hilsen Vale and having spent much of the last year walking across the Knownlands, Borrel's long stride ate up the miles. He extended his gait and went farther that night, hoping to catch up.

The late summer evening had crept up from the twilight under the great old trees the next night when he finally caught a gleam of the campfire in the distance. It was fully dark when he walked into the circle of light.

The Dragon Magician was waiting for him. "Hello, friend," she gave the traditional nyad greeting. "Please share my fire."

"Gladly, I thank you," Borrel dropped his pack and sat on a rock, smiling. "I haven't spoken Nyad in years."

"Nor have I. Would you prefer Landish?"

He shook his head. "I'll need Nyad in the Verwood." He delved into his pack, considering the Dragon Magician without looking at her directly. Her nyad brown hair was laced with gray. She had wrapped a soft brown cloak around her shoulders because the wood was chilly even on a summer night, but Borrel could see glimpses of fine red silk at her sleeves and hem. The power of her magic bathed him in warmth as tangible as the heat from the small fire.

"I'm Borrel Starrish," he said, offering the Dragon Magician some nuts from his pack. "My twin sister and I left the Verwood many years ago."

The Dragon took some of the nuts and in turn offered some rabbit jerky. "I'm Halla Felstar."

"You are a great Dragon," Borrel noted.

"I am the Red Dragon, my friend."

"Sweet goddess," he breathed. Like anyone with Dragon force in his or her blood, Borrel knew that the Red Dragon wielded a power second only to the Dragon Highlord himself. "Up until today Dragon Cyril was the most powerful Dragon I'd ever met."

Halla took a long drink of water. "Dragon Cyril is in Kree."

"Aye."

"Aye...." Halla's brown eyes focused sharply on Borrel as her thoughts raced to surprising conclusions. "*You* are the nyad she wrote me about. You somehow befriended a prince of Kordon, a prince who is connected to the Weaver?"

"Uh. Yes." Borrel squirmed on his rock. "I didn't realize anyone was paying any attention to me."

Halla looked him up and down. In his homespun clothes and serviceable boots, Borrel defined ordinary. Ruled by an oligarchy of scholars, nyads preferred subtle outward expressions of rank or riches, but Borrel exhibited none of these.

"Surely you noticed that lots of people pay attention to the friends of princes."

Borrel shrugged. "The Kordish don't pay any attention to nyads no matter who their friends are."

Halla laughed. "That's not exactly true. They remembered you in Rippsbridge." She offered him some more jerky.

"Those people were horrible," Borrel noted. "Wouldn't even help a dying druid."

"How did you manage to attract the attention of a Kordish prince in the first place?"

"We didn't know he was a prince, and I guess he didn't consider himself one." The moon rose over the darkened trees as Borrel explained how he'd met a half-islish slave in Hilsen Vale, walked with him, Florin, and the druid Marith across the Knownlands before ending up in Kordon and realizing that their slave was a prince of both of Baria and Kordon.

"So, the Oracle summoned him to fetch the Weaver off Sageham and take her to Kree?" Halla asked for clarification of this interesting detail.

"Yes. The Kordish nearly executed him, nearly executed all of us, actually. But the Oracle came and convinced the king that Jax wasn't a traitor."

"The Oracle traveled to Kree?"

Borrel nodded. "They did. They said that Jax and Weaver Klaris are supposed to do something together to stop the dragons from returning, but when I left Kree, they hadn't figured out what that is."

Halla placed another log on her fire. "We are well met, then Borrel Starrish. The Highlord has also learned that the dragons are returning. He wanted to speak to the Weaver, but I believe he's decided to do something else now."

"Do what?"

"I don't know," Halla's whisper was painful. "I am traveling to the Verwood to speak to the nyad magi about something that I read in the archive long ago. A bit of prophecy, I think." She looked at him, her brown eyes a mirror to her fire. "I hope the magi can help us deal with this because if we don't...."

Borrel shifted uncomfortably. "You are going to the Verwood on a mission to save the world, Dragon Halla. I'm just going to ask a stupid question about my broken heart. I feel pretty callow."

Halla shook her head. "Truth be told, my heart is tied up in this too, my lad. You see the Highlord is suffering...terribly."

"Ah." Borrel heard the love and anguish in her voice.

For another fortnight Borrel and Halla hiked together under the shade of the giant trees. They shared the stories of their lives, their magics, their loves. It was the first time either of them had put words on the powerful emotions that colored their lives. Halla, with the long practice of a great teacher, tutored Borrel and in those few days increased his proficiency and his grasp of his magic, more than doubling his abilities.

For his part, Borrel felt the tightness that had bound his heart and soul begin to loosen as Halla laughed at his tales of adventures with the paradox that was Jax.

Halla had family in the nyad city on the shore of the vast Lake Cronkie. Borrel's aunt lived farther away to the north. Unlike the built environment of other cities, the nyad capital was a carefully planted and cultivated grove of trees. The nyads made homes in ancient oaks and pines: their markets and gardens framed by elms and aspen, flowering crabapple and fragrant chokecherry.

Together they walked among the tree-lined avenue, breathing in the scents of pine and flowers blended with the clean wind off the great lake.

Nyad brown eyes gazed at them from treehouse knotholes and breaks in hedges as they made their way to the central grove. Here, a semi-circle of white-haired nyads sat under the sheltering boughs of a tremendous oak. Borrel stopped, swamped with memories of the last time he'd been here. His Aunty Alpeth had dragged him and Florin into the circle before the nyad magi and asked to be released from the responsibility of caring for her cousin's orphans. Borrel's magic had grown too powerful for her to ignore, and she claimed that she lacked the resources necessary to have him properly trained. Borrel remembered his grief and fear and guilt that both he and Florin would be homeless because of the Dragon force that ran in his blood.

Neither Borrel nor Florin cared for Alpeth any more than she cared for them, but she was the only family they had, and although nearly adults by nyad standards, the twins had no idea where they would go or how they would survive.

"You will go west, Borrel Starrish," the High Mage had pronounced his doom in a voice as soft as the wind through the leaves. "There you will find a guide for your magic. Your twin may go with you or stay in the Verwood, as she pleases."

Together Borrel and Florin had left the magi feeling both abandoned and betrayed. They'd never set eyes on Aunty Alpeth again. Florin, more offended by the sentence of exile than Borrel himself, stoutly vowed to go with him. He was glad she did. Her skills as a tracker and a guide had provided their livelihood as they made their way first to Fort Rim and finally to find a home and a community in Hilsen Vale.

But Hilsen Vale wasn't home anymore. He glanced at Halla, but her gaze was unfocused, her attention clearly fixed on something far away.

Borrel watched a nyad supplicant kneel before the semi-circle of magi. He recognized almost all the faces of the magi, despite the intervening years. Only two of the magi were new to him. The High Mage was as willowy as ever, her white hair tightly bound around her head.

The other supplicant rose, bowed and turned away, tears spilling down his face. Borrel took a deep breath and stepped into the circle. He knelt.

"Borrel Starrish returns to the Verwood." The soft voice had not changed.

"I come to you with a mystery, Magi."

"Speak."

"I met a woman, a landish woman, from the desert south. I loved her. I still love her, and it's as if she is haunting me."

One of the newer magi snarled. "This is no mystery. You insult us by bringing such a trivial, personal problem to this sacred space."

"I beg you—." Borrel began, but the High Mage had raised a brown hand.

"This woman lives yet?" The leaves seemed to ask the question.

"I don't know."

"Can't you send her a letter?" another asked in a voice like snapping twigs.

"I haven't the magic to do that."

"A pen and paper take no magic."

"There's no way to deliver such a letter to the Rocredlands."

There was a long pause. The magi swayed very gently in their circle.

The High Mage rose and stepped to Borrel. Her brown eyes were rimmed with blue as she peered into his face. "Is it time?"

"Time for what?" he asked.

"Blood must mix and frontiers clear." The old Mage shook her head. Borrel realized that everyone listening was terrified by the ache in the High Mage's rustling voice. "I had not thought it would happen in my time."

"What would happen in your time?" the crackling twigs asked sharply.

"Perhaps Halla Felstar will tell us." The High Mage held out her hand.

Halla's gaze had regained its customary sharp focus. She stepped into the circle.

"Is it time, Halla?" asked the High Mage.

"I came to ask you that question."

"Go read the rings."

Halla bowed. "Thank you."

"And take young Borrel with you."

Borrel sat stiffly in the Felstar tree. He hadn't been in a traditional nyad home in a long time and the memories were unpleasant. But the Felstar family was generous and gentle, where his Aunt Alpeth had been stingy and mean. Halla's white-haired sister served Borrel the traditional nyad food that he'd always hated when Alpeth made it, but he choked it down thinking he'd had worse or certainly less.

"What are the rings the High Mage spoke of?" he asked when he could graciously claim to have eaten enough.

"Did you never visit it?" Halla frowned at him. "Surely someone should have taken you there when your magic became apparent."

Borrel shook his head.

"It's a great, ancient henge that was tumbled in an earthquake just before the dragon interregnum. The ruin still holds the rings."

"What rings?" Borrel was thinking of gold and silver bands, maybe some adorned with glittering jewels.

"Tree rings, of course." Halla smiled. "Remember to think like a nyad here, my lad. Someone should have taken you there. I spent many long hours reading the rings before I went away to study magic elsewhere."

Borrel shrugged uncomfortably. "My aunt didn't have the means to support my studies."

Halla rose. "It will be my pleasure then, Borrel, to show you the wonders of the nyad archive."

Golden summer sunshine spilled into a wide clearing. Vast moss-covered gray stones stood or lay in the ruin of a rough circle while bright green grass and blue and yellow summer flowers smiled at the blue sky above.

Halla wove her way among the silent stones. Borrel followed breathlessly. The magic here weighed on him, pushed against the Dragon in his blood. After a few moments, he sank to his knees in the soft turf, tears pouring down his face.

"What is the matter?" Halla turned to him, worried.

"This magic. What is it?"

"Mystic, of course. A very old type of Mystic. You're not suffering cross-magic?"

He shook his head. "No. It's like Lexyl's magic. Just like Lexyl's magic."

"Really? This Lexyl of yours is becoming more and more interesting."

A shadow fell across the two of them and the windy voice of the High Mage caressed Borrel's raw feelings. "Come to the archive, now. Let's see if we are remembering correctly."

At the center of the circle a tall stack of monoliths rose to the sun. The rock was honeycombed with openings, some tiny, some large enough for Borrel to stand in. Each niche held a round slice from the trunk of a tree.

Halla put a hand to her lips. "Which one was it?" she asked reflexively.

"Has to be this one, I should think," said the High Mage gesturing to a cave-like opening in the rock. "Give a hand here, lad," she said.

Borrel and Halla together rolled a tree ring taller than Borrel into the sunlight. The outer rim of the tree was black, and he rubbed soot off his hands onto his trousers.

All races of the Knownlands could count a tree's life in its rings, but the nyads could read a much richer history here. Halla ran her long brown fingers over the rough surface that had formed the heart of the huge tree. The High Mage and Borrel watched. He felt Halla's magic flare and mingle with the innate forces of the magi and the tree itself.

Borrel's own power snagged in the flow and recognition flooded him. "This was once the sacred oak," he whispered.

"Did you think they lasted forever?" the High Mage's voice was sad.

"Here!" Halla sang. "This is what I remembered." Her fingers read the rings. "There are dragons here." Her fingers swept outward from the center of the ring. "And again here, but they don't stay."

"Dragons?" Borrel looked at the distance between the rings, seeing the millennia.

"And here." Halla had closed her eyes. "Here's the fall of Axterre."

Halla's fingers reached the edge of the ring. She pulled them away and looked at the soot blackening her fingers. "This tree fell when the dragons burned the Verwood."

Borrel had grown up cringing at the horrific tales from the dragon interregnum. The beasts had burned almost the entire Verwood a thousand years ago. Over half the nyad population had been killed. The remnant fled to other, smaller forests, returning slowly as the trees grew back over the centuries.

Like all the other peoples of the Knownlands, the nyads produced few children. Longer lived than most, their numbers grew slowly, but even a thousand years later, the nyad population was much smaller than it had been before the dragon interregnum.

The High Mage's crooked fingers ran along the tree. "See this, Halla. The Axterrans banished the dragons here and here again."

"How?" Borrel leaned closer, reaching his own fingers to touch the rings. The words leapt from the rough wood like a shout. "This is the poem that Lexyl gave to Jax."

"What is?" Halla turned to stare at him.

Borrel touched the tree again and read aloud:

> *"Oracle, speak the Mother's truth:*
> *Dragons come with claw and tooth.*
> *Your purpose for one thousand years:*
> *Is to remember fire and tears.*
>
> *A Paradox who can't be found.*
> *The Mother stirs and shakes the ground.*
> *Oceans rise to touch the trees,*
> *And bring a ruler to his knees."*

"Your Lexyl gave this poem to Prince Javix?"

"Yes." Borrel felt a little self-conscious when she put it like that. He wasn't used to being important or knowing people of significant power. "Lexyl had the bit about the paradox, and she gave it to Jax because he's so many contradictory things."

"As you have explained," Halla nodded, placing her own fingers on the rings near Borrel's.

> *"The opposites must now adhere*
> *And blood must mix while frontiers clear*
> *Align the magic, love and fae*
> *To turn the dragon threat away*
>
> *The Weaver and the Paradox*
> *A child born among Redrocks*
> *At Axterre the Cornerstone*
> *Holds lyrics to the Dragon Song."*

She stopped reading, frowning. "It looks like a couple more lines have been scrubbed out." Halla raised her eyes to the High Mage. "What is this?"

"The Prophecy: The key to the banishment."

"I bet this is what Jax and Weaver Klaris were looking for," Borrel muttered. "It names them, for goddess' sake." He stood away from the tree ring, thinking.

"Scry for them," the High Mage ordered.

With a new ease learned from his time with Halla, Borrel crafted a small fire in the lee of one of the fallen stones. He focused his magic and called for Jax. The flames darkened but revealed nothing.

"May I?" Halla stepped in, adding her magic to Borrel's. The intensity of the fire increased and the High Mage backed away, but still the flames showed nothing.

"It's just like when the Highlord tried to find the Weaver. She and this Javix can't be found," Halla said.

"Try finding someone else," suggested the High Mage.

Borrel felt Halla's magic redirect the intent of the scry and quite suddenly the flames turned red and Highlord Raggar looked up at them. He clearly recognized Halla's magic and smiled sadly. Borrel felt Halla send a wave of love over the scry and then it was gone. A small, blackened patch of grass gave lazy wisps of smoke up to the sun.

"I haven't done many scries," Borrel confessed quietly. "Do you think maybe Jax is dead?"

Halla shook her head. "Scry for someone dead and the flames turn blue."

Borrel sighed. "Jax is the paradox. *Child born among Redrocks.*" He grinned. "I know who can help us there. No one knows Axterre or the Rocredlands better than Lexyl St. Clare."

"Scry for her," suggested the High Mage.

Again, Halla and Borrel joined their power. The flame again glowed in the gray shade of the rock, but again dimmed and no image appeared.

Borrel's heart clenched.

"Another of your friends who can't be found." Halla closed the scry, frowning at the younger nyad. "Strange company you keep, Borrel."

"I hadn't tried to scry for her before," he slumped against a standing stone. "It seemed invasive, since I probably will never see her again."

Halla and the High Mage rolled the tree ring back into its slot in the rock.

The High Mage raised her arms and swayed silently for a moment among the rustle of leaves in the center of the ruined henge. Finally, she lowered her arms and turned to Halla and Borrel. "Your names aren't in the banishment, but your hearts are entangled with those who are." She paused and Borrel heard implacable resolution in her voice as she whispered his doom: "Go to Axterre."

Jax walked among the trolls bound in the hold and considered each one by the light of a lantern. Finally, he stopped in front of a young troll whose face was still marked with streaks of ochre powder and azure eye shadow.

"Use this fellow," he said to Lieutenant Warrix. "He's someone of status."

"Aye, my lord." Warrix motioned to several sailors who came to separate the troll from the others.

Jax stood back, watching, coughing.

"What are they doing? Where are they taking me?" the troll demanded. The Barians made no effort to understand the troll's Landish.

"You might have to go for a little swim," Jax told him.

"You can't drown me!" the troll exclaimed. "My mother is Velga Bladdervork, the Opposition Leader! She's important! *I'm* important."

Jax smiled. "I thought so." He turned away from the troll who began to wail. "I can't swim! You can't do this to me! I demand that you set me ashore!"

Jax motioned to another troll on the edge of the group. "I'll take this one in the jolly boat. Make sure he's bound hand and foot."

"Yes, my lord."

Just moving through the holds of the ship exhausted Jax. His lungs felt thick and heavy. He returned to his cabin and slumped at his desk, his head in his hands.

"Must you do this today?"

He looked up at Klaris. "If the dragons are coming at Darkfest, we don't have time to waste."

"We don't have time for you to fall at the feet of a bunch of trolls either."

"I'll try to stay afloat," he smiled.

Goddess, Klaris longed to kiss him. But the assistant druid entered followed by Jax's steward. They fed him a big mug of broth and a bit of fishcake along with the henbane and spiderwort tisane improved with mint. Klaris stood by the big stern windows and watched as they got him dressed.

He turned to Klaris. "Give me a kiss for luck," he said, smiling. "This is the day I put an end to slavery in the Hanter iron mines."

She didn't have to be asked twice. Her lips met his, her hands tangled in his hair, not wanting to let him go.

He pulled away finally. "I guess we shouldn't play with that fire," he said softly, the loss clear in his blue eyes.

"You and your damned bargains," she snapped.

"Barians love bargains, you know." He teased. "It's the merchant in all of us."

He nodded to Captain Blanx on the quarterdeck. They'd all been through the plans many times. He glanced at the two boats waiting in the calm, dark waters of the lake. The nameless troll lay bound in the bottom of the launch. They'd had to gag him to stop his shouting.

"My lord!" the aristocratic troll, bound by the rail called frantically. "My lord, what are you going to do to me?"

"Use you as bait," Jax said succinctly. He smiled at the look of terror on the troll's face, knowing quite well the interpretation the troll would put on this.

Gingerly, he climbed down into the launch and took his place in the stern. He braced himself against a thwart and nodded to the coxswain. The rowers bent to their oars and the boat swam into the sun-spangles. Behind him, the *Sharkin* and the *Eagle* swung on their anchors, their decks lined with silent Barians watching the two ships' boats pull toward the Hantish shore, the troll at the rail still howling. The other two galleons sailed back and forth further out.

As the land grew closer, Jax noted the familiar beach, the same wind-twisted trees, the same sulfuric smell overlaid with the bitter smoke belching from the smelting fires within the low gray mine compound that brooded up the slope.

The dock he had built under Oblek's lash had suffered only minor weathering in the three Risings since the ferry had sunk. Jax squinted against the sun and remembered the dark pit up there in the mine compound. He took a deep breath, steeling himself against the horror of his memories. His beleaguered lungs rejected the familiar, acrid air and he coughed violently.

The wooden boards of the dock creaked under his boots and swayed a little with the weight of forty Barians as they disembarked from their boats. The Barians moved onto the grass covered slope. The path had disappeared from disuse. Jax motioned to his crew. The troll, still tightly bound, was brought forward.

"Tell me your name," he demanded.

The troll spat at Jax's feet.

Jax raised an eyebrow. "Very well, Spit, you are to speak on behalf of your fellows in our holds. Tell the mine boss that we have ninety-four of you and we're willing to make a deal with him."

"He won't deal with you thievin' pirates!"

Jax shrugged. "If not, we'll toss those trolls overboard and see if any of them can swim."

"You wouldn't."

"I would. Now fetch the mine boss and thank the goddess that you were chosen to speak for your fellows."

The troll looked at Jax's face for a long moment then he put his head down and stomped up toward the gray building.

Jax turned back to look at his ship, anchored in the deep dark water about 100 yards offshore. Even at this distance he could hear squeals and shouts from young troll Bladdervork, who had now been hoisted into a sling and swung out over the water.

Admiral Hix snorted. "I hope they call your bluff, lad. They need to pay for what they did to you."

"Boss Taint won't bargain," Jax answered crisply. "Our loud friend out there will definitely get wet."

"You'd make your point more clearly if you let him drown."

"It's not about making the point, Hix. I'm going to need every single troll we have to trade for the slaves."

"My lords," Lieutenant Warrix said softly. "My lords, they're coming."

"Stand close now," Jax said to the Barians. "Draw your weapons." The slink of metal on metal whispered through the summer air as the sun glinted on forty sharp blades.

Boss Taint hadn't changed. He waddled his massive bulk down the path, his orange eyes spitting fire.

Behind him bounced the slave wrangler and ten more overtrolls. The last troll was dragging a ragged slave.

"Dragons, that's a Barian," Hix muttered, noting that the prince's expression had only grown colder.

Jax stepped forward to meet the mine boss.

"Fishman!" Taint snorted. "Look at you, all fancy now."

"We sold you for bait!" the slave wrangler squealed, apparently delighted to see her half-isle again.

"You tried to," Jax corrected. "But I have another bargain to offer you today."

"Bargain, smargain," snapped Taint. "I don't give a damn about the trolls you've captured; I want our iron back."

"I'm sorry to hear that. I can't give you the iron."

"That will be the death of this one, then." Taint waved a hand to the overtroll holding the slave.

"We got ourselves a new fishman, Fishman," the slave wrangler said cheerfully. "He don't help the others the way you did, but he's more cooperative."

Jax looked at the scarred young sailor on his knees in the sand and recognized cringing submission taught by abuse.

"Alright, Taint. You've got one of ours. If we make an even trade one for one, I still have ninety-three trolls in the holds of my ships."

"I told you, Fishman. I don't care about those idiots. If they're dumb enough to get captured by a bunch of puny Barians led by an ex-slave, then they deserve what they get. I WANT MY IRON!"

"Sorry," Jax shrugged.

"Kill him!" Taint screamed, pointing to the Barian slave.

Jax raised his hand. With a splash the bellowing troll fell from the sling into the water next to the *Sharkin*.

"Oh dear," said the slave wrangler. "Was that young Gorgon Bladdervork?"

"I believe he's the son of your loyal opposition leader." Jax said conversationally.

An overtroll was choking the Barian slave rather effectively. Two of the sailors raised their shining swords, but they made no further move.

Jax took another step forward and cleared his thick throat. "Stop strangling our Barian and I'll see if we can fish that troll out of the lake."

Taint grunted. The Barian slave rubbed the red welts on his neck. "Sweet goddess," he gasped in Islish.

Jax lifted his arm again and the Barians on the *Sharkin* hoisted Gorgon Bladdervork, still bellowing, out of the water.

"Let's start over, Boss," Jax suggested. "I have ninety-four trolls, including the loud and wet Gorgon Bladdervork. I will give them all to you in exchange for all the slaves in the mine's works."

"No. How am I supposed to run the mines without slaves?"

Jax shrugged. "In other countries we pay our laborers."

Taint growled.

The ground rumbled as suddenly a group of trolls on heavy horses pounded around the mine compound and galloped toward the gathering on the shore.

"What is going on?" Hix grunted. He didn't understand the way the trolls spoke Landish.

Jax answered in quick Islish. "The mine boss doesn't want to bargain, but I think more reasonable heads have just arrived."

The trolls who swung down from the thick horses wore colorful silks under light riding cloaks. The leader was a broad fe-troll with an orange headdress that matched her eyes. Two semi-circles of vermillion paint covered each cheek and clashed with her maroon lipstick.

"Thank you for alerting us to this alarming situation, Boss Taint." The fe-troll's teeth were marked with the maroon lipstick.

Jax noticed the grooves in Taint's face deepen.

The fe-troll turned to survey the Barians. "I am Gellaruth Loup, Premier of the Hantland. I don't believe we've met."

Jax bowed. "Premier. I'm afraid I did not have the pleasure of your company during my previous visit to The Hant."

"And who are you?"

The bow caused Jax to erupt in violent coughing, so Taint answered for him: "He's the Fishman, Premier."

"We had him here in the pens for some three years, Ma'am!" gushed the slave wrangler. "He's the most durable slave we ever had."

"A slave?" The premier looked Jax up and down.

"Durable, but a lot of trouble," Taint grumbled.

Jax had caught his breath. "Premier, I am Javix Sharkin, the lord admiral of Baria. I have a business proposal for you."

"I heard you had hostages."

"Indeed."

The premier's lips formed a bloom of maroon. "Go on," she said finally.

"I have ninety-four trolls in the holds of my ships. I will exchange them for all the slaves in the mines."

"Preposterous!" snapped Taint. "He also has a week's-worth of fat midsummer shipments of iron meant for the southern markets."

"Preposterous?" The premier turned toward Taint. "Why?"

"I can't run the mines without slaves."

"You could," Jax suggested. "And if you did, Baria would help you transport your ore to your markets."

"As if we'd ever trust you!" Taint snarled.

"I spent two years ferrying iron," Jax said. "I know how hard it is to get the ore to profitable markets, and what you've been willing to risk to get it there."

"Just because Oblek was willing to risk his neck with boats, doesn't mean the rest of us are that foolish."

Jax shrugged. "No troll would have to go to sea. We'd ship from The Hant."

"But Barians don't come here," Premier Loup noted.

"Because we don't condone slavery."

"So, are you saying that if we release our slaves and use paid labor, you will undertake to transport our iron?"

"For a small percentage of your profits," Jax nodded. The sun was hot, and the familiar smells of sulfur and smelter smoke made it hard to remember who he was today.

The premier looked from Jax to Taint and back to the group of ministers that had ridden down with her.

"You have a very interesting proposal, Lord Admiral. It would represent a major change in the way we operate the mine."

"I hope so."

"Who would work the mine, if not slaves?" Taint demanded.

"Well, there are ninety-four trolls in my ships who will need new work."

"Those fools," Taint spat.

"Fools indeed," the premier looked down her nose at Jax. "And what about the iron ore you've already seized?"

Jax took a slow, careful breath. "That's a small fee I'm extracting."

"Stealing," the premier corrected softly.

Jax smiled. "Money from the sale of that ore will be given as wages to slaves from the pens, when you release them to me."

"Release them?" Taint threw his hands in the air. "You make me regret the day I bought you, Fishman."

"Not nearly as much as I do."

"If we don't release them?" The premier kept her focus on the problem.

"I have no use for the trolls in my ships. They'll be tossed overboard."

"Would you really?"

Jax shrugged. "We already gave that one a swim. What's his name?" He looked to the slave wrangler.

"It's Gorgon Bladdervork, Premier." The slave wrangler gave a brief curtsey. "He's been working on our transport crew."

"Ah," the premier nodded, and the ministers with her stirred.

"He's just another troll to us," Jax said blandly.

"He is the son of our loyal opposition leader, as you probably know." Loup paused, considering. "You folks from down south get very snooty with us trolls over the slavery issue, but we elect our rulers here in the Hantland, while you are still governed by hereditary tyranny."

"For better or worse," Jax conceded. He knew he had to wrap this up or he would, as Klaris feared, fall down at the trolls' feet. "Premier, we cannot stand here all day. Give us the slaves from the mines."

"Fine. Bring them out, Taint."

"What!? No! This is insane!"

"You are probably right, Boss, but we have no choice here."

"Begging your pardon, Premier, but we do have a choice. Tell the Fishman to go home."

"I can't let him drown ninety-four trolls."

"Worthless trolls!"

"Interesting point, Taint," Jax said. "You appear to value your slaves more than your fellow trolls."

"Yes! Well, no. But. Oh, *damn* you, Fishman."

"I've told you many times, my name isn't Fishman."

"Taint, get your slaves. All of them. Now," the Premier ordered. She turned back to Jax. "You've won the round today, Admiral Sharkin." She smiled, showing the maroon-marked teeth. "The electors will have to consider your proposition regarding shipping. I'm not sure they'll agree. You see, one reason trolls justify the practice of slavery is that our political system is far superior to the other races, so we assume that we are superior as a race."

"Perhaps you are, Premier, but surely a superior and enlightened race would not resort to such brutality."

"You don't think so? Well, take the slaves today, *my lord*. And come back to discuss shipping."

Jax bowed again, his head spinning. A line of hunched figures filed out of the mine compound and walked slowly toward the beach. Trollish guards came out too, milling around in a crowd. Jax turned to Hix, grabbing his arm for support and speaking in rapid Islish. "Hold me up while I explain the situation to the slaves."

Hix pretended to take Jax's arm jovially. "I didn't understand three quarters of that, but it appears you convinced them."

Jax raised his voice to speak to the shuffling crowd of slaves. "Listen. We Barians have just bought you all your freedom. We are going to take you on our ships to get you away from here as quickly as possible. We also have extracted some wages for you. I know most of you don't like boats, but you won't have to be onboard for long. Please cooperate with my crew, and we'll get you headed for your homes."

"What'd ye mean, we're free?" asked one slave, her oily hair hanging lank in her face.

"The trolls have decided not to use slave labor in the mines anymore," Jax answered. "They've agreed to let you all go free."

"Thank the goddess!" someone breathed.

"Hooray!" shouted another voice. But these were the only responses. Unsure of what awaited them on the strange Barian boats, and in a future outside the walls where they thought they would die, the slaves silently, fearfully lined up as the Barians instructed.

"Let's get you in the launch, lad," Hix said, supporting Jax down to the beach.

"Be careful now," Jax muttered as he splashed through the waves. "Keep the crews together. We're outnumbered, and some of those slaves aren't too happy to be going on a boat."

"I understand." Hix nodded. "Lieutenant! You heard the lord admiral!"

Twenty slaves packed into the boat, looking about them with frightened eyes. Jax forced himself to keep his feet as the boat began to row back to the *Sharkin*.

He saw the Barian slave sitting on a thwart near him. "What's your name?" he asked to distract himself from his personal misery. "How did they catch you?"

"I'm Ladix Jeffian, my lord. They took me last fall. I was on the *Drixa* when the sealord came here looking for you. While the sealord talked to the mine boss, they invited me into another room and popped me on the head. Next thing I knew, they're calling me 'Fishman,' telling me they had a half-isle slave before and they wanted more of them."

"Did they send you into the tunnels?"

Ladix shook his head. "No. Kept me shoveling fuel into the smelting fires. But the worst of it…" he stopped and glanced up at Jax. "I'm sorry, my lord. I guess the sealord found you somewhere after all."

"No, he didn't. I was the Fishman, for three years."

"Three years, sweet goddess." Ladix shuddered. "But it's your fault, then. Your fault they nabbed me and your fault what they made me do!"

Jax's lungs constricted even more. "What did they make you do?"

"They wanted to breed me. Wanted me to rape the girls. They locked me up and wouldn't feed me until I did it. I tried to explain to the girls, to be inviting and nice, they didn't speak Islish, and I can understand some Landish, but I can't speak it."

The launch thumped gently alongside the *Sharkin*. Jax was grateful to be able to steady himself on the rope latter.

"Goddess," Ladix whimpered. "Sweet goddess, what I've done…."

Jax let the crew hoist him onto the deck and the assistant druid swooped him away to his cabin.

Klaris found him there, wheezing on his bed, with his arm over his eyes.

"Jax?"

"Tell me what's worse, Weaver: The grim life of the poor, condemned to the bilge slums of Haven by an inflexible social hierarchy, or the degradation of slavery? And how can I justify changing one and not the other?"

9

An hour later after another big mug of henbane and spiderwort, Jax stood on the quarterdeck and looked along the length of the *Sharkin* at the dirty, fearful, expectant faces staring back at him. He hardly noticed the Barian crew hanging from the rigging or the midsummer sun spangling the waters of Hanter Lake. The smell of sweaty bodies, musty from the dirt of the tunnels, and the ever-present reek of sulfur took him right back to his own dark memories of being locked away for days and even weeks in the pit Oblek had devised. The tightness in his lungs today was just like the constriction he'd felt at the bottom of that hole. He had to remind himself, just as he had reminded himself then, that the walls were not crushing him, that air would fill his lungs if he inhaled. So, he took a deep breath, coughed, and spoke to the crowd in Landish.

"My friends, today you are free."

Wary cheers, but mostly this statement was met with the stunned or suspicious silence of people who'd been long abused.

"I am Javix Sharkin, the Lord Admiral of Baria, but I spent three years as a slave, just like you, in the iron mines."

"You're Jax." A man's voice rose from the middle of the crowd. "The first Fishman."

Jax nodded, remembering that voice. He smiled at the lean, dirty face of Corvyd Cale. "I'm glad to see you, Lord Corvyd."

Corvyd did not smile as Jax continued to address the crowd.

"We have persuaded the trolls not to use slave labor in the mines."

The newly freed people looked from Jax to one another. Many of them turned to Corvyd with their questions. Could it be true? Could they go home? Were they really released from the horrors of the Hanter iron mines?

"I know that many of you are not comfortable aboard a ship," Jax continued. "But this is the fastest way to get you far from the trolls. They may try to retake you for other purposes, and I can't guarantee that they won't use slaves in the mines again someday. My fleet will disperse today and call at several ports all along the coast."

The people milled around. Some sat and put their confused heads in their hands.

"There's more," Jax noted. "We will give each of you two golden *drixas*. This represents your share of the iron ore we appropriated from the trolls."

"You're giving us money, sir?"

Jax nodded. "Yes. Wages. Use it to get home and start a new life."

Standing next to Jax, Klaris surveyed the crowd. Some folks cried with relief. Some still sat dejected or bewildered. "You'd think they'd be more enthusiastic," she muttered in Islish.

"It isn't easy to start thinking like a free person again," Jax answered. Again, he raised his voice and spoke Landish. "We'll be putting you ashore at either Southant, Brakkle, or at the Vrillbridge. Decide where you want to go and gather into groups."

"I don't like being on this boat!" A woman wailed. Five of the former slaves had already been sick, even though the ship hardly moved in the calm summer lake.

"The quicker we get you organized, the sooner we can get you back on dry land," Jax said briskly. He stood above them, watching as they shuffled around the deck discussing their options. Some wanted to stay with friends even though they came from different places. Others just stood or sat, unable to make a decision at all. Jax's eyes followed Corvyd Cale as he walked among them speaking quietly, and gently ushering them into the right group.

"Why that sly smile?" Klaris asked him.

"I'm glad to see my lord Corvyd Cale earning his privileges."

Klaris tapped her fingers on the rail and looked at the sun, which was well past noon. She didn't say anything, but Jax sensed her impatience and stepped down to the main deck. He moved among the former slaves, recognizing only a few of them, and realizing with horror that more than half of the slaves who'd been with him in the mines a year ago were dead now.

He found Corvyd talking to a man who was sitting on the deck, rocking back and forth, his arms wrapped around his head and ears. Together, they managed to get enough coherent words from the man to understand that he had come from Ohe, and so should go with the group headed to the Vrillbridge.

Corvyd stood finally and looked Jax up and down. "This explains a few things. Sir." He said slowly.

Jax's smile was wolfish. "I'm glad to see you still here, my lord. There aren't many others left that I remember."

"It was a bad winter." Corvyd said grimly. "And they had this new fishman and made him do terrible things. Brought us a lot of grief, he did." Corvyd stopped and fixed Jax with a hard gaze. "He made us hate you. My lord."

Jax accepted the injustice of this. "I'm glad you were there to take care of everyone."

Corvyd snorted. "Couldn't do a damn thing for most of them."

"What happened to Yory and the Crone?"

"The west diggings all collapsed." Corvyd's voice cracked. "Took about fifty slaves. Nearly took me. I was buried for hours in the dark before they came to dig us out."

"Goddess," Jax breathed. It was his own nightmare.

"No. Naught of the sweet goddess in anything that went on behind those mine walls," Corvyd said harshly.

Jax put a hand on his arm. "Agreed. Come below. We'll get you some clean clothes."

Corvyd's stomach rolled as the ship moved, but he followed Jax into the admiral's large cabin. It was a beautiful room.

Brocade-covered chairs, an elegant Darkwood desk, and crystal fixtures shone in the sunlight streaming in through the great windows.

Corvyd turned to Jax trying to connect the starved, disheveled slave to the fine nobleman before him now. The slanted, sea-blue eyes were the same, demanding, self-mocking.

"Who the dragons are you, sir?" Corvyd asked finally.

Jax had sat rather heavily on the sofa. "My father was the seal-ord. My brother is now. My uncle is King of Kordon." The crisp, aristocratic voice at last made sense to Corvyd.

Corvyd frowned, remembering his own haughtiness. "How did you survive? My lord." He demanded, chagrin making him aggressive. "I heard Boss Taint tell them to sell you for bait."

"I was sold to some Hantish druids instead." Jax coughed. "They healed me and freed me, more or less."

A Barian servant came in, said something in Islish to Jax then turned to Corvyd.

Jax shifted stiffly on the sofa. "Here are some clothes more appropriate for you." Jax's steward handed a pile of soft things to Corvyd.

Jax motioned to a screened corner of the cabin. "You can wash and change there. We're going to load the people onto different ships, depending on their destination. I assume you want to go to Southant?"

Corvyd nodded. That would be the quickest way for him to get back to his mother's lands in northern Ily.

"Jax—." The small, Black woman who had been standing next to Jax on the deck came into the cabin. Corvyd hadn't seen such beauty in a very long time. He noted the proprietary frown she shot at Jax, and he recognized the saucy way the admiral looked back at her.

"Weaver Klaris, may I present Lord Corvyd Cale of Norgren. My lord, this is Klaris de Farsouth, the Weaver."

He had been right about the definitive aura of power around her. As a noble, Corvyd couldn't expect to have much magic in his veins, but he'd seen people who did in his brief visits to the Ilyian Royal Court in Brakkle.

Corvyd bowed, feeling as if he'd like to sit down too. Jax Fishman had turned out to be a Prince of both Baria and Kordon. So many things from his first terrible months in the slave pens now made sense to him. He saw quite clearly that Jax had set him on the path to being lord of the slaves himself.

"You knew that troll was going to kill you."

Jax shrugged one shoulder. "I figured he'd put me in that hole for the entire Rising. I wasn't going to do that."

"So you took the ferry out into the Rising to sink it."

Jax nodded.

Klaris was considering him with her head cocked to one side. "But you would have drowned too." She spoke Landish with a throaty Islish accent that Corvyd found very fetching.

"I assumed so." He looked directly at Klaris and spoke quietly. "I hoped so."

A voice called something in Islish through the door. Jax took what seemed to be a rather painful breath and got to his feet. He answered in Islish and moved towards the door.

The Weaver snapped something impatient beneath her breath, but she followed Jax out.

Corvyd stepped behind the screen. He hadn't felt silk against his skin for a year and a half. He rubbed the soft fabric over his face, trembling. He could hardly believe that he was released from the horror of the iron mines. He could go home. He could be Lord Corvyd with good food, a warm soft bed, and choices. Choices.

When he came back on deck many of the former slaves had already been moved to the other ships of Jax's little fleet. A large group from northern Ily who would be put ashore at Southant now sat on the deck. They'd all been handed plates heaped with food and a foamy drink.

Despite the fact of their obvious hunger, the queer Barian food didn't appear to be popular. The dock ale, however, was going down fast and easy. Corvyd sat and tried the food, watching Jax speak to his officers.

Jax leaned against a rail and bowed his head for a moment. The Weaver frowned at this movement. She whispered something and got a grimace from Jax for an answer. She smiled at his scowl in such a way that Corvyd drew certain conclusions. That was one huge sapphire on the Weaver's finger.

Clarity came to Corvyd like a clap of thunder. Jax was wounded or ill. There was clearly something that the Weaver required of Jax, wanted of him. Lust had something to do with it, but that wasn't all of it, Corvyd was certain.

He had absently eaten the rather nasty, tide-tasting food, while lost in his observations of the admiral and the Weaver. He hadn't been paying attention to the Barians who'd been pattering all around the deck to the howling of several silver whistles.

With a crack and a bang, a giant sail fell into place over Corvyd's head. He, and the other freed slaves, cringed.

"Sweet goddess, what are they doing?" a woman shrieked.

"They have to put out the sails to take us to Southant," Corvyd answered, his own stomach objecting to the movement of the boat and the unfamiliar food. Almost all of the landish folk were soon at the rail, heaving the contents of their stomachs into the black, dusty water of Hanter Lake.

Eventually Corvyd collapsed onto the deck. Jax came and knelt beside him. The sea-blue eyes considered him for a long moment then slowly Jax smiled. "You'll be ashore in less than an hour," he promised. "Here's the gold for this group. I know you'll look out for them to make sure no one robs anybody or takes advantages."

Corvyd nodded weakly.

Jax paused for a moment. "There's another thing, Lord Corvyd. Dragons are returning to the Knownlands."

"What?" Corvyd sat up, his head spinning, not sure he'd heard correctly. "Dragons. Real dragons?"

"Yes, the beasts. The Weaver and I are going to try to send them away again, I guess, but if we don't or can't, I've been advising the rulers of the Knownlands to prepare. Stockpile supplies. Set up scattered shelters."

"Scattered shelters?" Corvyd was dazed.

"I don't know how much you know about Barian history, Corvyd. But a thousand years ago, Baria was devastated by the dragons because our government, our wealth, our people were all concentrated in one great city."

"Nez or something like that?" Corvyd muttered.

"Nec."

Corvyd visibly pulled himself together. "But how do you know this? How can you be sure?"

Jax pulled a golden chain from under his shirt. The Oracle's medallion flashed and gleamed. "The Oracle has spoken."

"Dragons," Corvyd swore.

"That was what I said." Jax stood up. "The Weaver and I are going now. Good luck, Corvyd." He smiled. "Goddess bless you."

"And you," Corvyd said softly, as Jax crossed the deck.

A tall, slender gray person stood next to the Weaver on the quarterdeck. Corvyd stood up as Jax joined them. "Watch!" he breathed to the other folk lying beside him. "Something is about to happen."

He was right.

Jax spoke a last time to Captain Blanx. He raised his voice and said something encouraging in Islish to the crew of the great wingship. They cheered in response, and Jax answered with a wide smile and a curious one-handed salute.

Then he disappeared.

Where he and the Weaver and the gray fellow had stood was now nothing but empty deck.

"Whoo!" whispered a woman with a trace of Mystic. "Whoo!" she repeated. "That was some amazing bit of magic, that was."

Corvyd stared at the empty deck. The sun shone down on the whitened planks. After a moment he closed his eyes. This morning he had woken up in the dark of Cave Three to a duty troll yelling. Now he was going home. He thought of his mother and his older sister, and then he remembered those odd islish eyes compelling him to assume a leadership he didn't think he was capable of. Then again, if he could lead the slaves, perhaps he could do something productive in the Norgren too.

Jax clutched at Klaris to regain his balance and blinked at the view that met his eyes. "It's Steppash," he said finally. "Steppash."

"Yes." Klaris moved forward, taking Jax with her. "It is exhausting and somewhat dangerous to teleport."

"Dangerous?"

"There's always the possibility that we'll land somewhere unexpected or inconvenient."

"That pretty well describes where you took me the last time," Jax muttered.

Klaris shot him a glance. "Kree might have seemed inconvenient for you, but you can't say it was unexpected."

Lad Yob had a far better understanding of the difficulties inherent in the type of magic Klaris was doing and the price she would pay, but he just picked up their bags and followed silently though the open gate and into the cobbled streets of Steppash.

"I somehow thought you'd take us all the way to the Vale," Jax was saying.

"We'll have to ride the rest of the way," Klaris answered.

"You ride. I'm going to hire a coach."

"We don't have time for that!"

"Then why don't you just use the Mystic and zap us there?"

She stopped and stared up at him. People were walking around them in the street, staring at the pair of beautifully dressed islish nobles, evidently arguing in their weird language.

"There's a price, Jax. Any magician has to pay for whatever magic he or she does. Not so much for the little things, the goddess gives that power freely. But the bigger workings are costly."

"Costly?"

"Of course!" She was clearly exasperated with him, and he wasn't really sure why. Jax stared at her for a moment, letting the impact of her point settle past his personal discomfort. But damn it, he *was* uncomfortable. His chest ached and he wanted to lie down for about two days, preferably somewhere where a decent druid could care for him. He had thought he'd be under Mother Marith's roof in Hilsen Vale this night. Finding himself in Steppash, three or four days on a bumpy road from the Vale, was more than disappointing.

"Weaver," Lad Yob spoke quietly. He was aware of the staring people and trolls of Steppash and thought it would be a good idea to get these two off the public street. Word of the Barians' actions against the Hanter iron mines could not have traveled all the way to Steppash in one day, but soon the news would arrive, and then people would remember that a couple of flamboyant islish people had been snapping at each other in the road.

"Weaver, Admiral, we should find lodging."

Jax glanced at him and finally noticed the curious faces surrounding them. "Aye. The inn's just here."

Kajjon was good at remembering faces. It was a skill that he had honed and used to build his business. The nobleman standing before him now was, he knew, the same half-isle who'd been a slave to the Valish druid Doc Appandel.

"Welcome back, my lord."

The nobleman smiled. "Thank you, Kajjon. I need three rooms, dinner, and your best wine."

"I'm happy to see your position has improved, my lord," Kajjon answered, pulling keys from the hooks behind the counter.

Jax put gold on the counter. "Indeed."

Klaris had the larger room with a view out over the city walls to the smoking geysers across the river. They ate their dinner there as the sunset turned the plumes of steam red and pink and violet.

Jax sat away from his empty plate and swirled the red stuff masquerading as wine in his glass. He remembered the table scraps he'd wolfed in the stable here last year. He thought of the ale and kindness from Doc and the comfort from the man chained next to him. But now, only a little more than a year later, he found his palate so spoiled by fine Kordish wine that he couldn't even drink the Hantish red in his glass. He coughed, wishing he could get the thickness out of his lungs, and thought about trying to ride three days up the mountains to Hilsen Vale.

He placed his still-full wine glass on the table. "What's the cost involved in using magic to get us from here to the Vale?"

"It'll warp my soul."

He shook his head. "You pulled enough magic to hoist you, me and Oblek all the way to Kree when you weren't even supposed to have any magic. Did that warp your soul?"

Klaris made an impatient gesture. "You didn't notice that I paid for that?"

"I thought that was from your Mastery or cross-magic."

"The cross-magic was something entirely separate."

Jax's blue eyes stared at her.

"Magical energy comes from the earth and the holy mother," she explained.

"Even Dragon force?"

"Even Dragon force. But it is the magician's soul that channels it. Powerful workings warp the soul, the way a flood changes the bed of a river."

"I don't like the sound of that," he muttered.

Klaris frowned at him. "Surely you know this? Every magician who goes to study at Caledra or at Dragonsholm must pass the Soul Test."

"I've heard of that."

"You've heard of it?" she grumbled, looking away, then turning back to him with mild fury. "Look, the Soul Test is the most unpleasant experience anyone can imagine. It's invasive and humiliating. We're made very vulnerable and exposed."

"Sounds kind of like slavery," he said quietly.

"It's not at all like slavery. We have a choice to take it or not. But it is unpleasant, and the experience never leaves us. Every time we work a great magic, a bit of that humbling, humiliating experience comes back to remind us that we are just people, with faults and strengths and sometimes illogical feelings."

"It's meant to be a good thing," Lad Yob added softly. "It's meant to keep those people with great power from misusing it."

"It certainly makes me think twice before I do something really powerful, because I know that I'll have to give up some of my soul."

"Is a soul finite? Can you use it all?"

She shrugged. "There are old stories in the very ancient archives of that sort of thing, but since we found the salutations to the sun and the moon, that doesn't happen anymore. These exercises restore us."

"Does warping the soul change you?" he asked finally.

Her green eyes met his blue ones. "Always."

He looked down and rose from the table. "I'll arrange horses for the morning,"

"No coach?"

"We'll get there a day sooner if we ride."

Given he could only get about half a breath at a time, Jax would have preferred to take a coach, and riding horseback meant that he was thrown to the ground three times before evening. Klaris magically called a small camp cabin up from the earth in a green clearing on the slopes of the Ledden Rises. His body throbbing, he collapsed into his blanket and coughed himself into oblivion. Klaris fell asleep listening to his wheezing.

The next day he awoke hot and aching from more than being knocked onto the ground. He said nothing, but Klaris's gaze darkened as the horse threw him again and yet again. Each time, he rose slowly, coughing thickly. By the third day when the horses crested the Roaring Pass and began to descend towards the boulders marking Hilsen Gate, sweat was seeping through his shirt, and his face was white.

"I hope they're home," Jax gasped, as they came upon the druid's burrow in the long summer twilight. "And not down at the pub or out at some farmstead." He slipped off his horse, which turned to bite him. He pushed the mare's head away. "Marith!" He called. "Doc?"

Klaris was dismounting, so she didn't see exactly how Jax ended up flat out on the grass underneath a dark-haired woman who was covering his face in ardent kisses. Klaris stepped into the yard, frowning. Lad Yob stood holding all three horses.

"Dylith, what are you doing?" a small woman came around the hill, carrying a clump of fresh greens, still dangling roots and earth.

"Jax is back!" The dark-haired woman sat up, straddling Jax's hips, and pushing her hair behind her ears. "Sweet goddess," she said, finally looking more closely at the man on the grass beneath her. "You're ill."

"It's always something with our Jax," Marith grumbled, but her eyes sparkled. "Get off him, Dylith. Ah, and here's the Weaver, too."

"Hello, Mother Marith," Klaris said, her smile a little brittle, as she watched Dylith carefully help Jax to his feet and brush grass from his hair and his clothes with a distinct familiarity.

"Mam," Jax pulled himself away from Dylith to embrace Mother Marith. "I need you."

"How gratifying. Come along inside."

Dylith turned at last to see Jax's companions. Klaris saw the joy on the woman's creamy face draining away. Neither of them spoke as they followed Jax and Marith into the burrow.

Jax let the poppy take him down with relief and gratitude. Sitting on a small stool next to the cot, Klaris listened to Mother Marith explain to Dylith the collection of herbs she'd given him to clear the congestion in his lungs and fight the infection that was giving him the fever.

"What's this?" Marith raised Jax's bandaged right hand.

"A long story," Klaris answered with resignation, not sure her Landish was up to it.

Marith unwrapped the hand, muttering and then growling. "Don't you islish have druids?"

"Of course," Klaris shrugged. "But the one on Jax's ship was not so good."

Marith bent closer to the wound. "Not so good?" she repeated. "This is criminal." She began a very technical explanation for Dylith, which went well beyond Klaris's Landish.

When they were done, Marith and Dylith washed their hands. Klaris moved to stand nearer the fire and watched Doc put a pan of greens on the blaze.

Marith turned to Dylith and broke the awkward silence. "Dylith, why don't you run down to the pub and bring back a few bottles for our supper."

"Will the nyad, Florin, be there?" Klaris noted that Dylith's eyes were violet.

"I don't think so, my...my lady," Dylith stumbled to find the proper honorific. "She took a group of tourists up to the Allerdale Falls yesterday and that's usually at least a three-day trek."

"You're in a hurry, Weaver?" Doc said, sprinkling goat cheese into the pan.

"Yes."

Marith glanced at Dylith. "Run along, Dylith. Dinner's almost ready."

"My husband won't want to miss you," Doc said, slicing bread at the table. "He's visiting a farmstead now, but he'll be back tomorrow night. He studied at Caledra. I'm sure you wouldn't have remembered him; he was far below your level, Weaver, but he goes on and on about how wonderful your Mystic is."

Klaris accepted this oblique praise. "What is his name?"

"Adgar Allerdale."

"Like these falls where the nyad has gone?"

"Yes," Doc grinned. "Come sit here, Weaver. And your man, Mr. Yob, you'll go there. It'll be the five of us here tonight."

Dylith returned with three fat black bottles. Deftly she cracked them open and poured dark liquid into the glasses waiting on the table. White foam rose to the surface.

"It's our famous Vale Ale," Marith said in answer to Lad Yob's curious expression.

Despite the ale and Doc's general volubility, the awkwardness between Dylith and Klaris pressed heavily on every pause in the conversation.

It was Dylith who heard the coughing from the cot in the surgery. She was up and at Jax's bedside before anyone else even realized he was waking.

"Do I smell Mam's goat cheese and greens?" he asked hoarsely.

"Aye." Dylith's heart ached. She'd forgotten how lovely his voice was, a little rough from sleep with that elegant Kordish accent.

Jax looked away from her eyes. "I love that."

"No, you can't have any." Marith had joined Dylith in the surgery. "You can have some broth and lots of it, but no solid food until tomorrow."

"But—."

"Hush. You know you can't put food on top of the poppy tea."

He sat up carefully, dizzy, but not so achy or feverish. He looked at Marith's lined face and blue eyes and smiled, his heart full.

Dylith saw the love plain in Jax's face, and she turned away to fetch the broth. Klaris and Doc came to look into the little surgery, both of them holding their glasses of ale.

Jax smirked at Klaris's nearly full mug. "Don't like the ale?"

She shrugged and, unable to find a polite response in Landish, said nothing.

"You get used to it," Jax offered.

Klaris took a dogged sip and changed the topic. "The druids tell me that Florin is not here now."

"She'll be back in a day or two," Doc said complacently. "You could use a little rest anyway, lad."

Jax sipped his broth and coughed. Klaris turned away, placed her ale on the table and walked out the front door. She strode back and forth amid the flowers in front of the burrow as the twilight deepened to night.

"There's naught you can do, Weaver." Lad Yob's voice came quietly from the doorway.

"I know. Jax does need the rest. But you understand...."

"I do, Weaver. I do."

Doc came out carrying chairs under both arms. "It's a beautiful night to watch the stars," he said. Marith followed, with a few blankets, and then Dylith came, supporting a wheezing Jax. They sat and watched the sky darken from blue to a sparkling black.

Doc had finally managed to engage Klaris in a discussion about some architectural improvements that Adgar had been contemplating. Before long, the two of them rose from their chairs and walked around the side of the burrow, Lad Yob trailing behind them. Jax felt Klaris's magic flare and build and heard Doc cheering.

"Let's get you back inside," Marith said to Jax.

"I'll help him, Mam," Dylith said quickly. "You go ahead."

Marith slipped into the house, well aware that neither of them made any movement to follow her.

Klaris felt better, having enjoyed using the Mystic to expand the burrow according to Adgar's plan. The residual glow evaporated as she came around to the front. Jax sat wrapped in blankets against the chill of the mountain night, his arm around Dylith's shoulders. Their heads were close together, Jax's voice was soft, gentle.

Klaris had no idea what he was whispering to the woman with those lovely violet eyes, but anger boiled through her. "It looks like you're feeling better, my lord," she snapped, Islish coming first to her tongue.

Dylith jumped up. "I'm helping Jax to his bed," she said quickly.

"I wish you joy of it," Klaris answered, flying away into the house.

"That's not what—," Jax started to answer. He did in fact let Dylith support him back into the house. He sat on the cot in the surgery, Dylith fussing around him.

A rapid knocking on the door startled them all. A small girl followed her knocks into the house. "Come quick, Mother! Aunty Ermis says her baby's coming now!"

Marith stood at the foot of the stairs. "You go, Dylith. I'll take the sun salutations in the morning."

Gratefully, Dylith escaped the burrow.

Upstairs in the new rooms, Klaris sat on her bed, disturbed at the violent emotions coursing through her. She went to the window and watched Dylith leave with a child. The burrow grew quiet as the others settled in to sleep. Klaris was exhausted herself. It had been a long ride today and she hadn't been as comfortable as usual in the saddle.

She twisted the sapphire on her finger. Damn him! Softly she slipped from her room and descended the stairs. A faint glow from the embers of the fire lit her way across the dark room to the surgery.

"Klaris." He wasn't sleeping either. "Can't you sleep?"

She sat on the edge of the cot and wrinkled her nose. Suddenly her anger exploded. "What do you think you're doing to that woman? To me?"

He sat up and tried to take her hand, but she pulled away from him.

"I'm trying not to hurt her."

"That's not what it looks like. Not what it smells like."

"Smells like?"

"You smell of her."

"Klaris.... Dylith was kind to me when I ended up here last summer."

"*Kind?* Is that what you call it?"

He leaned away from her and pulled the Dragon force within her Mystic to light a small candle by the side of the bed. The tears on Klaris's cheeks gleamed in the faint light before she wiped them away.

"I owe her the courtesy of an explanation."

Klaris stood up, her face stiff. "I see. You're very good about extending the benefit of your fine sensibilities to everyone, aren't you Jax? You'll sacrifice yourself for the Barian people or those xenophobic fools in Twistford, or some pretty village girl. Someday, I really hope to know the benefit of your generosity."

She turned away, furious, and ashamed of herself.

The sapphire caught the candlelight and flashed. Her attention focused on it, she didn't hear him slip out of the cot and come up behind her. She relished the strength of his arms and his warmth, even though she could hear the wheeze of his lungs. He kissed her hair, then her tear-salted cheeks and finally found her mouth. Her lips were soft in her distress, softer than he remembered.

He pulled her down to the cot. A fit of coughing brought him up short.

"Damn," Klaris sat up. "Damn, damn, damn."

"Yeah."

Slowly she rose from the cot, pulling her nightdress back into place.

"Never doubt that I love you, Klaris. You."

"But she's so beautiful, with those purple eyes. She's tall, and...."

"She's not you, Klaris. You light me up. Even when you're mad at me."

One corner of Klaris's lip quirked up.

"You wear my ring." He pushed his advantage.

She looked into his eyes and her heart eased. "I do not know how we are going to keep your promise to the sealord," she whispered.

Jax thought of the long road between the Vale and Axterre, of the many days and nights between there and here, and Klaris's sweet body beneath her nightdress. "Goddess help us."

11

"We'll levitate!"

"What?" Borrel leaned closer to the Red Dragon, afraid he hadn't heard her correctly over the thundering roar of the great falls.

She turned a wide smile upon him. "You heard me."

"I can't do that," he protested.

"You can."

Around him, shaggy pine trees rose hundreds of feet through the mist towards the clear sky above. Wide and green, the Barthrobar River rushed smooth and deep towards its great plunge over the Verfalls to the lower land of Ohe below.

Halla knelt in the long grass on the riverbank, holding the gunwale of their small skiff. Riding a boat down the turbulent river from its source at the great lakes of the Verwood had already taxed Borrel's tolerance for aquatic transportation, especially during the three days of rapids.

But Halla's proposal to use magic to lift the boat over the 300-foot drop was beyond Borrel's imagination and, therefore, beyond his skill.

Halla pretended to notice his dilemma for the first time, found the boat's bowline and tied it to a sturdy tree up the bank. "Alright," she said. "I shall wait."

"Look, Dragon Halla," Borrel began respectfully. "I'd rather you just did it."

"Why?"

"Because if I mess this up, we're going to end up smashed to pulp on the rocks down there."

Halla crossed her arms and shook her head in an expression Borrel had come to dread over the last two weeks since they'd left the nyad magi. She wasn't buying this excuse, and he knew better than to try others.

"I'm afraid I will fail," he admitted baldly.

"Are you afraid to fail or afraid to try?"

"Both."

Halla nodded. "Courage is not a lack of fear."

"So, what is it?" Borrel looked at the little boat. "Stupidity?"

Halla laughed. "Sometimes it appears that way."

Borrel suddenly remembered watching a rumpled Jax murmuring *dragons fry me*, in his crisp, aristocratic Landish as he stared longingly across the Rippbridge towards Ily. Borrel had watched Jax make the choice to risk a traitor's death in order to save Mam Marith. The nyad remembered how Jax had squared his shoulders and made his choice.

That was courage, Borrel supposed, and there was nothing stupid about it. He straightened his own shoulders, grit his teeth against the fear squirming in his gut and delved into the flow of Dragon force. He built a succession of spells; the boat remained gently bobbing on the surface of the clear water.

Halla sat on a smooth river rock and pulled her gray cloak around her thin shoulders. The mist rising from the crashing water was chilly, despite the sunshine of midsummer. A part of her chaffed at this delay, the part of her that felt Raggar every time he worked magic, no matter where he was. But she knew that each student must learn at his or her own pace, and with the intuition granted by her own great magic, Halla knew that Borrel needed the Soul Test to focus his training and give him the confidence to push himself to the edges of his own power.

That's what he faced here at the lip of the pounding Verfalls: the definitive test of his own unique character.

During the month they'd now spent travelling the tree-shaded paths of the Verwood, Halla had come to know Borrel Starrish far better than most of the young Dragon Magicians she tutored at Jezel. This knowledge gave her insight on how to devise a Soul Test for him here, far from the usual structure provided at Dragonsholm. As she expected, he was facing this test with his usual lack of confidence masked behind his self-deprecating humor.

She watched another spell build and fizzle. Borrel growled in frustration and stomped away. He came to an abrupt halt at the edge of the cliff.

The earth dropped away at his feet. Below, beyond the rising mist from the fall, the trees began to thin, and the river gleamed in the distance, winding its way across the rolling plains of Ohe.

Borrel looked back at the water of the river, moving swiftly and eternally to the precipice. He shuddered, imagining himself caught in that current, inextricably drawn to the edge then thrown out in the air, weightless for a moment, and then a scream and a fall and all the weight of the river pounding the breath and life from his body.

Fascinated, he stared at the apparently solid, green glass of the river above the falls. At the lip, sun shone through the cohesive body of water as it flowed over the edge. Then as it fell, the river fragmented and shattered into millions of droplets, each catching the sun.

Those droplets rose as mist to touch his face, cold but harmless. Droplets that moments ago had been part of the solid mass of river flowing almost eagerly to its own disintegration.

"Sweet goddess," he breathed as the epiphany ripped through him. He saw the river as a unity and the falls as the separation. He saw the power of the water as a river and the ephemeral beauty of each drop of mist making sunlight into rainbow. His breathing became rapid and shallow as the river and the falls became a metaphor.

"Sweet goddess," he repeated, rubbing his hands over his face, wet with cool mist and warm tears. He felt the thrill of the river as each droplet in the clear green movement hungered to fly free. He accepted the water's urge to become air and acknowledged the paradox of a wood-born nyad gifted with the fire of Dragon force taught the map of his own soul by water.

He did not consciously call his magic, but simply began to use the flow in a way he had never before considered. Behind him, the little skiff rose, dripping from the river. It floated above the bank, tethered by the rope.

Halla raised her head and opened her eyes. Her joy at the beauty of Borrel's magic was tempered with her awe at the increasing depth of Dragon force. Borrel had tapped into it, as she did herself. But he would not have the experience to realize that the flow of Dragon force was growing stronger, developing more powerful currents, undertows, and back-eddies. It was as if the magic was a river that had been joined by another river, just as large and just as deep.

Glowing with the force inside them both, Halla untied the boat and climbed aboard. It rocked gently on the air. Borrel joined her and they sailed off the cliff and slowly, gently descended through the glittering mist to land far downstream where the river once again gathered itself into a calm, glassy force, winding southward under the thinning trees.

Far away to the south, Highlord Raggar placed a handful of thorny sticks on the sand and backed away, paused, then backed further. He sat on a crumbling chunk of sandstone and watched the vast red ball of the sun touch the sand dunes in the west. Even then, he made himself wait until darkness had risen from the east and swept the minimal color out of the landscape around him.

Al-Sefir watched these preparations with resignation. It was only two days since the Highlord had last released his magic. When they'd begun this journey a month ago, Raggar had been able to buckle down his magic and keep it immobile for about a week at a time. Moving quickly, Al-Sefir hurried across the darkening sand to check their camels then found a larger boulder to shelter behind.

Tempered by his time with the Oracle and its joyful magic, Al-Sefir understood clearly that the Dragon Highlord struggled with something tortuous, tempestuous, and terrible.

Raggar had explained the arcane intricacies of great magic as they had slowly ridden on swaying camels' back across miles of dun-colored desert that shimmered in heat waves. Al-Sefir had offered prayers and sun salutations to console the Highlord's anguish. He learned to sleep while Raggar played his dragonpipe for hours into each night, understanding that the Highlord was fighting for his soul.

Suddenly the night exploded. Even behind his distant rock, Al-Sefir felt the heat. The camels made horrible noises of terror, and their harnesses jangled as they strained against their tethers.

A tower of flame rose to the night sky, growing higher, thicker, hotter, and hotter still.

And then it was over.

Al-Sefir, his eyes light-blinded, stumbled to the camels. They snapped and spat at him, but he crooned, and petted, and offered them bits of date until they calmed down. By then his eyes had readjusted to the desert night. Starlight was enough in the clear dry air to see the figure of the Highlord lying supine on the sand, spent by his organism of magic.

"Highlord? Here, a drink of water?" Al-Sefir put his arm behind Raggar's shoulders and helped him to sit. Raggar gulped the water mechanically. He was limp and wet with sweat.

Raggar sat, silent with his misery. He had unleashed a force that he could not control. These fires, built on just a few small twigs, were the only magic he dared use, and even these were increasingly dangerous, increasingly wild. If the magic continued to increase, he'd soon be able to burn bare sand.

And where was he in all this torrent of magic? Where was his center, his own soul?

Al-Sefir handed him some jackrabbit, roasted over the glowing sand where the inferno had been. Raggar ate without noticing. He gulped palm wine as if it were water.

The dragonpipe came to his hand and he moved himself closer to the glowing sand. Despite the summer heat of the desert, Raggar felt he could never quite get warm. He put the pipe to his mouth and played the First Tune.

The notes evaporated into the emptiness of the desert, so he played more and more. On and on he played, searching for his essence in the heart of harmony, hoping to find a lifeline in the chain of chord progressions.

Some distance away, Al-Sefir spread a carpet on the sand and wrapped his scarf around his head to mute the music. The Highlord played with rare virtuosity, and he seemed to know as many songs as there were stars in the moonless sky. But it hurt the priest to listen. The music was flawlessly executed, but soulless.

Blizzen stood on the balcony of the townhouse sipping a lovely glass of chilled Darkwood white. He let the wine linger a moment on his tongue as he smiled at the view of the lights of Kree spreading down to the edge of the bay. He so appreciated the luxuries of Kordon, the finest wines, finest homes, finest silks. This elegant townhouse he'd just bought was two streets away from Regent Avenue, where the Duchess of Chevvain and the Earl of Darkwood maintained their own townhomes.

A whisper behind him and he felt his mother's arms give him a brief hug. "Da and I are going home now," she said.

The common way she spoke irritated him. "You can stay here. I wish you would."

"Da likes his own bed, Blizzy. You know that."

Blizzen took a deeper drink of wine. He knew that his mother also liked her own shabby cottage and the dreary neighbors on her dingy street on the edge of town, despite his efforts to make something of a lady of her. She felt out of place here in this fancy house with servants and silks.

"I just want you be comfortable." He heard the whine in his voice, cleared his throat and started over. "You and Father worked so hard for so many years. Now at last the gift of my Dragon force – a gift you gave me – can provide something for you."

"T'was the Holy Mother that blessed you with such magic, Blizzy," his mother said. "And you studied so hard. Your Da and I know."

Blizzen nodded, but in fact his mother and father would never know just how hard he had studied and worked, what he had sacrificed, how he tested his soul even now, each time he used his magic to heal. He might have worried about this because the process of healing with magic caused such pain, but in the end the person was wholly healed, and his own once-empty pockets were full of gold.

He bent to put a kiss on his mother's cheek. The skin was loose with age, and he found it distasteful. He couldn't heal that.

Below them a carriage pulled up to the street door. He felt a tickle of magic from the passenger who alighted and a lick of a more earthy sensation when he realized who it was.

"See, you've company now." His mother peered over the balustrade. "That'll be Lady Venda of Caer Keff again. Good night, Blizzy."

"Night, Ma," Blizzen responded absently, tossing off the last of his delicate wine. Yes, his magic and his years of hard work had finally brought him benefits more tangible than the laborious honor of being the Orange Dragon at Dragonsholm. As the summer stretched on, he could envision more interesting and lucrative opportunities as his influence grew with the dowager queen and the Kordish court. Frankly, Blizzen felt he deserved the finest of Kordon's many luxuries: the wine, the fine home, the beautiful....He turned to see Lady Venda smiling at him, her dress a discarded pile of silk at her feet.

12

Golden sunlight crept down the peaks surrounding Daylor Lake and Hilsen Vale as the ten worshipers moved rhythmically through the poses and stretches of the sun salutations.

Mother Marith led the group with the ease of many years, opening herself to the energies of the morning and the people around her. Dylith's movements betrayed her sorrow at the irrefutable acknowledgement that Jax would never be hers. Doc's deep contentment and almost paternal pride in seeing Jax again was evident in the suppleness of his twists. Oddly, however, the young Weaver wobbled and wiggled through her poses.

Marith had tended Klaris back in Kree as she recovered from cross-magic and the effects of becoming Weaver. The druid had quickly come to respect the young Farsouthian. Despite her petite frame and her youth, Klaris possessed a strength of soul and character that Marith had rarely seen in any person anywhere, except maybe in Jax.

During those spring days in Kree, Marith had watched Klaris come into her own magic as Jax reclaimed his birthright. Both of them had struggled to accommodate the conflicts within the responsibilities that heredity and skill had bequeathed to them and their personal ideas and desires. Each of them had stood up to those exigencies, but their relationship with each other was still strained. With the complacence of an old druid, Marith wondered why they were fighting the obvious.

Despite Dylith's grief, Marith had long known that Jax needed a partner like Klaris de Farsouth: noble, clever, a little bit arrogant, and frighteningly powerful. In fact, someone rather like himself.

In Kree, Marith had watched the Weaver work through a number of emotions as she struggled to recover from the physical ravages of cross-magic and then the soul battering involved in seizing control of her new power as master of the Mystic. Frustration, anger, grief, and the beginning blossoms of love: all these had passed through the Weaver's heart.

But never confusion. That was what she felt today. It was clear in the misalignment of moves she'd performed perfectly for many years and in her inability to hold any balance pose. An unbalanced, confused Weaver was dangerous.

Marith bowed to the group for the final reverence and opened the circle. The others rose and quietly left the sacred grove, warily eyeing the Weaver who still sat, head bowed, tears streaming down her face.

The old druid waited.

Liquid, leaf-green eyes finally rose to meet Marith's compassion. "I do not say what's the matter with me," she said, her Landish as broken as her voice. Wearily she stood up and roughly wiped her eyes with the back of her arm. "I never cry, but now…. And I am exhausted no matter I sleep all night."

Marith linked her arm with Klaris and walked slowly toward the burrow. Absently, she noted Dylith sitting on a rock by the lake. "Your heart has been tested these past months."

"My heart," Klaris whispered. "My soul. But, goddess, I need to get control of myself."

Marith's well-honed druid's instincts caught on something in Klaris's tone. She stopped and turned, looking into her face. "Oh, my child," she ran her hand over Klaris' cheek. A slow grin deepened the wrinkles on her face.

Dylith jumped when she heard the shriek. She leapt off her sunny rock and turned to see the Weaver running away from Mother Marith as if the old druid had bitten her.

Defying her constant fatigue, Klaris ran all the way back to the druids' burrow and banged into the surgery.

Breathless, she looked down at Jax who opened sleepy sea blue eyes and smiled with drowsy warmth. Goddess, but he was beautiful.

"Are you panting for me?" He reached out a hand.

But she shook her head and backed away to the far wall. He pushed himself up and coughed.

"You are turning my life upside down," she snapped.

"Me? Or is it the Oracle, or the dragons, or maybe it's just who you are, Klaris. What you are."

"What I am? *What* I am is pregnant!"

"No." He laughed, disbelieving. "You can't be. We only had those few nights at Twistford, and we're not hand-fasted. The goddess wouldn't give us a baby."

She climbed onto the cot, straddled him, and shoved him roughly back onto his pillow. "Apparently, she would. Do you realize the implications of this?"

He smiled slyly. "It means my promise to Bryx is rather pointless."

"Well. Yes," she couldn't help answering that smile. "I hadn't been thinking about it that way."

"Seems the goddess blesses our adherence, or whatever it is," Jax noted, as his hands ran up her body.

She pushed them down. "Don't you see? This means I'll be six, no, seven months pregnant at Darkfest!"

The theoretical problems of facing the dragons pregnant or otherwise were too far from the reality of having Klaris on top of him, with the goddess' clearest blessing. He pulled her down to him, but she kept talking. "I'll have to face the dragons with this baby in my belly."

He paused, his mouth mere inches from hers. "Why would the goddess do that? She doesn't give babies into such danger."

"She did this time." At last Klaris let herself be drawn to his kiss.

"Unstick yourselves for a minute." Marith's voice startled them apart. Klaris jumped off the cot, and Jax pulled the blanket up to cover his lower regions.

"Congratulations," she said warmly, handing them each a cup of tea. "This is mint, ginger, and verbena for you, lass. It will settle your nerves a bit."

She turned to Jax. "Just plain tea for you, with honey."

"No milk?"

"Not while you're on the mend. Now let's look at that wound." She unwrapped the bandage and peered at the seared flesh and the stitches.

"Ah, excuse me, Weaver," Lad Yob stuck his head into the surgery. "Are you well?"

Klaris choked on her tea. "Why do you ask, Laddie?"

"I was walking around the lake and heard you holler."

"Ah. Yes. I am well, I guess."

"Perfectly, marvelously, healthy and well," Marith crowed, wrapping a clean bandage around Jax's hand.

"Jax is?" Doc joined what was beginning to feel like a crowd in the little surgery, followed by Dylith and Jelly, the cat. Jelly jumped up on the bed and settled among Jax's legs.

Marith smiled at Jax. "Yes, he is, too."

Jax hid his aristocratic nose in his teacup, but Klaris came to take Marith's hand. She looked into her sweet eyes. "Mam, why would the goddess do this?"

"Do what?" asked Dylith.

Klaris turned to look at the lovely woman and felt a moment of empathy for what this would mean to Dylith. She spoke words she had never thought to say: "I am pregnant."

"But...." Doc began.

Dylith choked.

"Every baby is a blessing," Marith answered Klaris's question.

"I wasn't," Jax said softly. "Not for my mother."

Marith lifted his chin and looked into his eyes. "You are to me."

Klaris set her tea mug down with a bang. "This is ludicrous! We have less than six months to figure out how to solve the dragon problem and then put the solution into action, and now I have to do it while pregnant! Sweet goddess, what does that mean?"

The cat answered: *"Opposites must now adhere."*

"Holy Mother!" Doc jumped.

But Klaris rounded on Jelly and quoted the rest of the stanza:

> *"Blood must mix and frontiers clear.*
> *Align the magic, love and fae.*
> *To turn the dragon threat away."*

She looked up at Jax. "You will notice that it doesn't say anything about being pregnant."

"In a way it makes sense." He paused and sipped his tea. "You and I could not *adhere*. All the temporal and secular powers of the Knownlands forbade it, from King Kodill to the sealord to any number of druids."

He leaned forward towards Klaris. "But this, this baby validates us, Klaris. It proves that our 'adherence' isn't unholy or unlawful or wrong."

"Well, of course it isn't," Doc blustered.

Klaris ignored him and stared at Jax. Finally, she reached forward and lifted the Oracle's medallion from his chest. For a long moment she gazed down at the disc and finally she murmured, "Adhere. Align."

She lifted her eyes to his, shaking her head. "We do not know where we have to go, what to do once we get there, and now, apparently, I have to do all of that and worry about keeping this baby safe too."

"I'm here for that," Jax said.

"As am I," offered Lad Yob.

"Excellent," Klaris snapped. "I shall require a daily foot massage and expect you to supply those hideous nomad candies I've been craving."

Dylith snorted in laughter and felt a sudden, surprising relief.

Marith smirked and began shooing everyone out of the surgery. "Babies are helpless, yes, but surprisingly hardy." She tossed a glance back at Jax. "Drink your tea, son, then I think you can have a coddled egg and some toast for breakfast."

Jax polished off his egg and toast and sat up looking around for his bags. He found trousers and a fresh silk shirt, but not his boots. Doc was finishing the dishes and handed Jax a damp towel for his face.

"Don't wet the bandage."

Jax rubbed the warm cloth over his chin. "I guess that means I can't shave."

"Still finding every avenue to antagonize the trolls?" Doc frowned.

"Absolutely." He smiled, thinking of the grimace on Boss Taint's face. He poured more tea into his mug and added milk while Doc's back was turned. His chest was still tight, but the fever was gone, and he felt remarkably well. He took the tea and walked barefoot to the front porch. Klaris stood there, leaning on the rail, gazing at the mountains.

Morning sun glowed on her hair and gilded her black skin. Jax had never seen anything so beautiful or desirable.

"Shouldn't you be in bed?" she asked.

"Why, yes." He grabbed her hand and hauled her upstairs to her room, pulled her down on the bed, kissing her face, her neck and nearly ripping her dress in his impatience to touch, to taste, to revel in her naked body.

"Holy Mother," Klaris breathed when it was over.

Jax pulled her sweaty body close.

She blinked at him, still trembling. Klaris had never felt such intensity, such depth to passion and its release, several releases. She ran her hand along his face.

He coughed.

"Did it hurt you?" she asked, still somewhat lost in pure physical bliss.

He shook his head, his smile lazy and cheeky with his own satisfaction. "That was worth the wait."

She licked his collar bone, tasting his salty skin. Happiness flared through her, and she smiled at him.

"Are you really craving nomad candy?" he asked suddenly.

"Oddly, yes. But there's something I want even more."

He did his best to indulge her.

Jax awoke a few hours later, judging by the slant of the sun on the trees outside the window. Klaris slept. He wrapped a soft curl of her black hair around his finger and let the joy of it fill him.

It came with terror. She'd always terrified him, he realized. This tiny woman held his heart, his magic, even his soul in her cold little hands. But those hands also held so many responsibilities, so many strands in the great weave of power in the Knownlands.

She faced tremendous challenges; any one of which might take her from him forever. He didn't want to think about that.

His stomach growled and he smiled despite his dark thoughts. A coddled egg and dry toast were not enough to sustain a man through such a vigorous morning.

He looked at the curve of Klaris's breast and began to envision an equally vigorous night. Gently he rolled himself out of the bed. Klaris did not move.

Marith looked up from the notes she was writing in her patient files as he came down the stairs drawing the laces on his shirt.

She sat back in her chair. "Let me look at your hand."

He sat down opposite her and watched as she carefully unwound the wrapping. "This is looking much better."

She watched him flex his other fingers around the gap and heard his stomach growl. "I thought you'd satisfied all your hungers."

Jax laughed as Marith rose to get her stinging ointment. She dabbed it over the wound then re-wound the bandage. "You're not wheezing anymore."

"No." His stomach growled again.

"You know where to find the bread and cheese, son."

"Son," he echoed, rising to find the food. "You're incorrigible."

13

Jax sat in the sunshine outside Aric's pub and sipped the dark, bitter ale, flexing his stiff fingers. He'd spent most of the afternoon toying with Marith's old lute and then his dragonpipe, trying to make music one finger short. It had been a difficult and discordant exercise, and painful too. He'd come to the pub for relief, but he wasn't finding it in Aric's black ale.

The taste transported him back to his days here as a slave. He remembered struggling against the entombing peaks and the equally confining affections of the two druids. His time frolicking with Dylith had been the one bright thing during those difficult months. Now what had once seemed good and healing was causing more pain.

Here he was once again faced with apparently irreconcilable dichotomies. He let his gaze rise to those stern gray peaks piercing into the blue sky and forced himself to see the beauty there.

"Enjoying the view?" Doc sat on the bench next to him.

"No."

The druid laughed and took a glass from the barmaid. "I just confirmed that little Callan Crane has Dragon force. That's the third Dragon confirmation this summer."

Jax shifted to look at him rather than the mountains. "Dragon force has been growing stronger."

"Mam says she's never seen so many babes born to the Dragon."

"To tell you the truth," Jax mused, "I had thought the increase in Dragon force might be the cause of Klaris's fatigue and, uh, moodiness."

Doc patted Jax's knee. "She'll feel better in the middle months of her pregnancy. That's a glorious time for most mothers."

"Glorious enough for her to face down the dragons?" His voice was tight with tension.

"If anyone can do it, it's your Klaris."

"She's her own Klaris." He paused for moment the spoke softly: "You know my mother died in childbirth."

Doc nodded. He took a slow sip of his ale. "There are things that we can chose, Jax, and things we can't. Things we can control and things that sweep us away. Often all of it is tangled together."

Jax frowned at him. "Fate, you mean."

Doc finished his ale. "Or destiny."

Jax set aside his empty glass and put his head in his hands.

Doc gently wrapped him his arms.

Some time later Doc saw people coming down the road. "That looks like Florin's party coming in."

Jax sat up and pushed his hands through his hair. "Good. That's why I was waiting here."

"I thought maybe you'd finally developed a taste for Vale Ale."

Jax shook his head.

Four wealthy Ilyian merchants, identifiable by the cut of their clothes and hair, strolled up to the pub, followed by a tight-lipped Florin leading a laden mule.

"Ale!" one of the men called into the building, as his companions sank onto several of the other benches. "Ale for five. You'll join us, won't you Florin?"

But Florin didn't hear him. She was staring at the nobleman sitting next to Doc. "Jax!" She looped the mule's lead around a post and launched herself into a tight embrace. "Goddess, but I'm still surprised to see you all fancy. Uh. Your Highness."

The Ilyians turned at the honorific. "Your highness, who?" one of them whispered to the others.

Jax ignored their speculation. "Where's Borrel? And don't your Highness me."

Florin took two glasses from the barmaid, downed one then pulled a stool up to sit with them. "He went to the Verwood."

"You didn't tell me this?" Jax turned to Doc.

"He couldn't get Lexyl St. Clare out of his mind or his heart," Florin explained, starting on her second pint.

"I thought his broken heart was mending in Kree."

"I did, too," Florin wiped foam from her lips. "But when we got back here, he seemed so lonely again."

"When did he go?"

"Just after solstice."

"Damn." Jax looked down into his glass, realizing how much he had been looking forward to seeing his friend.

"You have only me for nyad company," Florin kicked him gently.

"You're really the one we need," he looked up, grinning. "Klaris and I have to find the fairy queen."

"Klaris? As in *Weaver* Klaris?"

"Yes."

"You don't need me to find the fairies, Jax. Go out into the woods on a fine evening and the lascivious little bugs will find you."

"We've been waiting for you."

Florin emptied her glass. "Fine, but I'm not going tonight. I want to go home and clean up all this gear and eat real food."

"I thought you loved camp food." Jax grinned.

"Not."

"Come have supper with us," Doc invited.

"I will, thank you." Florin stretched, her back cracking. Then she rose and went to settle her bill with the Ilyians.

Jax walked beside Doc back toward the burrow through the lengthening shadows on the High Street. He could feel Klaris's magic like wind in his veins. "She's building something again," he muttered.

"Aye. Half the Vale has asked her to build or expand or reinforce some part of their burrows or barns or shops." Doc answered. "Berksheer Berkhoff even asked her to add a story to the hotel."

Doc and Jax moved out of habit to the side of the road to let two trolls march past them. Jax recognized Magistrate Vloggan and his young son.

Suddenly the big troll stopped, staring open-mouthed at the druid's noble companion. He took a breath to speak, but then confusion stopped him.

"Good evening, Doc," the boy said politely.

"Hello Gilbrick. How are you today?"

"We've been to watch the Weaver." The boy's orange eyes sparkled beneath their heavy umbrella of mascara. "She can pull buildings right up out of the ground all at once!"

"It's exciting to watch, isn't it?" Doc smiled. Most Mystics could make shelters, simple outbuildings, or cozy burrows. The more powerful ones could add rooms, designs, plasters, and water features, but the Weaver's skill was like a completely different art.

"Who are you, milord?" the magistrate asked suddenly.

"I am Javix Sharkin, Earl of Darkwood and lord admiral of Baria. And you, sir?"

"Oh." The troll's eyes narrowed. "I am Magistrate Vloggan, my lord. I'm in charge around here."

"I thought the Crone Council was in charge," Jax looked at Doc.

Vloggan considered the tone of that response. "I represent the Hantish government," he declared. "You look somewhat like a contraband slave our druids used to have: a slave that must be beaten, if I find him again."

"Magistrate," Jax bristled with affront. "I am a noble of Kordon and Baria, and I dislike your tone." He walked away, Doc hustled to keep up with him.

Behind them, they heard the young troll ask innocently: "Didn't the Crone Council forbid beating slaves, Da?"

Doc chuckled. "Young Gilbrick is a good egg, despite his Da."

Florin dropped her pack and suppressed a shudder as she gazed around the clearing. White-barked aspen held glittering green leaves to the evening sun. Three fairy rings rose from the soft bed of summer grass amid vivid pink and yellow flowers.

"This ought to do," Florin grumbled. "The moon rises early tonight. I suggest we eat and rest now, so we can be vigilant later."

Klaris pulled a small shelter up from the grass. She paused, considering her work, her head cocked to one side. Slowly she walked around the little structure. The stone danced under her Mystic, forming arabesques and curlicues until the shelter seemed built of lace rather than rock.

"That's beautiful," Florin whispered.

"Thank you. This is such a lovely spot. I felt we should have a structure to match it."

"The fairies will love it." Lad Yob smiled.

Florin snorted. "Have you met the little beasts?"

"Once. A long time ago."

"Really?" Klaris plopped onto a camp chair.

"The fairy queen came to Sageham to speak to the Weaver. She brought a large escort," Lad Yob grinned at the memory. "The little fairies were all over Caledra. We never knew when they'd appear or what they'd want. They were mischievous little things. It actually took several years to get rid of all of them."

"*Mischievous* makes them sound innocent," Florin protested. "And fairies are NOT innocent."

"This is going to be an interesting night," Jax said to Klaris. "Do you want a nap?"

Klaris looked up at him, her interpretation of his question clearly more mischievous than innocent. "Yes. That's a fine idea."

She rose and went inside the shelter. There were three private sleeping areas within. Jax followed her in and closed the door.

Lad Yob settled into Klaris's abandoned camp chair with a handful of radishes and a bottle of Aric's ale. "Join me, Florin?"

Florin sighed. "No ale for me. We'll want our wits when the bugs show up."

"I think the fire makes the clearing seem darker," Florin couldn't keep the nerves out of her voice. "Now that the moon is rising, we could douse it."

Jax pulled magic through Klaris's weavings, and the flames sank to darkness.

Indeed, the clearing did seem brighter under the silvery light of the moon. The four sat in silence. Jax suddenly wanted music. He could hear a tune in his mind. The melody seemed to come from the little clearing. He pulled his old wooden dragonpipe from his pocket. In the moonlight, his missing finger might have been a trick of shadows, except for the slip of white bandage.

He fumbled through the First Tune, still unsure how to compensate for the lost finger. Then he tried to play the music of the clearing. A series of notes came easily, then another. He repeated the phrase then found the refrain.

Klaris watched him. The interweaving of music and his magic sent a delicious, sensuous thrill through her. Goddess, but she'd had the man twice already today. She attempted to distract herself by looking up at the moon, which had cleared the treetops and floated round and full, echoing her own pregnant body. And then she felt the fairy magic.

The Weaver stood two seconds before the clearing exploded with a sparkling rainbow of fairies.

Jax let his last note fade into the darkness.

"Beautiful!" whispered Lad Yob.

Florin growled.

Bells tinkled and suddenly the fairy queen was there, floating before their eyes.

"What are you doing here?" she demanded. "The beasts are *coming*! You need to be there to meet them!"

"Be where?" Klaris's exasperation matched the queen's. "Your majesty," she added belatedly.

"At their mountain, of course!"

"Your Majesty," Jax intervened. "The Weaver and I know we are supposed to do something to thwart the dragons or send them away—."

"Banish them!" shouted the queen.

"Alright," Jax said evenly. "The Oracle gave us a prophecy, but it appears incomplete."

The fairy queen spun and flung a glittering rage of red sparkles around the clearing. The smaller fairies yelped and fled into the trees. "What prophecy?"

Klaris quoted the lines in Ancient.

> *Oracle, speak the Mother's truth:*
> *Dragons come with claw and tooth.*
> *Your purpose for one thousand years:*
> *Is to remember fires and tears.*
>
> *A paradox who can't be found.*
> *The Mother stirs and shakes the ground.*
> *The oceans rise to touch the trees,*
> *And bring a ruler to his knees.*
>
> *Opposites must now adhere*
> *Blood must mix and frontiers clear*
> *Align the magic, love and fae*
> *To turn the dragon threat away.*

The fairy queen crossed her arms and spoke in Landish. "That doesn't mention the song."

"It doesn't mention several salient factors," Klaris agreed.

"What song?" Jax asked.

"*The* song! The fairy song, of course," snapped the queen. "Those damned Oracles, just like the nyads, always thinking that words could actually capture the essence of a thing."

They stared at each other for a few minutes. The little fairies, peeping out from behind the trees, began to come forward.

"Did the Oracle at least give you the whistle?" the queen asked finally.

"Yes." Klaris called her magic and retrieved the ancient instrument from within Jax's pack. She held it out to the queen.

The fairy took it and stroked it sadly, but only for a moment. "Listen, now." She put the instrument to her lips and played. The smaller fairies came closer still. The tune grew through the clearing. Klaris felt Jax's magic react to it and leaning into his power, she heard joy and grief, loss and unity, pain and peace.

Somehow, she recognized the First Tune underlying the fairy's song.

The fairy queen stopped. In the deep blue silence, she handed the pipe to Jax. "You are the unseen paradox. You play. She sings. I think."

"Don't you *know*?" Jax asked, frowning.

"Goddess help us," Klaris choked. "I can't sing."

"It has been too long since we've had to perform a banishment in the original fashion," the fairy queen said finally. "I was born during the time of Axterre, and my parents, who would have known, perished in the claws and jaws of the dragons during the interregnum."

For several dark moments no one spoke. Florin frowned at the smaller fairies that were gathering too close for her comfort.

"So," Jax began finally. "We take your whistle, and I play your song while Klaris sings."

"No one sang last time," the queen noted. "The Oracle just played, but the music clearly wants a singer."

"Clearly," Klaris said, her tone implying no such thing.

"What does she sing, then?" Jax asked.

"Words, I suppose."

Jax spoke with disbelief. "So, we truly attempt to banish these huge, fire-breathing magical creatures with a song?"

The fairy queen floated closer and looked into Klaris's eyes. "That's the idea."

"Seems like a dumb idea to me," Florin muttered.

"I had truly hoped there would be more to it than that." Jax said grimly.

"Of course there is!" the fairy queen spun, scattering sparkles. "The song is the last part."

"It would be perhaps helpful if you could tell us the first parts."

"You already know that, Weaver! You're doing that – although you did take your sweet time."

"I'm not doing anything!" Klaris countered.

The fairy winked a violet eye. "Oh, yes, you are. Aligning the magic and love and mixing blood."

"Do you mean getting pregnant is part of the banishment?"

"Did you not listen to the song?" The queen frowned, perplexed. "It's all there in the music."

Klaris shook her head. "Some of us need words, your Majesty."

"Words, words, words," the fairy queen groused. "Slippery, tricky, and overused or forgotten until no one is sure what they mean or meant!"

Klaris gritted her teeth in frustration. When she spoke, her voice was hard. "I think we should seek the nyad magi."

"NO! NO!" yelled the queen, clearly as frustrated as the Weaver. "There is not time for you to go all the way to the Verwood and still get to the mountain before Darkfest."

"What mountain?"

"*Their* mountain! The mountain where they always land. At the end of the East."

"Axterre," Jax said grimly. "Goddess damn me, Klaris, you were right. I think we have to go to Axterre."

"Maybe those Oracles wrote something more useful," the fairy queen sniffed. "But I wouldn't count on much. Practice the banishment tune. All the answers are there. But hurry," she ordered. "*Hurry.*" The clearing seemed to pound with the sudden, silent darkness. The fairies had gone.

Four figures sat hunched around Jax's rekindled fire. Despite the cheery blaze, a black foreboding had settled around his soul. He fiddled with the fairy flute and finally, since no one was speaking, started slowly to play the fairy's tune.

The music was not fluid. He had to pause to figure out some of the notes. Fifths proved especially difficult with a missing finger.

Klaris listened to him playing, the words of the prophecy running over and over through her mind, as if repetition might make them clearer. True to the fairy queen's lament, they did seem to slip free of their phrases and recombine to form contradictory meanings.

Lad Yob was remembering the last time he'd seen fairies. It had been a different fairy queen who had visited Castle Caledra, but she'd been similarly panicked. Lad Yob had not been privy to the meetings between that queen and Weaver Bly, and so he had always assumed they'd spoken of Axterre's fiery demise. All the Knownlands were talking of little else in those distant days.

But now Lad Yob wondered if that fairy queen had understood the dangerous vulnerability that faced the Knownlands in the absence of the Oracle of Axterre.

Florin was wishing she had packed more ale. For her, Axterre was a memory of dirty air and dirty water, overlaid with the personal pain of watching her twin entwine his heart in an impossible match. But that gave her an idea.

"Let's go to Arandy."

Florin's proposal brought Jax's tune to a dead stop.

"Arandy?" Klaris asked. "This is the desert town where you went with Marith?"

"Yes." Florin swallowed the last of her ale with purpose. "Frankly, I'd like to have a little chat with one Lexyl St. Clare."

"That's a brilliant idea, Florin," Jax said, tucking the whistle away. "Lexyl hinted that she had access to ancient Axterran writings. It's where she found that bit of prophecy that she gave me."

Klaris turned to him. "You might have mentioned this sooner," she said sharply. "If she had part of the prophecy, maybe she has it all!"

He shrugged. "I wasn't thinking about Lexyl. I was thinking about Axterre and its ghosts."

Klaris rose to her feet. "Here we've been searching for answers and all along you've had two far better sources of information in this Lexyl and her archives."

"The Oracle told us to look in Kree!" Jax argued. "Lexyl called it a scrap of poetry when she gave it to me. And the damned ghost of an Oracle was not friendly or helpful. I caution even you to stay away from that thing, Klaris. It's malevolent."

"Stop arguing, you two." Florin stood up. "Go to bed. If we get an early start in the morning, we can be home by nightfall tomorrow."

Jax killed the fire, and they walked to the shelter by the light of the moon.

"How will we get to Arandy?" Lad Yob asked softly. "It's too far to walk all the way to Axterre between now and Darkfest. And too far to use magic."

"Maybe the Oracle will loan us the pegasi," Jax suggested flippantly.

"That's a good idea," Klaris said, shutting the door to their room. "Maybe I'm not a complete idiot."

"You do have your uses." He heard the smile return to her voice.

14

"That was unsettling." Klaris slumped into one of the wingback chairs and began drumming her fingers along the armrest.

Adgar, still glowing from the residue of sharing Klaris's magic, poured water into two glasses then handed one of them to the Weaver. "Did you speak to them?"

"I did." Klaris drank. Then shook her head and looked around at the others. "And they answered me."

A roar of thunder shook the burrow, and Klaris jerked, sloshing water out of her glass. Suddenly rain pounded loudly on the turf above their heads.

"This storm's been coming," Florin explained calmly. "You didn't hear it rumbling toward us?"

"No. I didn't."

"Will the Oracle send pegasi?" Jax asked the question everyone was wondering.

"They will."

Jax wondered at the distraction in her answer. "Did you tell them we wanted to go to Kree first?"

"They didn't like that." She looked up at him, her eyes cautious. "They said we should heed the fairy queen and go east from here."

"I can't miss Tallyn's wedding," Jax said. They'd been over this several times. Clearly it would be faster to head for Arandy, directly from the Vale rather than going first to Kree. But Lord Foby had asked Jax to be his best man, and Tallyn had made him promise to be there for their hand-fasting. "I'm giving everything else to the

Oracle's mission. Foby and Tallyn are my family, Klaris. I must be there for them."

She frowned. "The Oracle implied that this wedding would cost you."

Jax opened his right hand, displaying the absence of a finger. "Everything does."

"I worry about what might be taken," Klaris said softly.

Jax stared back at her, feeling his fears. He shoved them down. "No matter. I want to be there."

Klaris shrugged and took another drink of her water. Although she had no friends herself, she recognized what Tallyn and Foby meant to Jax. She changed the subject. "The Oracle also explained why the fairy queen was so concerned about the dragons.

"We knew that dragons eat fairies, but I hadn't realized that fairies are apparently their favored food, which may be why dragons migrate through the Knownlands. The Oracle told me there used to be large populations of fairies on Baria, Jezel, and throughout all the forests of the Knownlands. There was even a type of fairy that lived in the coves and harbors around Baria. But the dragons ate them to extinction."

Jax recalled his first encounter with the fairy queen and looked to Marith. "The fairy queen told us that, remember, Mam? She said their populations hadn't recovered from the last time, and that there were no fairies on Baria. Of course, we didn't know what she was talking about then."

"Goddess help us," Florin muttered. "I don't want to think what the Knownlands would be like with all the forests full of predatory fairies."

"Better than with the skies full of predatory dragons," Adgar answered softly.

Magistrate Vloggan had finally made up his mind to confront the druids and their arrogant noble guest. The law was quite clear on the matter, despite the meddling of the five oldest Vale locals on the Crone Council. Vloggan still received censure from the Prefect of the Ledden Rises because he had not dealt with the contraband slave. The prefect didn't understand that no one had slaves in Hilsen Vale, and that the human population there didn't approve, but Vloggan was a troll, and it was his duty to uphold the trollish law.

He stomped through the Vale, followed by two of the four trollish members of the town guard. The other two had come down with a highly-suspect illness when they learned of this morning's activity. He snapped his whip into the dusty road and gathered his determination.

"Mother Marith!" he called as he reached the path up through the druids' yard. He noticed that the burrow had been enlarged and hoped that the Weaver wouldn't get involved in this. Usually, he knew, Mystics stayed out of trollish issues.

"Hello, Magistrate," Doc stepped out of the cottage and came down the porch steps. "Do you need us?"

"I do, Doc. Where's that friend of yours?"

"Do you mean me?" Jax came from around the side of the house, followed by Marith and the little Weaver.

"Yes, I mean you." Vloggan turned to face the nobleman. He cracked his whip and the people stepped back. He motioned to his guards. "Take him."

The guardsmen stepped forward.

Jax shook his head. "I don't think so." The guards slowed at something in the nobleman's smile.

"Take him, I said!" Vloggan shouted.

The guards moved awkwardly; their feet stuck somehow in the soft summer grass.

The Weaver stepped forward. Vloggan glared down at her. She was so small that he was sure he could crush her with a negligent backhand. "You should move aside, Weaver. This is trollish justice here."

"There's no justice in slavery," Jax said.

"Yes, there is," Vloggan answered. "The druids paid for you, and our laws exist to protect that investment and the investment anyone else makes in a slave. You ran away from your owners. The law says you must be punished for that, no matter what the Crone Council says."

"But we, ah, punished him in our own way," Marith said.

Jax thought there was more truth in that than the troll could appreciate.

"That's excellent, Mother," Vloggan said. "But the law is specific. A contraband slave must be publicly whipped."

Adgar came from the house to stand behind Doc. "He's not a slave anymore,"

"Oh, but I am," Jax answered. "I just serve a different master now."

"I don't care—." Vloggan was interrupted by the sudden descent of a herd of flying horses. People from across the Vale came running to see. Klaris released the guardsmen from her weave, and they stumbled back to stand near the magistrate as the pegasi landed in the yard between the druids and the trolls.

Their coats gleamed white in the clear, bright summer sun and their wings shimmered, iridescent. Everyone, human and troll, marveled at their beauty. Even the magistrate was awed. He grinned as his son pushed through the crowd to stand beside him, gaping. "Did you bring those here, Da?"

"I asked the Oracle to send them," Klaris answered, stepping towards one of the mares. She smiled into its iridescent eyes.

Florin came running from her own home and hurdled the fence, her pack bouncing on her back. "I guess it's time to go?"

Lad Yob came out of the cottage, dragging everyone's bags and began fastening them onto the beautiful creatures.

"Wait!" Vloggan cracked his whip, and everyone jumped back. One of the pegasi reared and neighed. "I *must* have justice."

"You have it," Jax walked through the winged horses to speak quietly to the troll. "I'm not free, Magistrate."

"You were that slave."

"I was. And I remain bound to my people in Baria and Kordon. And thanks to the Oracle, bound to go with the Weaver to drive the dragons away from the Knownlands."

"What dragons?"

"The beasts. They're coming back."

The troll grew white under the saffron powder on his face. "How do you know?"

"The Oracle, the Weaver, and the greatest Dragon Magicians all feel them coming."

"That will be a disaster."

"It might be. The Weaver and I are required to go meet them."

"That's a death sentence."

"Probably. And your justice."

The journey between Hilsen Vale and Kree would take two months in a fast coach. The pegasi made it in ten days. They stopped to rest a few hours each night, but even so, by the time they reached the Kordish capital, the creatures and their riders were all exhausted.

Kree, already awhirl with preparations for a royal wedding, was stirred to frenzy by the arrival of the pegasi and news that the Weaver was pregnant.

Despite the excitement they caused, Florin, Lad Yob, and Klaris spent the better part of their first afternoon in Kree in bed recovering from the long flight. Tired as he was, Jax sat with his fleet captains and commanders, listening to reports and reviewing their progress on both the markets they were exploring for iron and sugar as well as the repairs to the fleets and the preparations to survive the return of the dragons.

The day of the wedding dawned grim and wet as a wild summer storm blew gales of rain across the town. Klaris left the *Sharkin* early and rowed to shore to dress at the palace. Jax watched her fade into the gray storm through his cabin's stern-lights then turned to let his steward dress him.

The voice of the sentry came through the cabin door: "Captain Blanx, milord!"

"Come!" Jax turned to greet the captain, disrupting the steward's efforts to perfect the knot on his cravat.

Blanx bowed. "The sealord has signaled for you to come to the *Drixa* immediately."

Jax was surprised that Bryx would be on his ship in this weather, and noted the concern on his captain's face, but waited until the steward had left to ask about it.

"The sealord has made no secret that he is displeased with you, my lord," Blanx offered quietly. "He says he ordered you to stay away from the Weaver, but you went off to the Hantland with her anyway."

Jax heard the gale ripping through the rigging of his ship, and felt his mood harden with the wind.

"Whatever happens, Blanx, keep the fleet dispersed. Make sure you continue with our plan to set regular meeting places in the open seas."

"Aye, sir."

Jax looked him in the eye. "I'm counting on you. All Baria may end up relying on you."

Blanx stared at his lord admiral with growing fear. "But sir, I'm not prepared—."

"None of us is," Jax cut him short. "Come on. Let's go see what the sealord's going to do now."

Despite venerable tradition, protocol, and the discomfort of the howling storm, Captain Blanx was not allowed to board the sealord's flagship. "Only the prince may come aboard!" Lieutenant Rixa shouted through the wet wind to the other officers in Jax's launch. "You're to return to the *Sharkin*."

Blanx saw a grim grin as Jax grabbed the rope ladder and began to climb. The launch pulled away from the great hull of the sealord's wingship. Everyone on board, from Captain Blanx to the youngest rower, noted that Rixa had referred to him as *prince*, rather than the lord admiral.

Bryx sat at his desk and did not immediately look up from his papers when Jax entered the cabin. The steward took Jax's dripping cloak and offered him tea.

"No," the sealord interjected. "He won't be here long enough for such pleasantries."

The steward fled.

Bryx finally looked up at his brother. "I would dearly love to feed you to the shark."

"Right. Because I've got the fleet back in ship shape, found new profitable markets, and made your subjects loyal again?"

Bryx deliberately set down his enameled pen and rose. "Because you broke your promise to me."

Jax answered carefully. "This prophecy about the dragons, this banishment, requires Klaris and me to be a unit, to be aligned, to adhere, Bryx."

"You may not address me as Bryx."

"My lord—."

Bryx continued as if he had not spoken. "From this day forward, I do not have a brother. You are no longer lord admiral."

"My lord!"

"Shut up. You will now be rowed ashore. If I find you on Barian soil, on a Barian ship or in any Barian embassy across the Knownlands, you *will* feed the shark."

"Who will run the fleet?"

"Not your concern."

Jax stared at the sealord and took a deep breath. This wasn't just about his own loss. He felt the weight of Logil and Dury's deaths and missed the solid oak of old Admiral Hix's convictions. He faced the wall of Bryx's closed mind and changed course.

"Yes," Jax admitted softly. "Yes, I broke my promise to you. I am sorry, Sire."

Bryx raised his eyebrows, but he pushed his advantage. "You are foresworn. Renounced. Exiled."

Jax nodded, grief heavy in his heart, but he fetched up a grim smile. "You don't need me, but the Barians need you. They already see the wisdom in your plans to provision the hard ports. They'll look to the flagship and to you."

Bryx saw their father in Jax's feral grin and wondered what he was missing. "Of course they'll follow me. I am the Sealord. Not you. Never you."

Jax bowed his head.

"Sentry!" The sealord turned away. "Take him ashore, now."

Jax stood in the launch as it pushed through the waves, his hood back, spray and rain soaking his head and face. He could not tear his eyes from the *Drixa* and the *Sharkin* anchored just beyond.

When the launch bumped against the wharf, he looked down, and was a little surprised that he wasn't bleeding, so deep was the pain in his chest.

"We regret this, my lord," Lieutenant Rixa said softly. "We need you."

Jax wiped the rain on his face. "Help him, Lieutenant. He means well, he just doesn't see…."

Rixa frowned. The prince was right. The sealord didn't see whether or not a ship was sailed with care; he didn't see how his people needed him; and he certainly didn't see how the Barians would miss their Prince Jax.

"Help him," Jax repeated then he jumped to the wharf and strode through the rain into the streets of Kree.

In his townhouse he called for a quick hot bath and let his valet dress him as a Kordish lord with no hint of Barian Blue in all his glorious attire. He stared at his reflection in a mirror, wondering if anyone beside Tallyn would notice the missing colors.

"All the wedding festivities have been moved inside due to the rain," his secretary was saying. "And the king has called a brief meeting of the royal council for a few moments right before the wedding."

"I don't have my speech ready," Jax muttered. He hadn't been able to keep his thoughts together since leaving the *Drixa*, and he certainly wasn't in the mood for the royal council.

The secretary grinned. "Make lewd jokes. That's what the best man is supposed to do."

Jax pulled at his sleeves, which felt a little too short and tried to smile. He flung a dark green cloak around his shoulders and dashed through the rain to his carriage. The secretary stared into the rain after him, frowning.

Jax stood behind his chair at the polished Darkwood table and refused both wine and tea. The other members of the royal council, elaborately dressed for the wedding, stood behind their own seats. Earl Oklan Kora asked Jax about his travels.

The king's entrance interrupted Jax's stilted answer. The dowager followed her son. Tallyn wasn't present for the meeting, as she was dressing for the hand-fasting ceremony.

The king sat, and the council took their seats. "I know we are all looking forward to the hand-fasting and the party today," he said. "I'll make this brief." He turned his pale blue eyes to Jax. "Prince Jax, you were forbidden to dally with the Weaver."

Jax mustered his best defense. "Your Majesty, the goddess has clearly blessed my relationship with the Weaver."

"Indeed," Kodill smiled benignly. "Indeed, she has."

"But the king forbade it," the dowager said with a smile.

Kodill sighed. "I probably shouldn't have."

The dowager cleared her throat.

Kodill glanced at her and found his resolve. "I understand, Prince Jax, that you and the Weaver plan to go east to find the dragons."

"Yes, my lord."

"Naturally our hearts and hopes go with you. We also ask that you take Blizzen, the Orange Dragon, with you. Perhaps his great magic will help you."

"Does he want to come?"

"Oh, yes." The dowager answered with a conviction that troubled Jax. "Yes, he does."

Jax gave a small bow to hide his misgivings. Then the blow fell.

The king sat up and looked him in the eye. "In the meantime, Jax, Darkwood is forfeit to the crown."

"I see." Jax felt like the floor had fallen away beneath him.

"You can't have Darkwood and the Weaver, too." The Duke of Vobury nodded. The others avoided Jax's eyes.

"Are we done?" the old Earl Von fidgeted in his seat. "I want a drink."

The lady chancellor answered. "Yes, and the ceremony will begin in a few moments."

In defiance of all that was proper, Jax remained sitting while his king stood and left the privy cabinet followed by the others.

Alone, he ran his hands through his neatly brushed hair. The missing finger ached. He thought about the curiously deep pain of absence.

"Goddess *damn* you!" he jumped to his feet and paced the room. Suddenly he stopped and a slow, wicked smile bloomed on his face.

Prince Jax's behavior at the reception following Tallyn's hand-fasting ceremony caused far more comment than the glories of the princess's dramatic wedding gown, or the shenanigans of the three ill-behaved flower girls, or the ribald comments that followed Jax's own brief, but rather touching toast to his two friends.

"He danced every dance with her," Carte Serge complained to a tired Priestess Mollish.

"And why shouldn't he? The goddess has blessed them in the clearest way possible."

"Psh," Serge snorted. "The king didn't."

"No," Mollish looked into her empty glass thoughtfully. "You'd think with what Prince Jax is going to face we'd all be honoring him. Instead, we're being about as ungrateful and nasty as possible."

Serge stared at her. "I'm just thinking of that poor, young Weaver."

Mollish sent him a very sharp glance. "Let her think for herself."

"Klaris de Farsouth shouldn't wear that color. She's too small to carry it off." Lady Raisha stood tall and regal before the mirror in Carden Yemmel's room.

He slid the light turquoise gown from her shoulders and bent to kiss the exposed skin.

Raisha sighed but continued her rant. "And I think its obscene the way Jax flaunted his affection for her."

"Obscene?" Carden murmured against silky skin of her belly. "Let us be obscene too." His tongue slid into her, and she forgot, at last, about the Weaver.

Foby lay replete and happy in his wife's naked embrace. He was drifting on the first soft clouds of sleep re-hearing the perfect lines from Featherfetch's poem that Jax had quoted in his brief toast. The thought of his friend woke him a bit.

He turned to look at Tallyn. "Did you know the king was going to take Darkwood from Jax?"

"I figured he might. Not that anyone told me, of course."

"Because you would have stopped them?"

"No."

In that simple syllable Foby heard how Tallyn would be a much different ruler from her father; he heard her awareness of the dowager's influence on the king's action and the political acumen that acknowledged her constraints as crown princess.

He closed his eyes, enjoying his pride in her and his joy that she loved him. Her voice startled him awake again.

"Jax doesn't need me to fight his battles for him. The sealord and the dowager have taken his titles, but he rubbed their noses in it tonight." She chuckled. "Both of them were as sour as lemons all evening. Did you notice?"

"Um." Foby hadn't.

"Wearing a sigil-gap, of all things!" Tallyn laughed. "Such a clever way to flaunt his status and the scar that represents all he's suffered for it."

"I did see that," Foby said. He had wondered why Jax would choose to resurrect a long-gone fashion where Kordish nobles left a gap in the clothing on their left collarbone to reveal the tattoo of their birthright.

"Everyone saw it," Tallyn rolled over and wrapped her arms around him.

"He still lost Darkwood." Foby nuzzled into her warm neck.

"They bloodied him," she grinned, "but he won this round."

Jax threw his clothes to the floor and flopped into Klaris's bed. Her maid pretended not to look and began to undo the complicated laces on the back of the Weaver's orange dress.

"You used me this evening," she said softly in Islish, as the dress came loose.

"I did."

"And now you'd like to share my bed?"

"I have no other."

Klaris heard the pain in his voice underneath the light tone.

"Perhaps it's my turn to use you."

"Everyone else does. Take off that damned dress and come lie with me."

The maid didn't understand Islish, but she didn't need to. Closing the door softly behind her, she thought only of the deep romance of renouncing all worldly position and wealth in the name of love. She didn't see the doubt, the grief, and the sense of failure that Klaris found in those sea blue eyes.

15

"Your grace! I cannot let you enter!"

Tallyn awoke to her lady-in-waiting's strident complaints.

"I will assure her of your loyal protest to my irresponsibility, Lady Quent." Jax's voice preceded him into the still-dark nuptial chamber.

Tallyn squinted as he ripped open the curtains, and Foby mumbled something into his pillow.

"Good morning to your Highness and to the luckiest man in Kordon," Jax said cheerfully. "I apologize, Princess," Lady Quent bustled about doing nothing other than admiring Lord Foby's naked chest.

"Go get us all some tea, please." Jax took her by the shoulders and steered her out of the room.

"Sweet goddess, it's the morning after our wedding." Foby woke enough to complain. "Go away."

"Aye, the first of many days of wedded bliss." Jax sat on edge of the bed. "I have to talk to you."

"Hand me my robe." Tallyn pulled the garment over her silken body and sat up.

"This had better be good," Foby grumbled, an arm still over his eyes.

"It's about securing the realm against another dragon interregnum." Jax said.

"Is that all?" Tallyn grinned. "You and the Weaver are going to prevent that."

"Of course, but the method for banishing the beasts seems tenuous at best. A great deal of information has been lost over the millennia and we may fail, as the last Weaver did."

Tallyn settled back on her pillows. "You're going off to meet the dragons, but you don't know what to do when you get there?"

"Exactly."

Foby finally sat up. "That's a dumb thing to do."

"Thank you," Jax noted. "That's why I'm intruding upon you this morning."

"Another dumb thing to do," Foby said without anger.

"I've given my steward in Darkwood a list of preparations that might help people survive a dragon attack. I recommend that you make such preparations across the realm."

"What preparations, exactly?"

"Stockpiles of food and supplies, diversified storage locations, a network of druids and officials to help direct people to emergency resources if we're attacked."

"Those are good ideas," Foby acknowledged.

"Darkwood is no longer your responsibility, Jax." Tallyn looked at him out of cool, colorless eyes.

He fiddled pointedly with the sigil-gap in his tunic. "Sir Arno Hyll in Twistford has the details of my plan. If you want them."

"The king will not endorse a plan of yours, and the royal council won't act without him."

"I know." Jax stood as Lady Quent finally returned with the tea. He took the tray from her and shut the door on her self-righteousness. "But you'll figure a way around that." He handed Tallyn a cup of tea.

She sipped it and considered him for a few minutes. Foby sat up to take a cup of his own. Jax heard a commotion in the anti-chamber. "Here comes Karric to arrest me for disturbing Your Highness."

The chamber door banged open and suddenly the room was crowded with guards.

Jax raised his empty hands. "I'm leaving, Captain. I just wanted to wish my foster siblings a long and joyful marriage."

"Well, you've got Lady Quent in quite a twist, my lord," Karric growled.

Jax sketched a bow to Tallyn. "I'll save my further comments for the breakfast then." He ducked between guards and slipped away.

Alone again, Foby peeled the robe from his new wife, and Tallyn temporarily forgot the wolfish grin on her cousin's face.

In Kordish tradition, the wedding of the crown heir was followed the next day by a late state breakfast. Immediately after the breakfast, the newlyweds set out for a month-long progress across the realm.

Klaris and Jax also prepared to begin their own expedition to the farthermost reaches of the Knownlands. Knowing Jax had been relieved of any duties to either Kordon or Baria, Klaris wasn't sure what he'd been up to early that morning, writing for an hour at her desk, and coming and going from her chamber in a cold silence.

She sat at the breakfast and smiled as Jax teased Foby and laughed with Tallyn about the miscreant flower girls. His arm curved casually around Klaris's shoulders. Understanding very well what he was doing now, she leaned into him and played along.

Bryx, sitting on the far side of the king, became increasingly sullen, and brooded malevolently like the sky before a violent storm.

"Look at the sealord," Foby snickered quietly to Tallyn. "Jax is killing him."

"Yes," Tallyn smirked into her champagne and orange juice. "Wait a bit and you'll see our Jax strike at Kordon too."

Foby looked up in surprise. "How do you know?"

"He warned us this morning."

Foby decided he must have missed something of the early morning visit due to hangover and lust.

Jax chose his moment with precision. The nobles had finished the feast and gathered in the courtyard. After yesterday's rain, the summer air sparkled freshly. Everyone waited quietly for the king to give his blessing to the newlyweds.

In the expectant silence, Jax's voice, conversational and friendly, carried to every attentive ear.

"Your Highness, I have here a list of my plans and projects for Darkwood." He handed the scroll he'd written that morning to the princess.

This wasn't what Tallyn had expected, but she smiled warmly. "Excellent, Prince Jax. I'll see that the crown continues your improvements. In fact, we'll begin our progress at Twistford and look in on things for you."

Jax bowed.

"Well played," the lady chancellor murmured to herself.

Standing next to her, Earl Oklan Kora whispered: "That rather draws the sting, doesn't it?"

The Duchess of Chevvain didn't answer, but her pale eyes gazed thoughtfully at Prince Jax as he rose from his bow and turned towards the Weaver. Chevvain had to admire the silky way Jax had just turned what was meant as a punishment into a blessing for Darkwood. In asking Princess Tallyn to follow his plans he'd put the crown to work for his own ends. When the royal council had taken his lands, it had expected Darkwood to languish under competent, though limited, management, but the prince had now enlisted the full resources of royal patronage to carry out his plans. The financial boon alone would be considerable.

The lady chancellor considered the princess for a moment and decided that Tallyn had not been forewarned of the prince's ideas. Still, he'd taken the gamble on her. Chevvain was not surprised. She had learned a new and deeper respect for the prince in the last few months as her position of lady chancellor gave her particular insight into the way he was running his new earldom. Like most Kordish nobles, Chevvain thought of the Islish as a somewhat irresponsible and certainly foolhardy race of sycophantic traders, with toothy smiles in their dark-skinned faces.

She remembered the charming way Sealord Rax had managed to be glib even in broken Landish. Young Jax's rascally wit had seemed a natural inheritance, although Prince Bryx didn't share it.

In truth, Chevvain had always dismissed Jax as a pretty face with a sharp tongue who profited from his association as Tallyn's foster brother. But now, as she read reports coming in from Twistford, reviewed the new earl's judgments, and analyzed his proposals, she found an unlooked-for acumen in the way he managed his people, his responsibilities, and his resources.

By contrast, the duchess had long ago learned respect for the crown princess's political abilities. She realized that far from merely tolerating her half-islish cousin, Tallyn recognized him as an equal and a valuable ally.

Now, while the king was bestowing a confused and long-winded blessing on the Weaver, the lady chancellor handed a small scroll to Jax. "This is a letter of free passage, your Highness. It will guarantee you hospitality in any manor, village, or castle in Kordon."

He looked down at the scroll for a moment. "A Prince of the Blood shouldn't need such a letter."

"True. But you and I both understand the politics of Kordon better than that."

Jax considered her for a moment, a little surprised by her unexpected honesty.

"Come back, Jax. You're a good earl. Tallyn will need you on her council."

"Funny way you have of showing that."

Chevvain's face betrayed her shame. "If you survive your encounter with the dragons, you'll get it all back: your lands, your titles, your seat on the council."

He stared at her, and for a brief second, she saw the hurt he kept so well hidden. "I'm going to confront a flock of dragons with nothing but a song. You're making a pretty safe bet."

The king had finished his farewell to the Weaver, and now he turned to Prince Jax. "Goddess go with you, lad."

Jax bowed one last time.

The dowager leaned around the king to speak to her grandson. "Keep the Orange Dragon with you."

"Yes, ma'am." Jax eyed her, instinctively alarmed by the old queen's mildness. She seemed oblivious to the slap he'd delivered to Kordon, but he knew she was not.

The king, who *was* oblivious, turned to the sealord. "It's going to be pretty dull around here without Tallyn and your brother."

Bryx smiled coldly. He spoke in Islish. "I have no brother."

"But you do have choices," Jax answered in the same language. He noted the hard looks the Barians in the crowd sent the sealord and turned away before Bryx lost his temper entirely. His heart ached.

"Look! The pegasi!" Cheers from the crowd swept away the possibility of more speech as the beautiful creatures circled down and landed softly behind the wagons, carriages, and horses that stood ready for Tallyn and Foby's progress.

"Goddess bless you, Jax." Tallyn gave him a hard hug. "You and Klaris both."

"And you," Jax didn't smile. "You and Foby both."

Lad Yob and Florin already sat astride two of the pegasi. A third and fourth carried packs of food and gear. Blizzen, his orange silks billowing, swung up on another of the creatures, glowing with excitement.

"Weaver," Lady Mollish took Klaris's hand and spoke quickly. "Dragon Blizzen knows how to heal."

"Really? That's wonderful."

The priestess shook her head. "I fear it imperils his soul."

"But healing is good."

"It should be," Mollish admitted. "Talk to him about it."

The crowd was cheering. Klaris saw the deep concern in the priestess' pale Kordish eyes as she mounted her own pegasus.

Jax sat on his own steed. "Here's one horse that won't throw me," he said, and the crowd, familiar with the prince's legendary difficulties with horses laughed, loving him on this beautiful sunny morning.

"Goddess go with you, your Highness!" someone shouted.

The rest of the crowd joined in shouting blessings as the Oracle's white horses spread their iridescent wings and rose to the sky.

The king's mumbled and tearful blessing to his daughter and her new husband was anticlimactic by comparison, although the people cheered dutifully. Later that afternoon the royal pair slowed their horses to walk under a tree-shaded avenue. After a few moments of silence Foby spoke. "Don't you rather wish we had a couple of those pegasi?"

Tallyn turned to look at her husband. "You do realize that he doesn't think he's coming back."

"When did he say that? He has all those plans...."

Tallyn resettled herself in the saddle. "The plans were for us, Foby. For us."

"Dragons," Foby swore and swallowed against the lump in his throat.

Jax had hoped to be out of Kordon by nightfall, but another violent summer storm blew across the green Kordish fields and forced the pegasi to land a few miles from Deepford in the Duchy of Clairo. Naturally, the greater nobles of the region were all still in Kree. Jax did not, in fact, need the lady chancellor's note to secure fine rooms and a delicious meal from the chamberlain at Deepford. Jax had been there as a child, on a visit to Lady Cheshir's family. The chamberlain remembered the prince from that visit, and he more vividly recalled how young Lady Cheshir had grieved when the lad disappeared.

Jax and his companions ate a delicious meal of fresh greens and grilled duck accompanied by a bright Clarovian red, while thunder and rain pounded outside.

"This isn't so bad," Florin said, watching a servant refill her glass.

"Better than trail rations," Jax agreed.

Replete with his own dinner and the wine, Blizzen leaned back in his chair. "Thank you, your Highness, Weaver, for letting me come with you on this quest."

Jax swirled the wine in his glass. "I'm surprised you'd want to come, frankly."

Blizzen sat up, his eyes cautious. "You are?"

"We're going to meet dragons. That didn't go well for the last people who tried it."

Blizzen relaxed back in his chair. "But no people had Dragon force in those days. Surely it will be different this time."

"We hope so," Klaris said dryly.

Blizzen eyed her sharply. He had to hold his magic very close to avoid getting stung by the vortex of Mystic that surrounded the Weaver.

Klaris cocked her head at him. "Priestess Mollish told me you've used magic to heal?"

Blizzen sat up with enthusiasm. "I have indeed, Klaris. Yes, I have indeed."

"How did you figure it out?"

"I'm not sure you can understand, since you don't have Dragon force."

"Try me," she said mildly.

"Actually, she has Dragon force," Jax said into his wine glass.

Blizzen frowned and Klaris shot Jax an exasperated glance. "Questions of magic always fascinate me," she explained. "I would love to know how you structure a healing spell."

Blizzen was clearly torn for a moment between wanting to keep his secret and wanting to brag about it. He tossed off his wine. "I use a person's own life flow, which is, you see, very much like fire. The flow identifies weaknesses, old wounds, as well as new ones. I add my magic to the patient's life force to close wounds or remove illness."

"You'll put the druids out of business." Florin poured more wine for everyone.

"I might," Blizzen said smugly. "You see the magic heals completely. There's no recovery. The patient is simply well again, which is why the temporary pain is justifiable."

"Temporary pain?" Klaris asked.

"The life flow energized by my magic can cause great pain as the wound or illness is cured. And I must be very careful if the patient has had any past wounds, because they can unheal."

"Unheal?"

"The magic seems to reopen the wounds."

"Keep your healing away from me, then," Jax muttered.

Klaris turned on him. "Did it hurt when I healed your finger?"

He shook his head. "Not at all." He glanced at the others. In fact, the sensation of Klaris's magic within him had been incredibly erotic. Just the memory stirred him now.

"You've healed also?" Blizzen was clearly disconcerted. He turned to Jax. "Can I see what she did?"

"I'm afraid not." Jax wriggled the remaining fingers of his right hand. "The wound became infected, and the finger had to come off again."

"Ah," Blizzen leaned back in his chair. "So, you didn't really heal after all, Weaver. It is apparently only something Dragon force can do."

Klaris heard the pride in the man's voice and was suddenly and unpleasantly reminded of Emmil Rohan. Mollish's instincts about the threat to Blizzen's soul were likely correct. She asked her next questions gently. "Can the Highlord heal also?"

Blizzen shrugged. "I'd assume so, but he's been overwhelmed with his own problems."

"Is he unwell?"

"I wouldn't say that exactly," he answered slowly. "But he wanted to see you, Weaver. That's why I left Jezel in the first place. We had hoped you would consent to meet the Highlord in Farsouth."

"Why did he want to see me?"

"He said there was too much power. In fact, I know he was growing fearful of using his force."

Lad Yob leaned forward and spoke to Blizzen for the first time. "Too much power because your magic is growing stronger as the dragons approach?"

Blizzen considered the gray Sagehamite with the typical Kordish distaste for anyone foreign. "Obviously."

"How did the Highlord think Weaver Klaris might help?" Lad Yob asked, ignoring Blizzen's curt tone.

The Orange Dragon shrugged. "I don't know. I'm not even sure the Highlord knew himself."

Klaris rose and went to look at the rain pounding on the window. "Farsouth."

Blizzen took a drink of his wine. "But he didn't go there."

Klaris turned back to consider the man.

He continued. "Halla, the Red Dragon you know, she scried for him. The Highlord left Jezel sometime before Beltane, but he was headed for Dranstyl. We don't know why."

"Where did Halla go?" Klaris asked.

Blizzen hesitated, not sure if he should reveal the discussions of the highest Dragon Magicians to the Weaver. "She went to the Verwood," he said finally. "She's a nyad, you see."

"I wonder if we should have gone to the nyad magi, too," Klaris said, drawing conclusions despite Blizzen's efforts to obfuscate the truth. She turned back to look at the wet, gray view. Something tickled in her belly. The veils of rain made her think of the glorious, glittering layers of diaphanous fabric that had made Tallyn's wedding dress.

She had never wasted time imagining her own hand-fasting, assuming that with all her Mystic, such a personal commitment would be impossible for her. Now she wondered why she'd made such assumptions. Clearly a crown princess faced great responsibilities, but these did not preclude the possibility of children as well. In fact, heirs were necessary.

The effervescence shimmered again through her stomach. Behind her she heard Blizzen quizzing Jax about how she had taken his magic. As usual, Jax did not mention what that had cost him. He inferred it had been a gift, but she knew it had really been theft.

Blizzen didn't quite mask his affront that a Mystic was able to take a Dragon's force.

Klaris turned from the window and watched Jax deliberately set his goblet on the white linen tablecloth. "I think we will need all that we have and all that we can give in order to banish the dragons." He was looking into Blizzen's ice-clear eyes.

"Maybe not," Blizzen answered with a grin. "As I said, maybe we'll understand the dragons better this time."

"Understand," Klaris breathed, her hand against her belly as comprehension flooded her. "I feel it, Jax. I feel the baby."

Lad Yob and Florin politely slipped away to let Klaris and Jax have a moment of privacy, but they were unable to get Blizzen to go with them. He leaned back in his chair and watched the prince and the Weaver. They were both royal, sure, but he was the Orange Dragon. They were born to their privileges, but he had earned his, earned the right to consort with the powerful people of Kordon.

Jax came across the room and placed his hand carefully on Klaris's flat stomach. Because Blizzen was still there, he spoke in Islish. "What does it feel like?"

"Bubbles." She smiled up at him and her breath caught as she saw the bleakness in his face.

He took her face in his hands and kissed her with such gentle intensity that tears came to her eyes. "I don't want to lose this," he whispered.

Her heart ached for what he'd already lost, and she took a shaky breath while the bubbles continued to tickle her inside. "I'll help you hold on," she promised. "Now, take a breath for the joy of this moment. When I need fear or frustration, I'll talk to Blizzen,"

Blizzen, still watching, thought he heard his name in the midst of their Islish gibberish, but since they both started laughing, he figured he must have misunderstood.

16

Al-Sefir looked at the plate of candied cockroaches and silently promised himself he'd never eat another date without first checking it for unwonted legs. The dish of nomad delicacies passed to other hands, and he cringed as he heard crunching from the nomad seated next to him.

A hot breeze wafted through the tent, shifting the blue and green shadows across the red and gold carpet. "I beg your forgiveness, Highlord," the nomad Dragon said. "I have never heard of such a place or this cat god you speak of." She looked around at the other, lesser magicians gathered in the tent. They shook their heads, their brown eyes blank.

Al-Sefir watched Raggar compulsively clench his fists.

The nomad Dragon continued. "I studied at Dishroc, but as you can tell, my magic did not warrant the training of Dragonsholm."

"That is precisely why I wanted to speak with you," the Highlord answered, through clenched teeth. "I already know there is no information at Jezel, or Dranstyl, or Seare that can help me."

The woman shrugged again. "Nomads have no archive, no library. Books and scrolls are heavy, and we move around too much to lug such things with us. We keep knowledge in our stories, our poems and songs. Even so, I don't remember anything about an ancient city."

The Highlord rose, and Al-Sefir jumped to his feet to steady him.

The nomad Dragons stood as well, their faces worried. "Try the priest, Highlord," said the woman. "The priests and priestesses keep the stories."

Raggar said nothing, but his grip was bruising as he and Al-Sefir left the tent. After the relative cool of the shadows, the blazing sunlight glaring off the few, white-washed buildings of Ropebridge blinded both of them.

"Where is the priest?" Raggar croaked.

"Probably at the oasis," Al-Sefir nodded toward the collection of colorful tents under the dusty green trees beyond the corral of camels. "And if he's not there, at least we can get a drink."

The priest was indeed taking refuge from the late summer heat in the shade of some thick-leafed thorn trees. Al-Sefir watched him sleep for a moment, disappointed. A young man like this seemed an unlikely source for lost tales of an ancient city and a forgotten god. He bent and shook the younger priest. "Forgive me, Father. The Dragon Highlord would like to see you."

"What?" The young priest sat up, his dark hair falling into his eyes. "The Dragon Highlord is here in Ropebridge?"

"He is."

The priest blinked and cleared his throat. "I'm sorry, Father. Who are you?"

"I'm Al-Sefir Hewish, oracular priest to Vitrus. I've been called to help the Highlord."

The young man finally recovered his drowsy wits. "Please, yes sit. Let me get you some wine. No? Water? Very well. Oh, and here I have a nice plate of candied—."

"No, thank you!" Al-Sefir said quickly. "Water will be fine."

The priest smiled. "I understand. The sweets aren't to everyone's taste."

Raggar had not taken a seat on the carpet. He stared up through the leaves of the tree. "You have a cat," he said.

"Yes, Highlord. That's Fierra."

"I recognize that word. It means fire in Ancient?"

"Yes. In Axterran."

"Ancient is the language of Axterre?" Al-Sefir gasped.

"You know the language of Axterre?" Raggar rounded on the young priest.

He looked startled by the Highlord's vehemence. "Just a bit of it."

Raggar grabbed the priest. His mouth worked, but no sounds came out.

Seeing the alarm in the young man's face, Al-Sefir gently pried the Highlord's hands from the priest's arms. "We've been searching for information about Axterre," he explained. "Searching vainly, until now, it seems."

The priest rubbed his wrists where the Highlord's grip had bruised him. "What do you want to know?"

"We don't think it's a myth." Al-Sefir said.

"No. Of course, it isn't."

The Highlord leaned forward, his eyes fixed upon the young man. "Where is it?"

"I don't know that exactly." He waved a hand. "Away to the East, right? Like it says in the poem. Only if you go east from here, you end up in the Maze. But that's where it must have been."

"What are your sources?" Raggar demanded.

"The poem, of course. And the water."

"The water?" Al-Sefir prompted.

"We drink from the oasis here, but never from the River Owh. The river is fouled."

The Highlord jumped up from the carpet and strode from the shade towards the spire of rock that marked the head of the bridge that gave this settlement its name. The two priests ran after him.

"Does everyone know this?" Al-Sefir asked as they sweated under the beat of the sun.

"Everyone knows not to drink or use the water. Even bathing in it can raise sores on a body. Animals won't touch it."

Raggar turned on him suddenly. "But why? And who told you?"

"No one told me." The priest frowned. "But when I learned the poem, the *Fall of Axterre,* I just put two and two together. I mean, we're already pretty far east in the Knownlands, right? So, the city itself must have been upstream from here."

They'd reached the bridgehead now. A long span of rope curved down across a chasm. Hundreds of yards below, a gray river zig-zagged back and forth in the confines of vertical red walls.

"I thought you didn't drink it because you couldn't get down to it." Al-Sefir said.

"No," scoffed the priest. "There are twenty ways down to the canyon floor."

"Not one I can see," muttered Al-Sefir.

The Highlord stared into the chasm. "How far downstream does the river retain its poison?"

"Once the Owh joins the Geitflow, which is clean, coming down from the Targheights, the water can be used for washing, but it still isn't potable until after it passes through Fumid Marsh. They drink it in Dishroc."

The rope-bridge swayed in the hot wind.

"Ha!" Raggar smiled for the first time in weeks. "At last, Sefir! At last we know where to go!"

The priest looked at them. It was his turn to be confused. "Go where?"

"Axterre!" the Highlord crowed. "We'll just follow the river east from here."

"But you can't," the younger man objected.

"Why not?" Al-Sefir took the priest's arm. "Why not?"

"The whole bottom land is fouled. Look, nothing grows down there. And you can't drink it."

Both Raggar and Al-Sefir turned to look again at the murky river running through the rocks below.

"You two are desert-bred," the priest reminded them. "You know any water should be lined with green, with trees and grasses. That's not."

"That's not." Al-Sefir agreed.

"Goddess damn it!" Raggar swore. "If Axterre is up that river, we must go there."

"Axterre *probably* is up there, the Maze certainly is." The priest answered darkly.

"What is the Maze?" Al-Sefir asked, wondering if this damned quest was going to be possible after all.

"The Maze is a labyrinth of canyons. People who go in don't come out."

Raggar seemed to deflate.

"Let's go back to the shade," Al-Sefir suggested, sweat pouring down his face.

They walked in silence. Al-Sefir watched the Highlord suck on his lips. They all sat on the priest's cushions.

Al-Sefir was surprised by the strength in Raggar's voice when he finally spoke: "Do you have any advice or know of anyone who can help us?"

The priest stared at them, his brown eyes wide and helpless. He shook his head.

Fierra dropped silently from the branches over their heads. She stalked to the Highlord, who froze, staring at her.

"Follow the river," she said. The priest gasped. The cat ignored him. "It's the only way you'll get to Axterre in time."

"In time for what?" Raggar asked.

"In time to help."

"Sweet goddess," breathed Al-Sefir.

The cat looked at him, her golden eyes unmistakably cool. "You might pray to the cat god also."

Klaris stood back from the house she'd just pulled from the granite of the soaring Targheight mountainside. Granite didn't give itself easily, and she took a sort of sadistic pleasure in making the work even more difficult by adding decorative touches and a wide veranda.

"Weaver, it is a joy to watch you work," Lad Yob whispered reverently.

Jax and Florin stood nearby with the bags, waiting for Klaris to finish, while Blizzen had retreated further away to the pine trees that covered the mountains to avoid suffering cross-magic. The pegasi cropped at the sparse bits of grass that grew down by the small tarn.

Klaris smirked in satisfaction and addressed Jax in Islish. "What's the Landish word for *veranda*?"

"Veranda," he translated.

Blizzen climbed the step to the veranda and flopped onto a bench. "Veranda," he echoed. "I have to admit, Jax. I had expected a half-isle like you would speak Landish with an accent like the Weaver does."

Jax found himself annoyed by yet another example of Blizzen's overly familiar tone and thoughtless xenophobia. This wasn't the first time Blizzen had crossed Jax's rather liberal boundaries of protocol. "You will remember, Dragon Blizzen, that I fostered with the crown princess. Our tutors were meticulous about proper elocution."

"Proper elocution," Florin repeated, capturing Jax's aristocratic accent. She pulled her bow from one of the packs. "I'm going to go elocute a rabbit for our stew this evening."

Jax laughed. "You'll have better luck with the bow."

She winked at him and dropped back into her broad Hantish drawl. "That's why I'm taking it, pal."

Blizzen stretched his cramped legs. "I'm surprised Klaris doesn't speak better Landish," he said.

Klaris had been using Ancient to discuss a technical detail of her construction with the lad. She turned a chilly green gaze on Blizzen, but it was Jax who spoke to the Orange Dragon in Islish: "And are you fluent at all in Islish?"

Blizzen shrugged. "What?"

"Excuse me," Jax returned to Landish. "You don't speak Islish, then?"

Blizzen laughed at the ludicrousness of the suggestion. "No."

"And how long, exactly, have you lived on Jezel?" Klaris asked in her husky accent.

"Nearly twenty years."

"Indeed," Jax answered.

Blizzen looked from Jax to Klaris, frowning. Had there been an insult in the prince's question?

"I'm going for a swim," Klaris said to Jax, in Islish. "Care to join me?"

"The water will be freezing."

"No colder than this conversation."

Jax laughed again and followed her down to the lake, leaving Blizzen to brood over the rudeness of people speaking a language others couldn't understand.

When Florin returned, she found both Klaris and Jax wet-haired and invigorated from their swim in the cold lake. Blizzen went inside the shelter saying, "Call me when dinner is ready."

Florin's mouth twisted in a grimace as she knelt to skin the rabbit. "I'm getting tired of being treated as an invisible servant by our esteemed Orange Dragon."

Jax organized kindling in the stone fire-ring Lad Yob had built. He pulled a flicker of Dragon force through Klaris's Mystic to set it alight. "Maybe you should apply your feminine charms."

"He'd probably still ignore me and think he was merely pleasuring himself."

Jax and Lad Yob laughed.

"What's the joke?" Klaris joined them by the fire.

"Florin is devising subtle tortures for our Dragon friend," Jax answered, still laughing.

"Let me know if I can help," Lad Yob offered.

Klaris eyed the lad with surprise. She'd never seen a glimpse of humor from any of the Sagehamites before.

Blizzen's head appeared at a window. "I can actually hear you."

Florin took a handful of gravel and tossed it at the window.

"Hey!" Blizzen's face left the window. A moment later, he came out the door.

"For goddess' sake, Florin." Jax grumbled, but he knew he had to settle this. "Blizzen, come help me check on the pegasi."

"The pegasi don't need us. And I've already taken off my boots."

Jax leaned against the veranda railing and struggled to keep his patience. "Put them on again, Dragon Blizzen, and come with me."

Blizzen sighed loudly, but he complied. Jax led the way through the twilight to where the white pegasi grazed by the lake that mirrored a pink and lavender sky.

"We're going to spend a lot of time together, Dragon Blizzen," Jax said finally. "I think we'd better make some things clear."

"That's always a good idea, son."

Jax bit back the sharp reply and took a slow breath. "I am not your *son*, Dragon Blizzen. You may continue to address me as my lord, or sir, or Prince Jax. Klaris will be called Weaver or my lady."

"But, surely—."

"Furthermore," Jax continued as if Blizzen hadn't spoken. "No one here is your servant."

Blizzen stared at the younger man for several moments. "But the nyad creature and the gray Mystic thing—."

"Are our companions. Not our staff."

"The Sagehamite brings you and the Weaver tea each morning."

Jax ran a hand through his hair and gripped for his patience.

Blizzen, thinking erroneously that he was winning the argument, let his logic slip. "The nyad doesn't use an honorific with you."

"No, she doesn't." Jax favored the Dragon with a sunny smile. "She calls Klaris 'my lady' but she has been given the right to address me informally."

"And you're withholding that from me?" Blizzen was clearly affronted.

"I am." Jax saw the indignation in Blizzen's face. "Friendship comes in stages, Dragon Blizzen."

"If it comes at all." Blizzen snapped.

Jax nodded.

"Dinner's up!" Florin called from the fire.

"Thank you for your understanding," Jax said. "Tonight, it's your turn to do the dishes." He turned and walked back to the fire.

Blizzen watched him go, torn. On the one hand he had to admit a certain respect for the young prince for speaking candidly to him. Still, he, Blizzen Kreeborn, had risen to be the goddess-blessed Orange Dragon. He knew all about hard work, unlike the prince or even Weaver Klaris, a princess herself. Slowly he walked back to join the others. He ate dinner in silence, noting the annoying way both Klaris and the nyad creature butchered the King's Landish.

As he washed dishes under the illumination of a glowing ball of his own orange mage-light, he began to understand the dowager's evident hatred for that damned, smirky half-isle. All the brat's charm and glamour just masked a selfish soul and arrogant pride.

17

Horrified, Chieftess Eleeza St. Clare, Speaker for All Eldars, gaped at her sister and spoke not at all. Finally, she closed her lips into a firm, unyielding line and turned away from her sister's agonized amber eyes.

For years Eleeza had dealt with the whispers about Lexyl's magic, whispers that suggested the chieftess' sister might not be quite sane and was possibly very dangerous. After all, reasonable people had long since ceased to bother with a true vision quest; reasonable people had the sense to stay away from haunted ruins; reasonable people did not need magic and didn't trust it either.

Eleeza placed her palms on the windowsill and stared without seeing at the hot summer day. Lexyl had always been an unconventional thinker, which made her a challenge for the conservative Eldar people. Unconventional, but brilliant: Eleeza had a profound respect for her sister's mind. She couldn't count the times that Lexyl had suggested a solution to some problem that was so simple and clear that Eleeza had been amazed no one else had seen it. Her learning seemed to encompass all Eldar experience: history, geography, plant and animal lore, and of course, the Mystic. Because she loved her sister, and because her information was so often useful, the chieftess had refused to consider where Lexyl had attained this knowledge.

But now, Lexyl's admission crossed the limit of Eleeza's tolerance. The speaker struggled for words as she sought a safe argument.

"For the moment," she began, "I'll overlook the crime of reading the Axterran scrolls in order to discuss their validity. First of all, those documents are ancient, so you can't be sure what you've read there applies today. Second, the Axterrans clearly didn't know everything, thus their horrible demise. And finally, how can you think that something written over a thousand years ago could possibly apply to you?"

"That's what a prophecy does," Lexyl said to her sister's back. "It speaks across time."

Neither sister spoke for a few minutes. Eleeza finally shook her head. "Often enough over the past few years, people have suggested that I should send you to exile in the desert."

"Ashande is a foolish old man," Lexyl said succinctly. "Don't tell him I've actually read the scrolls, or he'll come after me with some kind of perverted holy crusade."

Eleeza finally turned. "Of course he will! And he'd be justified. The scrolls are forbidden for a reason, Lexyl."

"Knowledge isn't as dangerous as ignorance."

"Right. That's why Axterre is now a haunted ruin."

"It *was* ignorance that caused Axterre to fall. Willful, prideful ignorance. Just as the Shaman Lyrech prophesied."

"Shaman Lyrech?" Eleeza hadn't heard that name since her history lessons some thirty years ago. Lyrech had been the priest whose visionary oratory had gathered a group of disaffected Axterrans and taken them away from the city several generations before the tragic destruction. This small group of people found a refuge in the forested canyons north of Axterre, between the primitive Caveharts who lived simple lives in the tunnels under the Dragon Perch Mountain and the gray and brown constructed landscape of the City.

By the time Axterre fell, the Eldar people had established their refuge. Over the years the desert crept further north, the trees died from lack of water. The Eldar people, having learned the terrible lesson of Axterre, were closely attuned to the changing environment, adapted, and thrived.

But Lexyl hadn't been talking about Axterran history, or even Eldar history. It was her talk of dragons that had horrified Eleeza.

"Look at the murals out there," Lexyl said. "Our ancestors knew that written words are perishable, only as durable as a scrap of parchment. That's why they made those paintings on the wall. Look out there, Eleeza, and tell me what you see."

Eleeza knew very well what the murals were, but she turned away from the vulnerability of her sister and looked again out the window. "Dragons," she said.

"And?"

"And other mythic creatures. Fairies. Nyads."

"I think we've established that nyads aren't mythic," Lexyl said dryly. "But the point is our ancestors knew that the dragons would return. The murals just confirm and reinforce the information in the scrolls."

This was where they'd begun this argument. Eleeza considered the apocalyptic implications of another dragon interregnum and grasped at one last point.

"Lexyl, if the dragons really are returning, then clearly our refuge here is the best place for all of us."

"For you, and the people, yes. Not for me."

"Why not?"

Lexyl gestured toward her desk. "Read that scroll."

Eleeza stared at the yellowed parchment laced with a dance of purple script and frowned. As heir to the speaker, she'd been shown the forbidden scrolls and recognized this as one of them.

"I can't read it," she admitted. "And something's missing at the bottom, she pointed to a edge of the parchment where another line of script had been mostly excised.

"This details the millennial cycle of dragon migration to the Knownlands," Lexyl said. "Before Axterre, the creatures of the Knownlands developed a banishment. The prophecy there contains some of the instructions."

"The prophecy that involves you."

"They are coming," Lexyl said, anguished.

"Dragons?"

"Dragons, yes. But also the Weaver and the Paradox."

"Sweet goddess, Lexyl." Eleeza snapped. "You know the people are saying you've lost your wits. Talk like that, and I might start to believe them."

"You've met the Paradox, Eleeza. It's Javix Sharkin."

"Right, Borrel's friend, that half-isle."

"Exactly: Half islish, half landish, prince and slave, and he can't be found in a scry."

"What does that mean?"

"Listen to the prophecy!

> *Oracle, speak the Mother's truth:*
> *Dragons come with claw and tooth.*
> *Your purpose for one thousand years:*
> *Is to remember the fires and tears*
>
> *A paradox who can't be found.*
> *The Mother stirs and shakes the ground.*
> *The oceans rise to touch the trees,*
> *And bring a ruler to his knees.*
>
> *Opposites must now adhere*
> *Blood must mix and frontiers clear*
> *Align the magic, love and fae*
> *To turn the dragon threat away*
>
> *Weaver and the Paradox*
> *A Child born among Redrocks*
> *At Axterre the Cornerstone*
> *Holds lyrics to the Dragon Song.*

Jax is the paradox who can't be found. And I am going into the desert, despite your objections, so I can't be found either."

Eleeza's mind whirled through her battered arguments but could find no solid way to deny Lexyl's conclusions, so she took refuge in her own authority. "I won't allow them to take you. You're my heir."

"It's not me they want."

Eleeza looked away from the deep pain in her sister's eyes and down to the baby in Lexyl's arms.

"They want the baby born among Redrocks. *My* baby."

Borrel stood beside Halla and gazed at the giant rock formations that marched away to the horizon.

"Sweet goddess," Halla muttered. "What I wouldn't give for a tree."

Borrel smiled. Halla had noticed him smiling more and more often as they traveled south across the vast prairie of Thequis and into the fissured land of canyon and mesa.

"It's a powerful landscape," he said. "Bare earth, sky, wind."

"We can't eat the rock or drink the wind," Halla groused.

"But you see the effects of water everywhere here. It's more present by its absence. If these washes were filled with water, we'd see trees, and frogs, and birds. But here, there's no water, so we're not distracted by the things that go with water."

Walking in the dry wash ahead of him, Halla smiled with the pride of a teacher for an apt student. "I see you understand the concept of paradox."

Borrel heard the smile in her voice, even though he did not see her face. "It's not hard to understand if you've spent any time with Jax Sharkin."

"The paradox who can't be found."

"Goddess help him," Borrel said softly.

"Goddess help *us*, if we don't find a wetter manifestation of water pretty soon, my friend."

Al-Sefir squeezed the moss to get enough water to fill the tin cup. He returned to the small fire he'd built the hard way, with twigs and flint. The Highlord slumped against a rock, the small flames reflected in his glazed eyes.

"Drink, Highlord."

Absently, Raggar sipped the liquid. "Tastes green."

The priest smiled. "Not enough green here, is there?"

The Highlord didn't answer. Al-Sefir fiddled with the sticks he was using to roast a lizard. Before it was cooked, Raggar had rolled into a ball and closed his glassy eyes.

Al-Sefir ate most of the lizard, saving some for the Highlord, hoping he would decide to eat. The man had taken little beside water for days. As the flesh sank beneath his skin, revealing the angular bones beneath, Al-Sefir feared the Highlord would die before they reached their destination.

At least Raggar still drank. Like all desert-bred folk, Al-Sefir knew the green moss water held powerful sustenance. For this reason, the priest gave all of the moss water to the Highlord and drank himself from their diminishing supply of water from the oasis at Ropebridge.

For five more days, the two trudged through the rocky bottomland. Several times each day they had to cross the foul brown river where it curved up against one of the vertical canyon walls and blocked their path. After each crossing, their skin and clothes dried quickly in the hot air, but a gray layer of grime clung to them. Al-Sefir noticed a rash on the Highlord's legs and watched a blister develop a nasty infection on his own left foot. He was relieved when finally the canyon widened into a broad valley.

He stood next to the Highlord and squinted at the strange brown haze that filled the flat. "Sweet goddess," he whispered.

The Highlord stepped forward and choked, his magic flaring. "Dragons," he gasped. "Do you feel it?"

Al-Sefir didn't feel magic, just horror.

18

Florin stood, hands on her waist and a scowl on her face, glaring down the embankment at the thick brown water in the River Rysk. "I'd love a bath, but I think I'd come out dirtier than I went in."

Jax ran a hand through his own sweaty hair. "Aye, but it's the last water we're likely to find."

Florin raised her eyes to the blocks of red rock massed across the river.

"Surely the Herders have clean water in Stede," Blizzen said.

Florin made an exasperated noise and rounded on him. "We're not going to Stede, Dragon Blizzen. It's been decided and you can stop complaining about it."

"You haven't had a civil word for me since I healed you, Nyad. I am the Orange Dragon, and you will respect me."

"Or not." Florin walked back toward their packs.

"No more healing for nyads," Blizzen grumbled, turning his attention to Jax, who continued to gaze at the distant monoliths. "I understand the Herders practically ran you and your Hantish companions out of Stede, my lord, but surely they'd be more respectful now that you are in the company of two of the most powerful magicians in the Knownlands."

Jax sighed and finally turned away from his survey of the Rocredlands and the fears and memories the landscape evoked.

"Dragon Blizzen, the Herders accused a simple druid of manipulating the weather. Clearly Mother Marith has no such powers, but there's no way I'm going to take a magician – or two – who *do* possibly possess such power into that hostile environment."

"But—."

Jax raised a hand and Blizzen stopped. "No. Now, excuse me, I'm going to practice the banishment tune again."

"Fool." Blizzen grumbled as he watched Jax walk away pulling that dingy wooden dragonpipe from his pocket.

Florin dried her hair, listening to Jax build his tune.

"Did you bathe in the river?" Klaris asked softly.

"I did. We aren't likely to find enough water to wash in once we get into the Maze."

Klaris stood at the window and considered the odd treeless landscape. It looked like something composed of a child's set of blocks, and yet the red stone underneath the deepening purple of the twilight was starkly beautiful.

Jax's music stopped in the middle of the tune then resumed repeating the phrase a little differently. Blizzen must be coaching him again, she realized, marveling that Jax had the patience to even listen to the man.

Over the past few days, Klaris had found herself increasingly annoyed by Blizzen's constant complaining that they weren't going to Stede, that the late summer heat was so uncomfortable, and that doing menial chores was beneath the dignity of someone in his position. She'd taken refuge in her magic, claiming Blizzen's Dragon crossed her, even though she was perfectly capable of shielding herself had she wanted to be in his presence.

Tolerating his presence had become more difficult in the few days since Florin had cut herself on the blade of her hunting knife and Blizzen bent his magic to heal the wound.

"It will be fine in a day or two," Florin had protested, wrapping a bit of cloth around her bloody palm as Blizzen offered to heal her.

"If you let me do this, it will be fine now," he'd argued.

They had all been gathered around the cooking fire, and Klaris couldn't hide her curiosity about the process. "How would you do it?" she'd asked.

"This would be quite simple," Blizzen had sniffed. "Compared to some of the healings I've worked. You see, you pull on the flow of her life, her blood, and use a bit of flame to—."

"I don't think so," Florin interrupted. "Someone go get the plates. This stew is about done."

"Ah, Florin, don't be a coward," Blizzen challenged, eager to show what he could do.

Florin looked at the fire-lit faces around her. Only Lad Yob seemed to share her reservations. Both Klaris and Jax seemed curious about how Blizzen would use Dragon force to heal.

"Fine," she spat, taking a seat and holding out her bandaged hand. "Do it quickly or the stew will be ruined."

Blizzen sat down opposite her and unwound the bloody cloth. The cut was deep, exposing white ligaments beneath the open skin.

Klaris and Jax both felt Blizzen draw on his considerable magic. The Weaver shielded herself, as Blizzen made no effort to contain his forces.

Florin sucked in her breath then screamed.

She tore her hand free of Blizzen's grasp. Jax leapt towards Florin, steadying her trembling shoulders.

"Sweet goddess," she gasped, tears in her eyes. "Holy *mother!* What the dragons was that?"

"I know it hurts a bit."

"Hurts? *Hurts* doesn't half describe it!"

"The pain lasts only a minute," Blizzen said curtly. He held out his hand and snapped his fingers. "Let me finish."

Florin stared down at her own hand, shaking her head. "It's worse. Look, it's like my wrist is broken again."

"Let me see." Blizzen grabbed her arm. "You broke that wrist some time ago."

"Years ago," she choked.

"You should have told me. Now take a deep breath. Hold her tightly, Jax."

Florin screamed and screamed again. The magic flared and died. The nyad collapsed, shaking in Jax's arms.

"There!" Blizzen crowed. "It's better now, isn't it? Completely better."

Still breathing heavily, Florin blinked tears out of her eyes and looked at her hand. The wound was gone, as if it had never been. Cautiously she flexed her wrist and made a fist, relief flooding through her belly. "It is better."

Klaris handed her a cup of wine, then filled three more. Florin took a deep swallow and wiped the sweat and tears off her face. "Holy mother," she swore again.

Jax let her go, as the shaking subsided, and took a drink from his own cup. "Is it always like that?"

Blizzen raised his cup. "To the dragons!" He smiled and drank before answering Jax's question. "It is always painful and can be more so if I'm not forewarned about previous wounds."

"Because the process can 'unheal' them?" Klaris asked.

"It can." Blizzen drank again.

"Perhaps you should speak to the patient about this before you start your torture." Florin snapped.

Blizzen frowned. "Why are you so upset? There's absolutely no pain now, right?"

Florin shuddered. "Not now, but sweet goddess...."

"I guess nyads aren't very strong, or stoic," Blizzen said.

Florin rose and might have kicked the cup right out of the arrogant man's hands, but Jax caught her arm and pulled her away. "Let's walk a bit," he suggested. "Blizzen, you can serve up dinner. We'll be back soon."

"Serve dinner?" Blizzen shook his head and drank off his wine. "Do I have to do everything? Heal wounds and dish out stew?"

"Allow me," Lad Yob offered quietly, leaning toward the fire.

Klaris sat silently watching. She heard Jax's voice in soothing tones as he led Florin away from the camp. Because she had appropriated Jax's magic, Klaris could now see the way Dragon force worked, how it flowed and how it bent matter. Indeed, Blizzen's grasp and command of that magic was impressive and even beautiful.

She stared now into the subdued fire and took the bowl of stew Lad Yob offered her, but she did not eat. Her thoughts had resurrected Emmil Rohan. He too had used his magic with similar strength and similar arrogance. That disregard for the loose edges and the lack of respect for the subject, whether stone or light or person, had killed Emmil. Klaris lifted her green eyes to consider Dragon Blizzen, his face content in the orange glow of the fire.

Surely healing ought to be a blessing. Klaris shuddered, remembering Florin's agonized screams, and worried what Blizzen's flawed soul might kill.

"Damn." Borrel frowned down into the unfamiliar canyon. He turned to look back the way they'd come. There were those weird spires, sticking up out of the sand, like giant fingers. And off to the east rose that big blue mountain Lexyl had called Dragon Perch. But this was not the Watcher's Plateau, where he and his twin, and Jax and Marith had first met Lexyl a year ago. And this, he stared down the Redrock wall, was not Nkai Canyon.

"We're lost?" Halla resettled her empty water skin.

Borrel looked around again. Surely, they couldn't be that far from the watcher's perch. But if the Eldar on watch duty happened to be someone other than Lexyl, perhaps he or she would simply be content to let him and Halla succumb to the rigors of the desert.

"Let's go down here," he said finally. "There's a couple cottonwood trees in that side canyon, which probably means water."

"Let's hope so," Halla grumbled in unison with her empty stomach. She scrambled down the rocks behind Borrel, wondering what good it was to have potent, powerful magic that could provide neither food nor water. Although Borrel had managed to find water several times, and foraged food from the small areas of green amid these rocks, both of them were about at their limit.

It took them all afternoon, winding through canyons, to find the cottonwood trees Borrel had seen from the rim rock. He and Halla had to climb up a fall of boulders to get into the broad sheltered bowl. A spring splashed rainbows into a small pool surrounded by green grass and the cottonwoods. Vertical Redrock walls towered up on three sides of the bowl, while the western side was open to the vast view.

Borrel stopped suddenly. The glade was not empty. A blanket had been spread in the shade and a small creature wriggled upon it.

"What's that?" Halla asked.

Three blue lines of fire crackled suddenly around the two nyads.

"Lexyl!" Borrel shouted.

A woman dashed from the small shelter under the back wall of the glade and ran to the blanket. "Go away, Borrel!"

Borrel stared. He took a step toward the blue bands that cracked as he touched them. "Lexyl, let me in."

"No! No, Borrel."

He pushed forward, pulling on his magic that was stronger than it had been a year ago, thanks to Halla's tutoring. The bands moved with him towards Lexyl and the bundle she'd lifted gently from the blanket.

Halla, her brown eyes thoughtful, followed.

Lexyl pulled more magic and wove a fourth band. Borrel, now only a few feet from her stopped. "Lex, my love." He was elated to see her but wounded by her clear rejection.

Her shoulders slumped at the nickname and the endearment.

"Let us in," he said softly. "You know we won't hurt you."

She looked into the longing in his eyes and saw his lips form that familiar, gentle smile.

"We need you," he said. "I need you."

By the cat god, she needed him too. But the blue bands did not fall. She let her gaze drift from Borrel to the woman behind him. Another nyad, this one, but older with long stripes of gray in her chestnut-colored hair.

"Why have you come?" Lexyl demanded.

"There's a prophecy about dragons," Borrel answered. "That bit of poem you gave to Jax is part of it. We need to know more and thought you probably had the answers."

"Probably," she snapped. The bundle in her arms gurgled.

Borrel stared at it for a moment. "Why do you have a baby out here?"

She clutched the child to her chest and shook her head.

Borrel took another step toward her, his heart failing him. "You've hand-fasted someone," he said in a strained voice. "That's why you didn't want to see me."

"No," Lexyl choked.

Halla decided this difficult discussion had gone on long enough. "Lady Lexyl, I'm Halla Felstar. I'm the Red Dragon, and I promise you, Borrel and I intend no harm to you or the baby."

"You don't know what you intend," Lexyl said with such tragedy in her voice that Halla blinked and paused.

Borrel heard the pain, too. "Lex, let me in. I'm here now. You're not alone."

"I'm not alone." She shifted the baby, and Borrel got a better look at his brown hair and blinking brown nyad eyes.

"That's my baby," he gasped.

"My baby," Lexyl clarified.

"Our baby?" Borrel's heart began to work again, as relief and joy flooded his blood. "What a blessing!"

Lexyl shook her head, her face hard. "It's not a blessing. It's a curse."

Borrel spread his fingers against the blue bands. "Please, Lex. Take these down and let me in."

Halla watched Lexyl's amber eyes harden. The nyad knew she could dismantle Lexyl's blue bands with a little effort. The Eldar was powerful and her magic definitely Mystic, uniquely so. But it was also untutored and no match for the Red Dragon. Still, Halla kept her power sheathed. It would serve little purpose to force themselves on the Eldar woman. Lexyl would have to decide on her own to let the nyads in.

Borrel's eyes glowed. "Goddess, I've missed you, Lex."

She looked up at him again and saw the tousled hair, stirred by the afternoon breeze, the intensity of his gaze, the lips ready to laugh or kiss.

"I've missed you, too," she admitted.

The baby cooed.

Borrel opened his arms.

Lexyl closed her eyes. If anyone else had come, she could have refused, but not him. She let the magic drop. He was there, his arms around her and the baby, his mouth on her lips, the warm, lovely scent of him filling her.

Halla stepped around them and went to the pool where she took a long drink and splashed her face. Since Borrel and Lexyl were still communicating silently, she walked into the little shelter in search of food.

She found a pear and a bit of some type of jerky and a lot of very old scrolls. She ran her fingers along them, frowning at the dark sting of the ancient magic. What could have caused such a taint to last so long?

One scroll lay unrolled on a table under the window. Halla frowned at it. The script was so archaic that the words were difficult to recognize. What language was this? Unlike the Mystic weave, which had been around as long as there had been sentient creatures in the Knownlands, Dragon force was relatively young, and its texts were written in only the last eight or nine hundred years. The most powerful Dragon Magicians still learned the ancient languages, but not with the same intensity as those with Mystic.

Halla swallowed the last of the pear and bent to look closer at the open scroll. Understanding hit her like a slap in the face. She stumbled back, into a stack of scroll cases, their dark magic reaching out to her.

Choking, she fled the shelter, her stomach heaving to expel the pear.

Borrel was holding the baby, admiring his little hands and soft cheeks. Lexyl glanced at Halla as she came out of the hut.

"Sweet goddess, Lexyl, you've got some nasty stuff in there."

Lexyl squared her shoulders. "Did you read it?"

Halla shook her head. "I can't read Ancient."

"Perhaps you're fortunate, Dragon Halla. It's definitely worse when you understand what it says."

19

"We camped here with Lexyl." Florin jumped off her pegasus. "There's the little shelter."

Klaris walked toward the structure examining its magical format. This was her first opportunity to review something touched by Lexyl and her unique Mystic. Indeed, the little shelter bore the unsettling imprint of a magic at once ancient in style yet obviously recently woven. In fact, Lexyl's weavings felt almost more like Oracular magic than Mystic.

"I'm starving," Blizzen announced, sitting down and doing nothing to help unload the pegasi or further preparations for dinner.

Both Florin and Klaris tossed exasperated glances at him. Jax, helping Lad Yob unload packs from the pegasi, didn't look at the man. "I wonder if the dowager expected him to foil our mission simply by annoying us to death."

"The dowager, sir?" Lad Yob lifted the harnessing gear off the steed.

"Aye, Laddie. She insisted he come with us." Jax hefted three of the packs. "I don't know what game she's playing this time, and that worries me."

Lad Yob watched Jax walk toward the shelter under the burden of their baggage and felt the magic move with a deep foreboding. He turned back to brush the pegasus, thinking someone should keep a close eye on Dragon Blizzen.

The chieftess rubbed her hands over her tired eyes and wished yet again for her sister's acute intellect. "You've made your concerns quite clear, Ashande." She managed to keep the fatigue and most of the exasperation out of her voice.

"Good, then, Speaker. You will surely order the people to prepare arms."

Eleeza glared him into silence. "War, Shaman? I am not yet prepared to use one blasphemy to thwart another."

The Shaman sputtered.

Eleeza let her amber eyes sweep the room. Runners from the other three Eldar Collectives stood listening with wary attention.

"Chieftess," a young man, his rust-colored clothing trimmed in green, stepped forward. "It will take me two days to reach Farloste. The intruders will descend upon us at any moment. If I and the other runners are to fetch help, we must be off now."

Eleeza turned to the window. It was far too late to run for help. The streets below seethed with people bulky with packs filled with food or treasured possessions. They weren't leaving yet, but they were panicked and balky. At best, the runners would be able to report what happened here this morning.

The chieftess had been Speaker for All Eldars for nearly half her life. She well knew that indecision in a leader could be worse than even a poor choice.

Goddess, she wished Lexyl were here to put sensible words on Eleeza's instincts. Of course, she had obliquely warned the chieftess that outsiders would be coming. But Lexyl had fled, and it would seem reasonable to the other Eldars to do the same, never mind the situations were not the same.

The chieftess opened a narrow door that gave on to the Speaker's Balcony. From here, her voice would resonate out to the people in the street and back to the advisors and runners in the room behind.

"People of Arandy," she began, breathing deeply of the gentle morning air. "As you all know, a flock of pegasi have come to the

Rocredlands. It is possible their riders want something from the Eldar people, but I do not think they bring either war or treachery."

"What do they want from us?" someone shouted from the street below.

"We shall have to ask them." Eleeza answered. "We will hide our fears and greet them with courtesy."

"They come!" A voice echoed down the canyon from the rimrock high above. "The pegasi are coming!"

The people in the streets scrambled for shelter. Eleeza turned back to the runners. "Go to the edges of Arandy. If this goes amiss, you will report that to your collectives. If it goes well, return here and the council and I will prepare missives for you to deliver."

By the time the winged horses flew into view above the canyon rim, the only Eldar in the open was the chieftess. She wore her white robe of state with thick blue and gold trim. The morning's soft breeze stirred the iridescent feathers in her tall headdress. Amber Eldar eyes watched from every window.

Just as the pegasi's hooves clattered onto the cobbles, Shaman Ashande stepped from the shadows raising his gnarled staff. "Magic!" he howled. "Perfidy!"

Eleeza made a small motion and four large Eldars stepped from the palace to corral the Shaman.

"I am the speaker," she noted. "You will hold your tongue now or lose it forever."

Ashande pressed his lips together, his eyes flashing.

Eleeza turned back to the pegasi, her trepidation growing. Indeed, she believed these riders wanted little from Arandy, but what they might want from her and Lexyl personally was inexpressibly dear.

Five people dismounted from the seven pegasi. She recognized Jax immediately. He stepped forward and bowed fluidly.

"I understand you are Javix Sharkin," the chieftess said sternly. "Prince of two western realms."

He rose. "Yes, your Majesty. May I present the Weaver, Princess Klaris de Farsouth; Blizzen Kreeborn the Orange Dragon. Also, Lad Yob from Sageham Isle and you may remember Florin Starrish, who was here with me last winter."

Eleeza knew that the magicians would be the most dangerous and problematic of the strangers, but neither of them seemed at all threatening. The Dragon fellow looked around with the air of someone ready to indulge a number of physical appetites, while this Weaver person was little more than a girl. So Eleeza turned to Florin. "Where is your brother, Florin Starrish?"

"He, ah, went to see the nyad magi, ah, milady. I don't know exactly where he is now."

Eleeza thought this news would be profoundly disappointing to Lexyl. But it was time to move this conversation out of the public eye and ear.

"Please come inside, Weaver, Your Highness, all of you. We have prepared a breakfast."

"You knew we were coming?" Dragon Blizzen asked.

"Your Majesty," Jax added.

"Of course." Eleeza answered.

"The Eldars have watchers stationed across the Rocredlands," Jax said softly to Blizzen as they followed the speaker into the palace. "I'm sure they noticed the pegasi days ago."

"We knew you were coming long before the flying horses were seen." Eleeza's sandals tapped on the tile as she led the group to an elegant room roofed only with a trellis covered by carefully trained green vines that dripped lightly scented purple flowers.

"How did you know, Your Majesty?" Klaris asked.

The chieftess considered the tiny woman. She couldn't feel the girl's magic but there was something about the way she carried herself and spoke that, despite her difficult accent, reminded her of Lexyl.

Eleeza sat at the table and gestured for the others to join her. Servants brought plates of food and the thick dark keffa that the

Eldars preferred to tea. When the food was distributed, Eleeza finally answered Klaris's question: "My sister, Lexyl, told us that the Weaver and the Paradox were coming."

"She has more of the prophecy than she gave you," Klaris said to Jax.

Bred to rule in his own countries, Jax felt the tension of all the people who were not in this room, had not been in the plaza or the street, but who were filled with questions and fears. He knew that for centuries Arandy had seen no outsiders other than himself, Marith, and the nyad twins, and having grown up among the xenophobic Kordish, he had a profound understanding for how unsettling his return would be to the isolated Eldars.

"Chieftess," he began. "I will again thank you for your mercy and generosity. My companions and I would certainly have perished last year if not for you and Lady Lexyl."

Eleeza sipped her keffa, and her expression clearly indicated that she now doubted the wisdom of her decision to let them go the last time.

Jax continued. "We trouble you again only because we believe the Knownlands face a terrible danger, and we think salvation might be found in Axterre."

"Salvation found in Axterre?" Eleeza snorted. "You haven't seen those ruins, my lord. Or touched the tainted relics of that place."

"Actually, we have."

Eleeza leaned forward in her chair, her eyes sharp. "I specifically asked you not to let Lexyl go there."

"She was our guide, Chieftess. I didn't know where we were until we were among the ruins."

Eleeza placed her cup back on the table with a calm gentleness that belied her anger.

"It was awful." Florin said. "A ghost attacked Jax."

Blizzen, unaware of any tension, enjoyed the food and downed four tiny cups of the bitter black keffa and now felt oddly jittery. "An Axterran ghost attacked *you*?"

"Things often do," Jax's eyes never left the chieftess. "Ma'am, we are here to ask you for permission to visit the ruins again. We'd like to talk to Lexyl too, of course."

"Because?"

"Because dragons are returning to the Knownlands."

"This is the threat you speak of." Eleeza toyed with her cup. She had been able to doubt Lexyl's allegations when they were based only on some ancient ramblings from the forbidden scrolls, but now apparently other forces in the Knownlands, great forces, had come to the same conclusions.

Dragons. The Eldar people had survived last time, nestled deep in their canyons which were too narrow for dragon wings. But the beasts would devastate the other peoples and cities of the Knownlands. It seemed to Eleeza vastly unfair that after all the care the Eldar people had taken for centuries to build security for themselves, without relying on help from the other peoples and cultures of the Knownlands, the first sacrifice should be theirs, Lexyl's, hers.

The chieftess looked around the table at the foreigners. All of them except the Dragon Magician watched her with some level of concern. The Blizzen fellow watched her too, but he seemed most interested in the cleavage revealed by her bejeweled neckline. She reflected for a moment on the various ways a man might be impertinent and how some of them were offensive while others were amusing.

She rose, and her guests stood from their chairs. "I will consult with the Eldar Council. Lexyl is not here. I believe she does not wish to see you."

"Why not?" The words popped out of Florin before she could couch them more politely.

The chieftess turned amber eyes to the nyad. "You are not prisoners, but I suggest you remain here, in my palace. The Eldar people are suspicious of outlanders, as you know, and consider some of what you are saying to be blasphemy."

"Blasphemy?" the Dragon repeated. "Did you say *blasphemy*, Chieftess?"

Jax put a hand on Blizzen's arm, but the Orange Dragon continued. "Really, I have a hard time understanding the speaker. Her accent is almost as muddled as the Weaver's, or the nyad's."

"Sweet goddess, Blizzen," Jax began to laugh. "I beg your pardon, Chieftess. Perhaps if the Eldar Council has questions, you will allow me to attempt to answer them, since our Dragon friend here has difficulty with the language."

Eleeza noted the emphasis on the word friend and the invisible lines of tension binding this odd group of travelers. "Thank you, Prince Javix." She left the room, not inviting the group to follow.

Jax sank back to his chair and lowered his head into his hands.

"Nice, Dragon Blizzen." Florin stomped to a large chair in a corner and flopped into it. "Last time we were here they nearly executed us, you know. It was Lexyl who saved us then, but she's possibly regretting that now. And what do you do? Go insult the speaker. She's the queen here, you know."

"Why don't they call her the queen then, for goddess' sake?" Blizzen paced back and forth. "And I don't know why you people can't speak proper Landish."

"How much of this keffa did you drink, Dragon Blizzen?" Lad Yob tasted a drop with a long gray finger.

"I don't know," Blizzen snapped. "Four or five of those tiny cups."

Jax laughed again, behind his hands. "You won't sleep for days."

"What? Is it some potion?"

Jax dropped his hands. "Keffa, Dragon Blizzen, banishes sleepiness. It's far more powerful than tea."

Klaris put her hands out to a wall and lost herself in the strange and ancient Mystic that had built this palace.

Blizzen strode around the room, toying with the hanging flowers, moving the chairs back around the table, lighting the wall sconces with his Dragon force then extinguishing them over and over again.

"I wonder why Lexyl doesn't want to see Borrel." Florin mused. "He'd sure like to see her."

"I have an idea," Blizzen announced brightly, ignoring Florin's thoughtful comment. "I shall go forth to these people and heal some of them. My art will subdue their fears about magic!"

"Or not," Florin said.

"And they will embrace us for the good we can do now as well as the good we'll do when the dragons come."

Klaris pulled herself away from the stone and her study of the ancient power. "That's a great idea, Dragon Blizzen," she said in her most throaty and accented Landish. "Especially as we know how these Eldar people are not at all familiar with Dragon force or Dragon Magicians."

Jax opened his mouth to protest, but Blizzen spoke first. "These backwards people don't have much Mystic either," he sniffed. "You stay here. I shall be back when I've shown these Older people what I can do for them."

"*Eldar* people," Lad Yob corrected softly. But Blizzen was already gone. Jax saw the small smirk on Klaris's face and began to laugh.

"Sweet goddess," he said. "They'll eviscerate him."

"Let's hope so," Florin growled.

Jax wasn't so amused as he blinked against the strong afternoon light streaming over the hard-eyed members of the Eldar Council. He had already explained several times, in several different ways, that Dragon Blizzen had *not* been trying to kill those four already injured people, that in fact he could immediately heal them, that Dragon force was *not* inherently evil – no magic was – and that no one yet knew if people like Blizzen who possessed Dragon force would have any influence with the beasts themselves.

"And yet you can't even guarantee that this murderous Dragon will contain himself." The shaman fixed Jax with an implacable stare.

"He has realized his services are not needed and agreed to leave Eldars alone," Jax answered. In fact, Klaris had finally used a wily weave of the Mystic in conjunction with the bit of Dragon she'd taken from Jax to force Blizzen to leave off his attempts to heal the Eldar people. Undeterred by either reason or screaming, Blizzen was facing fifteen drawn bows when Klaris had extracted him from the murderous crowds and immured him within the palace in such a way that his own magic could not free him.

Blizzen howled and set off a lot of fireworks, but when he'd exhausted himself, the others forced him to listen. He wasn't stupid, and once the keffa had worn off leaving him drained, he'd sworn to stop trying to heal the damned, ungrateful Elders. No sense wasting his powers if he wasn't wanted, he complained. Jax was relatively sure that Klaris had planned this from the beginning.

But Klaris wasn't used to councils. Jax listened as the Eldar Council debated exposing Blizzen in the desert to die. Shaman Ashande turned to the outlander prince. "We should have executed you last year and saved ourselves this trouble."

"Chieftess," Jax said, ignoring the shaman. "We are all headed for the ruins of Axterre, surely that is punishment enough."

"That is blasphemy," the councilor with the yellow scarf noted sharply.

"I understand," Jax said soothingly. "But we know that the dragons are returning, and we know the Axterrans had a method to banish them. We must find out how they did it."

The council looked at him, their faces showing skepticism at best.

"How do you know the dragons are returning?"

"The Oracle—."

"Blasphemy!" The shaman interrupted. "The Oracles are corrupt."

Jax spoke quietly. "Shaman, I understand that the Axterran Oracles failed, ultimately, in their duties to the goddess and the people, but the current Oracle has warned us and tried to prepare us."

The shaman shook his head and turned to the council. "We need hear no more. This outlander's information is a collection of false prophecies at best and perfidious lies at worst. We should expose them all."

Several council members endorsed this suggestion. Jax jumped into a lull in the debate. "My lords and ladies, I know you have good reason to doubt an Oracle, but Axterre fell fifteen-hundred years ago, and we must not blind ourselves to current dangers because of ancient failures."

For a long moment no one spoke.

"The Eldar people are here today," Ashande said crisply, "because they had the strength and vision to reject the Oracle."

Jax's response was spoken in gentle tones. "I would suggest that the Eldar people are here today because they thought for themselves. Rather than follow blind tradition, they recognized that the long-standing authorities had become untrustworthy."

In the silence that followed this comment, the growing commotion from the streets below finally carried into the council chamber.

The councilor from Mazedge rose and went to the window. "It's Lady Lexyl, Chieftess. And more outlanders too, evidently."

"We're being invaded!" Ashande snapped.

"We are certainly being challenged." Eleeza rose. "I will speak with my sister."

"Is that wise, Chieftess?" Ashande said carefully. "Perhaps the outlanders have some type of hold over her. And she has no respect for our traditions, so she is perhaps not the best person to advise you on such critical issues."

"Thank you, Shaman." Eleeza gathered herself. "This council will reconvene in the morning."

The others, including Jax, bowed as she left the room. Shaman Ashande followed her, but not before firing a venomous glare at Jax.

Despite the shaman's disapprobation, the councilors from Mazedge and Farloste waylaid Jax before he could leave the room.

"Ashande is immoderate," the man sporting the black scarf of Mazedge said. "We expect our shaman to espouse the fundamental truths of our beliefs. But you make valid points."

"It's just that none of us wants to believe you," the woman from Farloste said softly.

"I didn't want to believe it either," Jax answered.

"What convinced you?"

"The Oracle is compelling," he said dryly, following others slowly out of the room and down a flight of stairs. "But the fairy queen and other powerful, knowledgeable forces are convinced as well."

"Fairy queen?" The black-scarfed collective leader stopped and faced Jax.

"Yes, she exists." He answered before the question could be asked. "But ultimately, we won't know for certain that the dragons are coming until they're here. By then it will likely be too late to do anything but perish. It really costs us little to prepare to face them, and if they don't come, we'll go back to our homes in the west and leave you alone." He suppressed the pain that came with the thought that he no longer had a home in either Baria or Kordon.

Oblivious to Jax's inner anguish, the green-scarfed leader shrugged. "It won't cost us anything to let you go be haunted in the ancient ruins, will it?"

Jax didn't answer, trying not to think of what costs he might yet have to pay.

20

"Borrel! You goddess-damned, long-lost, lovelorn—." Florin's further deprecations were lost as Borrel wrapped his twin in a huge, suffocating hug, ignoring the shouting Eldars who came streaming out of the houses and shops to ogle Lexyl and frown at her companions.

"Don't you go traipsing off across the Knownlands without me ever again!" Florin snapped, when she could breathe again.

"Someone take advantage of you?" he teased.

"Damned Jax dragged me out here to face a fiery death by dragon."

Borrel stopped. "Jax is here?"

"And the Weaver, and this idiot Kordish Dragon fellow."

"Dragon Blizzen?"

Florin finally took a moment to consider Borrel's nyad companion. She was stunning. Stripes of gray lightened her brown hair and seemed to highlight her careful brown eyes. Before Florin's mind could even begin to frame questions about this woman, she noticed the bundle in the sling across Lexyl's chest.

The chieftess had pulled back from her embrace and Florin stepped forward. "Hello Lexyl." She stared at the face that had caused her twin such grief. "We were told you didn't want to see us."

Lexyl adjusted the sling. "I have some reservations."

Borrel moved to take the bundle from the sling. "Look, Florin. Meet your nephew."

Florin opened her mouth. "Goddess, not another baby."

"There's another?" Borrel looked to his sister's obviously flat stomach.

"Klaris is pregnant." Florin's frown swept from her twin to Lexyl. "None of you is hand-fasted, but the goddess is giving out babies left and right."

"Who is Klaris?" Lexyl asked.

"The Weaver," Borrel explained.

Florin reached out and took the baby from her brother. "He is beautiful," she smiled. The baby reached his chubby hands up to her face. "And he's smart enough to love his Aunty Florin already."

"Lady Lexyl!" The shaman stood on the steps of the palace, his ruddy robes swaying with the tension of his body. "These Dragon Magicians are not welcome in Arandy!"

"Dragons?" A shrill voice called from the milling Eldars who'd gathered to stare at Lexyl and the strangers. "No more Dragons!"

"No more Dragons!" The crowd took up the chant. "No more Dragons!"

"Sweet goddess." Halla looked at the angry faces around her.

Eleeza strode up the steps and faced the crowd, blocking the shaman with her body and her tall headdress. "People of Arandy, I am your Speaker by heritage and by right. Challenging times are upon us. In such times we must keep cool heads to make the wisest decisions. These outlanders will stay here tonight – all of them. In the morning, I will give you the decision reached by the Eldar Council and myself."

"Expose that Dragon!" some in the crowd recommended.

"That is under consideration," Eleeza said. "Good evening." She turned and, taking the Shaman firmly by the arm, strode into the palace. The others followed quickly. The only voice was the baby's happy coo.

"It wasn't magic that led us to Lexyl," Halla explained, leaning back in her chair, her belly full for the first time in weeks. "It was water."

Borrel and Halla sat with Jax and his companions around a low table in the same sitting room they'd shared during their first visit to Arandy. Dragon Blizzen claimed he was overjoyed to see Dragon Halla, but he had refused to eat with them and retired to his own room. Three large Eldar guards followed his every move, their bright swords unsheathed.

Halla had drunk enough water and now sipped the curious Eldar drink made of some sort of fermented cactus. It was bitter and sweet at the same time, and she rather liked the way it made her brain seem to glow.

"Be careful of that stuff, Dragon Halla," Borrel cautioned. "Its potency creeps up on you."

"It was another Eldar beverage that got our friend Blizzen in trouble this morning," Jax noted.

Halla listened to their tale of Blizzen's misguided attempts to heal, shaking her head. "He's over enthusiastic. The Highlord and I should have worked with him more closely, but we were both so busy trying to sort out the implications of returning dragons."

Klaris watched Dragon Halla and Borrel intently. Their accents challenged her Landish, even after weeks of listening to Florin. Florin spoke in short, emphatic sentences, but both Borrel and Halla covered more complicated topics, and Klaris had to concentrate to follow their thoughts as articulated in the nyad accent. She was fascinated by what she gathered of their journey to the magi, and when they spoke about the prophecy, she broke her silence.

"Can you show it to me? We lack this last verse. This is why we came here. We hoped Lexyl would have it."

"She has it, and more," Halla said darkly. "But the nyad magi had it in their archive, also." She rose from her couch finding that the drink had indeed gone to her head quickly. Rummaging in her pack, she found her copy of the prophecy.

She read the final verse:

"The Weaver and the Paradox
A child born among Redrocks
At Axterre the Cornerstone
Holds lyrics of the Dragon Song."

Klaris held out her hand for the paper.

Halla handed it to her. "There might be more. A couple more lines, maybe. They appeared to have been cut out from the nyad rings."

"Cut out?" Klaris cocked her head, not sure she was understanding the Landish. "You mean that someone defaced a part of the nyad archive?"

"It might just have been insect damage," Halla prevaricated.

For several moments no one spoke.

"The child is your baby." Klaris determined. Her accented Landish was soft with grief.

"Lexyl thinks so." Borrel poured more of the cactus nectar into their small glasses. "That's why she named him Tristan."

"Sorrow," Klaris translated.

"Sweet goddess," Florin breathed.

Klaris rose and stretched her back, moving her body around the baby in her belly. "Sorrow," she repeated, looking at Jax.

He drank off the liquor in his glass with grim efficiency then stood and went to Klaris. "Maybe it'll be a happy song."

"And maybe I'll be able to sing."

21

Lord Corvyd took off his hat and ran his hands through his hair. Usually, this movement calmed him and gave him great pleasure. He would never again take clean, well-cut hair for granted after his eighteen months as a slave in the Hanter iron mines.

But today frustration blocked his gratitude for the simple pleasures of freedom. He smashed the hat back on his head and kicked his horse to a gallop. His sister, well ahead of him and a better rider in any case, was already dismounting in the courtyard of Calehold by the time Corvyd caught up. She ignored him and strode toward the interior warmth of the castle.

She was seated, her cheeks still glowing from the ride in the cold autumn air, warming her fingers around a hot mug of wine and her heart at the sight of her toddler playing solemnly with her doll when Corvyd made it in from stabling his own horse.

"Have some wine, Cory, and leave it," she said, before he could speak.

He shook his head at the steward offering wine. "How can I make you understand?" he asked his sister.

"There is nothing to understand."

Corvyd sat on the floor near the fire. His niece, Lannez, toddled over to him, beaming. "Baby!" she announced, holding out her doll.

He smiled at her and took the toy. The child had not been so welcoming a few months ago when he had returned to Calehold after having been released from the slave pens. His mother, the Baroness, and his sister, the heir, had been delighted to have him back, of course. They had not been certain that he'd been taken by trolls that winter morning, nearly two years ago, but such things happened here in the far north of Ily, and they'd mourned him for dead.

To have him return on a glorious summer day was unlooked for and still, even after several months, the Baroness would find tears of joy in her eyes as she watched him pursue his duties around the castle and the barony.

His sister, Lady Zelanne, was glad to have him back too, but more troubled by his many improbable stories. She'd seen his scars and couldn't refute his tales of enslavement, although the idea that a full-blooded prince had also found himself victim to the trolls' brutish practices was hard to believe. And that was only part of it.

Zelanne was a practical woman, cautious, conservative. She'd hand-fasted the second son of the Duke of Lac-le-grand, who was himself a sturdy, conservative man with a florid face and a passion for nothing, as far as Corvyd could tell. Both of them thought they knew exactly how the world worked, although neither had been farther into the world than Brakkle or ventured out of their own social circle.

So Zelanne found Corvyd's report that this same supposed prince had returned to release the rest of the slaves in the Hanter iron mines simply ludicrous. No one could reason with trolls. This had been well established by centuries of Ilyian monarchs, nobles, merchants and peasants, usually to their own misfortune.

Worse even than these fibs about some half-islish prince who could bargain with trolls was Corvyd's obsession with the idea that dragons were returning to the Knownlands.

Much to her regret, Zelanne was becoming convinced that the trolls had somehow damaged Corvyd's mind. She watched him gently take Lannez's doll and its toy bottle. No doubt such an experience would change anyone, and it was entirely possible that some blow to the head along the way had quite literally knocked the sense out of her brother. At the very least, the trauma of enslavement could certainly make a person invent threats that didn't exist because he had lived for so long with threats that clearly did.

Corvyd glanced up from the doll to catch his sister's eyes upon him. "I know you don't believe me," he said. "But there's little harm in making preparations."

Zelanne rolled her eyes. "There's no proof! You're asking us to uproot our lives based on the ravings of a half-islish slave, who managed to convince you he was some kind of prince."

"The Weaver's concern might be taken as proof." Corvyd pretended to burp the doll, making a deep and manly belching noise. Little Lannez squealed with delight.

"And maybe you're right," he said, smiling at his niece. "Maybe they won't come, or if they do, the Weaver and Jax will successfully turn them away somehow. But if they are not successful—." He stopped and made another ringing belch. "Oh my," he said to the doll.

Zelanne finished her wine and set aside her mug. "You would have us stockpile food, set up shelters around the barony, disrupt our winter trade and cause potential hardship to our merchants all based on the stories of someone you met in the slave pens."

Corvyd handed the doll back to the child who fed it from the toy bottle. He looked up at his sister. "You'd believe Jax, if you met him."

She shrugged a shoulder, thinking of the dirty, emaciated figure Corvyd had been when he returned. She hadn't believed him then, and even now, clean and healthy again, she still didn't believe him.

"I'll make the arrangements," he offered. "And if you're right, and we don't need them, we'll sell the stockpiles next summer."

"When the prices are low."

The Baroness entered the warm room, smiled at her family, and took a seat by the fire. The steward handed her a steaming mug. "Are we still arguing about this dragon thing?"

Zelanne shot her mother a pointed look.

Corvyd turned away, his heart aching. He realized they'd always treated him with condescension. He knew he'd done little to earn their respect. He always had the disadvantage of being the baby, but in truth, he'd often been stupid and irresponsible. That was how he landed in the iron mines.

But he'd changed. Goddess knew that kind of experience would change anyone. He watched little Lannez pretend to feed her doll and wondered if the mines had changed Jax. It seemed more as if the experience had tempered him, hardened him into himself.

When Corvyd had seen him on that huge, heaving ship, Jax was better dressed, better fed, and clearly partnered in some way with the Weaver, but he had the same air of authority he'd carried in the slave pens, and the same dogged commitment to his self-imposed responsibilities.

Corvyd stood up. "I will arrange the stockpiles and the shelters. I will let the druids know so they can direct the people, if the need arises."

"You're wasting your time," Zelanne stood also. "Come along Lannez. It's time for your bath."

The child handed her doll to Corvyd. "You hold Baby," she said, her eyes serious. "You keep Baby safe, Uncle Cory."

Corvyd took the toy, its limp form warm from Lannez's grasp. "At least someone trusts me," he muttered.

"It's a toy," Zelanne snapped.

"Not to her."

Golden leaves drifted through the grove, catching the sun and spangling the crisp air. Lady Mollish's voice lilted over the wedding ritual.

As the bride's attendant, Tallyn faced the wedding couple and the elegant crowd of nobles gathered to watch the young Duke of Aychex marry Cheshir of Deepford.

Cheshir was speaking now, softly giving her love and life to Frinz of Aychex. Tallyn looked into her foster sister's blue eyes and saw contentment, even excitement. Still, the princess thought, it was just as well Jax wasn't here. His absence made it easier for Cheshir to appreciate Frinz and easier, much easier, for Frinz to have his moment of glory.

The thought of Jax and where he must be by now, however, focused the princess's mind. This trip to Aychex had provided the perfect excuse to organize this portion of the realm to withstand a dragon attack.

Frinz needed an outlet for his pre-wedding nerves, and he seized Tallyn's quiet, almost offhand, suggestions with zeal. He didn't need to know that most of the ideas had come from Jax Sharkin.

Priestess Mollish pronounced the couple hand-fasted. Tallyn, for the first and only time in her life, walked behind Cheshir toward the great gray pile of Caer Aynston. While all eyes were on the bride, Tallyn reviewed her progress on her preparations against the dragons.

Darkwood, Keffex, Rippsmarch, and now Aychex were prepared. That was not quite enough for her to take the plan openly to the royal council, since in Jax's absence Darkwood had no independent voice, and no one ever listened to the Duchess of Keffex at any time.

Tallyn knew she'd never get the king to sign on to any plan that admitted dragons might be coming. Despite the Oracle's visit and the conviction of Lady Mollish and the great magicians, both Dragon and Mystic, King Kodill continued to insist that such foolishness had originated in Jax Sharkin's imagination – an imagination understandably warped by his years as a slave, and not to be taken seriously.

Of course, the dowager would scoff at any talk of dragons from long habit of opposing anything Jax said, thought, or believed. If he said the sky was blue, she'd find a way to disagree.

On Caer Aynston's sunny patio, Tallyn found Foby and a bottle of champagne. He handed her a glass. "You're thinking about dragons again."

She lifted the glass to toast him and smiled into his perceptive eyes. "I need one more fief." Her clear eyes surveyed the nobles gathered in small knots in the late autumn sun. "One more region protected and one more voice on the council."

"Clairo, maybe?"

Tallyn found old Duke Von in the crowd. He was talking to, or rather shouting at, Vobury. "The old boys are devoted to the dowager. They won't oppose her unless everyone else does."

"Chevvain?"

"I wish." Tallyn took a long drink of her champagne. "Patrice is reasonable enough to see there are powerful forces who corroborate Jax's positions, but her chancellorship depends on pleasing the king."

"I was chatting with Pers of Traik this morning, while you ladies were dressing." Foby refilled both flutes. "He said Patrice has very quietly been making certain curious arrangements."

Tallyn smiled. "That's good, but I still need a voice on the council."

"You're down to Earla Stona," Foby concluded.

"Yes." Tallyn knew without looking that Stona was talking to young Orran Addle, the son of the late, treasonous Duke of Midipex. The Addles had lost their duchy as a result of Thorag Addle's actions, their title reduced to baron, and two thirds of their lands stripped to create the Earldom of Darkwood.

Foby watched Tallyn's smile grow more satisfied. He frowned. "You can't possibly think the Earla will openly support any plan devised by Jax."

Tallyn finished her champagne. "No one knows it's Jax's plan. The Earla of the Tarron March is unfailingly patriotic. Midipex used that fine sentiment to manipulate her."

Foby's mouth twisted. "You're going to do the same thing."

"I am. What's more, I'm going to get young Addle to protect his barony to prove his loyalty as well."

Foby took her empty glass. "Well then, with all your work done you can dance with me."

Patrice of Chevvain watched the princess dance and realized that Tallyn had come to some resolution. The lady chancellor knew that the princess was quietly working to prepare the realm for a dragon attack, despite the objections of the king. It was a delicate, subtle bit of work and frankly it worried Patrice. Tallyn was an adept politician: charming, wily, and acutely intelligent. The princess read people with an accuracy that was frightening and potentially dangerous in a future ruler.

Patrice knew that the realm ought to prepare for dragons. She admitted that the best way to do this was to follow the measures the princess was quietly advocating, but she looked forward to the day when Tallyn could rule openly instead of through guile. Then, realizing the treason inherent in this wish, the lady chancellor went in search of a tall glass of champagne.

Sven Narbonne had been the Oracle's high priest at the temple for fifteen years. For twenty years before that, he'd served as an acolyte, a priest, and finally as a teacher to the others blessed to be called to serve the Oracle. But never, in all those years, had he seen the Oracle so disturbed.

He sat in a low chair and breathed to calm himself so he could share this scry. Like most priests and priestesses, Sven had no magic of his own, but like an empty vessel, he could be filled with the Oracle's power. As high priest, he was often privileged to share the Oracle's work, and he relished the charge and the ensuing peace that working magic always gave him.

This evening, however, the Oracle appeared to struggle to center themself for the magic. They sat, rose, rearranged their gray robes, and sat again. They waved a claw-like hand and the large shallow silver bowl appeared on the table between them. Within the bowl a film of water shivered translucently.

The Oracle took a deep breath, then another. "Bah." They rose impatiently and stomped to one of the great windows. Sven waited, frowning.

After a few moments, the Oracle returned to their chair. They fixed Sven with their gray eyes. "Be ready to make notes."

"I am ready, Oracle." Sven picked up his paper and pencil.

Hours later the Oracle slumped in their chair looking like a discarded bundle of gray rags. Sven rang for tea and moved to lift the ancient creature.

"Stop fussing, Sven. Some tea will help."

Sven sat obediently while the Oracle drank, but he did not stop worrying.

The Oracle sat up a little straighter, finished a second cup of tea, and finally spoke. "Sum it up, then."

The high priest looked down at his notes. "Kordon is nearly prepared along with Norledge, Vitrus, Farsouth and Dranstyl. The Jezellians think they are, although we can't be sure the Dragon Magicians will actually be able to stay the beasts."

He flipped a page. "The nyads of Verwood have taken precautions and moved the archive to a cave where it will not be vulnerable in the case of a great fire."

The Oracle nodded at that but said nothing. Sven continued. "The Mystics on Sageham are in their rebuilt Caledra now and are warding it with everything they can think of. That worked for them last time, so they're probably all right."

He looked up at the old gray creature. The hollows under their eyes and cheeks were deep, and the lines of age severe. Sven poured more tea then continued to read.

"The trolls are doing nothing because the loyal opposition won't credit the threat, since it was announced by the Premier herself. Trollish druids are making some small preparations, despite the government's stalemate."

He turned another page. "Like the trolls, the Ilyians are divided, and the Ohites claim they have nothing to stockpile. The Sprites gather supplies but then decide to live in the moment and have a huge party, consuming all they've put aside."

The Oracle made a small noise. Sven paused, but when the Oracle still did not speak, he went on. "The fairies are dug in deep, of course, and the Herders think their bows will take down a dragon."

"They're wrong," the Oracle snapped.

"The sealord has put some energy into fortifying the Barian hard ports, but says he has faith that the Weaver will successfully banish the beasts. He appears to be living in Kordon. Still, it seems that our friend Javix Sharkin was less confident of his own success on this front and gave a number of precautionary orders when he was lord admiral that most of the Barian Fleet is pursuing."

The Oracle might have chuckled. "That's our paradox: backing all bets." They grasped the arms of their chair and tried to rise but failed. They paused a moment and Sven moved to help. The Oracle's arm felt like dry sticks beneath their robe.

Once on their feet, they again moved to the window. The sun had set behind the Barian mountains, and the view was of dark sky and darker sea as night rolled toward them from the east.

"Almost Samhain," the Oracle said softly.

"I pray it will strengthen you, Oracle." Sven stood behind them in the dark room.

"T'will be the last," the ancient voice whispered.

"No, Oracle!" Sven knelt and took the wizened hand.

"Yes. You don't feel it, my son, but the magic is shifting." They patted Sven's hand. "The babe has been born among Redrocks, and the dragons are close. Terribly close."

"What must we do?"

The Oracle took a long breath. "High Priest, you must go. Take the last pegasus and fly to those realms that are not prepared. Put the fear of the beasts in them and make them get ready."

"Yes, Oracle."

The old creature looked down into the devoted face of the high priest. "And Sven, know that the goddess blessed us all when she called you here."

"She blessed me, certainly," Sven agreed. He rose from his knees and bowed reverently to the Oracle.

The gray eyes watched Sven slip away into the shadows before they returned to the dark window. In their mind, the Oracle recalled the faces of high priests and high priestesses stretching back over the centuries. There had been over a hundred of them. All of them gifted by the goddess, and all of them a great balm and support to the Oracle themself.

Now, the Oracle felt Sven's commitment and also his worry, as he prepared for his journey. Sven was prescient. He sensed what the Oracle knew. They would not meet again.

Grief. It was the cost of immortality; the price paid for knowing the annual joy of the goddess's glories, and of meeting occasionally across the centuries a personality of such wit or vision or soul as to thrill an old heart.

There was one such now. The Oracle smiled in the dark, as grief gave way to relief. By now, that one would be together with the babe. Aware of the futility of attempting to scry for the Paradox, the Oracle bent over the silver bowl that had already shown so much this day. The magic swirled and the clear water darkened. From the shadow immerged the golden face of a desert lion.

22

Eleeza sipped her keffa and looked around the table at the members of the Eldar Council. "Yes, Shaman, we know that the scrolls warn against magic as it was deployed by the people of Axterre."

"Indeed," the shaman leaned forward to push his point. "We must not support these outlanders with their dangerous magic and blasphemous practices."

"But they are undoubtedly powerful," mused the representative from Oweshore cautiously. "If we don't help them, might they use their magics against us, as that Dragon Blizzen did?"

The representative from Mazedge adjusted his black scarf of rank. "They don't seem to be asking for much – just some food, and permission to visit the accursed ruins."

"Proof of their accursed intent!" snapped Shaman Ashande.

"I don't think so," said the representative from Farloste. "They are asking for permission, after all. And they see our Lexyl as an important resource. Maybe we've been missing something important, isolated as we've been all these centuries."

"We've been missing horrors," Ashande said crisply. "Criminal abuses of power, the destruction of the sacred connection to the goddess through sheer hubris."

The man from Mazedge pushed his demitasse away. "That was Axterre, Shaman. I do not see disrespect of the goddess in these outlanders."

"The Dragon had no respect." Ashande noted.

"But the others, the Weaver, contained him," the woman from Farloste replied. She paused, looking at Eleeza.

The chieftess took a slow breath. "I hear the Eldar Council and speak its will. We shall supply the outlanders with sustenance, and we will give them Lexyl of Arandy as their guide as long as they remain in the Redrock Maze."

"No," Ashande wailed.

Eleeza rose and put a gentle hand on his shoulder. "Bare witness, Shaman, our fears go with these outlanders, and also our future."

Ashande looked up at the chieftess' amber eyes.

"Pray for us," she said softly. "And for them."

Borrel leapt off his pegasus and looked around the rocky flat with a grin. "This is where we had our forath celebration."

"Yes." Lexyl returned his smile. "It took us a week to walk here from Arandy, but your pegasi made it in one day."

Klaris noted the sparkle in Lexyl's eyes. "What is a forath celebration?"

"Usually, it's a joyful celebration of the unity of the universe," Lexyl answered, pulling her baby out of the sling where she carried him.

"But in our case, it was rather more," Borrel said smugly.

"Forath is a desert plant," Jax explained, noting Klaris's confusion. "You inhale the smoke and it gives you visions."

"Lustful ones, if you're a nyad," Florin muttered, pointedly not looking at Jax.

Klaris noticed the unusual tension between them and decided not to ask further questions. Instead she turned to Lexyl. "Shall we build a shelter?"

The Eldar glanced up at the serene blue sky. "I prefer to sleep in the open when there's no moon, even without forath."

Klaris had never spent a night outdoors. Making shelter was, after all, the primary purpose of the Mystic weave. She looked a question at Jax.

He picked up her pack and shouldered his own. "There's a nice spot over here." He walked a little distance from the fire pit.

"You're not building a shelter?" Blizzen demanded. "Where will we sleep?"

The petulance in Blizzen's tone set Klaris's decision. It would do the damned Dragon good to live without the benefits of her magic for a night.

As it turned out, Blizzen slept soundly as a baby on the smooth sandstone, while Klaris was riveted awake all night long by the moonless dance of the stars as they swirled across the sky. She lay in her blankets, wrapped snugly against Jax's warm chest, and felt her soul fill with wonder.

The next evening found them in a much different place.

"I hope you're not proposing we forego shelter again tonight." Blizzen frowned at the haze-filled plain before them.

Halla saw Lexyl stiffen at Blizzen's lack of respect and realized she'd have to speak with her fellow Dragon. When had he become so arrogant?

"Blizzen," she said. "Come walk with me while the Mystics build for us." She took his arm and walked away from the alcove created by high cliff walls on the edge of the open plain. Behind her, she felt the Mystic rise and weave.

Both Dragons walked quickly to escape the cross-magic. Eventually they climbed a nob of rock. From here they looked over the plain. A thick layer of haze floated above the desert floor between the cliffs on this side and similar Redrock cliffs a few miles away. A collection of unnatural odd shapes slumped under the shrouding haze.

"You don't seem to have much respect for the Weaver," Halla said gently.

"Of course, I do." Blizzen sat on a rock. "She's clever and quite devious. You do know that she turned her magic against me when I was trying to heal those ungrateful Older people."

Halla sat next to him. "I've never heard of anyone using Mystic against a Dragon."

"She warped the bit of Dragon force she stole from Javix," Blizzen explained indignantly. "Warped it and used it with her weave. She actually imprisoned me!"

Halla put a calming hand on Blizzen's arm. "Perhaps she did it to help you. I know the Eldar people didn't understand your good intentions. Prince Javix had to beg their council not to execute you."

"That's what he told you."

Halla nodded.

Blizzen raised his eyebrows. "I warn you, Halla, all of them show a disturbing disregard for Dragon force and its benefits."

Halla watched the fat red sun drop to touch the angular horizon. "We're all going to have to respect each other if we're going to drive the dragons away."

"You might remind our Mystic friends," Blizzen snapped. "Besides, Halla, are you sure we should drive the dragons away immediately? Surely, you've felt the increase in power. It's grown even greater these past months – at least, mine has."

"Yes," Halla acknowledged. "All Dragon power has increased."

"And now that we can heal, our magic is perhaps even more beneficial than Mystic."

"It's not a competition, is it?"

"No, of course not. But why rush to expel the dragons when letting them stay a bit might actually provide substantial long-term benefits to all the Knownlands?"

The sun disappeared.

"You pose an interesting question," she answered softly. "But I caution you about sharing these views with the others."

"Oh, they've cautioned me themselves."

"You need to listen to them. Surely you understand that your points will be more persuasive if you are humble about your power."

"Why? Why must we down-play our power? Why shouldn't we be proud of what we can do, of the good we can bring?"

"Because pride is rarely influential."

Blizzen thought about that for a moment as the haze in the valley caught some trick of the vanished sun and glowed a sickish orange. "The Weaver shows off her power every time she adds some useless embellishment to our camping shelters."

"Is beauty useless?"

"It's not nearly as important as the ability to heal." He leaned forward to look into Halla's face. "Look, I am proud of what our magic can do. I refuse to hide behind some false modesty. I've shown that little Klaris how Dragon force can heal, but she and her friends retain their arrogance toward us. I don't intend to answer her condescension with humility."

Halla gazed at Blizzen. His fair Kordish skin glowed in the reflected light from the haze. He is the Orange Dragon, she thought, and saw both the unflawed logic of his arguments and their unacceptable conclusion.

She'd known Blizzen since they were both young acolytes, flexing their magic at Dragonsholm. She had studied with him, explored the magic with him, and risen just ahead of him up the ranks of Dragon force. He had always maintained a Kordish sense of his own racial superiority, along with this idea that Dragon force somehow needed to prove its superior value to the world. Halla had often found it easy to agree that Dragon force was a rare gift, but now she didn't know how to respond. Goddess, she missed Raggar.

The Highlord should be the one to address Blizzen's skewed views. She'd dreamed of him again last night as she'd slept out under the stars – a dream full of passion and anguish. She would scry for him again this night. Maybe, somehow, he could advise her.

"What's that light?" Blizzen asked suddenly. "Look."

Halla saw the small gleam far across the valley. There was no magic to that small fire, but.... "Oh, sweet goddess," she whispered. "Sweet goddess, Blizzen. It's the Highlord!"

"It's not his magic." Blizzen rose to follow Halla as she dashed down the darkening wash towards the camp. "It's nobody's magic!"

"But he's there!" She called. "He's there!"

"No!" Lexyl put both her hands on Halla's shoulders. "You do not venture into Axterre after dark."

"But the Highlord—."

"Can wait until the morning."

"That's Axterre?" Blizzen came huffing into camp.

Halla took a deep breath and glared at Lexyl, Blizzen's accusations fresh in her mind. "Lady Lexyl, I am the Red Dragon. Surely, I can walk in the night."

Lexyl stared at her for a moment then shrugged. "Indeed, Dragon Halla."

Halla paused for a moment, taken back by Lexyl's sudden capitulation.

Borrel cleared his throat. "There are ghosts out there, Halla. Malevolent ghosts. They attacked us. It was grim."

"But that was Samhain, right?" Blizzen didn't quite sneer. "And pardon me, Borrel, Lexyl, but neither of you has the magical power of Dragon Halla."

"Wait until morning," Lexyl urged. "We can all go together to find the Highlord."

"Come, Dragon Halla." Blizzen swirled his cloak grandly around his shoulders. "The Weaver does not appear to feel that the presence of the Dragon Highlord is significant. Let us, as his nearest comrades, go fetch him out of the dark." He stepped outside the ring of firelight and walked toward the seething shadows of the plain.

Halla glanced around at the others. She paused, caught in Jax's sea blue gaze. "The Oracle's ghost is out there," he warned softly. "It is full of pain. And fury."

Out on the open ground of the plain, Halla saw Blizzen create a small ball of mage fire. A queer green nimbus glowed around the ball.

Her loyalty to the Orange Dragon and her desire to see her beloved Raggar warred against her intellect that clearly sided with Lexyl's words of reason and Jax's voice of caution.

But Blizzen was now a hundred yards into the dark and she couldn't let him go alone. "Damn," she swore softly, and creating a light of her own, strode after Blizzen.

"Do you think they'll make it?" Borrel came to hand Lexyl the hungry baby.

"I hope so." She sat and began to nurse.

Florin and Borrel gathered ingredients for supper. Klaris built a table and benches, while Jax gathered the plates and utensils. Lad Yob checked on the pegasi. All of them listened to the silence of the desert.

Jax sat back from his empty plate and was thinking he probably had to wash the dishes in Blizzen's absence when a horrific scream ripped through the night.

All of them jumped to their feet.

"Sweet goddess," Borrel whispered.

They peered out onto the plain but saw nothing in the darkness.

Again, the scream split the silence. Tristan began to fret. Klaris felt Jax shudder. "Let's have some light," she said, calling her magic. A vast ball of white mage light burst into the sky.

Another scream, and then another tore through the air, echoing horribly off the cliff walls. Far out on the plain, two figures seemed to be running towards them, fleeing before what looked like a tall black wave.

"Hold the light for me, Lexyl," Klaris said calmly, ignoring the continued screaming. Lexyl handed the baby to Jax then pulled her magic to take Klaris's weave.

Borrel watched the Weaver with awe. He felt her shielding him from her own forces and was shocked that she now looked at him with such relaxed confidence. "Make a path of light for them to follow," she ordered.

"But what about this shield?"

"Create your spell as if it weren't there. I'll make a gate for you to shine it through."

Borrel saw the magic flicker. He did not have time to appreciate what she was doing, as he pulled on his own magic and did as she asked.

Klaris was already staring back out at the plain. She knew that the great black wave was a hoard of ghosts enlivened by some kind of ancient and unhappy magic, rising up to swallow the two Dragons. The bright glow of their own Dragon force surrounded them, but the hoard would engulf them, and Klaris didn't like to think what would happen then.

Jax felt the Mystic weave thwart the cresting wave of blackness. The two Dragons broke away from under its shadow and kept running up Borrel's path of light. Growls and shrieks now rose around the terrible screaming. Flashes of green light lashed out from the seething black wave, but Klaris's force held.

Halla and Blizzen ran. Finally, they arrived gasping for breath in the light of the camp. Borrel, exhausted, closed off his path of light and Lexyl, similarly drained, let the white mage light go.

Darkness crashed around them. Blizzen closed his eyes and moaned raggedly.

Klaris took a deep breath. She rewove her spells, drawing a thick, protective barrier all around the camp. With a flip of the Mystic, she set the spell free to stand on its own, like a building.

She stood staring into the dark, feeling the grim magic of the ghosts. Her shelter blocked their eerie screaming, but she still felt the powerful residue of an ancient horror.

Halla and Blizzen panted, shuddering by the small fire. Florin, remembering Marith's cure when Jax had been ghost-ridden, brewed a foul tisane.

"I'm not drinking that," Blizzen said weakly.

"You will." Jax took him gently by the shoulder and led him into Klaris's shelter. After he'd been violently ill, Jax put him to bed. It wasn't easy to maintain a tactful silence, but he managed it.

Florin helped Halla through a similar, unpleasant exorcism, but with less tact and less silence. Halla didn't even try to defend her foolishness.

None of the others felt comfortable lingering outside. They gathered in the central room before one of Borrel's bright fires.

After a few moments, Klaris rose slowly and began to move through the moon salutations. Lexyl soon joined her and then the lad. Borrel and Jax exchanged a glance. Each found his dragonpipe and together they launched into the First Tune. Florin rocked the baby.

An hour later, their souls restored, all of them found their beds.

"That's quite a sigh," Jax pulled Klaris towards him.

"I was thinking of how short the days are, and we have no idea where to even start looking for the Cornerstone of Axterre."

"We don't want to be out there after dark."

"Clearly not."

"And Samhain is only a week away."

"Yes."

He moved his mouth to her ear, and she heard the smirk in his whisper. "Whatever will we do with all those long, dark hours?"

"Study."

His mouth was moving along her skin. "Good. I need a lot of tutoring."

23

Klaris rose in the predawn dark. She found Lad Yob and Lexyl already steadying themselves with deep, quiet breaths. Without a word, Klaris joined them. As silent and graceful as the coming dawn, the three moved in unison from pose to stretch.

A simmering anxiety pushed Jax out of the lonely bed shortly after Klaris left. He lit a fire and smiled gratefully as Florin took the teapot from him. "I like my tea potable," she grumbled at him.

The red rock cliffs became dimly visible as Halla and Blizzen joined the others to watch the day come. The two Dragons, both wan and pale as the new day, stared into the dark haze on the plain with misgivings.

Florin and Borrel came out of the shelter carrying a collection of packs. "Here's lunch." Florin distributed one pack to each member of the group. "Water and a blanket, too. Make the water last all day," she said pointedly to Blizzen. "Because there's nothing you want to drink in those ruins."

Klaris shouldered her pack. The sun still hadn't risen above the eastern escarpment, but the light now penetrated the murk in the plain to reveal the shadowy blocks of ruins. She considered her companions, sensing their magic, their wariness, and their conflicts. "I wish we had a druid," she said softly.

"Bless us, sweet goddess," Blizzen intoned. The pomposity of his voice was undermined by a residual tremor as he remembered last night's horror. "Help us find the Highlord."

"And the Cornerstone of Axterre." Klaris added.

"But first, the Highlord," Blizzen insisted.

"Yes." Klaris began walking. "It will be easy to find him. And I'm curious as to why he is here."

Halla stared across the plain of ruins as the sun finally poured golden light into the haze. "He's on the far side," she said in a choked whisper. "The far side of the ruins."

Lexyl resettled her baby in the sling. "We might have to spend the night over there, then."

Jax walked alongside Klaris, recognizing the cobble-strewn remains of an ancient road, the twisted skeleton of a long-dead orchard, and the empty black windows of the ruined houses. He'd walked this road before. He felt again the ice of the dead Oracle's finger touching his heart.

Blizzen slowed to a halt. "Perhaps someone should stay at camp," he suggested, warily eying the shadows within the ruins.

"Go on back, if you want." Jax answered.

"You can't seriously take a baby in there!" Blizzen shouted at their backs.

"I can't seriously leave him." Lexyl answered and kept walking.

Unwilling to be left alone, Blizzen ran awkwardly to catch up. "I'm sore."

"You ran quite a race last night," Borrel said gently.

"Why don't we ride the pegasi?" Blizzen complained.

"The Cornerstone must be among the ruins," Klaris noted. "I don't think we'll find it flying above."

"We're looking for the Highlord," Blizzen argued.

"Yes. And the Cornerstone," Klaris insisted.

"Single-minded, aren't you," Blizzen sneered.

"Generally, yes." Klaris admitted.

Blizzen had no rejoinder, so he walked along quietly, his strained muscles aching. He wondered if he could heal himself, but when he tried, the ache was worse.

"What are you doing?" Klaris asked, feeling the surge of Dragon force.

"Nothing. Nothing." He let his magic go and simply walked on.

Clusters of ruins thickened into suburbs. Jax thought he heard a windy wail, but none of the others reacted. Finally, they arrived at the old city wall. Stepping around the shattered capstone, they moved through the broken gate and into Axterre.

Klaris instinctively moved to touch the old wall, to connect to the magic that built this place.

"No, Weaver!" Lexyl snapped.

Klaris paused, her head cocked in question.

Lexyl explained quickly. "The magic that built this place is shrouded in the dark power that corrupted Axterre."

"I feel that," Klaris acknowledged. "The grief, the horror."

"This place has the same black feel as your ancient scrolls," Halla said to Lexyl.

Klaris was looking up at the great walls. They appeared not to be built of individual stones, but rather as one massive gray block. "We'll have to touch it eventually," she said.

"Let's find the Highlord, first," Blizzen pleaded. "I want to get out of here. My skin is crawling!"

Klaris nodded and walked on. Jax took her hand. "Tell you the truth, my skin is crawling too," he said.

She looked up at him. "Why did they build that wall?"

Jax blinked. Once again, he was struck by the way Klaris's questions sliced through layers of obfuscating detail to find the heart of a problem.

Unaware of his appraisal, Klaris continued: "They built that great wall. They must have feared something outside. But clearly the real danger lurked within."

"Questions," Lexyl said grimly. "I think the Axterrans were trying to keep questions out."

Klaris followed Lexyl deeper into the ruins. "I've not seen a wall that can do that."

They reached the river before noon. Thick and gray, the water sucked at the ruins of a bridge. Tristan fussed.

"I need to feed him," Lexyl noted.

"Let's all eat, then." Florin sat on a block of stone and delved into her pack.

Blizzen twitched, looking at the hollow black eye-sockets of the surrounding buildings. "No. Let's push on."

"We can take a few minutes to eat and rest." Jax didn't like stopping here either, but he realized that they had to take care of the baby. He peered at the surrounding buildings, absently eating a bit of Eldar travel cake.

"This is where the ghost pounced on you." Florin said.

"I am aware of that."

"I thought you said the ghosts wouldn't bother us during the day." Anxiety lifted Blizzen's voice to a whine.

Lexyl kept her eyes on her baby's dear head. "They've stayed away from me, but Jax seems to attract them."

"Naturally," Jax flashed a sunny smile.

Borrel brushed the crumbs of his travel cake from his hands. "Let's run a rope across the river, since we'll likely come back this way."

"Good idea." Florin burrowed into her pack.

"Yes, it is a good idea." Lexyl lifted the baby to her shoulder and patted his back. "But it won't work. The ghosts, or something, will take it down."

All of them looked at her. Tristan burped and Lexyl continued. "I've tried to make a few small alterations around here: leave a rope, as you suggest, or brush away sand and dust from a mural, but when I come back my ropes are gone, and the sand is back."

Florin looked at the thick coil of rope in her hands. "I'd hate to lose this."

"We'll give it a try," Klaris announced, and Jax saw a light of challenge in her eyes. "These Axterrans made a lot of bad choices. Their time is done."

Florin began to tie the rope around a fallen lintel. Jax watched for a moment then took the rope in his own hands and retied it with a sailor's efficiency.

Meanwhile, Klaris and Lexyl wove a series of exorcism spells around the lintel and the rope itself.

Florin, the rest of the rope coiled like a giant snake in her arms, had just stepped into the grimy water when a voice sent icicles into everyone's blood.

"Arrogant! Arrogant, you are!"

Jax shivered, recognizing the voice of the last Axterran Oracle.

"What are they saying?" Blizzen demanded, not understanding the Ancient language.

Lexyl whispered a translation, while she, Borrel, Blizzen, and Halla all reached for their magic. Klaris raised a hand to stay them. She stepped toward the transparent figure that floated from the ruins. "Help us," she pleaded in fluent Ancient. "You were the last Oracle who might have banished the dragons."

"I *am* the Oracle of Axterre."

Klaris tilted her head to one side and considered the angry, malevolent force. "You were the Oracle, based here in Axterre," she qualified. "But an Oracle's responsibility is to all the goddess' creatures across the Knownlands."

"You presume to lecture me?" The ghost inflated, rising gray and malevolent like a thundercloud above the small Weaver. Jax stepped forward to stand with Klaris, but she stared up at the ghost, apparently unafraid.

"No, Oracle. I beg your help. How do we banish the dragons?"

"Look around you, young one," the ghost resumed a more human size, but their voice resonated with magnificent scorn. "My world was destroyed. Destroyed more horribly and with more anguish than any visitation of dragons. I'm pleased to let the beasts spread a tiny bit of grief and despair to the goddess' creatures, after she forsook me."

Tucked in the sling across Lexyl's chest, baby Tristan craned his neck, striving to face the ghost. Impelled by something she didn't understand, Lexyl lifted him slightly so he could see.

"Not *I*, Oracle. *We*," the baby said in distinct Ancient.

Lexyl screamed and muffled the baby into her chest. Borrel gently took the child from her.

The ghost rose to loom over the small family. It reached out for the baby but both Lexyl and Borrel shielded him with their bodies. Tristan squawked, but not in fear.

"I am the Oracle of Axterre!" the ghost bellowed. "As you will never be! You, aptly named Tristan. You horrify your mother, and your *holy* mother too."

"Not I." The baby's voice was muffled by his parents. "Not I."

"I—!" The ghost screamed then streamed away into the ruins.

Lexyl sobbed. Borrel tried to comfort her.

"Queer baby, that," Blizzen said.

Klaris, her hands on her hips, stared into the ruins where the ghost had fled. "That went well," she muttered in Islish.

"The ghost doesn't scare you," Jax noted in the same language.

"The ghost? No." Klaris hitched up her skirts and turned toward the river. "What scares me are the lessons the ghost teaches." She grabbed the rope and stepped into the filthy water.

The Highlord knew they were coming. Both he and Al-Sefir had watched the bright flashes of magic over the murk of Axterre last night. Raggar had recognized the power of the Weaver, and with a desperate joy, also sensed Halla's magic among others there.

He had risen early and made the first effort in weeks to eat and cleanse himself. Al-Sefir dug cleaner robes for both of them from the bottom of his pack and prayed that the Weaver had food. He was mightily sick of lizard.

Together the priest and the Highlord shuffled down from the camp they'd shared for the last week in the cliffs above the ruins.

They had reached the rubble-strewn avenues when Raggar's head snapped up.

"What is it?" Al-Sefir asked.

"Oracular magic." The Highlord's voice crackled with disuse.

"Is the Oracle here?" Al-Sefir felt a flood of relief at the idea. Raggar glanced at the priest's hope-filled face. "Not the Oracle you know."

"There's more than one?" The priest frowned.

Raggar grunted and stepped more quickly. "They may need us."

Al-Sefir easily kept up with the wizened Highlord. "Why? Surely the Oracle, any Oracle, would help us."

"Surely not."

The avenue they'd been following plunged over the river bluff in a straight, steep fall to the riverbank. Crumbling blocks of smaller, older buildings clogged the road.

"I see them!" Al-Sefir pointed to the far shore of the river.

Raggar peered through the haze and growled. "Do you not feel that Oracle's magic, Priest?"

Al-Sefir closed his eyes. He felt the ache around his heart as he did each time he'd followed the Highlord into these blighted ruins. Then suddenly, like an unexpected slap to the face, he felt another force. It was painful, angry, malevolent. The priest cried and fell to his knees.

Raggar stopped and put his hand to the priest's shoulder, while keeping his eyes and his magic focused on the opposite shore. "Get up!" His voice grated like the sound of tumbling rocks. "Get up, Al-Sefir. She is there, and I must speak to her."

Al-Sefir forced himself to stand, despite the crushing pressure of the very wrong Oracular magic. "What has happened to the Oracle?" he gasped, stumbling alongside Raggar down the broken road. "Their magic never felt like this before."

"What happened?" Raggar snorted. "Look around you."

The strange, sickening weight of the Oracle's magic vanished suddenly as the two arrived at the riverbank.

"Here she comes," Raggar breathed, collapsing heavily to sit onto a block of ruin. "At last."

Al-Sefir watched the group wade the river towards them. A tall man gave an arm to a very small woman to help her stand against the current. She was clutching a fat rope. Behind them came others, all clinging to the rope as well. The priest gasped.

"I think they have a baby with them!"

"And Halla." Raggar's voice was a prayer of relief. "Dear, blessed Halla."

As if hearing the Highlord's words, Halla plunged through the water, splashing past Klaris and Jax. She tore up the bank and enveloped the bony Highlord in a dripping embrace.

"Raggar! Oh, sweet goddess, what has happened to you?"

The others were up the bank now, wiping away the greasy residue from the river with towels Florin had packed for this purpose.

"Halla," Raggar mumbled, kissing her deeply. "I am so glad to see you, but I must speak to the Weaver."

Klaris straightened her skirt, arranged her magic so as not to cross the Highlord's and stepped to face him. He was a skeletal sketch of the man she'd met in the Oracle's temple, his eyes as distracted as his unkempt hair and beard.

Moved by the desperation emanating from him, Klaris reached out a hand, but stopped short of touching him. Even with her protect spells in place, such contact would sear them both.

"How do you manage all the magic?" the Highlord demanded without prologue. "It grows, it increases every day, and I am lost within it. I can't hold it all anymore."

"What are you saying, Highlord?" Blizzen knelt at Raggar's knee. "You've lost hold of Dragon force?"

Raggar waved the question away as if it were an annoying fly. Halla frowned at the tone of Blizzen's question, but before she could challenge the Orange Dragon, Klaris began speaking in her careful, accented Landish.

"I, too, have been lost in the magic." She paused and glanced at Jax. "It is a terrible feeling."

"Yes," Raggar breathed. "It is too much. Too much."

This was difficult ground for the Weaver. The emotions, the illness, the soul wrenching that Klaris had felt when the Mystic first returned after her Dark Fortnight were not easy for her to express in any language. But Raggar's distress astonished her. She began in Islish.

Jax interrupted her with a translation. "Otherwise," he said. "Or *before*."

Klaris nodded and managed to form her question in Landish. "Before, Highlord, before the magic grew, you held all Dragon force within you?"

"Of course."

Klaris sat back on another block of stone, her head tilted to one side. "This is magnificent, yes. Incredible."

"No! It's awful!" the Highlord yelled.

Klaris shook her head. "I did not think anyone could hold all the magic of either Mystic or Dragon within."

"Of course, I did." The Highlord snapped. "But now there's too much! Too damned much! I can't control it. It's not within me anymore!"

Although she'd been listening to the entire conversation, Lexyl felt she'd missed something critical. "Is there more Dragon force now?"

"Yes!" Raggar rose, trembling. "They are close. And the magic billows, roars, rages!"

"Indeed," Klaris answered calmly. "They come at Darkfest."

Raggar collapsed back onto his rock. "Help me, Weaver," his dark eyes flashed in his drawn face. "If they come and I have no control, all of Dragon force will erupt in fire and chaos."

Klaris caught a look of greed on Blizzen's face. She stared at him for a few minutes before realizing that the Orange Dragon could have no concept of what it was like to be lost in a flood of magic, unable to find oneself, unable to distinguish one's own body from that vast seething mass of power. She shuddered.

Lad Yob bent to frown at a set of large paw prints in the dust. "Highlord, Weaver, may I suggest we continue this conversation back at our camp?"

"The lad's right," Lexyl noted, handing the sling with her silent, wide-eyed baby to Borrel. "We need to move out of the ruins now."

Klaris tucked up her skirts again. "Back across the river, then," she muttered.

"Is that ghost still there?" Florin squinted through the haze over the river. "The thing is worse than fairies."

"It might be more helpful," Klaris said, grabbing Jax's arm to steady herself against the current.

"Or it might just suck the soul out of each of us." Blizzen grumbled.

Klaris caught his eye. "If we still have souls."

Behind them, the foul water swirling around his emaciated thighs, the Highlord began to laugh hysterically.

24

The setting sun enlivened the cliffs around camp with a bright red glow as the group gathered around the table, resting tired legs and frayed nerves.

Borrel made a fire under Florin's spitted rabbits. Lad Yob returned from the pasture up the canyon. "The pegasi are content," he announced.

"If we'd ridden today, it would have taken half the time and spared us the confrontation with the ghost." Blizzen grumbled, considering the blisters on his bare feet.

"I doubt they'd go," Lad Yob answered. "Not into the ruins."

"They're beasts," Blizzen said dismissively. "They go where you point them. If you know what you're doing."

Jax pulled out his dragonpipe. "You can try them tomorrow then, Dragon Blizzen."

"We're not going back there again so soon?" Blizzen frowned.

"Of course, I am." Klaris did not look up from her knitting. "And I am glad to have met that ghost."

Blizzen shook his head, as if the woman was daft.

The other Dragons retrieved their dragonpipes from pockets and packs and joined Jax's music. The sound echoed off the red canyon walls.

Florin turned her spits, the baby gurgled on her hip. She looked down at him. "Listen little guy; I'm not the maternal type. If you start chatting in some goddess-forsaken language again, I'm likely to drop you on your soft little head."

Tristan smiled at her, one small tooth gleaming as sharply as his nyad-brown eyes.

Both Al-Sefir and Raggar stuffed themselves on Florin's roasted rabbits, corn cakes, and pears.

"We've had little else but green water and lizard for the last weeks," Sefir noted. "I'm not the hunter Florin is."

Somehow the food seemed to weaken the Highlord. He began to tremble.

"Raggar?" Halla put her arm around his shoulder.

"It's all of you," he gasped, and Halla drew back, wounded by his angry tone.

Raggar stood slowly, shaking on his thin legs and raking his bony fingers through his stringy gray hair. "It's your magic: *all* of your magic. I cannot manage it! Help me, Weaver! Help me!"

Klaris tucked her knitting back into her bag and rose. "Come sit up on the cliff with me, Highlord." She walked up the thin path that led away from camp.

"I don't understand how the Mystic can possibly aid a Dragon Magician," Blizzen noted.

Florin smiled sweetly. "Funny how much you don't understand."

The Orange Dragon spitefully snuffed the campfire and stomped away to find his bed.

Halla relit the fire and the others gathered around it, holding warm mugs of Eldar thorn tea against the cool night air that came up with the shadows.

"I will admit to the same lack of understanding," Al-Sefir said gently. "The Highlord has been searching for Axterre for months, and I've seen him try to control the magic until he no longer could."

"The poor man," Halla whispered.

"Aye, but how can the Weaver help him?"

Jax leaned his elbows on his knees. "I think they share a similar experience, even if the magics are different." He looked at the fire-lit faces around him. "Klaris's mastery spells accessed more Mystic than had ever been available before."

"That's the truth," Halla confirmed. "We felt it at Dragonsholm."

"Well, she couldn't contain it," Jax continued. "She was sick and cross-magicked, and I think her soul had been lost in her mastery process. I'm not sure of everything that she did to finally grab hold of the power. But she managed it."

"She took your magic," Borrel reminded him.

"Yes."

"I'd give Raggar mine, if it would help him," Halla said fervently.

Jax took a deep breath and watched Borrel holding Tristan. The loss of his tiny bit of Dragon force seemed insignificant in the light of what others stood to sacrifice, but it still hurt. He remembered Klaris's comment about their souls. His own felt reduced by the theft of his magic and further withered by having been exiled from the places that he loved.

The others around the fire had also faced circumstances that eroded their souls and corroded their hearts, just as the eons of wind and water had withered away the Redrock of the landscape that surrounded them. Weakened within, how would they withstand the cunning vengeance of a long-dead Oracle and the overwhelming power of a flock of hungry dragons?

He swallowed the last of his tea and felt Klaris's magic swell then withdraw as she evidently tried to make some point to the Highlord out there in the dark.

Jax awoke before dawn, cold. He pulled up the covers, drew Klaris into his chest, and reached for his disembodied magic. The wood in the small grate burst into flame and gradually began to heat the small bedchamber as gray light rose outside the window. Eventually Lad Yob appeared, as usual, with two mugs of tea.

"Goddess love you, Laddie." Jax sat up to take the tea.

"Surely she does, my lord." Lad Yob grinned. "But she's given us a cold day."

Klaris blinked at the window. "And windy." Another gust of wind battered the shelter. "I think we will do the salutations indoors this morning."

An hour later the group ate their hot corn gruel and fried Elder sausages in the main room before a roaring fire. Raggar ate a great deal, but then sat staring hollow-eyed into the flow of magic, which engulfed him.

"Tell me how to help you." Halla begged. "Do you want my magic?"

"Dragons, no!" The Highlord blinked at her in horror. "There's already too much Dragon force. It isn't more that I need."

"What then?"

"She said it's all one." Raggar shook his head. "That seemed to make sense for her, but it's still too much for me."

Klaris stared into her tea. She was amazed that the Highlord claimed to have at one time carried all of Dragon force within himself. Certainly, she had carried her own Mystic within her before her mastery, but Weavers had always accessed more power than one person could contain. Many of them had written about taking the power once the Dark Fortnight was completed. None of Klaris's extensive reading had, however, prepared her for the task she'd faced to grasp hold of so much magic. Unlike the previous Weavers, Klaris didn't really hold all the Mystic, for there was far too much for two hands. Instead, she'd had to change her perspective which allowed her to see the entire seethe of power as a whole that she could move and work and weave, but not exactly grasp.

Lexyl had emptied her bag onto the table and was now repacking it. "We shouldn't have to wade the river today," she explained. "The oldest part of the city is on this side. If there's a cornerstone, it's probably in what they called the Ur."

"What's an Ur?" Blizzen asked.

"It means spring in Axterran." Lexyl pulled the pack's laces tight. "Like the start of a creek."

Blizzen stretched. "Let's take the pegasi today."

"Are we all going?" Al-Sefir smiled ruefully. "I'm in no hurry to return to those ruins."

Klaris rose. "I go. Lexyl, too, of course. And Jax."

"You don't need me," Raggar said softly. "I'm useless."

Klaris looked at him with deep concern. She spoke her broken Landish slowly, grasping for the right words. "A puzzle comes together one piece at a time. And if you look at one piece you will not see the picture that will be made. But once it is whole, you no longer see the pieces."

The Highlord stared her, his mouth gaping. Eventually he shook his head, comprehension still evading him.

Jax realized it was time to make decisions. "Let's do this: Weaver, Lady Lexyl, Lad Yob, Borrel and I will go into the ruins today. Highlord, you stay here with Dragons Halla and Blizzen, Florin and Priest Al-Sefir. Blizzen, you can see if the pegasi will fly into the ruins. If so, come meet us."

"And the baby?" Lad Yob asked.

Jax considered the deep nyad eyes staring at him from Borrel's lap. "If the ghost Oracle comes at us again, I'd like Tristan to be there."

Lexyl frowned. "He's not yours to sacrifice, Jax."

"I hope there is no sacrifice," he answered. "But Tristan spoke to that ghost, which was more than I could do."

Lexyl frowned at him then finally shrugged. "I'm not leaving my baby, in any case."

In the bustle as they moved to get their gear, Florin caught Jax. "Don't leave me here with all these Dragons."

"I'd rather you were coming with us," he admitted. "But you're the only other one of us besides Lexyl who can survive out here. If we get in trouble in the ruins, you and Halla and maybe the priest can either rescue us or save yourselves."

"I'm not likely to save the buffoon."

Jax flashed her a smile. "Also, we'll need food. You and Al-Sefir can hunt while we muck around in the ruins."

The sun burnished the Rocredlands without warmth as the explorers bowed their heads and shoved into the sandy wind.

"Down this way!" Lexyl called against the wind, leading everyone off the main thoroughfare.

The Ur was a small hill, wrapped on three sides by a curve of the river, and covered with broken buildings. The stone of these buildings was different from the rest of the city. Here, instead of the smooth gray monolithic rock, blocks of red sandstone formed the walls. Remnants of shiny tiled mosaics covered the walls with fragmentary pictures of trees, rivers, lithesome people, fairies, and dragons.

"This place was beautiful," Klaris whispered, ignoring Lexyl's injunctions and running her fingers over the crumbling walls. "And this magic was deep and clean and so elegantly simple.... Pure even."

"It's not pure now." Borrel looked around nervously. The sense of malevolence that always assailed him in Axterre was particularly acute here.

"Indeed." Lexyl said crisply. "The corruption started here, somehow."

Klaris considered the Eldar woman, who was looking at her baby to avoid everyone's eyes. "How did you dare to come here alone, Lexyl?"

"I read about the Ur in the scrolls. The Oracle's temple was here somewhere."

"Did you find it?"

Lexyl shook her head. "To tell you the truth, I never stayed more than an hour or so. The grim gets worse the longer you stay."

"Let's push on then," Klaris said. "Down towards the river."

Klaris kept reaching out to touch the buildings. "Older and older," she reported. The street ended in an open area at the riverbank. The force of the current ran along the far shore here, leaving a calm back eddy, swirling slowly past the ruins of a dock. Jax stepped onto the ancient pier.

"I didn't think any Landish people ever built a dock or a boat."

"The first Axterrans were islish." Lad Yob explained quietly.

Everyone turned to look at him in surprise. He shrugged a little self-consciously.

Klaris nodded slowly, as an old puzzle suddenly resolved itself for her. "That's why Islish is so similar to Ancient."

"Islish?" Lexyl frowned.

"Yes," Jax answered, understanding Klaris's epiphany. "Islish has a similar structure to Ancient. Landish is completely different. But how did Islish people get here, so far from the sea?"

Lad Yob spread his arms out toward the river. "The sea used to be here. A long gulf extended all the way to this place. Landish folk came here too. Axterre was a confluence of peoples and elements."

"The *Confluence of sea and air*," Klaris quoted, understanding for the first time the meaning of the line from the old poem.

Jax was looking at the surrounding desert. "What happened to the gulf? The sea is a very long way from here now."

"An earthquake, many millennia ago," Lad Yob explained. "The earth rose, and the gulf drained."

Jax nodded, gazing west. "Must have been quite a quake."

Lad Yob continued the story. "Many people abandoned Axterre, but many stayed to build a great city. They were proud of their resilience and their independence. They believed they did not need the sea or the other people of the Knownlands. They thought they didn't need a confluence to be powerful."

Klaris knelt to the plaza, brushing away sand and rocks to find pavers underneath. They were black. She reached out her red-stained fingers. "Ouch!" she jumped back in shock.

She brushed her hands on her skirt, trying to get rid of the sting. "This is where they started to go wrong."

"How?" Lexyl peered at the black paving stone but didn't dare touch it.

"Go ahead, touch it," Klaris encouraged. "Feel the...the...arrogance," she finished in Ancient.

Lexyl touched the paver for a brief second, snatching her fingers back from the sting. "Arrogance," she agreed in Landish.

"I have to figure out a language," Klaris grumbled.

"How about some lunch?" Borrel suggested.

They moved away from the riverside plaza, off the troubling pavers. Eventually they found what had once been a garden. An ancient fountain dribbled a clean trickle of water into a basin. Nothing grew here of course, but Lexyl declared the water fit to drink. All of them, however, preferred to stick with their water skins.

They spent several more hours exploring among the ruined streets. Klaris began speaking Ancient with Lexyl. Jax could follow most of their conversation, but Borrel, left out, found himself speaking softly to the baby, who now snuggled against his chest. Several of the larger buildings intrigued Klaris and she stopped to discuss them with Lexyl. These were apparently the most important buildings to the people who'd lived here, and they were crafted with a stunning beauty: elegant, graceful, and decorated with carved stone and colorful tiles.

"It is somewhat like your Arandy," Klaris said softly.

"Arandy is a shadow of this," Lexyl admitted, marveling at a particularly ornate building.

"Let's go in here." Klaris stepped through the broken door and into the dark shadows while the others hesitated. Her voice came to them out of the building. "Oh! This was their Caledra! Oh my...."

"Klaris!" Jax strode into the dark. Beyond the shadowed entry, the building opened to a central courtyard. Klaris stood there, bathed in sunlight, her arms outstretched as the Mystic reverberated through her.

"Come out of there, Jax!" Lexyl ordered from the street.

Klaris dropped her arms. She came towards Jax, took his hand and led him back out into the street.

"The scrolls speak of this as a place of terrible evil," Lexyl said in Ancient to be sure Klaris understood.

The Weaver considered Lexyl for a silent moment then turned and placed both her hands against the ancient wall.

"Don't!" Lexyl started, but it was too late.

Klaris shuddered as her magic encountered the ancient forces that had called this building up out of the earth. Here again the primeval construction magic was clean, precise, honest. As she pushed against the archaic weave, Klaris began to feel something else there, something foreign to the pure Mystic, like a thin strand of gray in a weave of white warp and weft.

Suddenly Tristan began to cry. It wasn't the typical baby fret of hunger or fatigue, but one of pure, inconsolable grief.

Borrel rocked the child and tried to soothe him. "Hush, Tristan. We're here."

Klaris suddenly thrust herself away from the wall, tears streaming down her face. "Sweet goddess, he's right," she whispered.

Jax wrapped Klaris in his arms. "Who's right?"

"Tristan," she sobbed. "Oh, my sweet goddess, the sorrow...."

"Enough," Lexyl snapped. "Let's go back."

Both Tristan and Klaris wept most of the long way home.

"Well, you look like you enjoyed your day," Florin drawled, as the group, tear-stained and windblown, reached the shelter. A hearty Dragon force fire warmed the room, scented with roasting venison.

"We've warmed water for you." Al-Sefir noted their wan, dirty faces.

Blizzen, his stocking feet propped near the fire, looked up from his reading. He let the ancient parchment roll itself up with a crackle. "Don't know why you're interested in reading this type of drivel, Lexyl."

Lexyl snatched the scroll from his lap with her cold fingers. "You took this from my room!"

"I noticed you had a lot of them, and I didn't have anything else to do here all day."

"You took an Axterran scroll from my room?"

"What, are they secret?"

"The Eldar people consider it a crime to read them," Jax said, testing the water in a pot with one finger.

"They probably haven't read them," Blizzen scoffed. "Damned difficult to wade through the Ancient, anyway. I didn't see anything wrong in what I read."

"It isn't always the content that's dangerous," Lexyl said sharply. "It's the assumptions, the tone."

Klaris had slumped, exhausted into a chair, but now her head came up. "Just like with those pavers, and that castle."

Lexyl nodded.

Klaris stood up. "We must all acknowledge the danger in that." She felt as if the wind had blown grit into her teeth, her curls, and the very pores of her skin. Even the Mystic felt somehow dirty. She turned to the priest. "Will you lead us in sun salutations, Al-Sefir?"

"Again? Now?"

"More now than ever."

Later, her soul cleansed, Klaris washed away the more prosaic dirt with the last of the warm water. Jax came into their room as she was teasing the tangles out of her hair. He noted the strength of her movements despite her fatigue.

"You'll go back there tomorrow, won't you?"

"Yes."

"Blizzen says he couldn't make any of the pegasi take him over the ruins, but he tried each of them and apparently even beat one. It threw him, so now he says he's injured and can't move beyond the fire."

"He can't heal himself?"

"He says no."

Klaris set down the brush and pushed on her belly where the baby was wiggling. "He managed to steal a scroll from Lexyl's room."

"Maybe you should add locks."

Klaris smiled. "Lexyl already did."

Jax placed his own hand on Klaris's stomach and marveled at the movement he felt there. "I don't think I trust Blizzen to read those scrolls."

"I'm not sure I trust myself," Klaris sighed. "But I'm going to read them anyway."

In the end, she and Jax both read more of the ancient scrolls than either of them would have wished. During the night the cold wind blew a fierce storm across the Rocredlands. Morning rain turned to blinding snow, keeping all of them huddled in the warm shelter, now enlarged with a wing for the Highlord and Halla. Florin, Lexyl, and Lad Yob ventured briefly into the storm to construct a barn for the pegasi.

Then Samhain was upon them, and they elected to stay out of the ruins while the veil between the worlds was thin.

Lexyl and Klaris, both fluent in Ancient, read and spent hours discussing the scrolls in the language of Axterre.

Jax sat holding the baby and tried to explain to Halla and Raggar how Klaris had taken the Dragon force out of his soul. He tried to tell them how he was still able to draw upon it to light fires and play his music, but he couldn't really explain the difference as clearly as he felt it.

Tristan sat and cooed on Jax's lap, displaying a clear affection that left Borrel feeling jealous.

"You can't fight the Jax-attraction," Florin told her twin softly as they watched the baby giggle for Jax. "You should know by now how everyone loves him."

"You think so?" Blizzen's voice was mild. "Plenty of people see past the half-isle's surface of charm."

"Past it to what?" Al-Sefir considered the Orange Dragon with his priestly instincts.

Blizzen shrugged and smiled. "I'm sure Jax means to support the Weaver in her endeavors here, but many people in Kordon doubted his loyalty to anything but his own gratification."

Florin made a rude noise and moved away to tend her bow and arrows.

Al-Sefir watched Borrel gaze across the room at Jax. "No," the nyad said finally. "He attracts people because he's not thinking about himself." Borrel left the priest and Blizzen to join Jax and the others. Jax gave Borrel the baby. Tristan cuddled into his father's chest, melting Borrel's heart.

The priest smiled then caught the expression on Blizzen's face and frowned.

25

Six days after Samhain the autumn sun had finally melted most of the snow, but the late dawn was still chilly as Jax, Borrel, and Lad Yob followed the two Mystics back out onto the Axterran plain.

They found the temple in the center of an old ring of stones later that morning. It was a ruin. Once it had stood tall and round, but now the remaining walls were broken off in jagged masonry twenty or thirty feet up.

Lad Yob touched one of the standing gray monoliths and fell gasping to his knees.

"Laddie!" Klaris called in alarm.

"No, it's alright, Weaver," he answered breathlessly. "These stones are the first.... The beginning."

"The cornerstone?"

He shook his head. The Lad's skin and hair were very nearly the exact color of the giant slab of granite. "My ancestors."

Klaris herself reached out to the rock. "Oh," she murmured, sinking to her knees, head bowed. The stone did not speak to her Mystic, the way a building block did. She felt, instead, the convergence of powers that characterized stone circles across the Knownlands. Like the Oracle's magic, the stones here radiated joy and peace and a profound sense of connection with the forces of earth, air, fire, water, sun, moon, and the goddess herself.

"Who placed these stones?" she asked Lad Yob.

"We did." His answer was gentle. "We placed all the henges to protect the Mystic of the Knownlands."

Klaris stared at him, thinking of the other circles she'd visited: one on Farsouth, one in Kordon, one in fact on the south side of Hanter Lake near where she'd first met Jax. Of course, there was also one at the Oracle's temple on Baria and at Caledra.

Klaris got to her feet and brushed the damp sand off her skirt. She walked around the monolith. "Yes," she said almost to herself. "Protection is here. And memory."

Lad Yob leaned his whole body against the stone and closed his eyes. "Memory," he echoed.

"Memory," Jax repeated. He was staring at the ruined round tower in the center of the henge and seeing again the fiery vision the ghost Oracle had shown him of the destruction of this place. In that vision, he'd watched the round tower engulfed in flames. The top had tilted sideways and then collapsed into the flaming river, leaving the stunted stub broken and charred amid its circle of stones that had not protected it on that day.

Jax ran his hands over his eyes, hoping to subdue the images, but he feared that this memory would continue to trouble his heart the way the fallen blocks of the tower broke and troubled the otherwise smooth flow of the great river.

"Memory," Klaris said finally, "is what we need." She moved towards the ruined tower. "Who remembers where the cornerstone sat? Who remembers how to banish the dragons?"

No one answered her, but Jax thought of the Oracle's ghost.

The tower, roofless, was half full of fine red sand. Arched windows opened to the cardinal directions. The plastered walls had been covered with the same, beautiful murals of green landscapes and dancing creatures that decorated the other walls within the Ur, here all darkened by soot.

As they stepped into the tower, each of them felt a surprising sense of peace.

"I remember that it's time for lunch," Borrel said, resonating with the sense of relief inside the round walls. He delved into his pack for their food.

Klaris ate a bite of cheese, still standing and looking around at the walls of the place.

"How can a round building have a cornerstone?" she asked abruptly. She took a long drink from the water skin. She walked slowly to the doorway, brushing sand away from the base of the building. All the stones were smooth and covered with frescos.

The others, one by one, finished eating and rose to join Klaris in her search, but by the time the sun was bowing towards the western rim rock, they'd found nothing but frustration.

At one point, Borrel had leaned up against a wall to rest, with Tristan on his shoulder. The baby had reached out his little hands to the wall, cooing happily. Borrel looked at the blocks his child touched. The wall was exposed here, where the plaster had fallen away. The red stone underneath the plaster had once been painted, he noted. Stylized flowers and geometric patterns lay like a mere breath of shadow on the red rock.

This design seemed at first much simpler than the lurid art of the frescos, but the closer he looked, the more he thought that the interweaving patterns here were more elegant and more sophisticated.

"Pretty, isn't it?" he asked Tristan, whose clear eyes had fixed on the revealed wall.

The baby laughed.

"We must go!" Lexyl called, shouldering her pack and stepping out of the round ruin.

Klaris, noting Tristan's gaze, smiled at the baby. "Yes," she said. "I prefer the older art too."

But as they walked back through the ancient city, her frustration grew. "Where's the cornerstone of a round building?" she asked again.

"You think the Cornerstone of Axterre will be the cornerstone of the Oracle's temple?" Borrel asked.

She turned to look at him. "I'd assumed so, but now that you put it like that, I'm not so sure."

"The temple is the oldest building there," Lexyl noted. "Only the standing stones are older."

"Maybe the cornerstone was the foundation block for the ruler's palace," Jax suggested. "At least those buildings are square, so they have corners."

"Maybe," Klaris conceded, unconvinced. She said no more as they walked through the lengthening shadows. Jax's idea made some sense, but she couldn't shake her conviction that the key to the puzzle lay somewhere in the round temple.

The next day Klaris and Lexyl decided to magically transfer themselves right into the Ur. This saved them three hours of hiking in and out of the ruins. Noting that the two of them together had enough "wherewithal" as Klaris phrased it to defend themselves, they went alone, leaving the others at the shelter, caring for baby Tristan.

Lad Yob climbed alone to the cliff above the plain and sat there all day, staring into the ruins.

Jax and the priest took a few pegasi back to Arandy for more supplies.

The Shaman Ashande leaned on his staff and stared at them with undisguised loathing as Jax reported their activities and needs to the chieftess.

It wasn't until they had returned to the shelter that Al-Sefir asked about the Shaman. "The Eldars don't trust the Oracle," Jax explained, carrying a heavy pack of supplies down from the pasture. "You can hardly blame them."

Fervently the priest led the Mystics through the purifying salutations that evening, sensing that his one wordless encounter with the Eldar Shaman had drawn down his soul, perhaps even more than the Mystics' use of great magic to transport themselves across the plain.

By the end of the week, Klaris's frustration with their lack of progress was infecting everyone.

The Highlord had sunk further into himself as he faced his personal failure to deal with the magic. He was humiliated that Klaris, young enough to be his granddaughter, had been able to manage a much greater amount of magic, while he had proven unequal to the challenge. It gnawed at him and left him despairing, with no tenable resolutions.

Unable to help him, Halla too felt her patience evaporate. She tried to continue her lessons for Borrel, but Dragon force, still growing stronger, was becoming dangerously unpredictable since the Highlord was unable to grasp it anymore.

Florin took her twin on long expeditions into the maze of canyons. Borrel carried Tristan in the sling.

"Lion," said the baby clearly one afternoon.

"Sweet goddess!" Florin stopped walking up the sandy wash. "That's just wrong."

"He's not wrong," Borrel defended his son.

"Babies that small aren't supposed to speak, Borrel. It's not natural. And you know that unnatural things upset the balance of the forest." She quoted long-standing nyad beliefs.

Borrel smiled gently. "But we're not in the forest here."

"He's still dangerous," Florin snapped.

"Lion," Tristan said again, more urgently.

Florin looked up, her sharp nyad eyes scanning the cliffs that rose around them. A chill ran down her spine that had nothing to do with the oddly talking baby. She drew her bow in a smooth movement and an arrow clattered off a rock a hundred yards away. The sleek, golden body of a great desert cat bounded out of a red shadow and raced away into the canyon.

Borrel followed his sister as she turned back towards camp. "Do you think balance would be preserved if we were eaten by a lion?"

"Shut up," she grumbled. "*Both* of you."

Blizzen planted himself in the best chairs each day and asked the others to bring him variously drinks, snacks, a blanket, or his dragonpipe. He played for hours. The Highlord occasionally joined in, his virtuosity, deft but soulless, was actually painful to Halla, who spent hours up on the rocks next to the silent lad, carving some pieces of gnarled wood.

Jax didn't enjoy playing his instruments short-fingered, and he couldn't keep up with the Highlord, but he did spend hours with Blizzen practicing the fairy tune until he could play it almost perfectly.

"You manage the left hand surprisingly well, but you're still late on that last chord in the bridge," Blizzen told him testily. "And the chorus begins thus...." Here he played the complicated passage that defeated Jax's remaining fingers every time.

Deciding there was no point in blunting Blizzen's meager praise by admitting he was left-handed, Jax simply tried the bridge again.

"No!" Blizzen cut him short. "Listen."

"I hear it, Blizzen, I just can't figure out how to go from the third to the fifth without my fourth finger." He played the passage again. In fact, while he was slightly off the beat, he managed the chord progression almost perfectly.

"Probably good enough if you're just playing for courtiers," Blizzen scoffed. "But you'd never pass anything at Jezel with such sloppy technique."

Jax's patience finally snapped. "I'll take my practice somewhere it won't offend you, Dragon Blizzen."

"It doesn't offend me, lad. I'm just accustomed to more perfect or perhaps more innate talent."

"I see." Jax's voice remained mild. "Surely then, you'll be happy to use your talents to organize our dinner this evening."

"I—!" Blizzen realized he was trapped into the chore.

"I'll go practice up the cliff so as not to trouble you." Jax ambled up the canyon towards where Halla carved and Lad Yob, immobile as the standing stones, kept his vigil for the distant Weaver.

"Will it bother you if I play?" Jax's tone implied that he wasn't really asking.

The lad didn't move. Halla shrugged.

He settled himself onto the sun-warmed rock and began the First Tune again. He played while shavings of wood fell on the rock at Halla's feet. The sun crept across the sky, melting the last of the snow. Finally, he once again tried the fairy tune.

He played the tune over and over again and began to feel the music's emotions just below the level of consciousness. As he practiced, a story started to form in his mind. It was a tale of struggle and peace, of love and grief, and catastrophic change at the bridge, which was where he had to admit that, though ungracious, Blizzen's criticisms were absolutely correct.

Everyone's nerves were raw and tempers short as they gathered around the dinner table that evening. The mood was not improved by the meagre, poorly prepared rations Blizzen supplied.

Klaris left the table, gathered her knitting and sat by the fire.

"Pardon me, Weaver," Blizzen said smiling. "But I fixed dinner, you know, and that's my chair."

Klaris's green eyes did not move away from the dance of her needles. "Thank you so much for letting me use it."

Jax sat on the floor next to Klaris's chair, the fairies' pipe in his hand. A phrase from the tune kept repeating in his head. He looked up at Klaris. "You haven't seen the ghost again?"

"No." Her answer was curt and a little absent.

"Maybe they can help."

"Probably."

"Maybe we need to give them an incentive."

"What kind of incentive do you give a ghost?" Blizzen demanded.

"Revenge?" Florin flopped down next to Jax.

"They've had that already," Jax explained. "The dragon interregnum was their revenge."

"What then?" Klaris asked, her needles still.

"Rest." Jax said simply. "They've been lurking out there with their hideous memories and their horrible guilt for centuries. They must want relief, release, rest."

The others considered him, sitting there on the floor, his face half in shadow.

"How does one give relief or rest to a ghost?" Halla asked, coming away from the shelves where she'd stacked the cleaned dishes.

Jax looked at her and gave a small shrug. "I think someone has to take their burden."

"Oh, no," Klaris breathed.

He reached up and disentangled her fingers from her yarn. "They need me to. I think that's part of this whole seen and unseen thing. And part of the paradox. I am somewhat familiar with burdens."

Klaris leapt from her chair, her knitting spilling onto the floor. "No! They will subsume you."

"That wouldn't help them. They need to give their burden away – or maybe they need to fulfill their purpose. We – I – can give them that opportunity."

"Jax—." Lexyl began, remembering how the ghost Oracle had touched Jax so grievously last year, but then she stopped. His logic followed Axterran principles more closely than he could know.

"In truth," Al-Sefir said softly, "In truth, we think that ghosts exist when something continues to tie them here. Severing those ties is thought to release their spirits to seek the Holy Mother at the Isle of the Apples."

Jax smiled. "For once my views are actually supported by theology."

"Wouldn't Marith be proud of you?" Florin spoke sarcastically to hide her terror.

26

The red rays of dawn brought no warmth to the group who walked with grim determination into the ruins. Jax had insisted that Tristan come along, and Borrel wouldn't let the babe go without him. Al-Sefir thought he too might be useful as a representative of the current Oracle. Lad Yob followed silent, his relief at being again with the Weaver almost palpable. Klaris didn't want to use magic to teleport such a large group into the ruins because she felt it wise to harbor her strength to face whatever challenges today would hold. They walked away from the rising sun into the seething haze.

Despite the unspoken gestures of support from Borrel and the priest, Jax couldn't get the sourness out of his heart. He wasn't sure he could get the ghost Oracle to reveal themself and even if they did, he wasn't sure they would tell him anything useful, but the angle of Klaris's head made her own opinion of this idea to lure the ghost into the open quite clear. She'd used words in Islish and Ancient well into the night, so he understood that her attitude came mostly from fear for his safety. Eventually she'd been convinced that they should seek the ghost's help, but she withdrew from him in anger. He knew she was worried for him, but he couldn't understand why she couldn't be more supportive. Obviously, he was doing this to help her, and he knew all too well that any encounter with the Oracle was likely to be unpleasant at best.

Why couldn't she just kiss him and smile up at him with those bright eyes? He'd do anything to see those eyes smile at him, but without either smiles or kisses, they arrived eventually at the ruined temple.

Jax dropped his pack beneath a fresco veined with fissures that marred the once-lovely picture of a green mountain stream. He closed his eyes to the picture and let the ghost's memories flood through him. He could smell the smoke, feel the heat, hear the cries of anguish.

Klaris watched him shudder under the onslaught. He put a hand to the wall, then snatched his fingers away as if burned. His gaze focused on a patch of wall where the newer fresco had chipped away. He stared at it for a moment.

"Jax?" Lexyl asked softly.

He didn't answer. Instead, he stepped out of the temple. "Oracle!" he called in Ancient. "Oracle! We seek you!"

"Of course, you do." The gray shadow coalesced beyond the ring of standing stones, their voice petulant. Even though she didn't understand the Ancient, Florin thought the tone very similar to Blizzen's.

Jax bowed and managed to procure a smile for the ghost. "Thank you, your Eminence."

"Eminence?" snorted the ghost. "Come out here, Paradox, where you can be seen at last."

Klaris's heart pounded, but she noted that the ghost Oracle had remained outside the henge. She watched Jax step toward the gray shadow. He showed no fear, no reluctance. Behind her, she heard Lexyl translating the Ancient for the nyad twins and Al-Sefir.

Again, Jax bowed. "You honor us, Eminence."

"Indeed."

"We humbly beseech your aid. We're looking for the Cornerstone of Axterre."

The ghost moved closer to Jax.

Klaris saw him steel himself against the reek of the corrupted magic.

"The Cornerstone of Axterre?" the ancient voice sneered. "That's no mystery. Go ask your present Oracle."

"They do not know." Jax drew on years of experience of courtly flattery. "Only you can help us, Eminence."

"And why should I?"

Jax's friends saw the wolf grin flash and realized he'd been maneuvering for this question. Softly he quoted:

> "Oracle, speak the Mother's truth:
> Dragons come with claw and tooth.
> Your purpose for one thousand years:
> Is to remember fire and tears."

The ghost expanded like a thunderhead to tower above Jax, blocking the hard desert sun and swallowing the lonely figure of the Paradox in seething black veils.

"No," Klaris breathed.

They could all see him swaying within the gray shrouds as if buffeted by great winds.

"Yes," Tristan answered softly in Ancient. Borrel stared at the baby in his arms.

Jax tried not to breathe the dark fog that swirled around him. He blinked against the visions of Axterre's fiery death that merged with images of dragons: dragons disgorging vast sheets of flame. The sulfuric air rasped in his throat and burned his lungs.

"Where is the cornerstone!" he shouted. "Tell us, Oracle! Tell us and be free!"

Suddenly the huge shadow plunged into themselves. Jax stumbled back to one knee, breathing deeply of the cleaner air.

Klaris took a step forward, but Tristan put up a pudgy hand. "Wait."

The Oracle had shrunk to the size of a child. Denser, darker, the ghost stood now eye to eye with Jax on his knees.

"Saucy, aren't you?"

"So I've been told." Jax cleared his throat.

"You think I can ever be free?" The wizened head shook side to side. "I am damned."

Again, the wolf grin flashed, grimmer this time. "The goddess doesn't damn anything."

"She *damned* Axterre! She *damned* my beautiful city, and my glorious people!"

Jax looked into the opaque gray eyes, thinking of Marith. "I would not presume to argue theology with you," he said softly. "But I believe we damn or save ourselves."

The ghost stared at him.

"Where's the cornerstone?" Jax asked softly.

The gray eyes glittered, and three large tears slipped slowly down the hideous face. "We are not damned. We are not free."

"Paradox," Jax whispered.

He felt the release coming before he heard the ghost's final words. "You've found the cornerstone," they said. "You fools have been snuffling around in it all week. The temple *is* the Cornerstone of Axterre. Or it was...."

Joy unexpected, lush, almost orgasmic washed through Jax, but it was laced with sharp sorrow. He gasped. Something icy lifted his sweaty hair. The sun went dark, and he raised an arm as if to ward off a blow that never came.

Silence.

Sunshine.

Relief. Gut-weakening relief.

He opened his eyes. The others crowded around him, where he sat in the sand. Drained, he heard their voices as if from very far away, speaking words in a language he couldn't seem to understand.

"We should have realized that," Klaris took his hand and spoke in Ancient, which slipped into comprehension through the haze around his mind. "There are other references to the goddess' worship as the basis of the city. How blind we've been! For goddess' sake, the temple is within a sacred henge."

"It's my fault," he whispered still in Ancient. "I'm the one who sees but can't be seen. I'm the one who should have known…."

"Any of us should have known," Lexyl said crisply. "It really makes perfect sense."

Jax stood slowly. He had something in his hand. He opened his fingers and stared at the three opalescent stones.

"What are those, in Landish if you please?" Florin demanded.

It took him a minute to change languages. "Oracle's tears."

They stared at the rainbows within the stones.

"That's a heartbreaking gift," Al-Sefir whispered.

"Mine usually are." Jax slipped the stones into his pocket. "I could use a drink."

"Couldn't we all." Florin pulled a skin of Eldar cactus nectar from her pack. She took a long pull before handing the drink to Jax.

They gathered again inside the round temple. Florin packed the flat, empty skin away. The sun, now straight overhead, filled the temple and all of them felt lighter, better, except Jax, who still couldn't quite seem to hear them clearly or rid himself of the Oracle's ache of grief. He stared without seeing at the ruins beyond the henge, wishing desperately for Marith.

The priest and Borrel sat down on either side of him. Florin cut some fruit and cheese for lunch. Lexyl nursed Tristan. Klaris stood in the center of the temple, the sun pushing down on her.

"Marith would be proud of you," Borrel said.

Jax flinched.

The nyad put a comforting hand on Jax's shoulder. When he spoke, the relief they all felt was evident in his voice. "I didn't think you really understood her theology lessons."

Jax shrugged.

"Who's Marith?" Al-Sefir asked.

"Our druid in Hilsen Vale," Borrel answered.

Jax ran his hands through his hair still trying to clear his head. "She saves me," he mumbled. "From trolls and ghosts and myself."

The priest exchanged a worried glance with the nyad over Jax's dark muttering.

"You might need another exorcism, Jax," Borrel warned.

Jax shuddered like a man with chills. His voice was so low, the nyad almost didn't hear. "I miss her."

Klaris walked to one of the walls. Her magic flared and a portion of the fresco crumbled to colorful sand. The original red stone blocks gleamed in the sunlight. Purple designs flourished across the red stone. She pulled on more magic and a larger section of the vivid plaster slipped away to join the sand on the floor.

"You're ruining the picture," Florin noted. Indeed, the fresco had depicted a sybaritic scene of nude men and women graphically enjoying an enthusiastic ritual to the goddess. Klaris had peeled away the most prurient portions of the scene. She didn't answer Florin, but slowly walked to Jax.

"Look," she said in Islish. "Look."

He stared at the exposed wall and the purple lines and curls that twisted rhythmically across the stone and disappeared behind the remaining fresco.

He took a deep breath. "It's script."

She nodded.

"What are you two talking about?" Florin snapped.

"We've found it," Klaris answered in Landish, her smile growing and filling her green eyes with relief and joy. "Read it, Lexyl."

"*The Weaver and the Paradox; A child born among red—.*" Lexyl choked to a stop as the words ran under the obscuring plaster. She bowed her head over the baby asleep in her arms and closed her eyes. Tears slipped free beneath her lashes and fell to the small dark head.

Jax looked into Klaris's smiling eyes. She bent down and kissed him. "You did it," she said.

Jax took the kiss gratefully and felt a little of the aching grief release him. He stood up, clutching Klaris to him. "Take me home."

Buoyed by the triumph of having found the Cornerstone at last and by the release of the ghost Oracle's malevolent force, Klaris summoned her magic in a tremendous wave and transported all of them back to the shelter.

"You could have warned me," Florin grumbled, following the others inside. "I wouldn't have left our lunch out for the ravens."

The sun had just risen above the rimrock the next morning as Klaris retrieved a roll of parchment, a quill, and a bottle of ink from her pack.

She sat on a stone, her implements ready.

Lexyl frowned, took off her wide-brimmed hat, then put it on again. "I'm not sure where to start."

Klaris set her pen down and joined the Eldar in the middle of the temple's floor. Together they surveyed the newly revealed walls of the old temple while baby Tristan slept in the sling across Lexyl's chest. From floor to where the walls gave jaggedly to the open sky the stone was covered with a flowing, intricate design. Both magicians were well versed in ancient scripts and the runes that predated Axterran writing. All of that was here and more.

The design reminded Klaris of the embellishments of Castle Caledra before it had been destroyed. The pattern linked symbols and beauty to weave a spell without magic.

"See?" Lexyl was explaining. "It doesn't begin or end. The lines circle back on themselves."

Klaris followed Lexyl's finger along a line of verse. There was much more here than the Oracle's prophecy. Words danced around the walls singing of all the goddess' glories: of full moons and rosy dawns, fields abloom and baby cheeks, lover's smiles and music, wind and birdsong, and long, silent nights. The words painted images, but there was no clear link between them, or any coherent message.

"We're missing something," Klaris decided. "Let's start by translating the runes into Ancient, then see what we have."

Lexyl appreciated the methodical nature of Klaris's approach to the problem and bent to the floor. "Start here. A pennywhistle, or a pipe?"

"A dragonpipe?"

"They didn't have dragonpipes in those days."

"Um," Klaris agreed, noting how her own perspectives had been changed by her association with Jax. "Let's say a pennywhistle, then."

Methodically, they unwound the runes.

"Here is the prophecy," Lexyl noted as she translated. "*Oracle speak the Mother's truth....*"

Klaris followed her work closely. "Oh, Look! Look!" she exclaimed. "There's another couplet, here! As there should be."

Lexyl bowed her head. "What do you mean?"

"The form of the poem." Klaris noted, as if this was obvious. She saw the confusion on Lexyl's face. "You know how Mystic spells are woven into poems that mirror their meaning, and there are forms used regularly, like this: four stanzas and a final couplet. That's standard. I knew we were missing something when we had only three stanzas, and even with the fourth one from the nyad magi we were still missing the final two lines."

Lexyl frowned at the runes. While Klaris wrote the words in Ancient:

> *Theory into action sings,*
> *Praxis life to lyrics brings.*

"Are you sure that's right?" Lexyl asked. "It doesn't make sense to me."

Klaris took a deep breath. "Yes," she said slowly. "But we still need to figure out which words are the lyrics. That's the key to the banishment."

Hours later the two walked away from the temple through the lengthening shadows. Around them the city still ached, but the sense of evil menace had vanished with the ghost of the Oracle. After the day spent crouching under obscure runes and parchment, both Klaris and Lexyl enjoyed the breath and stretch of walking.

Klaris battled her returning frustration. "There must be another poem within the poem. Another riddle within the riddle."

Lexyl didn't answer.

"I promise you, Lexyl, if we are able to solve this puzzle and actually weave the banishment spells, I'm going to write the instructions down in every language and in every type of medium from stone to tree so that whoever is here in a thousand years only has to face the beasts, not solve a bunch of ancient mysteries as well."

Lexyl looked down at her baby and said nothing.

Klaris felt the pain in Lexyl's silence and hoped that Tristan would prove to be a more useful Oracle than either of the last two. Her own baby rolled within her belly.

They came off the Ur's small hill and into the greater ruins of the city. Tristan gurgled then spoke one word in Ancient. "Paradox."

Klaris saw the anguish on Lexyl's face but didn't know what to do about it. "He's right. We need Jax out here again."

"You are merciless, Weaver."

"You will remember that none of this is my idea."

Florin watched Halla meander up the wash toward her favorite spot far up the canyon, her adz and half-formed wooden thing in her hands. The nyad turned to the Highlord, whose eyes likewise followed the Red Dragon.

"She has lots of magic, right Highlord?" Florin's eyes now swept the surrounding canyons.

"Her power is second only to mine own," he answered gruffly. "Although my own is...."

"Good," Florin said crisply. "A lion has been lurking hereabouts. I wouldn't want someone vulnerable out here alone."

"Lion?"

"Yep." Florin shouldered her bow and stalked down a different canyon.

Raggar didn't speak. His eyes watched two of the pegasi rise into the clear desert air. Jax and Borrel were returning to Arandy for yet more supplies.

The Highlord leaned back in his chair and felt the autumn sun warm the wall behind him. He closed his eyes and tried to calm his whirring thoughts, but lions and dragons and running flames of power seethed behind his eyelids.

An insect buzzed. Far away a raven screamed. These few sounds only emphasized the vast silence of the desert that seemed to provide space for his own dark imaginings to mushroom in vast and grotesque forms.

His heart pounded. Finally, he opened his eyes and gasped. A tawny desert lion sat before him, its golden eyes liquid and sentient.

"Help!" Raggar squawked, gripping the arms of his chair. "Al-Sefir!"

"You have found us," the lion said in clear Ancient.

Raggar's head swam, but he grasped the meaning. "Sweet goddess," he prayed.

The great cat's ears twitched. "Yes."

Years of dedicated discipline finally provided Raggar with some control over himself. "The magic," he gasped. "The magic isn't in me anymore. It cracked my soul, and I fear it will incinerate me."

The lion blinked but said nothing.

Raggar leaned forward. "Help me."

"The power has been split, divided like a river approaching the sea," the lion said slowly, softly. "It must lose itself to become the sea."

"What power?" Raggar asked.

"Dragon and Mystic; god and goddess."

Raggar licked his lips and looked into those great golden eyes. "I don't understand."

"You are in the shadow, Highlord, between theory and practice. Ideas must become actions."

"Dragons!" Florin's cry of alarm rang from the canyon walls. "Don't move, Highlord!" She stood above them on the path, deftly knocking an arrow to her bow, her eyes never leaving the lion.

"No!" the Highlord jumped to his feet. "Don't shoot!"

The lion's paw flew through the morning air, lacerating the Highlord from cheek to belly. It bunched its great muscles and bounded away into a canyon. Florin's arrow skittered off the rock where the lion had sat, just a second before.

Raggar's howls brought the priest running from inside. With Florin, he carried the Highlord back inside the shelter and up to his room.

Blizzen, his blond hair rumpled and eyes still droopy with sleep, stomped into the bedroom. "What's all the yelling about?"

"The Highlord was attacked by a lion," Florin answered tersely.

"Ah," Blizzen yawned and stretched. "I shall heal him. He'll be fine in a moment."

"Better ask him about that," Florin said.

The priest had gotten the Highlord settled on his bed, removed the torn and bloody shirt, and was now swabbing at the claw marks with a handful of towels. "Easy, Highlord," he crooned.

Raggar groaned.

"Stand away," Blizzen ordered. "Highlord, I shall use Dragon force to heal you now. Are you ready?"

At that moment Halla crashed into the room, having run down from her perch. "Raggar!"

"You might make some tea," Blizzen sneered to Florin. "I haven't had mine yet this morning."

"If you'd get up with the rest of us, you'd have had a full breakfast by now," Florin grumbled, but she went downstairs to prepare some food, having no wish to witness the suffering she knew the Highlord was about to experience.

"A lion dared to approach the shelter?" Al-Sefir was asking, incredulously. "That's unexpected."

"Not a lion," Raggar gasped, reaching out to grasp the priest's arm.

"Whatever it was, it had sharp claws," the priest answered gently. "Let's get you bandaged, my lord."

"Pooh." Blizzen pushed the priest away. "There's no need of bandages. I'll handle this. Are you ready now, Highlord? It will hurt briefly, but you will be completely restored in a short moment."

The Highlord blinked at Blizzen, his thoughts clearly elsewhere. But his brown eyes gained focus as Blizzen kindled his magic and began to direct it.

"Sweet holy mother!" Raggar gasped as Blizzen's magic sliced into his wounded flesh. "By the cat god...."

"Hush." Blizzen ordered. "Courage, Highlord."

Raggar screamed.

"Stop, Blizzen!" Halla cried. "These wounds aren't fatal. He'll heal."

"All done," Blizzen brushed his hands together. "See?" He grinned down at the trembling, sweating, wild-eyed Highlord. "Not even a scar left."

"Blizzen," Raggar breathed. "That's terrible."

"But you're completely healed now."

"Here, Highlord." Florin pushed past the Dragon Magicians and the priest to kneel next to the bed. She handed Raggar a cup of chamomile tea laced with some cactus nectar. "He healed me, too. It's...." She stopped, unable to find words for the experience.

"Horrific," Raggar supplied. He sat up and took the mug in shaking hands. He touched his unscarred face and looked down at his bare chest. As he watched, one thin, livid line reappeared on his skin from his collarbone down across his heart.

"Not quite scar-free," Florin noted wryly.

"He wanted to mark me," Raggar whispered.

"Who?" Blizzen turned to Florin. "Where's my tea?"

The Highlord found the priest's eyes and smiled. "The cat god."

"I'm glad I wasn't here," Jax said softly to the dark window, after listening to the others' story of the day.

"We didn't need you," Blizzen said with blithe condescension.

Jax ignored him. "What's going on here? Ghosts and gods come out of the desert to speak to us?"

"The return of the dragons upsets the equilibrium," Lad Yob spoke almost dreamily as he ladled more hot honeyed wine into Klaris's mug and handed it to her, "just as boulders disrupt the smooth flow of a river."

"A river must lose itself to become the sea," Borrel repeated the cat god's words and thought about his own epiphany above the Verfalls. "A river is always the same and always different."

"Enough with the paradoxes," Jax said slamming his own empty mug on the table. "I will face kings and trolls, ghosts and even dragons for you, Klaris, but divinity? Goddess, I wish Marith were here."

Al-Sefir looked at Tristan, who was sleeping in his mother's arms. "The divine is all around us all the time."

"I prefer the kind that exists silently in rocks or flowers or sunsets," Jax said crisply. "I don't like this special attention."

"You're a prince," Florin noted. "Doesn't that make you special?"

"No. There are lots of princes."

"If it wasn't you who was the Paradox, we'd still need one," Lexyl said grimly. "The prophecy is implacable. And at least you're old enough to recognize the necessity of participating."

The Highlord cleared his throat and spoke with a voice none of them had heard from him before. "The cat god said we are in the shadow between theory and practice. It's time for us to move out of that shadow and put our ideas into action."

"*Theory into action sings,/Praxis life to lyrics brings.*" Klaris quoted. "But we still don't know the lyrics."

The Highlord was rubbing the new scar on his chest. "I see what you mean, now, Klaris, about it all being one. Like the indistinguishable drops of water in a river; or all the rivers who lose themselves to make up the sea."

"I'm about drowning in your watery metaphors," Jax turned back to the darkened window. He could see nothing but his own muted reflection.

He was quite sure that someone, possibly many people, somewhere in the Knownlands would be better equipped, better qualified, with real magic and enough fingers to play the fairy song, to help Klaris and Tristan do whatever they were supposed to do to banish the dragons.

Klaris came up to join him looking out into the darkness. He put his arm around her.

"You can't swim against this current," she said slyly.

He laughed unevenly. "I'm going with you, of course," he said. "But I'm not sure I'm your best bet."

"Oh, I bet you are."

27

Sealord Bryx was in trouble, and he knew it. He glared across his desk at the lords and ladies of the Floating Islands who glared back. Crystal lanterns lit against the dark day cast dancing shadows as they swung on their hooks, rocked by the vicious waves of a brutal winter storm. Goddess, but Bryx hated a house that moved.

"Janil," he said through gritted teeth. "You're the next in line. You must take the job."

"I'm *not* next in line, begging Your Majesty's pardon."

"In the absence of Prince Javix, you are heir to the Helm. I fully appreciate that you might wish to do other things, but Baria needs its lord admiral, and *you* don't get to choose. None of us gets to choose."

Every noble in the room was thinking in one way or another of the sealord's choice to banish Jax, but none dared voice an objection.

Bryx rose and steadied himself on his desk. He read the silence accurately. "We will not harbor traitors. Lord Janil is surely more capable of being lord admiral than a disloyal prince." He watched with frustration as their faces clearly told him otherwise, but he knew as well as they did that Janil had no option but to take on the responsibility.

"Furthermore," he sat down again. "There'll be no more traffic with trolls and iron ore."

"Majesty," Lady Villar protested. "We've just begun to recover from the economic doldrums of the last four years. Trollish iron is critical to maintaining that recovery."

The sealord shook his head. "It's too dangerous, obviously. We can't afford more losses like the *Seaeagle*."

This was the crux of today's horrible meeting. Old Hix Sharkin, called to be lord admiral yet again after Bryx banished Jax, was hurrying back to Baria with no time to sell the *Eagle's* cargo of heavy iron ore. This storm that now shook the Floating Islands had caught the over-laden ship and de-masted the craft so that it broached to, taking Hix, his load of ore, and most of his crew to the bottom of the heaving sea.

Barians all lived with the possibility of shipwreck, but for such a tragedy to happen to an old and wily sailor like Hix was nearly unthinkable. Lady Villar, following Hix's *Seaeagle*, had almost lost her own ship as the storm winds twisted and shifted, but her wing-ship was larger, and more property weighted. She'd rescued a handful of Hix's crew, but the old admiral wasn't among them.

Bryx rang for his steward and stood up again.

"Janil, I'll expect you at Valla's Palace tomorrow morning to review the fleet lists with me." His round, Kordish-pale eyes swept the room, noting the disgruntlement and defiance on the faces of his lords and ladies. "Good day." He let the steward drape the Barian Blue cloak around his royal shoulders and headed into the driving sleet for the walk back to Valla's Palace.

"Goddess damn him," Janil swore as the door slammed shut.

Neben went to the window and looked out at the dark storm. He watched the hooded figure of the sealord, surrounded by his four guards, splash through the puddles.

"I'm not giving up the iron trade," Villar said crisply. "It's too profitable."

"*I'm* not going to be his damned lord admiral," Janil vowed. "He leaves everything to the admiral, and I don't have time to do all his work, run Helm's fleet, and the Phlyx fleet too. No one has that kind of time."

"You will, Janil, and you know it. You too Villar." Koralixa leaned back in her chair. "Or risk the sealord's wrath. If he's willing to banish his own brother, he'll have no qualms feeding anyone to the shark. Even you, Janil."

Janil put on a show of bravado, but no one was fooled. Sealord Bryx had fed the shark three times already since banishing Prince Jax last summer. While none of the traitors had been as elevated as the lords and ladies of the Floating Islands, they had learned that this sealord was not afraid to resort to public execution to display his will and his power. The sharks in the pen had grown fat and rapacious, and the people increasingly callous.

Neben watched the rain fall in the now-empty street. Bryx didn't govern, he just punished. Anyone who offered help trod on slippery decks. The sealord didn't think he needed help. To suggest otherwise was therefore treason.

Neben turned from the wet view and refocused on the problem at hand: "Appoint a good vice-admiral," he said to Janil. "Or several of them. One for each of your fleets."

"You've got such fine ideas, why don't you take the admiralty?" Janil sneered.

"The sealord's right about one thing, and we all know it." Neben said softly. "It's not a choice."

No one answered this. They looked at the storm, at the fire, at the dissatisfaction on each other's faces. Finally, Janil took a turn to look out the window at the ships bouncing in the harbor. "I wouldn't mind having the helm of the *Sharkin*," he said. "But damn it, I don't want the job!"

"That's the problem," Neben snapped at him. "No one wants to govern here. Bryx doesn't. *You* don't."

"We need Jax back," Old Lady Esmee said quietly.

All eyes in the room turned to her.

"Don't let the sealord hear you, Esmee," Villar grumbled. "He'll feed you to the shark for mentioning his brother's name."

"Have you been listening to your crews?" Esmee looked around at the faces of Barian power. "You'd think young Jax was some kind of savior the way they talk about him. And they're not far wrong.

He was here for a few summer days, rebuilt the fleet, reopened trade with Kordon, solidified new markets with both The Hant and Farsouth, then off he goes with the most beautiful islish girl in all the archipelagoes of the Knownlands – never mind she happens to be the Weaver."

"Beautiful?" Janil snorted. "She's terrifying with all that Mystic."

"Jealous?" laughed Esmee.

"Not one of us should be jealous of Jax," Neben noted. "Think about what he's facing."

"Dragons," Janil stated. The others weren't sure if he was answering Neben's question or cursing, or both.

"It will snow tonight," Kodill patted his winded horse, while looking up at the dark clouds riding the cold wind in from the sea.

Tallyn shook her head free of her hood, relishing the fingers of wind in her hair. Father and daughter sat, while their horses blew plumes of feathery steam into the cold breeze.

Tallyn waited in the windy silence for a few moments before speaking. "You know, Papa, the Earla said something interesting during our visit to Tar Baravel last week."

The king glanced at his daughter.

"She mentioned that you shared her concern for the people if the dragons really do return to the Knownlands."

"I'm always concerned for our subjects," the king answered.

"Of course, sir, but I hadn't realized you were taking steps to secure food and supplies against a possible dragon attack."

"Food and supplies?"

Tallyn found her gaze focused on some detail of her reins. "It was prescient of you, sir, to take such precautions."

The king, unused to receiving praise from his sharp-eyed daughter, smiled benevolently as she raised those ice blue eyes to him. "Yes," he said. "We can hope that our Jax and that little Farsouthian will send the dragons away, but we don't want to put all our trust in a pack of foreigners, do we?"

"Certainly not, sir. It's much wiser to take the cautionary measures you've instigated."

"Yes. And of course, we sent that Kordish Dragon fellow along with them."

"Ah yes. Dragon Blizzen."

The king's stallion took a step and shook his mane. Kodill grinned into the wind. "Race you to the river!" He spurred his horse and got a jump on his daughter. He raced the wind, rather proud of himself. It wasn't often that anyone got the jump on Tallyn.

The princess followed her father, making sure her horse didn't catch him. Already she was planning how to present the "king's plans" to the royal council tomorrow.

Bitter cold followed the winter storm on Baria. Icicles gleamed in the cold sunlight as the islish of Baria gathered at Helmsquay to bid farewell to Hix Sharkin. The sealord spoke briefly, but the cold wind snatched away his words, leaving the crowd with a disgruntled and unfair sense of Bryx's insincerity.

The Priestess Ayslic managed to make her prayer heard, but it too was short, and the crowd soon scattered as if blown by that wind onto various taverns and homes and palaces where warm fires and seaspirit heated their fingers and inflamed their anger.

"That was acutely inadequate." Neben stretched his stocking-clad toes toward the grate where firerock burned brightly.

Shallyx moved their toddler back from the heat. "Careful. Hot."

"I wish you could give the same warning to Bryx."

"So, we can sail first thing tomorrow." The Sealord concluded.

The *Drixa*'s first lieutenant gave a small bow. "Very good, your Majesty. The ebb will begin just past noon."

"Fine," Bryx snapped. "First thing tomorrow *afternoon*." His damn Barians always knew the schedule of tides. How they kept track Bryx didn't know. They didn't seem consciously aware themselves, but every time he got ready to sail, he realized that here again was yet another critical Barian competency that he lacked.

He turned to look out the wide window at the sunny day. Whitecaps bloomed and faded on the blue sea. It would be a lumpy crossing to Kordon, but goddess help him once there he'd stay there. The new palace should be livable by now. He knew it would take years for various Mystic weavers to improve, decorate, and grace the structure to befit the monarch of Baria, but it would be habitable now.

He returned to his desk and looked down at the large painting of mother and child that had been removed from the wall and sat ready to be packed. He smiled into his mother's painted eyes. "Tomorrow," he said in Landish. "Tomorrow we'll go home, Mother."

"You know he spent hundreds of our coins and hours of his time," Lady Zelanne Cale groused. "Even after you told him not to bother."

The baroness watched her heir gaze grumpily at the snow falling heavily on the Ilyian pines outside the window. "Why does it trouble you so?"

"He disobeyed you." Zelanne turned to face her mother.

"That's not unusual," the baroness answered dryly. "If he followed my rules, he never would have been abducted by the trolls."

"You'd think he would learn," the younger woman muttered.

"What's the real problem here? Is it that he took the initiative to make these preparations against a dragon attack, or that such preparations might actually be the right thing to do?"

"You're not doubting your own decree, Mother?"

The baroness shrugged one shoulder and moved a couple of papers among the tidy piles on her desk. "Aren't you?"

Zelanne sighed deeply and faced back to the snowy view. "The Oracle's high priest convinced you."

"He did," the baroness admitted. "And frankly, I was glad I could tell the king that the Calehold had already made preparations."

"So Corvyd's disobedience saved your face."

"Our face."

Zelanne considered her mother. "But you're the ruler here."

The baroness leaned forward. "The title doesn't come with omnipotence, my sweet."

"So, now we think dragons are coming?"

"We do."

Zelanne answered with heavy scorn. "And do we believe the rest of Corvyd's improbable tales about a half-islish slave prince who's attempting to save the Knownlands from this threat?"

The baroness gazed past her daughter to the blowing snow. "Something or someone changed our Corvyd. Whoever could do that clearly has some unusual skills."

Zelanne turned away so the baroness didn't see her roll her eyes, but the old woman knew anyway.

28

Jax stood in the center of the temple and turned in a slow circle. The space seemed larger now that the colorful frescos had been magically peeled away to reveal intricate patterns traced in ancient purple on the red stone walls. The patterns clearly represented a variety of scripts and languages. He recognized runes similar to those on the Oracle's medallion. Higher on the wall, the formal and precise writing of ancient Axterre marched around the circular room and he could pick out the words of the prophecy. A different circuit was written in Old Nekkian, which he could only understand if he said the words aloud. Interspersed among the various written words were lines that appeared to be simple decoration: a scrollwork of flowers and leaves, symbols of stars, moons, and spirals.

He stopped his slow spin, facing Klaris. "No Landish?"

"Thank the goddess for very small mercies."

"Does all the writing say the same thing?" he asked.

Lexyl shook her head. "Not exactly."

"Not exactly?"

Klaris had unrolled the new parchment that she and Lexyl had covered with a copy of the words on the walls. She used rocks to hold down the corners. Red sand dusted the document but did not obscure the Weaver's tidy writing.

She stood, brushing the sand from her hands. "Here's the prophecy." She pointed to the lines Jax had read on the wall. "It reappears here in Old Nekkian, and here in the runes. But then it's as if the words are unwound and reassembled in these lines here and here. They're set apart by the decorative work."

"What are we looking for?" Jax was puzzled.

"Lyrics," Klaris snapped, exasperated that he hadn't instinctively followed her line of discovery.

"*Lyrics of the dragon song*," he quoted.

"Which is why we need you," Lexyl explained. "If you play the fairy tune, we think the lyrics may become clear."

"The way the prophecy emerged from that Axterran book you found in Kree." Jax nodded, understanding at last.

"Exactly," Klaris noted.

Jax seated himself on one of the fallen blocks and pulled out the fairy pipe. "First Tune, first," he said and launched into the familiar music.

Klaris began to tremble as the sound reverberated with the old magic of the temple. "Sweet goddess," she whispered, stunned as the earth beneath her, the crumbling walls around her and the standing stones all resonated to the tune. Magic poured into the temple, filling her.

Lexyl cried out and fell to her hands and knees.

Jax stopped playing abruptly. "What's the matter?"

Klaris blinked at him. "Oh. Don't stop," she begged, her voice thick. "Please don't stop."

Jax's own response to the music had also been fiercely physical. He took two steps forward and pressed himself to her, bulging belly and all, gripped her curls and plunged into her impassioned kiss.

Klaris dug her hands under his shirt.

Lexyl, breathing heavily herself now sat on the ground, her arms wrapped tightly about her knees. "Stop it, you two. Unless you want an audience."

Jax lifted his head. He saw the look in Klaris's eyes. Without a word, he took her hand and together they dashed out of the temple. He threw down his cloak behind one of the standing stones and pulled Klaris down on top of him.

Inside the temple, Lexyl closed her eyes and covered her ears against the cries of Klaris's release. The potent magic of the tune and temple had not ignited lust in Lexyl, but a gut-wrenching fear.

The silence afterward seemed thickened, as the sun moved higher into the clear blue sky.

Klaris returned to the temple, her face glowing. "Sorry," she said without contrition.

"Is that what you two are going to do when the dragons are descending upon us?" Lexyl asked tartly.

"We are aligning," Jax grinned, unrepentantly. Lexyl couldn't help but laugh.

Klaris put down the water skin and attempted to tuck her dark curls behind her ears. "The connection between Jax and me is part of the banishment, Lexyl. You know that and we know that, and the goddess has acknowledged that." She patted her belly. "And it is undeniable."

"Clearly," Lexyl's voice was as dry as the sere desert air. "Can we try again, or will it drive you two mad?"

Jax shrugged. "Won't know until we try." He resumed his seat on the rock. He winked at Klaris. "Ready?"

She took a breath to steady her magic. "Ready."

Again, the music rose and resurrected the potent, ancient magic. Prepared this time, Klaris rode the waves of power, sorting through the various weaves of this place. The music opened portals to layers upon layers of magic. She found not only the Mystic, but also fairy and Oracle, and even a very ancient strand of Dragon force that had come from one of the great creatures itself.

Lexyl held her hand over her mouth and squirmed.

Jax got to the end of the First Tune and stopped.

The gut-wrenching terror evaporated, leaving Lexyl dizzy and nauseous. "Sweet goddess," she blinked tears from her eyes. "Don't you feel that fear?"

Klaris and Jax both stared at her.

"Fear?" Jax shifted on his rock. "It's not *fear* I feel."

Lexyl hugged herself.

Klaris cocked her head to one side. "I don't sense a threat here," she said in careful Landish. "But there is all magic. Even Dragon."

"That's Jax," Lexyl's voice crackled as she strove to contain her horror.

"Jax has no magic," Klaris said coldly. "The Dragon force here comes from one of the beasts. Very ancient."

"All I feel is fear," Lexyl repeated.

Klaris considered the implications of this information.

"Shall I try the fairy tune?" Jax asked, ignoring the pang he always felt when he had to face the loss of his magic.

"Yes." Klaris turned away from Lexyl's troubles. "I'm curious to see what that song brings us."

"That makes one of us," Lexyl grumbled.

Jax blew a scale into the pipe, paused to gather his breath then launched into the fairy song.

The tide of magic evoked by the First Tune was a mere puddle compared to the flood released by the fairy song. Jax watched Klaris raise her arms and sway in an invisible hurricane of power.

Lexyl first fell again to the ground then gathered her own considerable will and ran from the temple.

The song drew to its wailing finish. The last note disappeared into the sunlight. Klaris let her arms fall to her sides.

"Play that again, Jax."

He did.

Outside the encircling henge, Lexyl listened to the fairy song repeated three, then four, then five times. She faced away from the temple, but nothing moved among the ruins. Out here, beyond the standing stones, the terror was reduced to an insistent sense of dread. She could manage that well enough to examine the storm of magic contained within the henge. Lexyl wasn't sufficiently familiar with the other magical forces to be able to name the strands of fairy or Oracular magic that rippled through that tempest, but she realized that all magic was somehow present there and that Klaris was seeking ways to weave it.

The audacity of this was stunning and appalling.

It seemed unfair to Lexyl that anyone should have such a gift, even as she recognized that having to face a flock of dragons was no entitlement. She still resented that Jax and especially Klaris could somehow manage to exist and even function within that vortex.

In the silence that finally swathed the temple and ruins when Jax stopped playing, Lexyl swore she'd never give her precious Tristan to that maelstrom.

"Lexyl?" Jax stood in the temple's ruined doorway. "Lex! Are you alright out here?"

The Eldar stood slowly and came out from behind her shelter. "I'm fine. Have you finished?"

Jax nodded. "We're having some lunch."

Lexyl joined them, noting a sharpness in Klaris's green eyes. "What did you find?" she asked the Weaver, just managing to keep the resentment out of her voice.

"The lyrics."

"Truly?"

Klaris smiled briefly and handed the water skin to Lexyl. "Among other things."

Lexyl waited, but Klaris did not elaborate. "There was a tremendous amount of magic," Lexyl prompted finally.

"Yes."

Jax frowned at Klaris's unfriendly responses. He'd felt her find the lyrics that went with his fairy song. They were there among the other words, highlighted by the scrollwork of flower and leaf. Klaris had found them the second time he played through the song.

Now she knelt in the sand and added the symbols to her parchment to delineate the words that formed the lyrics. "It can be sung in Ancient, or Old Nekkian," she explained. "See these symbols tell you which words of the prophecy make up the song."

"So, you will sing to the dragons?" Lexyl asked in a flat voice.

"No."

Both Jax and Lexyl stared at Klaris, surprised by this answer.

She glanced at them and that brief, cold smile flashed again. "You know that Mystics have no music."

"I thought the Oracle told you to learn how to sing," Jax reminded her. "And the fairy queen did too."

"We've already established the fact that no one knows all the details of a proper banishment."

"I can't sing either," Lexyl offered softly.

Klaris dipped her quill in the ink and turned back to her work.

"Klaris!" Jax said, frustrated by her rudeness. "Tell us what's going on."

Klaris made one last mark on the parchment, corked the ink bottle and rose slowly. She put the quill into her pack.

"The Oracle sings, of course."

"They're coming here?" Jax asked, wondering how the tiny ancient creature would manage to withstand the rigors of such deep magic.

"The Oracle is already here."

"No!" Lexyl stiffened.

Klaris considered the Eldar with a mixture of compassion and anger. "You've known this."

"He's just a baby."

"He can do it," Klaris said firmly. "Now that we know at last what must be done."

Jax heard the accusation in Klaris's voice and looked his question at her.

"I finally understand the wall around this goddess-damned city," Klaris kicked at the dust that remained of the frescoes. "They had the knowledge, Jax. Lexyl knows they held all the keys to the banishment process. But the Axterrans wanted that power for themselves. That's why the prophecy in that book we found in Kordon is incomplete." She gestured to the walls. "That's why the frescoes were painted on top of the banishment code here. Even the writing in Ancient here doesn't contain the final couplet of the Prophecy, that's only found in the older parts, in the runes. And that's also why walls were raised around Axterre to hide from a curious world."

"To keep the banishment spells secret?"

"To control access to the knowledge. Look," she motioned to the walls. "Initially this information was written in every language. It appears the banishment was developed by a collection of creatures from across the Knownlands, even apparently a dragon. *Blood must mix* and all that. There had to be cooperation, initially. But the Axterrans hoarded this knowledge and *hid* it.

Jax whistled softly, understanding the power this would have given the ancient Axterrans over all the other races and peoples of the Knownlands.

Klaris took a step towards Lexyl. "And the descendant of Axterre continues to hide important secrets."

"Can you blame me?" Lexyl growled.

"It is *I* who must face those dragons," Klaris snapped. "Jax and me and your Tristan. We must know what to expect and what to do."

"And I who must give something more precious than my own life!" Lexyl cried.

"So why not help us succeed?" Klaris demanded.

"I have, haven't I?"

Klaris gave half a shrug. "You have. But I think there was another scroll. I don't know if you destroyed it because you do honor these ancient things."

"It held no answers to your many questions, Weaver," Lexyl admitted tacitly. "No lyrics. No methods. Just a name."

"Tristan."

"Tristan," Lexyl sobbed.

Klaris felt her own baby roll and was suddenly exhausted. She bent to remove the rocks from the corners of her parchment, which curled in upon itself. "We have answers now. More, perhaps, than we wanted." She held her hand to Jax and began to summon her power. "Let's go home."

Jax stared into his empty mug as Klaris explained what she'd finally discovered to the rest of the group.

No one spoke when she was done explaining. A log crackled in the fireplace. At last the Highlord cleared his throat and sat up a little straighter. "So, you will harness all the magic of the Knownlands and channel it into the banishment spell."

"Yes, using the music of the fairy's song as the focus. It's actually the dragons' song."

"And Tristan, somehow, will sing?"

"Yes."

"So, it's just the three of you standing at the top of Dragon Perch Mountain on solstice morning?"

She nodded.

Jax took a breath as if to speak but let it out without a word. He stood up and went to the window. The sun had gone. "I really had hoped there was going to be more to it than that."

Klaris saw the dejection in his stance. "Lexyl, do we truly have it all?"

"Alright, yes!" Lexyl admitted finally. "I did leave one scroll in Arandy, but truly, it had nothing more to tell us about the banishment process. You can see for yourself when we go back there."

"We are in the shadow," the Highlord said softly, quoting the cat god. "The shadow between theory and action."

Borrel cuddled Tristan to his chest. "We know what needs to be done, but where do we find the courage to do it?"

They did not linger in Arandy, resting only for one night within the comfort of the chieftess' palace. Lexyl did produce the ancient scroll naming Tristan, and Klaris found herself agreeing that it held no additional useful information.

Eleeza turned back to the palace after the last pegasus disappeared into the icy morning air and sought refuge in her private sitting room. Lexyl's small gray cat curled before the bright fire that burned in the hearth, and Prina opened her arms. The chieftess settled into the embrace on the sofa and finally let her tears fall.

Prina rocked her lover, her own cheeks wet.

Their private grief was interrupted by a short knock. Prina rose and opened the door. "Not now, Shaman."

"I beg you, Prina," his voice was unusually gentle. "I have found something the chieftess should see."

Despite her personal misery, the chieftess' interest was captured by the unusual note of contrition in Ashande's voice. "Come in, Shaman." She wiped her face.

Ashande saw the grief evident on both women's faces. He took a deep breath. "I know you fear for Lady Lexyl," he began gently. "And even more for Tristan, your heir."

"For all of Arandy."

"Indeed, Chieftess." He paused and opened the ancient scroll he'd brought with him. "As you know, our ancestors wisely repudiated the foul magic of Axterre."

The chieftess and Prina nodded, sitting side by side, fingers intertwined.

"The Axterran scrolls are forbidden because they contain so much information about the evil magic that eventually destroyed the city."

"Yes?" Eleeza well knew her history.

"But they have a great deal of other facts within them as well," Ashande continued. "History, theology, maps, and such." He turned the scroll to face the chieftess. "Read here, my lady."

Eleeza looked at the crabbed script. "My Ancient is rusty," she said, knowing that Prina had never been taught the language of Axterre, which was only permitted to a few members of the royalty and high clergy. "Translate it for me."

Ashande cleared his throat and read: "*When the dragons return to the mountain, keep the people safe in the canyons while the Oracle of Axterre performs the banishment. This duty is the one justification for the Oracle's great power. It is believed that in ancient times the banishment was performed by a coalition of individuals representing the various races of the Knownlands. The Axterran Oracles have consolidated that power these last two millennial cycles, and to good purpose. The dragons have been successfully banished, and a new Oracle created each time.*"

Eleeza stirred. "Lexyl mentioned something like this to me."

"Listen," he went on: "*You will know the millennium approaches by several portents: Cats will speak with human tongue. A paradox will roam the Knownlands, invisible to magic. A great earthquake will shake a center of power into rubble, and a half-breed babe, half nyad half Axterran will be born. And its name will be Sorrow.*" The Shaman lifted his head and pronounced the last word in the original language: "Tristan."

Prina covered her mouth to stop her cry of shock.

Ashande's inexorable voice read more. "*That babe will be the next Oracle. If the child is born amongst us, we must give it up to the forces at Axterre. For without the mixed blood babe, the dragons cannot be sent away and unimaginable devastation will result.*"

Eleeza stared at the Shaman. "Have you known this all along?"

The man let the scroll rollup and shook his gray head. "No. Lady Lexyl showed it to me before they left this morning."

Eleeza stared at the fire for a long moment. She thought of her nephew's precious bald head and lovely, precocious eyes. She'd been so sure he would grow to be an exceptional Speaker for All Eldars, but now she had to acknowledge that he was destined to speak for a much greater force and a much larger population.

She rose and rang for her servant. "Let's have some tea, then."

"I apologize for trying to thwart the outlanders," Ashande said, his amber eyes steady on the chieftess. "I thought my duty was to protect the secrecy of Arandy, and I have always disapproved of Lady Lexyl's fascination with Axterre."

"Yes," Eleeza resettled herself of the sofa. "But it appears that her blasphemous obsessions were perhaps warranted."

"She faces a terrible loss," Ashande admitted gently.

Eleeza accepted the Shaman's apology and his change of heart. She watched her steward pour steaming thorn tea into green glass mugs. When all had been served, she cradled the mug in her cold fingers and pushed aside her personal troubles. "If Tristan cannot be the next Speaker for All Eldars, then I must identify another heir."

The Shaman and Prina looked into their own mugs of tea, as if the answer might be found in the green depths.

The cat rose and stretched. "Patience," it said, and began to clean itself, oblivious to the startled amber eyes that glared at it.

29

Klaris and Lexyl built their shelter in a clearing surrounded by tall pines on the western slope of Dragon Perch. Klaris felt the spidery remains of very ancient magic and realized that previous shelters had been built here and then returned to the mountain. This realization gave her comfort. Others had gathered here to face the dragons and survived.

Jax stood back with the Dragon Magicians and stomped his cold feet in the snow. A few hundred yards up the slope the pines gave way to rocky, rime-covered scree and then above a cornice of blown snow, the peak itself.

"The pegasi can't stay here," Florin said. "There's no forage for them. I'll take them down the mountain where grass still grows."

As Klaris moved inside the new structure to add finishing touches, Lexyl and Florin mounted the pegasi and sailed down slope to create a barn for them beside a greener pasture.

Al-Sefir pulled his thin, desert-made cloak around his shoulders. "I wish I was going with them."

"I have a thicker cloak, if you'd like to borrow it," Jax offered. He turned back to the shelter, where smoke now drifted from several chimneys. He paused then began to run.

"My lord? What is it?" Al-Sefir stumbled through the snow after him.

"Sweet goddess!" Klaris snapped, waving ineffectually at the smoke that filled the room. "We're all cold, but the flue's not large enough for an inferno!"

Halla pulled her force into herself. The fire, which had roared up the chimney and spilled onto the hearth, shrank to a bright blaze.

Lad Yob used a small shovel to lift the smoking embers back into the grate.

The Highlord lay writhing on the floor. Blizzen knelt next to him. "Highlord! Raggar!"

Borrel, his own magic fluctuating wildly within him, helped Blizzen lift the trembling figure to a sofa. Jax threw open the windows to clear the smoke. The priest found a skin of Eldar Cactus nectar and bent over the stricken Highlord. "A sip here, Highlord."

Raggar drank and coughed.

"I'm sorry." Halla slumped to a chair, her head in her hands. "I'm so sorry. I was just lighting the fire, but then a wave of magic flooded into me. I could not control it."

"I know." Raggar's voice ached. "By the cat god, I know."

Klaris stared at the stream of water running into her newly crafted sink. She closed the faucet and turned to the others in the room. "They're very close. Solstice is just two weeks away."

The winter wind blew through the shelter dissipating the smoke. All of them shivered, though not from cold.

"Here you are again." Borrel pulled up his hood and sat down next to Jax on the rectangular altar rock at the summit of the mountain. The constant wind had scoured the peak of snow. The nyad followed his friend's gaze away to the distant east. He noted the Oracle's pipe in Jax's short-fingered hand.

For a long time neither spoke. Below them, the bare rock of the summit gave way to pines contorted by the relentless wind. Lower still, the pines grew taller and darker until they thinned as the snow gave way to red desert rock, wrinkled and sliced by canyons and cliffs. The air was astonishingly clear. Borrel's nyad senses told him he was able to see nearly fifty miles, beyond the horizon of the Knownlands.

"Do you think Blizzen might be right after all?" Jax asked finally.

The question confused Borrel. "He's not right about much."

Jax quirked a small grin. "What if the dragons were to linger again in the Knownlands? What if Dragon force did increase? That might be a good thing. Maybe more powerful Dragon Magicians would learn to heal without causing such pain."

"Maybe," Borrel conceded without conviction. "But there's little doubt that another dragon interregnum would cause considerable devastation."

Jax kept his gaze on a hawk that circled far above the desert. "But pain isn't always unredeemed. I remember drinking with you in that Nomad tavern last Darkfest. You said that knowing Lexyl was worth the pain of losing her."

Borrel didn't want to remember the hollow ache that had followed him from Dishroc to Kree and back to Hilsen Vale and finally driven him to return to this desert landscape in search of wholeness for his heart. "It's not quite the same," he said softly. "I had the joy as well as the grief. If the dragons are not banished, if they do stay here for another interregnum, the creatures who will die will not share any benefit that might come from an increase in Dragon."

Jax took a deep breath and exhaled slowly. "The air is so dry here," he said very quietly.

Borrel watched the hawk gather in its wings and plummet to earth. He couldn't see if the raptor caught its prey. The nyad chose his next words carefully. "Lexyl is confident that she and Klaris finally understand the banishment. The spell and the lyrics and the magical laws or theory all agree."

"I know."

"It will work, Jax."

The sea blue eyes never left the horizon where the hawk again rose to the clear sky. "I think it will."

"So why are you worried?"

"Aren't you?"

Borrel thought of his precious son and the anguish in Lexyl's amber eyes as she held him. "Sacrifice."

"And sorrow." Jax's voice was just as soft. "Tristan will survive."

Borrel and Lexyl had covered this ground, both of them weeping. The banishment required the making of a new oracle. A mixed-blood babe. They presumed Tristan would survive, but his life would be altered beyond all normalcy. How else could he live a thousand years to fulfill the prophecy for the next banishment? Borrel finally repeated the article of faith he and Lexyl clung to. "The goddess doesn't demand sacrifices."

Jax looked at him finally. "But perhaps dragons do." He saw the look of horror on Borrel's face and took the nyad's arm.

"Tristan has to survive," Jax repeated. "He's not the sacrifice."

Borrel blinked. "Who is?"

Jax looked down at the pipe in his hands. "It can't be the Weaver. It can't be her unborn baby – the goddess wouldn't do that."

"It's you?" Borrel's whisper was snatched away in the wind.

Jax shoved himself off the altar stone. "Klaris holds the magic; Tristan holds the future; I'll be the idiot facing the dragons holding naught but a fairy pipe and a breath of tune." He stood for a moment then grinned. "That's the paradox again, isn't it? Sacrificed to a goddess who doesn't demand it."

"Best let me do that." Florin took the tin of tea away from Jax and began to measure the black strands into the pot.

Jax sat on the bench near the fire and watched Florin cut some sandwiches while the kettle simmered.

The nyad glanced at him. "What do you need, besides tea?"

He took a minute to answer. "After we've banished the dragons, Klaris will likely need some healing, and her baby is due around Candlemas."

"Yes." Florin moved to take the singing kettle off the flames and poured the boiling water into the pot.

Jax turned to look her full in the face. "I wanted to ask you to take Klaris back to the Vale. Back to Mam Marith."

"Is that where she'll want to go?"

"Maybe not."

"Well, I'll be happy to go home with both of you."

Jax snatched a sandwich, and Florin swatted his hand with the flat of her knife.

"She's tough as rocks, you know," he said. "She'll be fine eventually, but she might need a druid after facing the dragons."

"I'll be right here," Al-Sefir joined them.

"Yes," Jax gazed at the priest. "As I said, Klaris is strong, brilliant, fearless. But facing down the dragons is bound to leave a...mark."

Al-Sefir frowned.

Florin set a cup of tea in front of Jax and looked into his blue islish eyes. "Borrel told me," she whispered. "I'll take Klaris home to Marith."

Jax gripped Florin's hand. "Thank you." He rose and took his tea to the other side of the room, where Tristan was pestering the Highlord.

Al-Sefir watched him distract the child. The Highlord settled himself more easily. The baby played with the ties on Jax's shirt, and he smiled, ruffling the thin baby hair.

Florin poured her own tea, added a liberal dollop of cactus nectar, and sat next to the priest.

"How could you ever mistake him for a slave?" the priest asked softly.

Florin considered how someone might see Jax today: dressed in silks, acknowledged as a prince, addressed as a lord, and a damn fine-looking man. She swallowed half her tea and faced the priest. "It's not so different."

Jax climbed into bed that night and held his hand gently on the bulge of Klaris's belly that was their child. It wasn't moving.

"Make sure it knows I loved it," he said softly.

"*Loved?*"

"And you." He moved and covered her mouth with a deep kiss.

Klaris frowned up at him. "I love you, too. Note my use of the present tense."

Jax ran a thumb down Klaris's soft cheek and grinned. "Yes, present tense. But next week this will be past tense."

"And your fickle love will be, too?"

"It's not fickle, Klaris." He rolled onto his back and pulled her on top of him.

Klaris pushed his arms down and sat up. Her wild hair shadowed her face from the light of the last single candle.

"Why do you assume the dragons will kill you, but not me?"

"You have all the power. Tristan is the next Oracle. I'm just a puzzle."

Klaris pushed her hair behind her ears and stared at him. She had become increasingly confident in the last few days that they would survive the banishment. Previous Weavers and Oracles obviously had done so, and since the Paradox and his music was so integral to the whole process, she'd assumed that Jax would, too. She now realized that this assumption was not based on any evidence.

She saw the resolution in his beautiful face and the sorrow. Terrified, she determined to go back to the scrolls, to read more closely, and to practice more deeply the interweaving of magic into the lyrics of the fairy song.

Something was wiggling on the outside edge of Klaris's weave, so she moved to strengthen the careful bonds that she'd constructed. She felt Lexyl recognize her action and move with her. Half a moment later, the Highlord too adapted his rigidly controlled magic.

Together they built a spell like a wall out of a string of lyrics and the geometry of a tune.

But still there was that niggle, a bit of pressure that changed the flow of power.

Having re-woven the foundation of this practice banishment, Klaris pulled back a bit to consider the odd, outside force. Halla was playing for them today. The nyad played with a virtuosity that Jax couldn't match, and yet the weave was never as strong when someone else played.

Klaris sighed, knowing it was her fault, not Halla's. When Jax played she wove the magic with her soul and his as well. She knew this was what the prophecy required, but still wished someone else could play when the dragons came in a few days, someone less dear.

The niggle became a sudden hideous tear. With a gasp, Klaris let the magic go. Lexyl, Raggar, and Halla reeled away from the circle they had created, each aching with the wrench.

Klaris felt Jax pull what had once been his magic and then an overwhelming surge of Blizzen's smooth orange power obliterated it.

"What is Blizzen up to?" Raggar grumbled.

"It feels like he's healing someone," Halla said, pocketing her dragonpipe.

"Healing who?" Lad Yob asked from his usual spot at the window.

Blizzen's magic soared and throbbed. Klaris sensed Jax struggling like a small boat on a storming sea, almost lost in that magnificent torrent.

She jumped to her feet. "He's doing something to Jax."

Everyone there immediately recognized the multiple consequences of such an interaction. Klaris dashed out of the shelter, forgetting to grab a cloak. Outside nothing seemed unusual, but the magicians all felt the epicenter of Blizzen's magic. They ran for the peak.

Florin wrapped her cloak more tightly around her shoulders, enfolding the baby in his sling on her chest. She knelt to look more closely at the tracks in the snow. Sweet goddess, she'd never cat prints this large. She stood, surveying the woods around her, sniffing. The baby gurgled.

"Yes," Florin said, dryly. "Lion."

She gazed up the slope, following the direction of the tracks. What was a lion doing here? There was precious little prey.

Then she heard the terrible, inhuman scream.

Jax pushed back his hood, hoping the icy wind might freeze away his fears the way it had blown all the snow from the peak. It did not.

Too cold to practice the fairy tune, Jax walked in meditative circles around and around the altar rock. He picked up certain smaller stones and began placing them in the cardinal directions, praying for protection.

He was not, somehow, surprised when Blizzen showed up, muffled to his nose in several layers of wool and fur. The Orange Dragon negligently kicked over one of Jax's little cairns.

Jax looked into Blizzen's ice blue eyes and realized his danger. He pulled on his bit of dragon magic, but it was enmeshed in the work Klaris and the others were doing back in the shelter, practicing the banishment weave yet again.

Jax pulled the magic again, desperately.

"That really is pathetic," Brlizzen scoffed. "Your magic is insufficient, as is your music."

"I appreciate your confidence," Jax said, circling to keep the altar rock between himself and Blizzen.

"Give me the fairy pipe, my lord." Blizzen held out a gloved hand, and Jax felt the force of his magic pulling the pipe from his inner pocket.

He held his hands across his pocket. "Why do you want it?"

"I don't want it," Blizzen knocked over another little cairn. "But I don't want you to have it."

"Because you don't want us to banish the dragons."

Blizzen shrugged. "Give me the pipe."

Jax felt Blizzen's magic tugging at the pipe and then suddenly, horribly, the dragon force was inside him. The bones of his hand cracked and broke.

Again, Jax wrenched his magic, trying to set Blizzen's clothes afire.

The Orange Dragon laughed, took Jax's own force and pressed it further into his veins.

"Stop," Jax gasped, falling to his knees. But the magic did not stop. It roared through his blood, exploding into centers of pain as ribs broke, ligaments snapped, and old wounds erupted.

"My, my, my lord." Blizzen smirked. "You've truly injured almost every part of yourself. He bent down to Jax, who now lay bleeding in the icy gravel, and plucked the fairy pipe from Jax's pocket.

"Why does the dowager want the pipe?" Jax croaked.

"She doesn't even know about the pipe or the banishment. It's just you she wants dead, or nearly so."

The "healing" magic crashed into Jax's face, rebreaking bones. Blood clouded Jax's vision, so he wasn't sure what he saw poised atop the altar rock.

Jax cringed as a terrifying scream broke over his head. Blizzen, screaming himself, reeled away. Jax felt Blizzen's magic rise and build and suddenly disappear.

Jax smeared the blood off his face. A great tawny lion stood above him on the altar rock.

They blinked at each other for a moment while Jax gathered his breath.

"Did you...save me?"

"Maybe."

Jax tried to get up, but his knee wouldn't bend, so he lay back on his side. The cat watched him.

"You're not going to...eat me?"

The cat blinked. "We don't like the taste of princes. Too gamey."

Jax licked blood off his lips. "Who's we?"

No one answered. Jax was alone again with the frigid wind and his failure.

Once again, he had miscalculated the dowager, and this time the cost would be paid not just by an arrogant, idiot of a prince, but perhaps by every creature across the Knownlands.

He moved to cradle the broken arm against his chest and saw something astounding. Blood covered both hands and was running into his eyes. He blinked. His laugh was brief, as broken ribs sent off ripples of stabbing pain.

Florin got to him first. Following the lion tracks up to the summit, she didn't see anyone. She trotted to the eastern side of the rectangular altar rock and almost retched. Blood had splattered on the snow and rocks.

"Jax!" Florin knelt to her friend.

The sea blue eyes opened, and Florin frowned.

"Jax!" Klaris's voice echoed up the slope.

Florin stood. "He's here! Come help."

Lexyl, Halla, and Lad Yob slowed, while Klaris dropped to her knees. "Sweet goddess, Jax, why can't you ever keep your blood inside you?"

"He took the pipe." Jax whispered.

"Took it where? Why?"

He couldn't muster a response.

"Weaver, let's get him back to the shelter," Lad Yob put a hand on Klaris's shoulder.

Helped by Al-Sefir, the Highlord arrived breathing heavily with exertion. "Look," he gasped, pointing to a bloody paw print. "The cat god was here."

"Did the cat god do this to Jax?" Halla looked at the bloody mess.

Al-Sefir pushed the blood-sodden cloak aside and assessed the wounded prince with the eyes of a practiced healer. "This isn't the mauling of a lion."

"No," Jax confirmed breathlessly. "I'm not to his taste."

"Please move aside," Klaris said to the Highlord and Halla. She took Jax's hand and also the priest's.

Jax felt the Mystic weave, and the world tilted. He recognized the room he shared with Klaris and the bed. The priest immediately began removing the bloody clothing from around his wounds, calling down to the others, who returned on foot, to bring him his satchel and prepare hot water and poppy tea.

Klaris sat next to him, probably in the way of the priest, but Jax was glad she was there.

"Why did he do this to you?" she asked.

"Dowager."

"And he took the pipe?"

"He wants the dragons to stay." Breathing was agony; speaking was nearly impossible.

"But the cat god saved you?" Al-Sefir wondered, threading his needle. "Where did Blizzen go?"

As usual, Klaris's mind leapt ahead to the greater question. "Does the banishment require us to use that particular instrument? Could you use your own dragonpipe?"

Jax had neither an answer to her question nor breath to say so. He bit back a groan as the priest's needle stabbed into a gash. Borrel came into the room with a steaming mug of poppy tea and began to spoon it into Jax's mouth. Lad Yob arrived with hot water and white linen bandages. Jax swallowed the tea, and Klaris watched a feral smile form on his face. How could he find a smile in a crisis like this?

"What's funny?" she demanded.

"Look at my hand."

She looked. Al-Sefir had washed away the blood, but the wrist and hand were swollen and purple. It took her a moment to understand.

Then she too smiled and bent to very gently kiss the whole fourth finger.

The poppy was working. Jax couldn't keep his eyes open, and he did not want to. Amid the agony everywhere else, he focused on the warmth of her lips on that restored finger and let go.

The discussion had gone on while four large logs burned to ash in the grate. Still, they had come to no resolution. Now they sat in silence, subdued by the hours of reviewing esoteric magical theory and the stark suffering apparent in Jax's labored breathing upstairs. Florin and Al-Sefir quietly prepared some food that no one wanted to eat; Lexyl moodily nursed her baby; Lad Yob stood like a stone in a henge, staring out the window at the deep, midwinter night.

This morning Klaris had taken her magic to Jax's fractured bones in an attempt to heal him. She could get the bones to straighten, but the breaks did not mend. Wracked as he was by the multiple wounds, Jax still writhed with erotic pleasure of her magic moving within him.

"Sweet goddess, Klaris," he blinked at her, confused and overwhelmed by the mixture of agony and delight.

Al-Sefir had set the straightened bones, sewn up the lacerations and bandaged wounds. But despite all these efforts, it would be weeks before the wounds healed and Jax could draw a breath without pain or use the restored compliment of fingers on his right hand.

Which was where their long debate had run aground. No one wanted to subject Jax to the kind of pain involved in using Dragon force to heal, but he could not play the dragon song on Solstice, only three days away.

Klaris felt the magic two seconds before the fairy queen exploded in glowing color into the shadows of this stalemate. At first the queen said nothing. She floated in the center of the room, turning slowly to survey the silent, sullen group.

"Where's the Paradox? Has he gone to bed already?" the queen asked finally.

"You could say that, your Majesty," Klaris answered dryly.

Raggar rose unsteadily then bowed. "I'm honored to meet your Majesty."

"Naturally." The fairy queen hardly glanced at the man. Instead, she floated to baby Tristan who lay awake in a cradle near the fire. "Hello, Oracle." Her voice was soft and gentle. "May the Holy Mother bless you." A gentle mist of golden sparkles floated from her fingers to drift across the baby.

Tristan cooed.

The fairy queen turned back to Klaris. "You're ready then, Weaver?"

"We had thought so, but we now face an obstacle." Klaris explained how Blizzen had stolen the pipe and wounded Jax.

"Why? Why do such a treacherous thing?" the queen demanded.

Raggar answered, shame in his voice. "He thinks it would be beneficial if the dragons stay and more of their magic remains here."

The queen stared for a moment as if she didn't understand. At last she spoke very slowly. "It comes with a price."

"We know, Ma'am," Raggar said contritely. "We're not willing to sacrifice any creature of the Knownlands to have more Dragon force. It's why we're here."

"Good to know, but not what I meant," the queen snapped. "There is never more or less magic in the Knownlands. The cumulative power is always the same. When Dragon force seeped into the stones here and then into the creatures, other, older indigenous magics weakened." She turned to Klaris. "You know the history, Weaver. The Mystic weave has been waning, as Dragon force has grown in the Knownlands."

"True," Klaris acknowledged.

"And furthermore, Dragon force has been able to increase because the beasts killed so many fairies during the dragon interregnum. Our magic, like our people, was decimated."

Klaris's nimble mind leapt. "So how was I able to access so much more Mystic at my Mastery?"

The queen shrugged. "Caledra fell almost immediately after your Mastery, yes?"

Klaris frowned.

"You now wield all the Mystic of those who perished," the fairy said. "And you will need it. Also, the old Oracle weakens at the end of their millennium, so power moves to other forms." She turned now to the Highlord. "And you. You have lost control of what was yours. That has led to this treachery."

"But there's more Dragon force as the beasts approach, Majesty," Halla argued.

"That's their magic, not yours." The queen's voice was dismissive. "It won't stay here, *if* you banish them. And if you fail, then Dragon force will increase at the cost of the fae and probably Mystic as well."

Raggar dropped his head to his hands. "I have proven to be an unworthy Highlord." He clutched his fingers into his hair. "I should not have seized the high throne. I should have stood aside and let Halla take it."

Halla jumped to her feet. "No. I don't have the strength, Raggar. It wasn't for me, Raggar. Not ever."

"You could have. And I knew it. But I wanted it. I wanted the glory. But now I will have the ignominy I deserve."

"It is too late for remorse," the fairy queen said coldly. "We must solve the problem at hand." She settled for a moment near the fire, thinking. Without warning she began to sing. Her voice was clean and lovely as it moved through the fairy tune. Klaris recognized the words in the ancient language, but the queen didn't seem to be singing words so much as sounds. For her, the melody spoke.

After a few bars the small voice of Tristan joined in. He carried a harmony that amplified the joy, the sorrow, the fulfillment of the song.

"Oh," Raggar sobbed. Indeed, all three Dragons, including Borrel, had tears streaming down their faces. Klaris closed her eyes and swayed in the potent flow of magic.

Upstairs in his dark room, the flow of magic pulled Jax out of his poppy-induced cocoon. He groaned as he felt his wounds and the soul-ache of the song.

The fairy queen seemed to hear him. She stopped singing and Tristan fell silent. Her eyes, violet then blue then green, considered Klaris carefully. Without a word she floated out of the room and up the stairs. She settled on the edge of the bed and shook her head.

Jax swallowed and gathered his voice. "I lost the pipe, your Majesty. I'm sorry."

"You can't play if you can't breathe." Her eyes were hard and her voice almost cruel.

The others crowded into the room.

"Must it be Jax who plays?" Halla asked. "I could play the song." The offer was brave, but her voice trembled.

"You are no paradox," the queen answered. "But I know of four others in the Knownlands who could be."

"Four others?" Klaris asked. "There are four others who are invisible to magic?"

"Of course. You didn't think Javix was the only one? Besides, we had no way of knowing who the Weaver would be, and since the two of you have to align, we must make sure that there are options."

"Can we get one of the other paradoxes here, then?" Lexyl asked. "Since Jax isn't in any shape to play."

"I could get the half-troll here, or the new Cavehart Keller." The fairy queen frowned. "But neither the half-sprite nor Bryx Sharkin—."

"Bryx?" Jax choked. "Bryx is a paradox too?"

"Of course, he is."

"But he is not *aligned* with me," Klaris noted crisply. "Majesty, the Oracle told me that they played the tune last time, but we know that a Weaver tried to banish the dragons first. Why didn't you give her the pipe, or the song, or the Paradox?"

"She did have the pipe," the queen answered softly. "We'd sang the song for her, but she couldn't make any music at all, not with her voice or the instrument. After she was killed, we retrieved the pipe from the peak at tremendous loss of fairy life. We then gave it to the Oracle."

"And the Paradox?"

The queen turned her multi-colored eyes to Jax. "Couldn't be found, of course. The Axterran Oracles had managed the process for so long we forgot to track possible paradoxes. I wasn't going to make that mistake again."

The figures around the bed seemed to waver in Jax's vision. He heard their words but couldn't marshal his own thoughts into any coherence beyond the recognition of pain and the overwhelming sense of failure.

"Your Majesty is quite certain that we must have the Paradox who is aligned with me to play the banishment tune?" Klaris summarized.

"Don't you *hear* the song?" The queen was clearly perplexed. "It's all there."

"I don't hear music with that type of clarity," Klaris snapped. "I can't imagine that any Weaver ever did. We're notoriously unmusical."

The fairy queen's glorious voice sang the heart-rending middle passage of the song. It was the same notes that had particularly stymied Jax's missing finger.

Through the haze of poppy, Jax heard the heartbreak and sacrifice and a powerful, enduring love as the fairy sang.

Klaris shook her head, the music was lovely, but it did not move her heart or her soul.

"I hear it," Jax croaked.

"Good," the queen said rudely. "But how can you play it? You can hardly breathe, and the beasts are just beyond the horizon. I can hear their hearts beat."

"Can we wait?" Jax asked. "Give me a couple of weeks to heal?"

"NO!" roared the queen. "If they're allowed to stay the long night, the banishment will not work. The thing is tenuous enough as it is. If they're allowed to settle, to feed, the dragons will be able to withstand the banishment spell, and it'll be a century before the urge to migrate will give us another chance."

Raggar slumped to his knees next to the bed. Like all of the Dragons, he had heard more than words in the fairy queen's singing. "We will have to heal him," he said in a voice heavy with resignation.

"Heal me?" Jax breathed. "With Dragon force?"

The Highlord would not meet his eyes. "We will blend our force with the Weaver's Mystic, and maybe that will make it better, so that it won't tear so...."

Jax pushed himself up. "No."

Raggar stood up with determination. "I know the horror of what you have been through already, my lord. Believe me, I know."

Jax looked at Klaris. "Can you do that? Cloak the dragon force?"

"I don't know."

Jax licked his split lip. He pulled his gaze away from Klaris and found the fairy queen staring at him, and oddly Tristan was too. He had failed them all. He had ignored his personal problems, thinking them unimportant in the larger issues that faced him, but clearly that had been unwise. So now his only option would be to submit again to the fire of Dragon force tearing through his body.

The fairy queen floated above him, her smile unusually tender. She ran a cold hand along his bruised face. "Our beautiful Javix. I will fetch you my pipe."

Everyone felt the wrench of magic as the queen vanished.

Klaris took Jax's un-bandaged hand. "Sleep tonight, Jax. We'll do it in the morning."

He took a shaky breath. "Alright."

Klaris bent to kiss him softly. "It's not alright."

"Let's pretend it is." He could only manage half a smile.

"What are you doing?" Lexyl wrinkled her nose as she watched the Weaver carefully drawing on her own arm with a thick white paste. The smell of it cleared Lexyl's sinuses.

"I don't know a word for it in Ancient or Landish." Klaris's eyes never left her careful work. "In Farsouth we call it *henna*."

"*Henna*." Lexyl repeated the strange word. She watched in silence for a few minutes as the Weaver traced a scrollwork up one arm and then the other.

"You're copying the banishment spell!"

Klaris glanced up at her then but only briefly. "On Farsouth we use the *henna* for spells without magic. There is power in symbols and in beauty, as you saw within the Cornerstone."

"This part on your foot is flaking off," Lexyl noted.

"The paste comes off, but the design stays stained on the skin."

Indeed, Lexyl could see a white mark on Klaris's black skin where the *henna* had fallen away. The Weaver held out her bare arms and legs and surveyed her work. She pulled at the neck of her dress. "Will you help me?"

Lexyl nodded cautiously.

"I need the last line here, I think." She drew a finger around her neck. "Will you write it?"

Lexyl took up the small bottle with its narrow tip and paused. "You want the fairy symbols, too?"

"Yes. Like this." Klaris pointed to the parchment bearing the copied lines from the Cornerstone.

Lexyl quoted the words as she drew the graceful script in a white pasty necklace on Klaris's black skin: "*Praxis life to lyrics brings.*"

When it was done, Klaris held the bottle up to the light to see how much paste was left within. "I think it would be a good idea to put some on Jax and Tristan."

"You'll be hard pressed to find a whole patch of skin on Jax."

Klaris rose, letting her dress fall back into place over the dried paste. "Where's Tristan?"

"Outside, with Borrel." Lexyl hedged. She wasn't sure she wanted her baby's lovely skin marred with Klaris's smelly stuff.

Klaris considered Lexyl's tone for a moment then started upstairs. Lexyl followed her. They found Jax drugged asleep.

"That's a mercy," Lexyl muttered, as Klaris pulled back the blankets revealing a body wreathed in bandages.

Jax's eyes fluttered a flash of blue as the smell of the *henna* cut through his poppy haze, but he did not wake. Klaris drew four symbols, one each on his left hand, over his heart, on his belly, and at his temple.

Lexyl read the shapes of power and shook her head. "He needs a lot more help than a few ancient runes."

Klaris pulled the blankets back into place and considered the sleeping face. She was not confident that Raggar's proposed entwining of magic would work. Blizzen had said, dismissively, that it was the patient's own life force that caused the pain, as if that somehow excused him from the anguish he caused. She saw the necrosis these justifications left on his soul.

"I can't do it," she whispered. "To put him through the horror of a healing and then offer him up to the dragons. It would be better to go up there alone, like Weaver Seldona did. You take Tristan and the others and—."

She stopped, seeing the fault in her own arguments.

Lexyl pulled her away. "He won't let you go up there without him, even if he is not healed."

Klaris allowed herself to be drawn back down the stairs, acknowledging the truth in Lexly's observation. She would sit with Raggar and Halla tonight and attempt to weave a mask of Mystic around their Dragon force.

But that didn't answer the nagging of her soul. She shook the last of the *henna* in her little bottle and went to find Tristan.

"May I give you some?" she asked the baby.

Tristan waved his pudgy hands. Klaris opened herself to Tristan's clear, unstructured magic, searching for the right sign to draw on him.

"Soul," Tristan suggested.

Goosebumps shivered up Klaris's back, but she nodded reverently. "Yes, Oracle."

Lexyl choked and turned away, while the others watched the white henna stain words of inexorable power on the sweet, tender skin.

31

"Blizzen!" His mother screeched as her son suddenly appeared and fell to the kitchen floor, his shoulder burning and bleeding.

The father came running. "Mother? Blizzen! Oh, my lad! What has happened to you?"

Blizzen slowly sat up. He rubbed his shoulder. "I'm alright, Ma." He pushed her back, his smile tight. He hadn't been sure he would be able to teleport himself all this way. But he'd been inspired to pull on the growing power of the beasts themselves, and sure enough, it had worked.

"The dragons are very close." Shaking, he surveyed the scratch on his shoulder.

"Let me give you some tea." The mother began to gather the kettle.

"No, Ma. I must report to the dowager queen." He pulled the cloak over the wound.

"But you're bleeding." The father looked at the red smears on his own hands that had come from Blizzen's cloak.

"Yes. I will heal myself." Blizzen's voice wavered. "I will do that at my own home."

His parents continued to protest, but Blizzen only allowed them to take his bloody cloak in exchange for a clean one. He walked through the snowy streets of Kree to the better section of town, letting the cold air steel his nerves and calm his mind.

In the privacy of his own room he turned his magic to healing the bloody scratch. His servants, running a hot bath and organizing court attire, cringed at the howls coming from his chamber.

He was still trying to settle himself with deep gulps of rich red wine as his valet fussed with his blond hair. Healing himself had been almost impossible. He congratulated himself on his personal strength in withstanding the hideous pain and wielding Dragon force through it. It had been horrific. Of course, he was sure that he suffered more acutely than a normal patient, as he was both the healer and the healed.

Two hours later, he presented himself to the dowager, and an hour after that he returned to his townhouse a much, much richer man. Glowing with triumph, he was pleased to seek an early bed with an especially enthusiastic Lady Venda. He wanted to be up early the next day to make sure he had time to prepare for the audience with the royal council that the dowager had arranged for him. Certainly a title awaited him: a title more noble and durable than the meretricious one of *Orange Dragon*.

Still, it was a tremendous achievement to walk fully garbed in rich orange silk into the gleaming paneled cabinet that was the heart of Kordish power. The greatest nobles of Kordon rose to greet him: Him! Blizzen Kreeborn, a nobody from the hovels along the edge of town. He wasn't nobody anymore.

"Please take a seat, Dragon Blizzen." The king himself gestured Blizzen to a chair. "We are anxious to hear if the dragons will arrive."

"They will arrive, your Majesty. Most certainly they will arrive within a day or two."

Blizzen didn't notice the ice that sparked in Princess Tallyn's pale eyes as she assessed the undisguised joy in the Orange Dragon's tone. Nor did he sense the reserve that grew within others around the polished table as he related how Prince Javix, the Weaver, and their companions had dallied in the ruins of Axterre, how the Dragon Highlord was rendered impotent, how a nasty, backward people lurked in dry canyons far to the east, and how he was convinced that the dragons would come, and the proposed banishment would surely fail.

The Oracle sat shrunken, shriveled and nearly lost in the large chair that faced the east window and looked out over a sea as gray as the old creature themself. A fire burned in the center of the round room, but its heat didn't reach this chair that faced the brief cold day. The Oracle breathed quietly, their magic fiercely concentrated.

The fairy queen burst into this cold colorless room, scattering rainbows and frustration.

"You were entrusted with the pipe!" she launched into her accusation without preamble.

The opalescent eyes turned very slowly to face the glow of fairy magic. The Oracle smiled. "You feel so good." The voice cracked. "Warm."

The queen moved closer to the small figure in the chair. She stared at them, seeing a baby, a young man, and a lost soul. She remembered her own parents and the great sacrifice each of them had made.

The queen pulled strands of color from the gray room and from the dark ocean. She braided them into a glowing blanket and settled it around the thin shoulders.

"Listen, Oracle," she said softly. "And add your voice when the time comes."

"This voice is nearly gone," they whispered.

"Yes." The queen felt a unique and largely unprecedented surge of empathy. "Yes, but not yet."

She was gone. The eyes turned back to the view and the heaving winter sea. Further back in the room, un-regarded, the priests and priestesses argued in whispers about whether that had been the Weaver or the fairy queen herself, weaving rainbows for a fading Oracle.

All the fires of Dragonsholm had been snuffed. The torches, bonfires, even kitchen fires sat black and cold. Many of the Dragon Magicians that had been pursuing higher studies here had left in the last months to return to their homes across the Knownlands. Others, craving the comfort of their own kind, huddled in the damp huts and wished their Highlord, or their Red or Orange Dragons would send them some direction.

As autumn had turned to the typical rainy Jezellian winter, one Dragon, a tall thin fe-troll, had organized an election to determine their leadership and found herself chosen to rule the remaining magicians.

Her latest decree was now being vehemently argued, and she wondered why she'd agreed to be the Overseeing Dragon in the first place.

"We're tired of cold food!" Old Vikker complained. "Surely we could ask some native Jezellians to cook us some fish."

"Nothing is ever *cold* on Jezel," the fe-troll answered. "Not compared to The Hant."

Vikker opened his mouth to reply and squealed, "Dragons!"

The fairy queen had appeared in the middle of the crowded, humid hut. "I am certainly not a dragon," she drawled, her green and violet eyes moving slowly around the room.

The fe-troll rose and bowed. "Your Majesty, how may we Dragons serve you?"

"Where is the Orange Dragon?"

"We don't know, Ma'am. We've scried for him and the Highlord and our Red Dragon too. None of them can be found."

The queen made an undignified noise. "That's because they're all with the Paradox – or they were."

The fe-troll frowned. "I don't understand."

"I don't expect you to. The Orange Dragon has left the others now." The queen considered the skinny troll and her thin magic.

Powerful enough to deserve to study at Dragonsholm, the fe-troll would never have the capacity to be Highlord or even either Red or Orange Dragon. Still, she would have known this Blizzen idiot, which made scrying so much more simple.

"I want you to scry again for the Orange Dragon." The queen ordered.

The fe-troll pressed her lips together, then answered slowly. "I would be honored to serve your Majesty, but a scry requires fire, and we've established that Dragon force can no longer safely kindle flame."

The fairy queen moved to float next to the troll. A small, rainbow-colored fire suddenly glowed to life in the center ring of the hut. "Find him," she growled.

The fe-troll steadied herself and drew on her magic. The queen, noting the effort and the pathetic flow of the troll's magic, almost despaired, but then a face appeared in her obedient flames. It was a self-satisfied Kordish face, with those pale eyes.

"Where is he?" she hissed.

The image expanded to show a wood-paneled room, long windows letting in snowy light, and a group of nobles whose deep-hued, velvet robes were reflected in a polished, darkwood table.

The queen leaned toward the flames. "Who are they?"

"That's the King of Kordon, your Majesty," offered a gray-haired woman. "And the dowager queen, and lady chancellor, oh and Aychex. In fact, it looks like the whole royal council."

The fire vanished. The fe-troll shuddered as her spell fell to sudden shards. The fairy queen watched the troll gasp and try to regain her composure. She pulled a sparkling gem from thin air and tossed it to the troll. "My thanks."

Four golden sparkles drifted to nothing above the cold black remains of the fire.

"Your bravery, Dragon Blizzen, is astounding," the king concluded, but not as heartily as he might have. The magician was here, safe in Castle Kree on this Darkfest Eve, while Prince Jax must be far off on that strange mountain, bracing himself against the rigors he'd face tomorrow. King Kodill looked down at the document before him. He hadn't been thinking of his nephew Jax last night when his mother presented him with this decree to award the Orange Dragon with a barony and some land in northern Keffex.

"Indeed," the dowager was saying. "We are proud a Kordish subject has achieved so much in Dragon force and performed great services for Kordon in this matter."

"You've certainly seen a great deal of the Knownlands now, Dragon Blizzen," Tallyn said thoughtfully. "I never had the chance to hear Prince Jax's tales of those lands."

"Yes, and our young Javix is still out there, isn't he?" Vobury said.

"Goddess bless him," Earla Stona prayed.

Blizzen was pretty sure that their young Javix was probably well beyond the goddess' salvation. He had, in fact, assured the dowager of that happy situation yesterday. Now he wanted his reward. He'd certainly earned it, suffering through the long journey, the indignity and disrespect, and even his own wounds. He touched his unblemished shoulder and smiled.

"Yes," the king fingered the decree. "We shall ask Priestess Mollish for a special prayer at the Darklighting this evening for our Prince Jax. But now—."

He stopped, gaping.

The fairy queen, all eighteen inches of her glowing rose and gold, floated above the darkwood table. She smiled, and her eyes glowed. "Greetings, your Majesty."

"Bless me!" Vobury breathed.

Clairo choked, his face purple, and fell out of his chair.

"Sweet goddess, Von!" The dowager kicked him. "Get off the floor. It's just a little fairy."

Tallyn had risen and curtseyed. "Not *just* a fairy, I believe."

The fairy queen's smile sharpened. "Very perceptive, Princess. I am the fairy queen. Perhaps I should apologize for making such a sudden appearance." She cast a laconic glance at Duke Von, now gone white, pulling himself back into his chair. "On the other hand, you appear about to reward a thief, and I wonder if Kordon has been complicit in this crime."

"Thief?"

"Crime?"

"Liar!" This last came viciously from Dragon Blizzen.

The fairy queen at last turned to face the Dragon. She floated toward him, menacing despite her beauty and glowing colors.

Blizzen scrambled for his magic, but found it blocked and his body paralyzed. "I am the fairy queen. You are insignificant by comparison."

"Your Majesty." Tallyn's voice was calm but forceful. "We have no knowledge of a theft or any crime. I beg you to enlighten us."

The fairy queen held out her hand. Against his own volition, Blizzen's fingers reached into a deep pocket and withdrew a thin, golden whistle.

"Is that his dragonpipe?" the dowager asked, innocently.

"It is *my* pipe," the fairy answered. "The Oracle has held this instrument since they banished the dragons and ended the interregnum."

"You stole something from the Oracle?" The lady chancellor frowned at the immobile Blizzen.

"No," Blizzen said without moving his lips.

"Indeed, he speaks the truth." The fairy queen held the pipe out so the council could see it. It was half as big as she was herself. "The pipe had been given to the Paradox, who needs it to banish the dragons."

"Isn't Prince Jax the Paradox?" Tallyn asked gently.

"He is."

The pale, clear eyes of Kordish power drilled the Orange Dragon. He said something, but no one could understand.

The fairy queen flicked a finger and freed his mouth.

"I was obeying the dowager!" Blizzen shouted. "She asked me to make sure the half-isle prince suffered. And he did, I swear to you! He did."

"Did you kill him?" Oklan Kora was on his feet.

"No! NO!" Blizzen could move only his mouth. "Of course not."

"What did you do, exactly?" The lady chancellor demanded.

"I just did what the dowager asked. I thought it's what you wanted."

"I did not ask you to steal things, Blizzen," the dowager said dismissively. She shook her beautiful head slowly. "I suppose you couldn't get past your gutter birth and had to rob Javix while you had the opportunity."

"What you took has endangered every creature in the Knownlands," the fairy queen said raising the pipe over her head. "You will not speak, you will not eat, you will not move until either the dragons have gone, or your own life has drained out of you." Again, she flicked a finger.

Blizzen bellowed but had again lost the ability to form words.

"Get him out of here." The dowager pulled a cord on the wall to summon servants who dragged a stiff and inarticulately screaming Orange Dragon from the room.

The members of the royal council resumed their seats, eyeing the fairy queen warily. "I'm sorry," the Duchess of Keffex said softly. "I don't understand. Did Dragon Blizzen commit some kind of treason by harming Prince Javix, or did he simply steal the fairy queen's pipe?"

"You have to decide if his attack on your prince equates to treason." The fairy queen shrugged. "When I saw him, Javix lived yet, but barely. I have extracted my own punishment from Dragon Blizzen for his interference with the banishment process."

"What did Blizzen do to Jax?" Kodill asked.

"He used magic to reopen every wound the prince had ever experienced." The queen spoke dispassionately. "His companions were preparing to heal him." She turned, her lovely eyes fierce. "He is the Paradox. You know magic can't see him."

"Yes, Ma'am," Tallyn confirmed. "We know."

"And he must play this pipe."

The dowager's polished nails tapped a tattoo on the polished table. "Rubbish."

The fairy queen floated toward the old woman. "Do not interfere again."

The room seemed suddenly darker; the fairy queen had gone.

Frinz, Earl of Aychex, leaned his elbows on the table to frown at the dowager. "Ma'am. Ma'am, you asked Dragon Blizzen to attack Prince Jax?"

"Shut up, Frinz." The dowager waved a languid wrist, as if brushing away a fly.

"Sire," Tallyn said in a voice of clear authority. "Sire, I respectfully request a private audience with you and the noble dowager."

The king, questions on his own tongue, realized the awkwardness that the wrong answers would cause. "Yes," he said. "Leave us."

The other members of the royal council filed out of the room, only to stand in a tight knot of speculation outside the shut door.

"We can't give him a traitor's death if he was following the dowager's orders," the lady chancellor shook her head. All their desires for vengeance continued to break on this immutable rock.

"Perhaps we could punish him for attempting to initiate another dragon interregnum," Frinz suggested.

"We have no laws about that."

"Isn't it treason to so endanger Kordon – all the Knownlands?"

"But Blizzen thinks it would be a benefit to have more Dragon force," Earla Stona noted. "*He* thinks he's doing us all a favor."

"It's an issue of magical ethics," the lady chancellor concluded. "We have no authority to render judgment on such a question."

"Who does?" asked Clairo, who was still feeling unsteady.

"The Oracle, of course."

They all remembered the small, eccentric figure that had visited Kree during the Spring Rising. Somehow none of them had any confidence in the Oracle's ability to adjudicate this issue. With vague excuses, they separated to prepare for the Darklighting that opened the Kordish celebrations of Darkfest.

Tallyn had turned away from her grandmother and closed her eyes, struggling to accommodate the truth of the dowager's confessions. It wasn't a surprise. Jax had already told her much of what the dowager now admitted.

But to Tallyn, the woman had always been generous, complimentary, proud and loving. Tallyn had always thought that if the dowager really knew Jax – the way she herself did – the old woman would love him, too. After all, he had many of the traits she clearly admired: quick-witted, politically adept, charming, and beautiful.

"But mother," Kodill sat back in his chair frowning. "He's Valla's son. You see her in him, don't you? I do."

"And I loathe him for it," she growled. "He makes me realize what I lost, what that damn Sharkin Sealord took from me, what that smirky, horrible child stole from me!" She had risen with her voice. "I hate him. He should *suffer*. And suffer again!"

The king sat silent, terrified.

Tallyn rose and wrapped her grandmother in a warm embrace. "He has, my lady. And I fear he will."

"Who are you?" Bryx dropped the brush he was using to groom his stallion and grabbed the bridal to keep the horse from rearing in shock at the glowing creature who sparkled in the dim light of the Kordish Royal Stables.

"Who am I, Sealord? I think you know."

"Fairy Queen."

The fairy glowered at the lack of an honorific. The horse stomped and shied.

"Why are you here, Sealord?"

"I like it here."

Her sparkles darkened to violet, but she held her slim golden pipe out to Bryx. "Can you play this, sire?"

Bryx snorted. "Isn't that what Jax is supposed to do?"

"He is compromised."

"So now you want me to pick up his pieces?" Bryx shook his head. "I don't play, Madam."

"Klaris needs the music from this whistle," the fairy queen offered, shrewdly.

Bryx bent to retrieve the brush from the straw. He stood again smiling. "Perhaps she chose the wrong brother."

The fairy queen tried one more argument. "If you knew that you, perhaps only you, could save the Knownlands from untold devastation and grief by taking this pipe and going with Klaris to banish the dragons, would you?"

"I told you; I don't play."

"It's not a game." The fairy said in a low, dark voice.

"Then why does everyone discard me?" Bryx turned away, and the fairy vanished.

32

J ax awoke with a shudder so violent the whole bed shook.

"Sweet goddess," Klaris mumbled. She sat up slowly, pushing the tangled curls off her face.

Jax didn't respond. He lay staring at the ceiling, his breath shallow, as if he was afraid or unable to fill his lungs.

Klaris used his bit of Dragon force to rekindle the fire and illuminate last night's bit of candle. He felt her use his amputated magic and turned his head away from her.

She pulled the covers up over her shoulders. This close to solstice, the morning was still black, and it would take some time for the fire to warm the small room. Solstice. Tomorrow. Her heart began to thump. She took several deep, steadying breaths then reached out to Jax.

He shuddered again as she touched him.

"Are you in pain?"

"No."

Klaris felt condemned by the flatness of his listless voice. She reached out to him again. This time he controlled the reaction to flinch and swallowed hard to suppress a growing desire to scream.

"Jax? What is it?"

He looked to her at last, amazed she didn't understand. A half an hour can slip away unnoticed, but the half hour he'd endured yesterday might have ruined him forever. For thirty excruciating minutes, Klaris had braided the fire of dragons into his own life force, and despite her efforts to shield him from the pain this naturally caused, the experience had been annihilating. Involuntarily, he shuddered again.

A knock sounded on the door. After a considerate pause, while Klaris unwrapped her arms from around Jax's chest, Lad Yob entered with two steaming mugs.

"Thank you, Laddie." Klaris sat up and wrapped her fingers around the hot mug, hoping it might warm the chill that had settled around her heart.

Jax shook his head to refuse the beverage, but Lad Yob wouldn't let him. "Here, my lord, I'll help you sit up. There. The priest says you'll need this broth to restore your strength.

Jax stared into the mug the Lad had forced into his hand.

Lad Yob went on: "When you're done with that, Al-Sefir will come remove your stitches, since you don't need them anymore."

Jax still gave no sign of comprehension.

Klaris turned to face him. "What is the matter, Jax?"

He could not summon the words to answer her. He felt as if the core of him had been scraped out with sharp knives, leaving him hollow and empty, except for a deep resentment. He shuddered again, spilling the broth.

"My lord, drink it up." Lad Yob found a cloth and dabbed at the stains on the quilt.

Jax obeyed the demand in the Sagehamite's voice. Klaris rose from the bed and went downstairs.

"Has the prince finished the broth?" Al-Sefir asked her. "Is he feeling whole again today?"

Klaris stirred her small bowl of porridge, eating none of it. She looked up at the priest. "I fear that's the problem. He's not whole."

"Is he in pain? Shall I brew more poppy?"

"Poppy won't help." Klaris pushed the bowl away and put her face in her hands. Guilt tore through her.

Al-Sefir watched her with compassion. He couldn't think of what happened yesterday as a healing, although Jax's wounds were now restored.

The priest had prepared the patient for the process. First, he'd given Jax a heavy dose of poppy. When that had taken effect, he'd carefully removed the bandages and splints that he himself had applied. He left the stitches in, not willing to risk any more blood loss. Jax lay on the bed, bruises and wounds exposed, his eyes half open. Al-Sefir settled into a chair at the head of the bed as the three Dragon Magicians summoned their power. Klaris bowed her head and wove the Dragon force into the Mystic. When her green eyes opened and focused on Jax, Al-Sefir felt the prince steel himself. But nothing happened.

"I can't get his life force," Klaris muttered.

"It flows," the Highlord said. "Not strands like Mystic, more like a river."

Klaris's eyes lost their focus. "I see his aura."

"Inside that," Raggar whispered.

Suddenly Jax jerked and gasped.

"Got it!" Klaris crowed.

"Yes, you do," Jax choked.

Al-Sefir was astounded that the prince could feel anything through that dose of poppy.

Klaris's hands hovered over the purple bulges of Jax's broken ribs. The lumps subsided and the bruises faded, but Jax writhed.

"Weaver, I thought you could shield him," Al-Sefir said.

"I'm trying,"

Her hands moved to Jax's wrist. "Try harder," he begged, then grunted as the bones moved.

Reknitting the cracked bones of the hand took a long time. Al-Sefir bathed Jax's sweaty forehead.

"Are you feeling less pain now?" Klaris asked rather plaintively as she moved to heal the torn ligaments in his knee.

"Stop."

"You can't face the dragons like this," Klaris argued.

"Please, stop."

Klaris's cold hands moved with a gentleness that belied the strength of her will as she moved to touch Jax's swollen face.

He was sobbing brokenly by the time they rolled him over to heal the flayed skin on his back. The welts and cuts subsided, but he shook with undeniable suffering.

"Just the last wound here where they burned off the tattoo," Klaris whispered, as she bent towards at the red blister. Jax went limp.

"I've lost it!" Klaris cried. "I've lost his life force."

Al-Sefir, with long healing experience, leapt to action. "He's not breathing." The priest thumped on Jax's newly healed chest.

"Did we use up all his life force?" Halla asked.

"Was that a risk?" Klaris let the Mystic go.

The priest was blowing air into Jax's mouth. "Help me!"

Borrel jumped forward and began to work with Al-Sefir, pumping Jax's chest in time with the priest's exhalations.

"Is he dead?" the Highlord asked. For a long minute no one spoke as the priest and Borrel worked to restart Jax's breathing.

Finally, Jax convulsed, gasped, and coughed.

"Thank the goddess!" Al-Sefir rejoiced.

"Thank the goddess," Klaris repeated, crumpling to the floor, her hands over her face.

Jax breathed heavily and opened his eyes, although he did not appear to see anything.

Florin came into the room. "Is it over? Are you done?"

"Not quite done," Klaris whispered. "We didn't heal that last burn on his collarbone."

Florin looked at the pallor on the faces around her and heard Jax's ragged breaths. "I think you've done enough, to him and to yourselves. Go on downstairs. I'll sit with him." She moved into Al-Sefir's chair, took up the damp cloth, and wiped Jax's face. Klaris fled the room, Florin's gentle, calming whispers replaying in her ears like an indictment.

Later, when Florin came down for dinner, she reported that she'd held him through a number of convulsions. She didn't mention the cold tears that had run down his face. Jax had finally slipped into sleep, but he had not spoken or acknowledged her.

Now, the priest sat on the bench next to Klaris, thinking of his long trek with the Dragon Highlord. He had been awed by the Highlord's commitment to managing his power, even as that became increasingly impossible.

Yesterday, after the healing, Klaris had gone for a long walk in the cold wind, then returned to perform hours of sun salutations. Halla and Borrel sat together playing their dragonpipes all afternoon and into evening, but the Highlord had not joined them. He had sat empty-eyed next to the fire and was there still.

"We should not have done it," Klaris said. "Or we should have done less, just enough to allow him to play the fairy's whistle."

"He'll be weak from blood loss, as well as the ordeal." Al-Sefir suggested an excuse for Jax's distant behavior.

Klaris felt her baby move violently. Unconsciously, she placed a hand on her belly. The joy of that new life could not mitigate her shame or her fear that Jax would never forgive her.

"This goddess-damned banishment is taking everything from us." She said with a sob. She turned to see the broken Highlord and Lexyl, nursing Tristan. "Our hearts and our souls."

"They weren't ours to lose," the Highlord whispered. "Everything is part of the whole."

Jax watched the day brighten and felt as ineffectual as the distant winter sun. He knew he should find the old wooden dragonpipe Doc had given him and practice the damned fairy tune, now that he had all his fingers again, but he felt too listless. The dragons would come tomorrow, and he would climb the peak to face them. In a way it would be a relief to be released from the messy, sticky web of his life. He would no longer have to grovel for favor in Kree, nor watch

Baria flounder under the helm of an incompetent sealord. Perhaps best yet, he wouldn't have to deal with Klaris and her sheer, unimaginable power. He wasn't sure he could negotiate a life with her after what she'd put him through yesterday. His heart ached with that thought.

Another great shudder racked his body.

A small bell twinkled and suddenly the fairy queen floated at the foot of his bed.

"All better, are we?" She smiled, holding her fairy pipe out for him to see. He did not move to take it, so she tossed it onto the bedcovers.

Klaris, having felt the fairy arrive, hurried up the stairs and burst into the room. The others, most of them also recognizing the fairy magic, followed her.

Jax just gazed out the window. He knew what he had to do, and didn't need everyone here talking about it.

The queen rounded on the Weaver. "You've closed his wounds but murdered his spirit!"

"What choice did we have?" she demanded. "Your Majesty."

The fairy floated closer to Jax and waved her hand in front of his face. "Choices? Sweet goddess, have none of you been paying *any* attention?" She snatched the pipe from the bed and played her beautiful tune.

They'd all heard it now an infinite number of times.

"Goddess damn it!" Klaris cried in frustration. "We know how the song goes. Even I hear its power now, but I need words."

The fairy queen stopped playing. Jax shuddered again.

"Master," Tristan said clearly.

Jax laughed softly. "Master," he repeated, finally looking fully at Klaris. "Master of our own destinies."

33

A throbbing drumbeat, low and potent, stirred his blood and other parts of him arose in the night. Deep darkness swathed the world, but the thrumming in his blood grew more powerful. He turned in the bed to find a warm, sleepy Klaris.

The doubts and heartache of yesterday were no match for the compulsion of that beat and the joy of Klaris next to him. He pulled her to him, pushing away her nightgown. She awoke to him fiercely, but he tasted tears in the darkness.

"Will you forgive me?" she whispered.

He paused, his pleasure intense and the aches of yesterday far away. "Anything, Klaris. I'll do anything for you."

"Love me."

"Always."

It was still dark when Klaris went downstairs to begin her sun salutations. Jax got himself out of bed, scratched at three days' worth of whiskers and stretched cautiously. The last unhealed wound on his collarbone stung, and he looked down at the blisters where Felona had burned away the sigil of his birthright so long ago. He resolutely refused to think further about burns and raised his eyes to the window and the darkest day of the year. The Morning Star sparkled in a black sky. He felt both strong and weak, centered and fragmented, resigned and inconsolable. "Damned paradoxes," he muttered.

The throbbing that had woken him so insistently still beat in his blood and he wondered if he could have Klaris again before they had to meet the fate this day held. He turned away from the window.

She'd need the strength of the sun salutations for all the magic she would have to harness today, so he couldn't bother her just now.

Borrel came up with warm water for a shave and his warmest clothes, washed of the blood. "You ready for today?"

"No." Jax lathered his face. "Yes."

Borrel stared at him as he bent over the basin. "Your scars are gone."

Jax paused in his ablutions and considered his arms. Sure enough, his skin was unblemished, marked only by the pale, henna-stained runes Klaris had drawn on him.

Involuntarily he shuddered again. "Yes. I'm all nice and whole." He resume shaving. Borrel heard the sarcasm but had no charity this morning, so he left to hold his baby.

Jax had just finished dressing, but his clothes came off quickly when Klaris returned. The *henna* designs flickered with the firelight on her dark skin.

This time they loved each other slowly, deeply, thoroughly. Afterward, Jax held her close, not wanting to let her go.

"I'm sorry we had to heal you," she said finally, moving away to get dressed.

"It's my fault." He watched her, loving the shape of her, the mess of her hair, her belly bulging with his future.

"It's Blizzen's fault," Klaris said.

"No, I knew he was the dowager's puppet. I always underestimate her."

"Seems to me, that she underestimates you." Klaris dragged a comb through her hair which lifted to frizzled heights.

He pulled on his own clothes again, noting a cold gray line out the window: Dawn. Warm scents of Lad Yob's breakfast preparations wafted up to them. They descended together and stood with the others as Al-Sefir cast a circle and invoked the goddess' blessings for Darkfest. No one seemed able to concentrate on the brief ceremony, and they fell to Lad Yob's meal absently, tasting little.

Jax sat back in his chair and looked around the table. He controlled a shudder as he considered the tension and grief in all of them. "Thank you," he began quietly. "Thank you for coming here, for believing with us that the dragons are coming and that we might be able to stop them. Thank you for taking risks with yourselves, your magics, and for helping heal me. I think you should take the pegasi and seek shelter in Arandy until you know whether or not we're successful today."

"We're staying here, Jax," Florin told him, matter-of-factly.

Klaris rose, considering the faces around her. "Theory into action," she quoted. "It's time."

Jax wrapped the sling for the baby around his shoulders and held out his arms to Lexyl. Tears poured from her eyes that were already swollen from hours of crying. She kissed her baby again and again.

Jax felt tears in his own eyes and saw Halla and Al-Sefir weeping as well. Klaris wasn't crying, but she stood at the door with a look of stark desolation on her face. Jax embraced Lexyl and the child. "He'll always be yours."

"Yes." Tristan said. "Mama."

"Oh," Lexyl gasped, her body shaking with sobs. "My baby. My sweet, sweet baby."

The remembrance of the physical pain of the healing faded to nothing compared to the anguish Jax felt as he pulled the child from his mother's arms.

"Yes," Tristan said again.

Jax had to wipe his own wet face. Lexyl collapsed, howling into Borrel's arms. Cradling the baby, Jax flung an unadorned cloak around his shoulders and followed Klaris into the cold gray morning.

"Goddess bless you!" Al-Sefir called as the door shut behind them.

Within minutes they were at the peak. A few high thin clouds caught the dawn and glowed rose in the pale sky. Klaris set to work. She faced the cardinal points and cast an encircling spell of protection.

"Look." She pointed at a trail of paw prints that also circled the altar. "He was here again."

"Do you hear that?" Jax asked.

"Hear what?" Klaris asked.

"Heartbeats," Tristan said.

Jax nodded. "I've heard it all morning." The steady, seductive, sensual rhythm still warmed his blood.

The orange orb of the sun appeared over the uneven horizon, bathing all of them in gold.

"I don't hear—." Klaris began.

The magic of the Knownlands ripped apart.

A terrible scream cut through the morning air, and something eclipsed the sun.

Jax saw an amazing smile on Klaris's face as she stepped forward. "Goddess," she breathed. "Sweet goddess, what power!"

Jax had gone cold. Hundreds of beasts swarmed in a great cloud coming towards them. Terror froze his blood, but his heart and breath raced. He glanced at Klaris. She stood a step or two in front of him, her face glowing in the dawn light, her eyes rapt as she let the incredible power of the dragons wash over her.

"You're one crazy woman," he muttered.

"Play for them, Jax. Let them hear you." Her smile was so fey and unafraid, he wondered if he really knew her at all. But she'd given him something to do, something to ground him away from the fear that made him want to run, to puke, to scream.

Jax licked his lips and pulled the fairy pipe from his pocket. He hadn't played with his full set of fingers in many long months, but the First Tune burst from the pipe, almost without his participation. The insistent rhythm of the dragons wanted music and matched that tune. Although he couldn't hear them, he felt Halla, Borrel, and the Highlord also recognize the compulsion in the dragons' power and raise their instruments to play in the cabin below. After a few opening bars, Tristan's reedy voice added a harmony to the tune. The music steadied Jax's breathing and calmed him down a bit.

Klaris let herself float on the flow of Dragon force as she watched the cloud of beasts descend toward them out of the rising sun. The cloud grew, splintered, and took color. Hundreds of dragons in a glowing rainbow of hues swirled in the cold, clear air. Jax thought of the leviathans that lurked under the seas. But whereas whales were rounded, these vast creatures were lean and angular. He lost a beat, coughing on the stench as they came closer.

Again, the great scream sliced through the morning, drowning the last notes of the First Tune. Then came the flame.

Long tongues of fire reached toward the peak. Ice became billows of steam, and the odor choked all of them. They felt the heat, but Klaris's magic circle held fast and protected them.

One massive golden dragon dropped out of the sky and landed on the altar rock. It did not seem to see Jax, Klaris, and Tristan beneath the magical shield. Its nostrils flared, and its cold green eyes swept around the peak. A forked tongue delicately licked the dried puddle of Jax's blood. The dragon rumbled.

Other dragons now landed, gathering around the peak. Still, they seemed unable to see the group awaiting them.

Klaris turned to Jax. "They can't see us."

"That's maybe a good thing?"

The dragons' heads lifted at the sound of voices. The beasts looked around.

"Is it your shield?" Jax wondered.

"Shouldn't be. It's not meant to conceal."

Klaris was wondering what would happen if she dropped the shield when Highlord Raggar stumbled up to the peak. He ignored Jax and Klaris, standing together with the baby but flung himself at the base of the altar rock, arms wide, rapture on his face.

"Ahh," the golden dragon blinked, clearly able to see the Highlord.

Raggar met the dragon gaze with a look of ecstasy. "I am with you!" he cried to the great golden beast.

There was a sudden brilliant flash. The Highlord became a streaming pillar of flame that climbed to the flawless sky.

The flock of dragons rose screeching, wheeling and angry. Led by the large golden one, they opened their mouths and poured flame onto the fire that had been Raggar.

Jax felt the magic build and crest like a vast wave. It crashed into the vortex of flame, flattened, drained, dissipated.

The flames died and the dragons settled again to the ground. A few blackened rocks were all that remained of the Highlord. Jax had to gulp to keep his breakfast in his stomach. Tristan wailed.

The golden dragon resumed its place on the altar rock.

Its eyes again swept the peak. It spoke slowly at last in Ancient. "Where are you then, my tasssties? We feel your magic. We sssmell your blood." It paused and licked again at the bloodstained rocks.

The only sound was Tristan's thin keening.

Klaris couldn't contain her curiosity. She stepped out of the circle.

"Dragons," Jax swore. But he couldn't let her face the beasts alone. He followed her two steps forward, out of the sheltering magic.

The golden dragon blinked. "Where did you go? I sssaw you for a moment."

Klaris looked at Jax. She shoved at him, whispering. "Back inside."

"No."

"They can't see me. It's you. It's your invisibility."

"I'm not leaving you."

The dragon sniffed and moved its head toward them. "What are you sssaying? Where did you go?"

Klaris stepped further away from Jax and spoke in Ancient. "I am here, your Majesty."

The dragon reared back. "A fairy! A *giant* fairy!"

Klaris put her hands on her hips and cocked her head to one side. "You've been gone a long time, Majesty. I'm not a fairy."

The dragon lowered its head toward her and sniffed. "No. You are not a fairy." The disappointment was clear, but craft gleamed in the green eye.

"I'm the Weaver."

"Yesss. Sssent to banish us again, are you?"

Klaris smiled. "You've been here before, Majesty?"

The dragon settled itself on the altar rock. "Of courssse. How do you know me?"

"Your royalty is obvious, my Queen."

Jax smirked at the sarcasm in Klaris's tone and marveled that no other creature ever seemed to grasp the extent of Klaris's scholarship.

"Yesss. Bring us a few fairiesss and we'll go."

"Where exactly do you go when you leave here?" Klaris asked.

"The Island of Wavring."

"Baria?"

"What'sss Baria?" The dragon queen sucked her fangs.

"A large island, with mountains and pine forests off the coast to the west."

The golden dragon shook her head. "That island is part of Faelyn. We ate all the fairiesss of that place last time."

"Faelyn," Klaris repeated. "That's your name for this land?" She swept her arms wide.

"Yesss."

"Where is Wavring?"

"Wessst. Far to the Wessst."

"Are there fairies there?" Klaris asked.

"No. Only here."

"Where do you go after Wavring?"

"Holy Mother, Klaris." Jax pleaded softly. "We're not here to talk to them."

The dragon scratched the ground below the altar rock. "Verddent."

"And that is to the west of Wavring?"

"Ssso many questionsss, little Weaver. Lasst time we ate you."

Klaris bowed. "Thank you for your answers, your Majesty. We don't live long, and too often our memories die with us."

"Are you ready then, my tasssty?"

Klaris smiled up at the dragon and spoke in Islish. "Jax, play now."

He was more than ready.

"What?" the dragon demanded, shuddering as the fairy tune rippled through the morning air. "WHAT!" It reared back on its legs, wings flapping violently.

Klaris dashed back to her protective circle, pulling Jax and Tristan with her. "Now, Oracle!" she commanded. "Sing!"

The sweet voice of the baby joined Jax's tune. The dragons were all on their feet now, clawing at the mountain. The Fairy Tune clearly disturbed them. Their restive eyes flashed, and heads swiveled on their long scaly necks, but they couldn't find the source of the music.

Klaris frowned. Something wasn't right. Something was uneven in the flow of spells.

The music was there. Tristan sang. She watched the weaves. Halla and Borrel, both laden with grief, were playing down in the shelter and she wove their power into the banishment. The strands braided together and glowed.

The dragon queen settled down on the altar rock again. Her eyes were half shut, dreamy. The tune came to its end.

Jax blinked at Klaris, who was clearly perplexed. Her confusion did not assuage Jax's fears. He dared a quick glance at the dragons all around them and shuddered, his innards still weak with fear. Tristan pushed at the sling and fretted.

Klaris's mind was flying. The magic was all there, even without Raggar. She'd harnessed Mystic, Dragon, Fae, and Oracle power. And yet the great beasts had not moved.

"Feed usss a fairy, invisible Weaver," the dragon queen said sleepily. "Feed usss a fairy or we'll eat you. Maybe we'll eat you anyway."

Klaris pulled her one trick out of her pocket. She stepped away from the circle and Jax's invisibility, holding a glowing orange crystal to the weak morning light.

"Ahhh," hissed the queen, her eyes finally finding Klaris. "That's mine."

"Play, Jax." Klaris ordered, dashing back behind her magical shield. As the tune began, she threw the crystal to the ground. As it shattered, she gathered the strands of Dragon force to her own weave and pushed against the beasts.

The queen raised her head and screamed to the sky. The other dragons joined the cry. Klaris covered her ears against the terrible sound. Again, the song came to an end. The dragons shifted on the rocks, uneasy, but they did not leave.

"Damn," Klaris swore. She glanced at Tristan, who continued to fret.

Jax absently soothed the child. He knew now what had to happen, but he didn't want to give it voice.

The dragon screamed again and raked the mountain top with foot-long claws.

"Klaris," Jax said with regret. "It's the circle. The shield. There can be no boundaries here."

Tristan looked at him and quoted *"frontiers clear."*

Jax explained, "The banishment only works if we're completely vulnerable. Like love."

Klaris saw the terrible truth in this. She glanced at the dragons. Some of them on the lower slope were starting to blow fire in their direction. Others were sniffing towards the cabin. The sun had climbed to the zenith of the short day. Dragon fire would bake them without the shield, but she had no choice, and yet she did.

"We have to drop the shield, but we'll still be invisible," Jax said, trying to strengthen his own dissolving courage. "We can move around, and they may not be able to direct their fire at us."

"They'll know where we are by the sound of the music." Klaris brutally erased this brief hope.

Jax had no answer. He pulled her close and kissed her. Her belly got in the way, but she wrapped her arms around Jax and Tristan. "Alright. Begin."

The tune started softly, plaintively. Halla and Borrel joined in again and then Tristan too. Klaris aligned the magic and opened the circle.

Earsplitting dragon screams almost drowned out the tune. The beasts leapt to the sky as if the earth burned them. Klaris continued to weave the magic, building the banishment, unfiltered and raw.

The great golden queen reared and took a great breath.

Jax saw her intent and shuffled to the other side of the altar rock, with Klaris's arms still around him. The queen poured a jet of flame onto the place where they'd been standing, and they felt the terrible heat. Klaris's *henna* tattoos glowed, but the fire did not burn them.

Jax continued to play, moving constantly with the babe in the sling and Klaris snug beside him. The dragons roared and blew fire across the peak, but never directly at the three.

The queen gathered her flock and mustered their power with more cohesion, pushing relentlessly against the Mystic with wave after wave of incredible force.

The tune ended. "Keep playing!" Klaris gasped. "Here they come again."

She held the weave, but just barely. Just when she feared her grip would fail, she felt the deep power of Lad Yob threading into the Mystic and Lexyl's ancient form of magic, too.

As the song began a third time, Klaris felt the fairy queen herself lending support to the weave, which was distracting because it tickled Jax and the other Dragon Magicians. She had to lace it carefully into the spell.

More magicians from across the Knownlands added their power to the spell. From Farsouth to Sageham, Mystics joined the Weaver's weave, while every town, village, city, and ship echoed with the sound of the fairy tune, as everyone with a drop of Dragon force in their blood found their dragonpipes and played along. Klaris even felt the low rasp of the ancient Oracle at their temple on Baria adding the last whispers of their power to Tristan's harmonies.

Klaris channeled all that force and focused it. Its depth and breadth awed her. The weave was flawless. But even so, the dragons continued to blast them, and the strands of her spell began to fray.

She continued shuffling alongside Jax in their awkward dance around the mountain peak at the center of the vortex as the threads began to snap. Goddess damn it! She'd done everything and more. She'd adhered, aligned, found the babe and the Cornerstone and the lyrics, and it still wasn't enough. The warp was going to break at any moment.

Again, the song ended. Jax took a deep breath and began again. The beasts roared, flapped their leathern wings and spat searing tongues of flame. The reek of sulfur rasped in Klaris's lungs. The tune moved to what Jax called the bridge. This was the part that had eluded him when he played short-fingered. Klaris listened now. The notes progressed smoothly, and suddenly her heart broke.

She heard the grief of exile, the longing for home, and she thought of her own mother, of the way old Mother Marith looked at Jax when he wasn't watching, of the way Lexyl had howled when Jax took baby Tristan from her.

Her thoughts snagged on the paradox of motherhood, how it came with incomparable power and uncompromising obligation. She shuddered as the underlying warp of her magic tore apart, and she knew that all the power in the Knownlands wouldn't be enough to banish the dragons. It would never be enough.

She turned to look into those sea blue eyes.

Jax knew the weave was failing. He let the pipe drop from his lips. "What can I do? Take whatever you need."

She stared at him. He'd already given everything short of his life, and she understood that he'd give that, too. He'd lost his lands and position in his homelands, offered up his blood, his magic, and his heart.

"Live for me, Jax Sharkin. Play."

The tune began again. Klaris turned back to the magic. She reached through the great hole as her banishment spell began to fly apart and seized the dragons' own magic.

The screeching and the fire stopped abruptly. Jax choked but kept on playing. Tristan's voice soared, his words suddenly more lucid.

With the same ruthless and relentless grip that she'd used to take Jax's magic, Klaris now harnessed the beasts' own vast power to her banishment spell.

The dragons dug their claws deep into the frozen mountain. The golden queen growled and lifted her glittering eyes to the west.

Jax felt the weave strengthen, rebuild as all the magic came together again.

The dragon queen leapt to the sky. The others followed her. The great wingbeats sent rocks and bits of ice to scourge the three standing on the hill, but still they played, sang, and wove the banishment.

The golden dragon sent one last terrible river of flame down onto the peak. "Next time we'll eat you first!" she screamed, wheeling on one wing and setting out after the dropping sun.

Klaris smiled, the *henna* shapes glowing on her arms. "Away, away west! Away, away home!" She echoed the lyrics Tristan had been singing all day as the cloud of dragons flew beyond their sight.

"Don't stop," Klaris warned. "We're not free of them, yet."

So Jax played and Tristan sang and Klaris wove the magic as the cold afternoon slipped toward evening. At last, the sun dropped to touch the earth. They could still feel the dragons' presence and the occasional flare of the beasts' magic, but Klaris kept pushing. The sun had gone from their view atop Dragon Perch Mountain.

In the dark, all three of them shivered with cold and exhaustion, "Play it one more time," Klaris breathed.

Jax began and then, abruptly, the beasts were gone, and their magic vanished from the Knownlands.

Disoriented by the sudden absence, Klaris tried to untangle her spells, but the power tore away from her. The Mystic that had been supple threads and strands began to solidify, like crystals forming in an alchemist's potion. The crystals spread as the magic solidified and fell like bricks.

Klaris fell to her knees, battered, smashed, crushed. She grasped for the threads of the weave that had always twined around her but found none. Blocks of solid magic that would not bend or flow entombed her, suffocating her in icy darkness.

Jax felt Mystic and Dragon force freeze together and heard the dead silence. He caught Klaris as she collapsed to the ground, cradling both her and Tristan against the icy, smashing blocks of magic. He shielded them with his body against the dark and the wall of solid power that weighed down upon them. Somehow, he found laughter bubbling up from his exhaustion. For months he'd thought he'd end up incinerated, but it turned out he was going to simply freeze to death.

34

The flock of dragons flew west from Dragon Perch in a wide "V" that swept across the Knownlands. They appeared briefly in the narrow strip of sky visible from the bottom of Arandy's canyon. Eleeza saw the rainbow-colored flock pass overhead and held her breath. But they flew west and did not return.

"They're gone?" Prina dared to whisper.

"Thank the goddess," Shaman Ashande muttered, relief evident in his voice.

"Thank Lexyl," Eleeza turned away, tears streaming down her cheeks.

A band of Herders shot arrows that rattled against scaly underbellies. One dragon spun negligently on a wing, dropped from the sky and scoured the Herders, horses, bows and all in a deadly jet of fire. The flames caught in the dry grasses and flared away in a widening black swath all the way to the Rysk Sink.

The northern flight of dragons veered among the peaks of the Barthrobar Mountains and out over the unbroken treetops of the Verwood. Two red dragons flew down among the trees, dodging and swerving at breakneck speed among the winter-bare trunks. They screeched to a stop above the ruined henge where the nyad archive had rested for a millennium. But they did not alight. Instead, they flew at tornado speeds around the clearing, screaming in frustration.

The fire they blew did not catch, and finally, baying with frustration, they rose to the sky and sped west.

In Hilsen Vale, Mother Marith stood in the silent, snow-filled holy-grove. The other Darkfest worshipers had returned to their cozy burrows. The magicians among them huddled by Yule fires, still giving their magic, in various forms and strength, to the Weaver's distant spells, but Marith felt compelled to stay in the sacred grove, watching the blue sky darken to purple. The magistrate's young son stomped through the snow to join her. He was only about ten years old, but already he stood eye to eye with the old druid.

"Are dragons really coming, Mother?" he asked, following her gaze to the dusky heavens.

"Look!"

The boy clung to Marith's bony arm as he realized what his orange eyes saw. Six dark shapes soared over Daylor's Peak. One of them dipped to the frozen flat of the lake, but soon resumed its position in the line. A fierce cry echoed among the peaks. Other people stuck cautious heads out of windows and doors.

Dragon shadows slipped over houses and trees and soon the beasts disappeared over the ridge to the west.

After a few moments, the boy spoke again. "Are they gone, do you think?"

Marith blinked into the empty sky. "Almost."

The boy let go of Marith's arm and stared at her for a moment, his face solemn, thoughtful. "Was it your old slave, that naughty half-isle, that made them go?"

"He helped."

"Hum," the boy sounded very much like his father. "It must have been scary to see those dragons up close." His nose wrinkled. "They stink."

Marith shivered in her cloak, her heart aching for Jax.

"I wouldn't have thought a slave would be so brave," the boy continued.

"It's a good thing the Magistrate decided not to whip him," Marith answered softly.

"But he broke the law," the boy argued. "You can't let lawbreakers go off scot-free."

"What's more important, son," Marith asked, turning to walk back to her burrow, "mercy or justice?"

"Justice!"

The old druid nodded. "The trouble with justice is that it isn't always kind. At least mercy is always kind."

The lad followed her, his deep frown foreshadowing the troll he would become. Marith didn't look at him, but she could feel his thoughts churning.

"That's what the goddess wants, isn't it?" the boy said finally. "Kindness."

Marith smiled. It had been a long time since there had been a trollish druid in the Vale. "Come have a bit of Yule cake, and warm yourself before you head home," she offered at the door of her burrow.

The boy hesitated.

"It's chocolate," she said slyly.

"Oh! Thank you, Mam! I will."

The great golden queen herself was the shining point on the front of the "V." She turned that point north beyond the Rocredlands, aiming over the Levenloes, north across the wastes of Ohe and the gray, bare trees in the Y-Gren across Ily. Her powerful, ancient magic tore through the Weaver's spell and she came to earth amid the steaming geysers outside Steppash. The resident trolls cringed inside their walls, few daring to watch the dragon bathe in a turquoise pool of scalding water.

But she splashed only briefly. The Weaver had rewoven the spell that echoed through the dragon queen's head like a migraine.

Impelled by that force, the queen rose with a howl, spraying flame across the already wasted landscape.

A purple dragon, the color of mourning, unable to fight the banishment as effectively as the queen, led a flight of smaller beasts west across Ily. The delectable scent of fairy magic rose to his smoking nostrils. He dipped low, preparing to blast away the bare trees with a gout of flame, but he could not. The banishment pushed him away from the treetops and pressed his sulfuric flames back into his face. Again, and again he dipped and was bounced back.

By the time he and his fellows flew over the Calehold, they were screaming with hunger and frustration. The noise they made terrified the cowering people. Three folk died when their hearts stopped from fear.

"Down!" Corvyd called from his lookout on the castle wall. "They're coming!"

In the damp shadows of a deep storeroom, Zelanne held her daughter and trembled. "Damn, but he was right," she muttered to her mother, who sat listening for sounds of destruction that did not come.

"I hear the dragons!" the child said, her eyes wide and haunted in the flickering candlelight. "Uncle Cory make them go?"

The baroness absently reached a hand to the toddler's dark hair. "Hush, Lannez. Corvyd can't make them go, but he's made sure we're safe."

The purple dragon managed to set fire to a large wooden barn that burned with satisfying towers of orange flame and sent billows of black smoke streaming back to the east, toward the impudent force that kept him from landing and pushed him ever further to the west. The beast did not see the Ilyians rush from their hiding places to douse the flames, nor the upturned face of Lord Corvyd, who paused in his organization of the firefighters to gaze thoughtfully after the fleeing shapes.

Far to the south, a group of dragons followed a fat orange dam-dragon across the fissured deserts. Ancient and crafty, she waited for a pause between the constantly repeating banishment song. In that half-breath, she dropped to the earth upon a collection of colorful nomad tents, setting them all aflame. When she rose again a few seconds later, she carried a screaming camel in her talons, which she ate as she continued to fly south.

The other dragons with her learned the trick and each time the song came to an end, they fell upon whatever hapless creature or settlement lay beneath them. In this way, they scattered the Darkfest celebration in Roadsend and blackened the garden baths of Zeezan, before soaring across the sea to Jezel.

Here the old dam-dragon circled the island, peering intently into the jungle. When the song ended again, she plummeted to the mass of firerock on the island's western slope. She licked the black rock with her forked tongue and raked through it with black claws. When the song began again, she tried to resist its compulsion.

The Dragon Magicians, huddled in their thatched cabanas at Dragonsholm, could not hear Jax Sharkin playing the fairy tune far away at Dragon Perch, but they felt the powerful magic and had grabbed their favorite instruments to join in.

The dam-dragon let herself be drawn into the Dragon Magician's power. This almost allowed her to resist the banishment spell, but not quite. She could hover over the pile of firerock but could not land until the music stopped.

Still, each time there was a break in the singing, she dropped down and dug through the sooty rubble. The dragons with her circled for a while, but less interested in the ancient remains of dragon eggs, they turned their frustrated fire to the circle of thatched huts and the fountain of their own magic, that was so hurtfully turned against them.

When the pause came again, they blasted the huts and the insolent creatures who would presume to use a dragon's magic.

As the Dragon Magicians died in flames, their magic dissipated in the smoke that billowed into the mild tropical sky.

The old dam lifted her head and gave a keening cry. Deprived of the Dragon Magicians' power, she could no longer get close to the ground. As she lifted off the pile of firerock, a gleam of orange among the black caught her eye.

"Ahh!" she cried, even as her leathern wings slowly beat to lift her away. She poured a hot narrow jet of flame toward that small orange gleam. The firerock ignited, glowing orange and sending small blue flames into the tropical air.

With one last cry of anguish or triumph, the orange dam submitted to the banishment and flew with old, wiry strength west towards Wavring.

The "V" turned inside out as the golden queen fought the banishment longer than any of her flock. She watched the other dragons lift their heads for the west and fly off the edge of the land and out over the open water.

But the queen wasn't ready to give up. From the hot pools of Steppash, she lazed through the steam above the Vrillian River to burst into the clear air over The Hant. Curiously, the slushy streets of the town were crowded with people, clinging together and shivering. Swooping lower, the queen noted that none of the creatures in the streets were trolls. But orange, trollish eyes gazed from the relative safety of stone buildings.

Too bad. The queen was hungry, and a fat, fleshy troll would be far more satisfying than the ragged folk stumbling in the streets. Her sharp claw snagged a laggard woman before the banishment spell forced her skyward again to take her stringy meal above the city.

With a roar, she dropped the bloody carcass on the largest building. She climbed higher into the sky and wheeled over the Forest Krill, where more geysers sent satisfying jets of steam into the icy sky.

But a great rock of Mystic thwarted her in that direction, so she banked her wings and flew south, her glittering court of great dragons streaming behind her like flags.

Gellaruth Loup, thrice elected Premier of the Hantland, stepped onto a balcony and watched them go. On the roof above, the shattered remains of someone's slave dripped blood into the rain gutter.

Gellaruth turned to the fe-troll beside her and held out her hand. "Peace then, Velga?"

The opposition leader took the premier's offered hand and shook it. "You were right. Dragons were coming."

"It was that half-isle slave that was right," Gellaruth answered generously. "And your smart idea to release the slaves into the streets to distract the beasts."

"Truth be told, Premier, I learned a thing or two about hostages from that same slave."

Gellaruth turned her orange eyes to the slaves still milling in the streets below. Some were slowly freezing to death in the slushy shadows, while a few hardier fellows were working their way out of the gates, hoping for freedom.

"Better round them up, Sergeant," she said to her adjutant, who lurked in the warmer, safer shadows of the room behind.

"Yes, Premier."

When the adjutant and his troops had left the safety of the First House to gather up the slaves, the premier finally went inside to the radiator and ladled up two steaming mugs of solstice wassail. She handed one to Velga Bladdervork. "That slave-prince fellow wants us to free all the slaves," she said thoughtfully.

"So? Puny southerners don't dictate to trolls."

"No. But he was right about the dragons."

"That half-isle is no more than a hereditary tyrant. He almost drowned my son!"

Gellaruth nodded, as if conceding the point.

Velga continued with vehemence. "But now the dragons have gone and done us little damage, thanks to our slaves!" She tossed down the last of her wassail. "I will return to my family, Premier, and my Party. A blessed Darkfest to you."

"And to you Leader Bladdervork."

The premier's husband entered as the opposition leader haughtily left the First House. He ladled more wassail into Gellaruth's stein and filled one for himself. "You don't usually look so smug after sharing a triumph with the loyal opposition."

Gellaruth sank deep into a chair by the warm radiator and grinned widely. "We'll win the next election."

"How do you know?" He took the chair across from her.

"She's dead set against abolition."

"Many trolls are."

The premier sipped her drink and admired the mark her new cherry-red solstice lipstick left on the stein. "Yes, some trolls are loath to give up the easy habits of having slaves, but the truth is the iron mines are actually more profitable using Barian shipping and paying trollish laborers."

"Really?"

Gellaruth nodded. "Purchasing perishable slaves and paying the overmasters was not economical. And now, I tell you, trolls will wish to show their better nature by rewarding the slaves who risked their lives for us today."

"Ah," the husband slipped out of his clogs and put his stocking-clad feet onto the hot radiator.

One of his own slaves, her cheeks still ruddy from her exposure in the streets under the dragons' wings, entered with a tray of sugared delicacies that he'd purchased from the last Barian ship that had come for iron ore.

He popped a treat into his wide mouth and closed his eyes, savoring the crunchy sweet.

"There are many advantages to opening our trade to Barian shipping," Gellaruth said, her own mouth full of a chili-spiced chocolate. "Our slaves will simply become servants, allowing us to claim the moral high ground."

"I see." The husband smiled, reaching for another candy. "The moral high ground and a stronger economy. All sugared with delightful imports. I, too, see yet another triumph, Premier."

"You *do* know what those are?" Gellaruth frowned as her husband crunched another lozenge-shaped sweet.

"They're some fabulous delicacy from the Nomads, I think." He licked his lips and picked up another one. I've eaten a whole box already today."

"They're cockroaches." Gellaruth told him.

35

The dragon queen flew a zig-zag pattern to the south. The banishment spell would push her west, out to sea, where she'd gather her own will and powerful magic until she could once again swoop over the land.

She ignored Spritely, but one of her consorts snagged a flag-waving sprite out of a tree. The dragon chewed briefly, but spat out the flag pole. The dragons missed Brakkle, being out to sea at that point, but they flew back on land at Foilfield, where they burned a field of winter wheat.

Over the rolling brown hills of Kordon they flew. Patches of snow gleamed in the shadows of copses and on the northern sides of villages and barns. They circled the gray castle of Twistford, the queen sensing something powerful about that place. She was gathering her breath for an attempt to blast the building from high above when she found a small hole in the otherwise inexorable banishment spell.

She forgot about the gray building below and turned south again, drawn by an independent bit of Dragon force that shone through that hole like a focused beam of lantern light on a dark night. The queen's golden wings beat with new vigor.

Dragon Blizzen could not speak or move, but he could collect his considerable power and hold it aloof and away from the rest of Dragon force that had been perfidiously co-opted to banish the beasts.

He lay on the small cot in the round prison at the top of the ancient keep. This was the same cell that had held that traitorous Javix Sharkin and centuries of Kordon's vilest enemies. It was blasphemous that he, the Orange Dragon, should be held here.

He was not alone. He'd been mortified when Princess Tallyn had escorted his parents up the stairs to the traitor's cell.

"He's not chained," Tallyn had explained. "But he can't move. He can't talk."

"Oh, Blizzy!" his mother had cried, falling to her knees to cradle his head. "What have you done?"

Blizzen could only blink his eyes in anger as he listened to Tallyn's flawed answer.

"He tried to thwart the banishment," she said. "We know he attacked Prince Javix, who is working with the Weaver, and the other great magicians of the Knownlands to make the dragons leave."

"Why, Blizzen?" His father frowned down at him. "Why would you harm a prince of Kordon?"

Blizzen's only answer was an inarticulate growl.

"You are not prisoners," Tallyn said gently to his parents. "You may stay here or go, as you like."

The mother held Blizzen's head close to her bosom, in a way that he found humiliating. He growled again.

"You are not our prisoner either, Dragon Blizzen," Tallyn told him. "We understand you were following certain directions. The stairs are not guarded, and this cell is not locked. Please remember that it is the fairy queen who holds you immobile."

"So, he can leave, your Highness?" the father asked.

"That's up to the fairy queen." Tallyn moved to the door. "You may not remove him from here, but if the fairy queen releases him, we will not hold him."

"We'll stay with you, Blizzy," the mother crooned. "We don't understand what ye done or why ye done it, but we'll stay with you."

"As you wish," Tallyn answered. "You may get what you need from the kitchen and see the chamberlain if you have other needs."

"Thank you, your Highness." the father made a clumsy bow.

Unaware of the magic their son was working, Blizzen's parents now sat at the small, round table sharing a glum cup of Darkfest wassail. The endless repetition of a rather mournful tune from the Dragon Magicians in the great hall below did nothing to improve their mood.

Everyone at Castle Kree knew dragons had arrived with the solstice dawn. The people in the kitchen had looked askance at Blizzen's grim parents, not sure whether to pity or fear them.

The two old folks weren't sure how to react themselves. For two days they'd watched their beloved son stare fixedly at the ceiling. Now, dragons were truly flying over the Knownlands, and no one could be safe.

Yet this was what Blizzen had wanted. Their son wasn't a bad lad; he wasn't evil. Surely there must be something that everyone else was missing. It wouldn't be the first time Blizzen's unique and extraordinary power took him beyond what other people understood.

Blizzen's strangled voice gurgled with triumph as something thumped onto the old slate roof of the keep.

"What's that now?" The father looked up, while the mother turned to Blizzen on the bed.

Again, he gurgled.

"Blizzy?"

The roof of the keep ripped open, letting in the cold wind and a shower of broken slates.

"Sweet goddess!" yelled the father, as he saw the massive claws that had lifted the roof.

Sulfuric fumes gagged all three of them. The parents wheezed and coughed. The mother stumbled to Blizzen to shield him.

"Help!" the father screeched as a vast golden head reached into the roofless room. The wide mouth opened, revealing fangs as large as he was. They snapped shut on the father, muffling his scream, but not stopping his kicking legs.

The mother screamed more clearly.

Blizzen blinked.

"Go away!" the mother shouted, lying on top of Blizzen and wrapping her arms around him. "Go away!"

But the dragon did not go. She pulled Blizzen's magic and tried to get her own back from that horrible Weaver.

Perched on the roofless rim of the keep, strengthened by the hot blood of the man she'd swallowed and this well of Dragon force in the prone form on the bed, she fought to rip her own magic from the Weaver's grasp.

But it would not come free. She shook her head to clear it from the ache caused by the wail of music rising from the hall below. That damned tune pushed at her. And the magic of the Knownlands, entwined with her own, aligned against her.

The glittering green eyes turned back to the bed and the deep Dragon force there. Her nostrils smoked and flared. There was fairy magic here, too: fairy magic that imprisoned this little dragon creature and held him.

That was wrong! Fairies fuel dragons! They ought not ever hold a dragon down.

The golden dragon leapt to the sky, gathered her fire and poured all her wrath and frustration onto the round, roofless keep. Her cohort, echoing her anger, added their fires to hers. Flames tore through ancient beams and melted stone.

When Blizzen died, his magic evaporated, and the queen could no longer ignore the compulsion in the banishment spell. She rose with a final terrible scream and fled west into the eye of the setting sun. Her court streamed behind her.

Dusk settled over the smoking mound of melted rock. Heat rose from the pile in shimmering waves, as people emerged from hiding and ran for buckets of cooling water. The water turned to steam as it touched the molten mass.

Sealord Bryx stood at the edge of the great hall with the other nobles and courtiers of Kordon. Behind them, the court's Dragon

Magicians continued to play that damn song, while in front of them they considered the baking ruin that had been the old castle keep.

The sealord stepped away from the king to look out a west-facing window at the last dragon soaring over the sea towards Baria. Bryx didn't think the beasts would harm the Floating Islands, because they'd left them alone the last time. But Valla's Palace might interest them. He could feel the heat still radiating from the ruined keep. Good thing he had a residence here in Kordon.

"Well." The dowager turned away from the wreckage. "Apparently our friend Blizzen was wrong about the dragons, too."

Baria was a deeper shadow in a dark sea as the short solstice day drew to its close. The dragon queen's great wings flapped through the cold air. She felt strong and powerful and indeed, the idea of seeing lovely Wavring was more and more appealing. Faelyn was, after all, damn cold.

Behind her, she sensed the mood of her flock echoing her own desire to find the warmth of Wavring. Faelyn was usually closed to the dragons, anyway. It was only that last time they'd enjoyed such a feast....

Ah, there was the center of power she'd been seeking. She dropped out of the sky like a meteor, slipping through the waves of magic, and came to rest outside a small henge on the headland.

Her flock pecked around the rookery where they'd stayed last time, scratching at the old, ruined buildings, sniffing vainly for the scent of fairy.

The queen faced the white temple that glowed with the last orange light of the day. A small figure shuffled from within. She blinked. How changed they were, after only one cycle! The creature bombilated toward her slowly.

She stepped back, unable to withstand the force of that tune. It shoved and pushed her away from Faelyn and made her homesick for the green peaks and white beaches of Wavring.

But she would not be cowed by this frail sack of bones! She snorted, and a jet of smoke rose from her nostrils. "We meet again," she said, digging her claws into the turf and hoping that that the creature would stop its infernal humming.

The creature bowed but continued to purr that irritating tune.

"Oh, very well," the queen snapped. "You've ssserved your purpossse, little one. Now I will give you the goddesss' blessing that you wishhh."

The Oracle looked up into the dragon's green eyes. It fell silent at last, but the queen felt its power even more keenly.

"We wish you to be gone," the Oracle whispered.

The dragon beat her great wings. "No. Ssspeak to me not asss the Oracle. Another now hasss that voice. Tell me what you want."

"I?" The word came out rusty with disuse.

The sun touched the distant sea and the dragon felt the implacable imperative of the banishment spells.

"Come away with usss. You may be a dragon now and for eternity."

"A dragon?"

The queen rose on her haunches and spread her wings. She was glorious, magnificent, powerful. "A dragon. Come, live forever!"

The Oracle was silent; the orb of sun was half gone below the horizon. A screeching roar rolled across the sea from the north. Focused on their debate, neither the queen nor the Oracle heard the roars or noticed the billows of smoke rising from Haven, the black cloud lit red from fires beneath.

"I," the Oracle said again, testing their own will for the first time in a millennium. "I do not wish to live forever."

"I didn't think you had what it takesss to be immortal," the queen scoffed.

The sun was almost gone. "Farewell, Majesty," the Oracle whispered and began to hum again.

The queen jumped into the sky, wheeled and flew toward the last glowing arc of the sun. Her flock rose from the ruins of Nec and came away from the cloud of destruction over Haven to follow her west.

The small gray figure watched her slowly recede into the rising night.

A priestess finally gathered enough courage to come out of the temple to find the ancient creature swaying in the winter wind.

"Come inside, Oracle," she pleaded, her voice full of both joy and deep concern.

"No." A bony claw patted the priestess' arm gently. "No. I'm going to the Isle of the Apples now."

"No, Oracle! The dragons are gone. You survived! We've all survived!"

The old eyes flashed in the last of the twilight and the priestess realized that they were not gray, but a deep, nyad brown.

"I see my mother," they croaked in wonder. "Mama! Blessed be!"

"Oracle!" the priestess cried. Others came running to her stricken voice, hoping to help. They found her kneeling in the dark, sobbing into an empty gray robe.

36

Lexyl lay flat on the cold stone floor of the shelter, breathing shallowly under the weight of the solidified magic. She couldn't move, but she watched the shadow of Florin stoke the fire.

"They're not dead," the priest's voice came from somewhere that sounded far away.

"Lexyl's eyes are open." Florin stood from the fire.

The priest knelt to the Eldar. "Lady Lexyl? Can you hear me?"

The solid magic still held her down like heavy, cold sand, but Lexyl would not give in. "Water," she whispered.

There was movement again by the fire and Lexyl pushed herself to hands and knees.

"Broth, my lady." The priest handed her a steaming mug.

She sat on the floor, feeling the cold stones beneath her and the frozen magic around her. She closed her eyes and drank. Someone was whimpering. Someone else was groaning. Florin and Al-Sefir whispered, but she couldn't make out the words.

The broth allowed her to move to her resolve. Slowly she rose from the floor, swayed and caught herself on the back of a chair. Her head spun, but she was able at last to survey the room.

Halla was a ball of weeping misery. Borrel, helped to sit by his twin, leaned his back against the sofa and drank from a mug. Lad Yob crawled stiffly on all fours towards the door.

"What are you doing?" the priest asked him. "Take some broth, Laddie."

The Sagehamite was more gray than ever. He jerked his head in a negative. "We must get them."

Lexyl felt as awkward as the lad looked, but at least she was on her feet. "I'm coming," she announced and managed to step to the door.

Lad Yob used the table to pull himself up. Florin helped Borrel.

"Did it work, then?" Florin asked. "All of you just collapsed when the music finally stopped. Are the dragons gone?"

"Gone!" wailed Halla. The priest bent to help her stand and gave her a hug.

Lexyl pulled her cloak around her shoulders, still feeling as if she were moving through thick sand. "My baby."

"We'll need some light," Florin noted, exasperated at the weird slowness and enigmatic answers of the magicians. No one responded.

"Can you make a light, Borrel?" she demanded.

He shook his head. "The magic is stuck. Frozen."

"Well, wait a damn minute, then." Florin deftly prepared two torches and lit them from the fire. She handed one to the priest, who was half carrying Halla towards the door. "Is this a good idea?"

"Tristan," Lexyl said in a voice thin with anguish. "I'm coming."

Slowly, painfully they climbed through the dark to the peak. Florin supported both Lexyl and Borrel. Lad Yob wobbled stiffly behind them, followed by the priest and Halla.

The snow had been scorched away from the peak, leaving the jumbled scree blackened under the clear starry sky.

"Tristan!" Lexyl cried.

"Here's Jax!" Florin raised the torch. Jax lay on the ground, his body sheltering and warming Klaris and Tristan.

"Baby!" Lexyl dove to retrieve her child. "Tristan! Oh, my baby." She rolled Jax's stiff form aside, pulled the child free of the sling, and cradled him to her chest. "You're so cold."

The child squawked and blinked. In the dim light of the torch, Lexyl saw only these wondrous signs of life. "Blessed goddess." She snuggled her cold nose to the warm baby. "Let's get you inside, my little sweet."

She still had to struggle against the stiffened magic, but her heart had thawed at last. The dragons were gone, and her baby still warmed her arms. Borrel wrapped his cloak around all three of them and together they walked slowly back toward the cabin.

Lad Yob silently scooped Klaris up from the ground and lurched after Borrel and Lexyl. Halla fell to the ground near the altar rock. "Raggar," she moaned. The priest bent to comfort her.

"Come on, Jax." Florin pulled at his arm. "You ain't frozen yet, but I'm not going to carry you."

He didn't want to wake from the warm cocoon. The light from her torch burned his eyes, and Florin was insistent: "Come on. Get up. It's too cold to stay out here."

His muscles cracked as she moved him. Ice water flooded through his veins. "D-d-dragons." He shivered.

"No more of those, I guess." Florin put her shoulder beneath his arm to support his numb movements. "You did it. Banished them, right?"

Jax stumbled, barely able to see through the ice on his lashes. "F-f-frozen," he muttered through blue lips.

"Yes, you are nearly."

"The magic," he clarified. "M-m-magic is frozen."

"Oh. That explains why all of you are so stiff and awkward."

"Heavy."

The windows of the cabin twinkled warmly. "Almost there," Florin encouraged. "Al-Sefir!" She turned to yell back up the darkened mountain. "Better get that nyad back inside. We've got one case of hypothermia and don't need any more!"

Jax flinched as the loud voice cracked his cold thoughts.

"You'll thaw," Florin promised him.

"Will the magic?"

"How should I know?" Florin did, however, know how to deal with hypothermia. She wrapped Jax in thick quilts, put his hands and feet in tepid water and forced him to choke down two steaming mugs of broth. Once his violent shivers had stopped, Florin put him to bed next to the Weaver.

Lexyl would not release Tristan. She nursed him and he snuggled contentedly into her and fell asleep.

Lad Yob fretted over Klaris. She'd been sheltered by Jax, so she wasn't hypothermic, but she would not open her eyes. "Drink some broth, Weaver. Please," he begged.

"I am not the Weaver anymore," she whispered. "There's nothing to weave."

The priest had built up all the fires within the cabin and tucked the exhausted Halla, Borrel, Lexyl and Tristan into beds under layers of thick quilts. Lad Yob refused his own bed but wrapped his quilt around himself then sat beside the fire in Jax and Klaris's room and watched the Weaver with immobile gray eyes.

Florin and Al-Sefir sat beside the roaring fire in the great room. Florin ladled steaming Yule wassail into mugs for them.

"The mother's blessing to you, Al-Sefir," Florin raised her mug and mocking tone. "This doesn't feel like victory."

"No." The priest looked into the dark red wassail.

"Did you see the marks on their skin?" Florin frowned.

"Yes." The priest shook his head and the memory of sooty shapes where Klaris had painted the henna runes on Jax and her own skin.

"It doesn't seem fair!" Florin rose and paced before the fire. "They did it, after all! The dragons have gone. There will not be another interregnum."

"True."

"Shouldn't we be celebrating? Dancing? Drinking? Making merry and what not?"

The priest shook his head. "I think we've all had enough music for a while."

Florin emptied her mug. "Fine. I'm going down to check the pegasi." She put a torch to the fire. "Such a ho-hum mumble dum," she groused as the door slammed behind her.

Al-Sefir poured himself more wassail and cast his circle to make his prayers. Comforted by the familiar ritual, he let the deep peace of the solstice flood him and returned it with gratitude. He offered prayers for Raggar's soul and asked for healing for those asleep upstairs.

Leaning back in his chair, he reflected on the Darkfest message of rebirth at the darkest time of the year. He closed his eyes and raised his power to offer one last prayer for the Oracle he had served for so many years. He let that power flow towards that ancient soul whose opalescent gaze had met him tonight from Tristan's sweet baby face.

A cold tickle ran down his spine. Jax rolled over, hoping to stop it. The tickle ran down his arms then up his legs.

He squirmed, coming more fully awake. Sunlight seeped into the warm room. Lad Yob sat in a chair by the bed, his eyes fixed, unblinking on Klaris. She lay on her back, eyes closed, face taut.

Jax sat up and shivered. The cold tickling ran through him. "What is that?" he asked, not expecting an answer.

"Thaw." Klaris said without moving.

Jax looked at the black mark on the back of his hand. He rubbed at it, and the black stain smudged, revealing a glittering golden rune beneath. "Dragons," he mumbled, pulling the comforter up around his shoulders. He didn't know how Klaris could lay so still with the thawing magic scintillating under her skin.

Lad Yob wasn't moving either and appeared to be in some kind of trance. Jax scratched his hair. Reluctantly, he opened himself to the magic. The giant blocks of power had softened, were weeping, melting. The tickling trickle became almost painful. This was not Mystic nor Dragon force. There was another force there too: the force causing the thaw.

"Who's doing that?" he asked.

"Oracle." Klaris answered through tight lips.

Several insistent physical needs compelled Jax to get out of bed. He moved stiffly to the guardrobe and then slowly pulled on some clothes. He wiped the black marks off his skin and frowned at the new golden scars underneath. "I'm going to see about tea," he said.

A blood-stopping scream from the next room made him jump. Klaris's eyes popped open.

Rainbows exploded around the room. Jax fell back onto the bed.

"Well done! Well done!" the fairy queen exulted, clapping her hands. A host of small fairies capered around the room, flipping, singing, and playing wildly discordant tunes on screeching pipes.

The scream echoed again.

"That's Lexyl." Jax stood up again. He felt the fairy magic skirling into the weird new power and was grateful to leave the room.

But he found little relief. Florin had beaten him to the room that Lexyl and Borrel shared. The Eldar was hunched on the floor, her baby clutched to her chest.

"What's wrong?" Florin asked.

"Is he hurt?" Borrel pawed at Lexyl to see the baby.

Lexyl looked up at them, her eyes finally focusing on Jax. "What have you done to him?" she screamed.

Jax backed against the wall. "I feel his magic." Indeed, a powerful, warm force filled the room and overflowed.

"Look at him!" Lexyl cried. "Look!" Her voice cracked.

Jax and Borrel both reached for the child. The blankets fell away, revealing the baby face staring up at them out of gray, opalescent eyes.

"Goddess!" yelped Borrel. "Oh, sweet Tristan!"

Jax took the babe and considered those familiar eyes and the thick warm magic in that small bundle. "Hello, Oracle."

"No!" Lexyl shouted.

"Mama," the Oracle said in a voice so full of peace and compassion that it brought tears to Jax's eyes.

"Oracle!" Al-Sefir came bounding up the stairs. "Oracle! I feel your magic."

The room was too crowded. Jax felt lightheaded from want of food and the exertions of the previous day. He bent to Lexyl, crumpled in misery upon the floor. "He'll always be your child."

Lexyl took the baby and whimpered into his warm soft belly.

"Let's go downstairs and get some food," Jax said to the rest of the group. He turned the priest around and nudged him towards the stairs.

The fairy queen lounged on the sofa wedged between Jax and Klaris. Everyone had eaten and was now relaxing with a third or fourth cup of tea. Lexyl still clutched her baby, and Klaris still sat with eyes closed.

"You should have shielded yourself," the queen chided. "You had to know the magic would solidify as soon as the beasts were banished."

"How were we to know that?" Klaris asked in a voice laden with fatigue.

"It's all in the song." The queen snapped her fingers, and the small golden pipe appeared. She put it to her lips and played the last few bars of the banishment song.

Jax shuddered. The tune carried a memory of searing smoke and terror.

Klaris stiffened, but her eyes did not open. "We don't understand music that way, Majesty. As I have told you."

The queen played the phrase again. "Don't you?"

Jax put his teacup on the floor. "Yes. I hear the thickening, the thuds."

"Of course *you* do." The fairy queen glanced at Klaris's closed eyes and ran a hand down Jax's arm.

"But what now?" Klaris whispered. "The magic is thawing, but it isn't Mystic."

"It isn't Dragon either," Halla said quietly, her face still ravaged by grief.

"Of course not!" The fairy queen shook her head, spreading golden sparkles across both Jax and Klaris. "Fairy Magic and Oracular Magic don't change, but your mortal power always does. Naturally!"

"Naturally." Klaris put a hand over her eyes.

The fairy queen rose from the sofa to float in the middle of the room. "Alright. I came to offer you our congratulations and gratitude. I will take the pipe you played, Prince Javix, to keep it safe until the next time, since the Oracle doesn't yet seem to have enough dexterity to hold onto anything for the next thousand years."

Lexyl whimpered.

The queen bent towards Jax. This movement opened the low-cut front of her gown.

Jax reached for her hand. Her magic tingled against his palm, just as the pipe had. "Tell us with words, Majesty. What happens now?"

She let herself settle onto his lap, her fingers entwining with his. "Now? You've resolved the dichotomies, my friend." Her smile was full of promise. "The Oracle and the Weaver will likely create new ones to last for the next millennium. But you...." She raised soft lips to him. "You might come away with us to rest and recuperate."

"Jax is needed beyond Faery." Klaris's eyes did not open. "The Barians need him. The Kordish need him. He'll go to them."

The queen moved against Jax's chest. "The sealord won't welcome you, and the Kordish will never trust you. Spend some time with the fae and let these petty mortal troubles pass you."

Klaris's eyes finally opened.

Jax released the queen's hand. "Thank you, Majesty, for your offer, but as the Weaver says, I've responsibilities elsewhere."

The queen shrugged and moved to the center of the room. She surveyed the faces around her: tear-stained, grieving, exhausted. "I offer you all congratulations," she repeated petulantly. "And the gratitude of all the fae. Should you – any of you – ever want us," here she turned to offer a blatant wink to Jax. "Want us for anything, you have but to wish it and we shall satisfy any desire that is within our power."

Jax cleared his throat. "It's our pleasure to please, your Majesty."

"It could be more pleasure, Javix Sharkin," the queen laughed and disappeared, leaving the room dark by comparison.

Jax burst out laughing.

"Only if I'm allowed to participate," Klaris muttered.

Jax laughed harder.

He collected himself, stood up and stretched, still amazed that nothing hurt. "The queen's right. We did it. The dragons are gone, and we're still here."

"Raggar is not here," Halla contradicted.

"My baby isn't here," Lexyl moaned.

"Our magic isn't here," Klaris finished.

Jax surveyed his companions, weighing the wounds and scars each bore on his or her body and soul against his own growing sense of jubilation. "But the queen is right," he said again. "We need to recuperate, rejuvenate, and figure out how to live in this new millennium."

Klaris had folded over on herself as the thawing magic moved from a trickle to a flood. "We need healing," she gasped.

Jax moved to the fire, shivering in the wash of cold magic but still smiling. "We'll go to Marith." The decision gave him a sense of relief that warmed him despite the frigid torrent of magic.

"Back to the Vale?" Florin looked up at him with a smile.

"On the pegasi," he answered.

"Today?" The priest rose, ready to begin preparations.

"Tomorrow," Jax decided. "And we'll go to Arandy first."

The small settee was already full with Lexyl and Tristan snuggled between Borrel on one side and Eleeza and Prina on the other, when Lexyl's gray cat jumped up to find his place on her lap.

"I don't know what I will do," Lexyl confessed.

"You'll come back," the cat said.

Prina leapt off the settee with a screech. "Goddess preserve us!"

"She already has," Eleeza said with some asperity. "But I'd rather our pets were less articulate."

"Meow," said the cat.

Borrel chuckled.

Lexyl had stared at the cat through all of this. "But Tristan.... Tristan won't be back."

The cat licked a paw and apparently shrugged. "Someday."

Lexyl shuddered and clutched the baby to her chest.

Prina poured cactus nectar into a small rose-colored glass. "Anyone else?"

"I will," Borrel accepted, and the others nodded.

Lexyl raised her glass with resolution. "To the cat god," she said, still looking at her cat.

He purred.

Eleeza choked but lifted her own glass to the toast.

"That's blasphemy," Prina objected.

"Not anymore," Lexyl tossed off her drink.

Jax awoke alone in the small room he'd shared with Klaris. He lay for a few minutes in the cool, rosy light. The monolithic, immobile magic weighed on his senses, and his bones felt exhausted. He knew that all of them were as confused and exhausted as he was. Resolutely he pushed himself out of the bed, got himself dressed, dared one tiny cup of keffa, and went in search of Klaris.

He found her sitting under a halo of crystal lantern light at the back of the Eldar Scrollroom. The sandstone walls here were honeycombed with thousands of long narrow holes to hold the ancient and forbidden writings of Axterre. Wrapped in a thick woven quilt, her legs splayed wide to give room to her drooping belly, Klaris sat, elbows on the table, her fingers entangled in her messy curls.

"No luck?" Jax asked, sitting beside her.

"Nothing." She wrapped the quilt more tightly about herself. "But that's the story of this entire adventure, isn't it? We seek answers on how to deal with a problem. We ask all the extant authorities, who often wonder why we're even curious. We turn to ancient resources to find only fragments of answers, and sometimes not even that."

"Maybe there's something about this change of magic at Caledra?"

She shook her head doubtfully. "Maybe. Maybe in among the things the Weaver Seldona had in her study. I didn't have time to read all of it." She winced and placed her hands on her belly.

Jax frowned. "The baby?"

"It's getting big and uncomfortable." She took a deep breath. "Sometimes it moves when I'm in a balance pose and it knocks me over."

"Children seem to do that to their parents." Jax answered, thinking of Lexyl.

Klaris began to re-roll the scroll. "I don't think the magic changed the last time the dragons left." She resumed the line of reasoning she'd been following before Jax joined her. "They were banished only nine hundred years ago, and there are numerous documents from that time as well as plenty of structures that were partially destroyed and rebuilt. If Mystic had been new nine hundred years ago, someone would have recorded that in words, *written* words."

"You sensed Mystic in Axterre, didn't you? In the ruins?"

Klaris wiggled her head in a noncommittal way. "Yes, it's Mystic, but weirdly so. Just as Lexyl's magic has a different resonance. I thought it was because the magic was so old, but now I'm beginning to think that it was a previous version of Mystic. It's as if the same idea is expressed in a different language."

Jax rose as Klaris stood to replace the scroll in the carefully labeled lattice work. She reached for the lantern and carried it with her.

"At least it's all thawed now." Jax followed her through the shadows. "That trickling and flooding was damned uncomfortable."

In the bright corridor, Klaris blew out the lantern. "Join me for some sun salutations?" She entered the parlor where the Eldars had often offered them tea.

"Your second round today?" Jax asked.

She took a deep breath, as he also found a mat. "I notice you're not playing your dragonpipe with the others."

"I'm played out."

Moving through the poses, Jax gazed out the window at the huge murals on the vertical canyon wall. An illustrated city rose to the canyon rim then clearly fell to smoking ruins; dragons writhed above a mountain that resembled Dragon Pearch; people danced around one massive menhir under the light of a full moon.

When the salutations were finished, Jax and Klaris lay side by side on their mats. He turned to look at her and grieved for the tears on her cheeks.

"What can I do for you?"

"Forgive me," she whispered. "For taking your magic, for failing to shield you in that healing, for requiring you to be the Paradox that I aligned with."

He cuddled her into his arms. As he did so, the Oracle's medallion slipped out of his shirt to rest between them. "I'd have to forgive you for being yourself," he said. "We were both compelled by the Oracle, by the prophecy."

She sat up and wiped her face with her skirt. "My soul is exhausted, depleted, but yours seems as whole as ever. How is that?"

Halla and Borrel began the First Tune in a room down the hall. Jax shuddered at the sound. "You gave your soul," he said, turning to face her. "I gave my heart."

"Raggar thought they weren't ours to give," she answered softly.

"It felt like they were."

37

"Thank you for the report." Sealord Bryx turned away from his lord admiral to look out at the winter-brown downs of Kordon. He'd go for a nice long ride once this unpleasant interview was over.

"I'm sorry the palace was lost, my lord," Janil offered, some sincerity in his voice. "We all know it was very special to you."

"Yes. Fortunately, I now have this palace."

"Indeed, sir."

Bryx could see that Janil wanted to say more and wondered why the man didn't just spit it out.

"So, the Floating Islands survived. We have great potential in the sugar market between Farsouth and Kree. All seems well," Bryx prompted.

"Sire." Janil faced the wind of what he had to do. "Sire, the people would like to see you."

"Why? They don't love me."

"You're their sealord, sir. The dragons were terrifying. We know the beasts are gone, but at a time like this, the people need to know their ruler cares about them."

Bryx pursed his lips. Janil sounded too much like his goddess-damned brother.

"That's a myth, Admiral. You and the lords and ladies care for the people and the people care for you. I'm just a figurehead, too far above everyone for actual affection to be felt on either side."

Janil sighed. "But you will come, Sire?"

"After the Spring Rising, sure."

"That's *months* away, my lord! The people *do* have feelings for you, just as you have feelings for them."

Bryx thought the lord admiral might be right, but the mutual feeling he shared with his people was contempt.

"Do come sooner," Janil begged. "Come for Candlemas."

"Aye, and blab about promises of the coming spring," Bryx sneered. He actually loved Candlemas the way it was celebrated here in Kree. But if he went to Baria then he'd likely be stuck there until after the Spring Rising. Besides, he hated a winter crossing. The seas were so high and damned cold.

Janil stared at his sealord's back. How could the man be so obtuse? How did he expect to rule a people who never saw him? And how would Janil ever get the sealord to lift his interdiction against pursing the Hantish iron trade if he wouldn't return to Baria to listen to his subjects. The lord admiral had invested heavily in refitting Phlyx's fleet to carry the heavy ore. Sugar wouldn't repay that cost.

He strove for a more compelling argument. Over the sealord's broad shoulder, the lord admiral watched a herd of Kordish horses galloping across the winter-sere fields.

"Your horses, Sire. Many of them actually survived the dragon attack, but your grooms and stable keepers did not. I fear your beasts are in a sorry state. No one knows how to care for them, sir."

"My horses?" Bryx finally turned away from the view. "My stallion? Windwing? Is he at least cared for?"

Janil frowned. "I'm sorry my lord, I don't know one horse from another."

"Very well, Admiral. I will come to Baria. You sail today. I'll follow tomorrow, weather permitting."

Janil bowed himself out. He wasn't nearly done with the trade arrangements he wanted to make with the Kordish, but he could leave Lieutenant Warrix here to carry on those discussions. In fact, if he got his people moving, he could weigh anchor on the evening tide. He stood in the stern of his launch as it was rowed back to the *Sharkin*, admiring the beautiful ship. With a crew well-schooled by old Admiral Hix and the trim finessed by Prince Jax, the great wing-ship could fly. Janil smiled in satisfaction. He could push the *Sharkin* far faster than the lubberly sealord would ever manage the *Drixa*, allowing him at least three days for politicking in Haven before the sealord turned up.

"I expect to be back after the Rising," Bryx told King Kodill and the royal council at the afternoon assizes.

"I quite understand your need to see the devastation the dragons visited upon your realm." Kodill nodded his regal head. "We'll look for you again in a few months, my lord."

Foby saw the look on Tallyn's face. "What?" he asked softly as the sealord took his leave.

"He should have gone to see his people immediately," she answered. "I was wondering what the new lord admiral had said to make him see that."

"New lord admiral." Foby grumbled. "It ought to be Jax."

"Wherever he is."

"There aren't enough pegasi to take all of us," Florin noted as they sat over a typical Eldar dinner of corncakes smothered in a colorful salsa of onions, tomatoes, and fiery orange peppers. The heat of the dish prompted Florin to drink more of the cactus nectar cocktail than was probably good for her.

Jax sipped his own drink. He was cognizant of the mathematics. Only five of them had ridden from Kordon on the pegasi. They'd had two of the flying horses to carry supplies on the trip out. Even without Blizzen, he didn't know how eight of them could fit on seven pegasi.

"I will not go to the mountains with you," Halla said slowly, pushing her uneaten food away. "I feel a call to return to Jezel."

"That's a long walk," Al-Sefir cautioned.

Halla nodded. "I think such a journey would be restorative." She looked around the table with a wan smile. "I don't know if I'll ever have magic again. But without Raggar, I'm the highest-ranking Dragon, or former Dragon. I'll go to Dragonsholm. At least for now."

Klaris fiddled with the last of her food. "Halla," she said cautiously. "Someday we will surely figure out this new magic. When that happens, people will need tutors and places to study. What do you think of creating more centers of learning, maybe places that don't require people to take boats?"

Halla, deep in her grief for all that was lost, only wanted to go home to Dragonsholm. But now she considered Klaris, her bulging belly viscerally connecting her to the future, a future with a different structure to magic and a new connection to the divine.

The nyad nodded. "Yes, Weaver. Those are good ideas. I will be honored to help."

"I am not sure I am Weaver anymore." Klaris admitted. "And I am not sure that such a single hierarchy will serve us if all magic is combined."

"Is it more magic than one person can access?" Lexyl asked, looking at her baby's sweet head.

"Maybe." Klaris admitted. "It's certainly more power than I controlled as Weaver."

"But it is all one," Halla choked on a sob. "Raggar was right."

"He was right," Klaris snapped, "and wrong. The magic is one, but this is not just a matter of perspective. There's an element I'm missing, and I fear...I fear my broken soul can't find it."

No one spoke for a few minutes. Florin poured more cactus nectar into everyone's glass. Halla sniffled. Lexyl rocked her baby.

The priest reached across the table and touched Halla's cold fingers. "I'll come with you. I walked the desert from Seare to Axterre with the Highlord. It will be my honor to walk back with you."

Halla's tears could no longer be withheld. "Thank you."

"We will find you an Eldar to guide you to Roadsend," Lexyl offered.

Jax turned to her. "You'll come with us then, Lexyl, to the Vale?"

"Yes."

Her gray cat leapt into her lap and butted his head against her chest purring loudly.

"That's six of us, plus Tristan," Jax muttered. "We'll have to be sparing with the supplies."

Al-Sefir raised his glass. "Merry meet and merry part and merry meet again."

The others raised their own glasses and drank rather dutifully.

"Not so merry," Florin grumbled into her glass.

Jax bent to put a piece of wood on the fire, but as he did so his eye caught again on the mural on the opposite wall of the canyon. The standing stone, the monolith in the picture, seemed to stare back at him with Lad Yob's face. "Sweet goddess." He blinked, opening the window to see more clearly.

"Brr!" Borrel complained.

Jax stared at the far canyon wall. The face had gone. The menhir stood in the middle of the dance, faceless and silent. He pulled the window closed. "Where's the Lad?"

"He's right here." Klaris motioned to the corner by the fire. "He's been here all along, Jax."

Jax cocked an eyebrow. "My apologies, Lad Yob. I didn't notice you there."

The gray creature barely moved, but his lips twitched in a sketch of a smile. Jax blinked, remembering his vision of a great standing stone featuring the Lad's benevolent face.

"It isn't finished." Jax finally put the piece of wood on the fire.

Klaris looked up at him, her green eyes cloudy.

"The banishment, the cycle, isn't finished," Jax clarified. "There's another step."

"Yes," Klaris agreed firmly. "The step where we get the magic back."

Weak winter sun shone down on the long, frost-sparkled shadows in the plaza outside the speaker's palace.

Hugs and blessings exchanged, Al-Sefir and Halla slowly walked down the canyon, following the Eldar man who served as the watcher in the southern part of the Maze.

Wrapped in soft blankets woven with geometric Eldar designs, Jax and the others mounted the pegasi. Borrel carried Tristan in a sling on his chest. Klaris climbed on her pegasus feeling awkward and heavy, but the beautiful creature seemed unconcerned. Lad Yob's pegasus, however, shook and rocked, trying to settle its stiff rider.

Klaris took one last glance at the mural on the canyon wall and noted the last image that Jax had pointed out to her: people dancing around the standing stone. The laddie didn't appear to note the mural or his pegasus' discomfort, lost as he so often was these days in some kind of internal vision.

"Thank you, Chieftess, and all of the Eldar people for supporting our efforts," Jax was saying graciously. "We could not have banished the dragons without your help."

The Chieftess smiled, despite the pain within her. "We're pleased to have been of assistance. May the sun always grant you his shade, and the...cat god grant you safe journeys."

"I will come back, Eleeza." Lexyl promised. "I will."

The pegasi walked, then trotted, then cantered down the cobbled street. First one then the others jumped into the morning sky, rainbows flashing from the great, iridescent wings.

38

"Your Landish is much more fluent," Marith said, while her gentle druid's hands carefully explored Klaris's distended abdomen.

"It's good to know that I have learned something over the past six months," Klaris grumbled, her eyes closed as Marith probed. "I just wish it was something more useful."

"Surely it's useful to be able to communicate."

"Yes," Klaris conceded. "Like Jax. He's fluent in everything."

Marith rose and pulled Klaris's dress back into place. She thought about the morbid aura surrounding Jax and the deep wounds that dragged him back to his bed every morning. Putting aside those concerns for now, she helped the Weaver sit up on the cot, then sat next to her, still holding the small, cold hand. "You'll be a mother soon, Klaris. That will open yet another way of communicating."

"Just what I need."

"What you need, my girl, is some long, gentle sun salutations and a deep winter meditation."

"Healing," Klaris whispered.

"Aye."

As Jax expected, Marith unobtrusively nudged each of the companions to find activities suited to restoring themselves. Florin strapped on long wooden skis and headed for a solo trip into the white silence of the mountains.

Lexyl joined Klaris in long sessions of sun salutations, stretching and breathing and releasing months of anxiety and heartache.

Borrel took Tristan to Aric's pub, sat by the big roaring fire and played tune after tune.

Tristan learned to crawl and spent hours going around and around Lad Yob, who stood silent and stiff beside a window, moving and speaking only to stop the baby from eating interesting things he found on the floor.

Doc, Adgar, and Dylith continued to treat the Vale residents for the usual winter ailments and occasional frostbite.

Once Jax trailed after the druids, slipping back into his role as their assistant, but it was too awkward to be with Dylith. He let Florin strap a pair of skis onto his boots and spent a few exhausting hours rolling in the soft snow. He went with Borrel to the pub, but the sound of the First Tune nauseated him, and he fled back into the cold winter evening. Refusing to travel the tunnels, he had to wade through waist-deep snow. Still, he meandered among the burrows, taking the longest route home before his stomach would settle.

Marith noted Jax's now unblemished skin. She listened to a long recital of that healing from Borrel and Florin and knew that Jax's invisible wounds were still raw.

"I heard clomping coming from up here." Doc stuck his head up through the trap door into the attic and peered around the gloom, seeing his mother hunched over a pile of stuff covered with an old blanket. "What are you looking for?"

"That old lute. Do you know where you put it?"

"It's out in the stable, I think."

"Ah. We need it." Marith straightened.

Doc retrieved the lute for his mother. She dusted it off and set it on the table. Every meal, someone moved it off the table, and after each meal she put it back.

"I won't play, Marith," Jax said to her one night after dinner as she replaced it on the table.

She shrugged. "Alright."

Petite as she was and heavy with her baby, it was difficult for Klaris to move around outside through the deep drifts of snow. So, between her exercises and meditations, she sat by a window and watched the light play on the surrounding mountains and dance through the falling snow.

Here in Hilsen Vale, there were no archives, no hidden sources of ancient wisdom, no magical resources. She saw dragon-shaped clouds race over the peaks, felt how the life inside her belly was completely its own, and finally stopped trying to grab that slippery sphere of magic.

With surrender came peace.

With peace came gratitude.

With gratitude came joy.

Marith too, had stayed in the cottage, tending the fires and brewing tea, enjoying her own deep winter meditations of stillness and restoration. Thus attuned to the energies in her house, she knew when it was time to take Klaris to the sacred grove. She found the young Weaver crying tears of joy and relief.

"Come, Klaris. Let's go to the holy grove."

Marith helped strap snowshoes onto Klaris's boots. She sent Doc and Jax to fetch Borrel from the pub and settled Tristan into Lexyl's sling. Adgar took Klaris's arm to support her as she waddled through the snowy drifts.

The boughs of the holy-grove pines drooped with the weight of snow. Marith paused for a moment in the circle of pines. She gazed through the trees and across the blinding white expanse of the frozen, snow-covered lake to the Winter Isle. She smiled. All these Islish folk were opening her eyes to different possibilities.

"Follow me," she said.

The others, wearing snowshoes or skis, followed her to the island where one lone pine tree rose toward the blue sky.

Marith wasn't surprised when young Gilbrick Vloggan joined the group, and the arrival of the fairy queen also seemed completely fitting.

"By the Earth that is her body...." Marith began the ritual. The thirteen others followed the familiar forms. Jax felt goosebumps on his skin that had nothing to do with the cold, and everything to do with the satisfied smile on Klaris's face.

Lad Yob stepped to the northern point of the circle. He raised his arms and his hands met in a peak over his head. He radiated strength, purpose, and even pleasure.

"Together," Tristan instructed in Ancient. The others had no trouble understanding and reached out to clasp hands. Power flared around them: oracular, fairy, and the deep abiding forces of the holy mother.

"Oh," Klaris gasped. The weird new magic slithered into her and seemed to inflate her.

Lad Yob appeared to be inflating as well. He was growing before their eyes, his legs widening into one solid mass, his raised arms stretching even higher, all of him solidifying into a great gray granite stone.

"Laddie!" Klaris cried, even as the new magic poured through her.

"Let it go, Weaver," he said, a smile cracking across his gray face. "Blessed be!"

Tears again ran down Klaris's face, cold in the winter air, but she did as the lad had asked. The magic flowed, poured, rushed through her. Lad Yob rose to become a standing stone, towering twenty feet above the earth, which began to shake and tremble as stones moved and rose like the Lad.

Twelve smooth dolmens fanned in a circle from the Lad.

Klaris was laughing. "I get it!" she crowed.

"It's about time," the fairy queen said with a large, congratulatory smile.

One of the dolmans began to writhe and morph and took on the geometric patterns common in Eldar weavings. "That's how it works!" Lexyl clapped her hands. "That's how we use the magic!"

Borrel pulled his dragonpipe from a pocket. He concentrated for a moment and a fire leapt to life in the center of their circle.

"Yes!" Klaris encouraged. "We don't need to grab it anymore or pull on it. We just let it through us."

Jax had sat in the snow with his back against one of the cold standing stones, his hand over his mouth to keep his rising gorge from spewing out. The magic was different, but he shook with the remembered horror as the magic all around him pushed into and through him. He tried to control his shuddering and take pleasure from Klaris's obvious joy, but the nausea would not subside.

"What's wrong?" Klaris asked. "You try it."

"I've had enough of magic."

Klaris frowned then gasped as pain tore through her body. "Ow!"

"You have finally finished," the fairy queen noted.

"Are we finally going to celebrate?" Florin asked, her eyes shining with anticipation.

"I don't think you're quite finished." Marith took Klaris's hand. "Let's get you home and help that baby come out."

Jax pushed himself up off the ground and lumbered through the snow across the frozen lake where he emptied his stomach.

Marith watched him with concern, but her focus now had to be Klaris. "Let's get those snowshoes back on."

"Don't be silly," Klaris gasped. "Hold my hand, Mam." She paused to let another wave of pain grip her and pass.

"Now." Again, the magic swelled and Klaris and Marith vanished.

"Where'd they go?" Gilbrick asked.

"Home," Doc answered. "Home to have that baby."

The fairy queen had followed Jax. She swirled around his head, dropping sparkles into the snow. This did nothing to relieve his dizzy distress.

"If Klaris doesn't please you, you know where to find me." She too vanished, leaving a fading fall of golden sparkles.

"Is anyone going to celebrate?" Florin asked

"Yes!" Borrel took Lexyl's hand. "It's good to have magic back."

"I'd like cakes and ale," Gillbrick piped, following the others across the snow towards the pub.

39

Absorbed in the act of creation, Klaris did not see Jax's anxiety. He held her hand, breathed alongside her, wiped her brow with cool cloths, and resolutely hid his own heart-stopping terror.

Marith was not fooled, but busy with the birth, she said nothing for the moment.

The labor was sharp and intense. Jax thought his own half-hour of "healing" agony was no match for the hours that Klaris endured. Deep in the night Klaris gave a great final push and a baby girl slipped into the world, her islish eyes wide open. After what seemed like a long time, she howled.

"Holy mother," Jax breathed.

"Ah, healthy and beautiful!" Marith quickly wrapped the baby and handed her to Klaris.

Jax kissed Klaris fervently. "Beautiful."

She stared at the tiny, wrinkled baby, agreeing with him. She'd never seen anything so stunning. "What will we name her?"

Jax looked into the baby's face. She blinked back at him: this unlooked-for child who'd already survived so much before ever taking her first breath. And what would her future be? Her mother was the most powerful magician in the Knownlands. But he could give her nothing: maybe Darkwood, if the Kordish gave it back to him, and maybe Lady Admiral of Baria for Bryx's eventual son or daughter, but not if she shared his exile and never learned to sail.

Klaris also watched the baby. "We could name her for your mother."

"Marith," he said softly. "Can we call her Marith?"

Klaris felt tears welling at the implications of this response, which was not what she'd expected. She looked at the precious bald head and whispered, "Marith."

"What?" Mother Marith came across the room with warm wet towels. "Do you need me?"

"Always, it seems," Jax answered.

"Take the baby downstairs," she ordered. "Show her off to Lexyl and Adgar, while I care for Klaris."

"Yes, Mam." Jax smiled, taking the tiny bundle. He bent to kiss the old druid. "Thank you, Mam."

She met his smile. "Thank Klaris."

"You're welcome," Klaris laughed as he covered her face with kisses.

In the early hours of the morning, Jax sat awake with his fears and watched Klaris and Baby Marith sleep. He wondered if his own mother had held him like that on the first night of his life. He wondered if she'd looked at him with the same visceral devotion that shone from Klaris's green eyes when she held the child.

Valla Brondon hadn't died right away. She'd survived his birth by about a week. He didn't know what had gone wrong, but too often he'd heard the dowager blame "Rax's big Barian babies." Little Marith certainly didn't seem large, but Klaris was much smaller than Valla Brondon had been. After all they'd been through, Jax felt as if his heart was made of thin glass, and this sleeping woman could so easily crush it.

He looked up as Marith came quietly into the room. She sat on the arm of his chair and squeezed his shoulder.

"I knew Klaris would survive the dragons," he said quietly. "She has such power and the precedents were all good. But this...."

Marith placed a wrinkled hand on Klaris's forehead and then ran her fingers along the baby's cheek. "All is well here, son."

Jax put his head in his hands. Marith saw tears seeping through his fingers. "Come downstairs with me," she said. There was a familiar firmness in her voice, and Jax followed her with resignation.

The old druid reached into the back of a cupboard and pulled out a dark brown glass bottle. She splashed some of the liquid into two cups and added a little water. "This is Baby Brandy, Jax. I got it a very long time ago off a visitor from Ily." She sniffed the amber liquor and smiled. "We drank it when Mrac was born."

"Mrac?"

"Doc."

Jax swirled the brandy in his cup and recognized the scent of fine, well-crafted liquor.

"We were saving the last of it to toast if Doc had a baby."

Jax looked up at her. "Did Doc and Adgar hope to adopt?"

"The Vale hasn't had an orphan in over twenty years." Marith gave a twisted smile, part proud and part sad. She raised her cup to toast but didn't drink. "Tomorrow we'll ring the bells for your baby and give her name to the world. I wouldn't ever have thought of you as lucky, Jax. But you are."

He shook his head. "I think not. And neither is she. I have nothing to give her. She's heir to nothing."

"You and Klaris have given her life. You've given her a world free from dragons."

"There should be parades and fetes for her birth, Mam. Heralds should be designing a new sigil for her tattoo. She's royal, but because I'm under attainder, she gets nothing. She'll watch her cousins rule three countries of the Knownlands, and no one will even call her *my lady*."

"Toast with me, Jax. Raise the baby brandy to this precious new life. No matter what we call her, she's here with us, and none of those supposed cousins are born yet."

Jax raised his cup at last and touched it softly to Marith's. The brandy was old and mellow. And despite the late hour and heart-wrenching day, he felt surprisingly strong. "We'll name her Marith," he said, looking into the old druid's eyes.

"No, son. Mine is an old Vale name. Not fit for the fine halls where you'll take her."

"I'm not sure where I can take her. Klaris suggested that we name her after my mother, so...."

Marith wrapped him in a deep, motherly hug and let her tears flow freely.

Jax watched with amazed relief as Klaris recovered. With plenty of advice and support from the druids and Lexyl, she settled into motherhood, bolstered and invigorated by the return of her magic. As she sat with the baby during late-night nursings, she'd let the magic flow through and around her, finding joy in both. The new magic was far more powerful than what she'd harnessed as Weaver. It ran through her now with such physical joy, refilling her soul as she used it, rather than depleting it.

Jax resolutely refused to use the magic, even though he could sense each time Klaris did. He learned to breath through the nausea and often sought a private space to shake the residual trauma out of his body. Music, so closely linked to his own amputated force, was unthinkable.

One morning, baby Marith was inconsolable. She wouldn't nurse, didn't want to be rocked, screamed if anyone other than Klaris held her.

Klaris looked at the baby with growing desperation. "What do you want?"

"Can you sing to her?" Mam Marith suggested. "A lullaby?"

"I can't sing," Klaris snapped. "Jax could."

Jax took the baby. He croaked the first line of an Islish lullaby, but the baby just howled even louder.

He handed the child back to Klaris and took the lute from the table. He plucked at the strings and adjusted the tune. The baby continued to wail. Automatically Jax's fingers moved to pick out the First Tune, but he shuddered to a stop. He looked around the room. Klaris walked back and forth trying to soothe the child. Marith appeared busy brewing tea. He took a deep, shaky breath.

Instead of the First Tune, he started with the lullaby. Slowly he found the chords and sang the words in Islish.

The baby hiccupped. She cried some more but finally fell silent, her eyes watching her father.

When the song ended, Jax gently set the lute back on the table and went outside to heave out the contents of his stomach. He heard the baby resume her wailing. Marith came out to him with a cup of peppermint tea.

"This will help," she said.

He drank it down, went back inside, picked up the lute and played lullabies in both Landish and Islish until the baby finally fell asleep.

Klaris put the baby in a bassinet and slumped in one of the wing-backed chairs before the fire. "Thank you, Jax."

He rubbed his hands on his trousers as if his fingers stung. "I'm going to need a lot of peppermint tea to survive fatherhood."

Klaris used her re-found magic to speak to her mother and the people at Sageham. She explained how the new magic worked, and she could feel the other magicians of the Knownlands, both Mystic and Dragon, learn from her example to let the new form of magic work through them.

She had also spoken to Sven Narbonne, the old Oracle's high priest, to Dragon Halla camped in the desert a few days yet out of Seare, and to Carte Serge in Kordon. But she hadn't been able to find any receptive mind at Dragonsholm.

Jax watched her reconnect to her life and wondered if he too could come back from exile. He asked her to get a report from Wexalay in Haven and Cart Serge in Kree on the dragon damage. Her answers inspired him to play something besides lullabies on the lute, but he still refused to play the First Tune. His dragonpipe lay untouched on a bedside table next to the three opaque crystals of the ghost oracle's tears.

Winter still lay deep and silent in Hilsen Vale, but Klaris knew it was time to leave the snow-cocooned comfort and return to her duties as Weaver, or whatever the master of magic should be called now. Those magicians who had been most powerful in the old systems had sensed how she let the new magic support her desires and were again using magic, but Klaris knew she'd need to establish new centers of learning. And she needed to codify and record all that she'd finally learned about the banishment.

She looked down at her baby's sleeping face. Here in the Vale, she'd had plenty of help with motherhood. Lexyl and Jax were both free to help. But Lexyl would stay here while Tristan grew. Aware of Jax's many talents, Klaris knew that the great powers of the Knownlands wouldn't let him languish or give him much time to bathe or rock a baby once they had access to his political acumen. Although he couldn't see a role for himself beyond Darkwood, he agreed with Klaris that it was time to leave the Vale.

"Will your mother come to Kordon again?" Marith asked, holding the baby while Klaris packed her bag.

"Yes."

"Good. You'll want help with an infant."

"Yes," Klaris repeated, hesitation clear in her voice. "But my mother can't stay away from Farsouth for long."

Marith stared at the child. "I don't think I can bear to let you go," she whispered, and Klaris wasn't sure if the old druid was speaking to her or to the baby. "I love the Vale, but Doc and Adgar can take care of the folks here. And Dylith's coming along just fine and young Gilbrick also. If you need help, maybe I can come along to give a hand to little Merry."

"Please do!" Klaris left her bag and came to wrap both druid and baby in a warm hug. "Please, Mam. It will make Jax so happy. And me, too."

Forewarned, Carte Serge had arranged the reception. King Kodill, Crown Princess Tallyn, and the royal council all stood by the roaring fire in the Great Hall to greet the return of the Weaver, Prince Jax, their baby, and the old Hantish druid. Still, everyone was awed as they suddenly appeared on a smooth wave of the new Mystic.

"Ah!" Kodill masked his surprise with regal joviality. "Welcome! Welcome, Weaver, Prince Javix, show us your pretty baby."

The assembled court was making appropriate cooing noises over the baby, but Jax noticed the mound of melted rock that had been the old tower keep. "Majesty, what happened here?"

"The dragons attacked the old keep. We had Dragon Blizzen up there because the fairy queen said he'd tried to thwart your efforts to banish the dragons and she'd immobilized him."

Jax considered the horrible shapes of melted stones and felt a residue of the dragon's power and an odd whiff of heartbreak too. He hadn't thought about what might have happened to Blizzen, but found he was grimly relieved.

Tallyn noted the wolf grin. She offered Jax a glass of hot mulled wine. "We've just heard that one of the big Barian ships has arrived in the harbor. Perhaps the sealord has come to welcome you back."

The wolf smile grew even brighter.

"Prince Javix!" A voice called in accented Landish from down the hall. All eyes turned to see the old Barian Ambassador, Grisham, hobbling through the crowd. "I am so relieved to find you here!"

"Ambassador, I'm happy to see Barian faces."

Grisham shook his gray head. "No, my lord. I bear terrible news from Baria!" Grisham panted as he pushed through the Kordish courtiers. Jax frowned at the pain in the old Barian's voice and noticed Janil of Phlyx dressed in heavy purple following the ambassador.

The Kordish nobles stood aside, respecting the tears on the lined islish face. Grisham took Jax's hand and fell to his knees. "The sealord is dead," he choked. "Long live the sealord."

40

Jax held his baby and stood looking down at Bryx's desk. He'd sought refuge here in the sealord's privy cabinet in this new palace on Kordish ground.

The walls were still plain and the hearth just simple blocks of unadorned marble. There was something incredibly sad about the room. Its unmet aspirations and its loneliness were emphasized by the large portrait of Princess Valla and her young, dark-haired son that hung on the white wall above the desk.

Jax turned away from the painting as he heard someone enter the room. Tallyn didn't speak. She simply put her arms around him, holding baby Marith between their bodies.

Jax finally pulled away and sat down in the big leather chair. The princess took a seat before the fire.

"It's inconceivable," he said at last. "At least, Janil's story is. There were two sealords and one seaqueen assassinated by rivals in the history of Baria, but none has ever been deposed by the people."

"You don't trust Janil?"

Jax shrugged. "I'm not sure. The Barians were frustrated enough to harm me last summer, but I thought when I left to deal with the dragons that we'd united them again."

"Bryx didn't help, you know," Tallyn said gently. "I was surprised he stayed here for weeks after the dragons had been banished, even after we'd heard that they'd destroyed parts of Haven."

"He should have been on Baria."

"Of course."

The baby gurgled in her sleep, and Jax resettled her gently.

"I don't think I can be sealord," he said finally in a voice full of grief.

Tallyn gazed at him, understanding that his reservations had nothing to do with ability. "Perhaps the goddess' former injunctions against liaisons between a sealord and a Weaver are no longer valid."

"She clearly condones the relationship between Klaris and me," Jax agreed, his eyes on the baby who was that proof. "But I think the basic policy is sound. We shouldn't consolidate so much power in just a few hands. Look at all that our little Marith here has to grasp. She's heir to Darkwood – if you're going to restore that to me. And now she's also heir Baria. If something happens to Klaris's brother, she becomes heir to Farsouth. That's too much."

"You're sounding dangerously republican," Tallyn drawled. "Have you seen the amazing sigil that's been designed for your little Marith?"

He shook his head.

Tallyn continued. "You're Earl of Darkwood and sealord. If you can do it, so can she."

"I *can't* do it."

"You find yourself in the same predicament as Bryx." Tallyn leaned back in her chair. "He didn't want to be sealord either."

"Worse. If I'm sealord and also your vassal as Darkwood, I put all Baria under the rule of Kordon."

Tallyn grinned knowingly. The fire crackled. Baby Marith gulped. Jax opened a desk drawer. Well organized trays of pencils, quills, and boxes of ink lay ready for use. In contrast to these tidy supplies for wielding power, stacks of reports with unbroken seals had been shoved into crumpled ruin at the back of the drawer.

"Do you want to give up Darkwood?" Tallyn asked. "The king was all set to give it back to you before Ambassador Grisham interrupted with this bad news."

"It would give me some vindictive pleasure to refuse it," Jax pulled out the crumpled dispatches and shut the drawer, trying to block the physical pain in his chest.

Marith awoke as the papers crackled. She yawned and burped. Jax had to push the papers far from her small fingers.

"Apparently little Marith is more interested in those dispatches than Bryx ever was," Tallyn said, considering the changes in Jax.

Of course, she had to expect this. He had lost everything he'd valued twice now: first when he was sent to slavery, and again when Sealord Bryx exiled him and King Kodill took the Darkwood from him, even as he was compelled by the Oracle to face down the greatest threat the Knownlands would see in a millennium.

The golden runes that marked his hand and temple, burned into his skin by the dragons were a small outward sign of far deeper marks he'd bear for the rest of his life. Now he also held something far more dear than privilege and title.

He'd been a harder man when he returned from slavery. She'd watched him channel his youthful impertinent attitude into political craft as he negotiated his conflicting responsibilities to the Oracle, the Barians, and the Kordish. The betrayal he must have felt when the sealord exiled him and the king took Darkwood had hurt him as deeply as any trollish lash. But he won those battles.

She watched him quietly play with the baby's little fingers and decided that Jax Sharkin had grown to be rather terrifying. She'd already heard her ladies calling him Jax the Unscarred, because the scars he'd brought back from his years as a slave had disappeared. Everyone had listened to the whole harrowing tale of the banishment, including the horror Blizzen had inflicted upon Jax. Tallyn had uneasily watched her grandmother smirk during that part of the story.

Jax the Unscarred. Tallyn felt that the name was aptly paradoxical. The outward marks of Jax's years as a slave had been erased, but the smooth appearance belied the truth of who her cousin had become. She watched him confront his grief in this uncomfortable room, while soothing a tiny baby with a gentleness and a joy made all the more poignant by Bryx's tragedy.

"I'll keep Darkwood." He glanced up at her. "My liege." The old, cocky smile flashed.

Some things, Tallyn thought, smiling back, hadn't changed.

Jax refused Klaris's offer to teleport them all directly to Baria, explaining it was more fitting for him to arrive in the *Sharkin*.

"Majesty!" Captain Blanx knelt to him as he climbed aboard. The line of officers followed Blanx's example. Jax saw welcoming smiles on a number of faces. And relief.

"Hip, hip, hooray!" shouted the crew. "Hip, hip, hooray!"

"Thank you," Jax acknowledged their pleasure at having him back.

"May I show you and the Weaver to your stateroom, Sire?" Lieutenant Warrix asked politely with a huge grin.

"Yes, Lieutenant." The lord admiral had the big cabin on the *Sharkin*, but a beautiful stateroom was always reserved for the seal-ord or seaqueen.

Kordon slipped into the darkness behind them as they sailed over the horizon and through the night. A small brazier cast only furtive warmth into the cabin. Jax snuggled into the rocking bed next to Klaris and the baby.

"Freezing," she mumbled. "I'm not sure Marith will sleep with such pitching."

"She's sick, poor thing." Jax wrapped his arms around Klaris and the baby.

"I was thinking about little Merry," Klaris clarified. "I'm sorry Mam Marith isn't doing well. Maybe you should have let me use the magic to send her to Baria."

"Yes, that would have been better." He looked into the baby's bright, sea blue eyes. "Little Merry likes the rocking, though."

The ship worked through the heavy winter sea, creaking and splashing. He smiled with pleasure, loving the way the bed moved. He settled the baby onto his chest. "Hear the ship sing?" he asked her. "Listen, Merry...." After a few minutes he began to sing a lullaby in time with the movement of the boat and the swaying cot, and neither of them was nauseous.

Klaris closed her eyes. Merry blinked at him in the light of one last candle. He let it burn, still unready to let magic flow through him again. He sang a few more verses until he was sure the baby slept as soundly as her mother. But he, thinking of what a failure his generation of Sharkins had been, didn't sleep until much, much later.

The door shut after the prisoners had been escorted out under heavy guard. Jax leaned back in his chair and considered the assembled nobles who faced him uneasily.

"Do you believe them?" Jax turned an opaque gaze on Janil.

The lord admiral shrugged. "I do, Majesty."

Jax didn't answer right away, but his sea blue gaze swept them all. Once he thought he knew them well, these lords and ladies of the Floating Islands. Now, he wasn't so sure. Had one of them, or maybe more, conspired to murder their sealord?

He reviewed the facts of Bryx's murder as they'd been presented and shook his head in some amazement. Since Valla's Palace had been destroyed, Bryx had been forced to stay at the Cabyn on Helm, but he'd gone each day to the Barian mainland to care for his Kordish horses, spending hours there, overseeing the rebuilding of the corrals and stables.

The people apparently Litly felt slighted, because he'd spent no time checking on them. The impression of disregard rankled and grieved, and eventually angered a few so intensely that a small group of them attacked the sealord as he made his way back to Helm one evening after tending to his horses.

Maybe they hadn't meant to actually kill him. Maybe they thought he'd survive being tossed into the cold winter sea. But his heavy furs and leather riding clothes dragged him under, and he hadn't come up, until they fished him out, blue and quite dead.

Goddess, of all the horrible ways for Bryx to go. Drowning would be the worst for the land-loving sealord.

Jax went to the balcony windows. In the plaza below, a crowd huddled in the cold. Someone saw him at the window.

"Let them go!" she shouted. "Let them go!"

The crowd took up the chant.

Jax turned back to the room. "How often did you feed the shark while I was away?"

"The sealord ordered four executions, Sire," Esmee answered.

"Four incidents of treason, just since last summer?" Jax returned to his chair and sat down.

Lady Villar shrugged. "It all started with the execution of Dury Axian. Sealord Bryx thought the people enjoyed the spectacle."

"And you agreed?" Jax gestured to include the assembled nobles.

No one answered. They could all hear the shouting crowd in the plaza.

"No," Neben finally spoke softly. "No, Jax, we did not agree. But Bryx was implacable."

"If you, the most powerful people in Haven, don't speak up, who will?" Jax demanded.

Again no one answered.

"Alright," Jax continued. "What about these six prisoners who killed our sealord. Do they deserve the traitor's death?"

"Yes," said Villiar.

"Yes," agreed Janil.

Koralixa was nodding.

"They broke our fundamental social construct," Neben argued. "We can't kill each other, certainly not our ruler."

Jax turned his gaze on old Esmee.

"Justice is not always easy," she said gently.

"These people are asking for mercy," Jax noted. "Do we give them justice instead?"

"It's not about us, Sire." Esmee noted. "It's about you."

Jax cocked an eyebrow, thoughtfully. He turned to Janil and, ignoring the chanting crowd outside, changed the subject. "Thank you, Lord Janil, for taking on the fleet responsibilities as lord admiral."

Janil bowed. "I but did my duty, Sire."

"Would you prefer to return to the Phlyx fleet then?" Jax asked.

"Aye, if you'll let us pursue the Hantish Iron trade."

"Sealord Bryx forbade it after Hix was lost?"

"He did."

Missing old Papa Bear, Jax took a deep breath. "You may trade with the trolls as long as you continue to verify that they use no slaves in the iron mines."

Janil bowed and smiled. "But it will be years before Princess Marith can be the Lady Admiral."

"Indeed." Jax smiled with such warmth that Janil was confused. It would be tricky shoals to be lord admiral to Sealord Jax: the man never said half of what he was thinking.

In fact, he was changing the subject again, turning to the Lord of Rillt. "Neben, everything is prepared for the coronation?"

"Aye, my lord." Neben's own smile was friendly. "Your staff here has it prepared for two days from now."

"Thank you. Then tomorrow we will deal with the assassins."

The lords and ladies of the Floating Islands gathered again in the reception room on Helm, whispering among themselves. They knew that Prince Jax had held meetings that morning with the burghmasters, followed by a long session with Captain Blanx and the Royal Barian Cartographer. Not even Neben seemed to know what the new Sealord was thinking, and that made them all nervous.

Jax waited in a small cabinet room, watching from behind a closed curtain as the crowd gathered, the nobles assembled, and the prisoners were brought forth amid shouts and curses.

He remembered Dury and thought about what happened when the wrong people took initiative. But someone had to. He turned away from the window. Klaris and baby Marith waited for him. "It's time."

Followed by Klaris, holding the baby, he left the small cabinet, crossed the reception room to the bows of the nobles, and opened the door to the balcony above the crowd.

"I greet you, people of Baria," he started formally. "We all want a Baria that is prosperous and safe for our children. As a people, we share the abundance of the sea and the wind. We know that everyone on a ship shares responsibility for a successful voyage. I recognize that crosscurrents have vexed us, impoverished and challenged us. We will not weather this storm by fighting amongst ourselves. We can change course, we can try new designs, but we will not succeed through violence or disrespect."

"We got what we wanted!" shouted one of the prisoners who was being held on the quay. "We got you as sealord!"

"Feed the shark!" Someone else in the crowd bellowed.

"Let them go!" Another voice yelled.

Jax raised his hands. "For generations the Sharkins have had both the privilege and the responsibility of holding the Helm for Baria. Some of us might be better at it than others. But murder is forbidden by the goddess, and the murder of a sealord must be punished."

He paused. Everyone waited in silence. He looked at his people, noted the worn cloaks against the late winter wind, the children clinging to parents, the merchants standing in the back. When he finally spoke, his voice was low. "We seek justice, but we also strive for mercy. Baria will no longer feed the shark."

A murmur ran through the crowd. One of the prisoners fell to his knees, trembling with relief.

Jax pointed at the prisoners. "By your own actions, you forfeit your place on the Barian ship. You are hereby banished to Rockagle Island to live in exile for rest of your days."

The guards dragged the prisoners away, but one repeated her claim: "We got what we wanted!" she shouted. "What everyone wanted!"

The pounding started slowly, but soon grew to a thunderous roar and the islish of Baria stomped their feet in their traditional form of applause.

Jax turned back to the room to face his nobles, who recognized a full force Sharkin wolf grin on his face as he strode through them and left the reception room.

"Was anyone expecting that?" Neben asked.

"Hard to know which tack he's going to take," Janil complained.

"Did you notice that smile as he walked out of here?" Viller swirled into her cloak. "Shades of Sharkins past."

Old Lady Esmee laughed gently, and slipped her arm around Lord Fellix, who she'd grown up with and who now had tears on his cheeks. "He reminded me of Seaqueen Pyrriv today."

"Unconventional," Fellix noted.

"Come have a glass of seaspirit, with me." Esmee said. "We'll toast to her, and you, and your grandson, too."

Chilled and drained, Jax returned from a long visit to the sanctuary where a new golden plaque now adorned the wall of Sharkin dead. He found Marith rocking the baby and Klaris at a writing desk sharing the warmth of his privy cabinet. All three of them looked at him with some exasperation.

"Do you know what you're doing?" Marith held the baby on her lap and rocked rather vigorously.

"Theoretically," Jax said tiredly.

"Some warm wine, please Bolo," he said, handing his cloak to the servant.

"Yes, sire."

"Sire," Marith repeated the Islish word.

"Sire," Klaris echoed.

"Master," Jax raised his goblet of wine to her with a cheeky grin. "Isn't this what masters do? Turn theory to action?"

"You are implacable," Klaris snapped.

"I learned that from you."

"You learned it from destiny," she argued.

"Destiny is an implacable master."

Mother Ayslic invoked the goddess and initiated the ancient coronation ritual. Jax stood at the head of Helm's Great Hall. Golden light from vast stained-glass windows streamed into the room and burnished his fair, anomalous hair. Next to him, Klaris stood with the baby Marith asleep in her arms.

Jax noted Klaris's well-hidden tension.

She watched the Barian nobles approach one by one to pledge their loyalty to Javix Sharkin. Jax had a word for each of them, letting each know that he recognized them and making each feel somehow special. Klaris couldn't even keep the lords and ladies of the Floating Islands straight, much less the rest of the privileged population of Baria.

Finally, the procession of nobles, merchants, magicians, and priests ended. Jax took the baby from Klaris. The child awoke and squawked. Jax patted her back and she settled into him comfortably.

Mother Ayslic approached Jax holding the Drixa Crown, the most formal and ancient of all the Barian royal relics. Encrusted with sapphires and aquamarines, the crown gleamed like the summer sea in the gold-filtered sunlight streaming into the Great Hall.

Jax's heart pounded. He'd seen that crown only on the gravest of state occasions, and never on Bryx's head.

He knelt, facing the crowd of Barians.

Ayslic lifted the crown. "Holy Mother! We ask that this reign be long and blessed!"

As she lowered the flashing symbol, Jax lifted baby Marith.

The crown slipped over the baby. Before Ayslic could react Jax stood and lifted the child and the crown in his arms. "Long live Seaqueen Marith!"

The nobles gaped. Someone laughed softly.

Jax surveyed the people. "I cannot be sealord," he explained. "I'm allied with the Weaver, and I hold a fief under the King of Kordon. I will be Lord Admiral and Regent of Baria until Seaqueen Marith achieves her captaincy and her majority."

For a moment the throng breathed in silence. "Long live Seaqueen Marith!" a voice shouted. Others took up the chorus. Jax smiled at the heartiness of the cheers.

An hour later as the band played yet another Barian stomp reel, Janil of Phlyx slid up to Jax and clinked his glass. "I'll miss sailing the *Sharkin*, my Lord Admiral," he admitted. "But I won't miss the Admiralty."

"That's very gracious of you."

"Apparently that assassin didn't get what she wanted after all," Janil mused.

Jax's grin was friendly. "I'm glad you noticed."

Klaris sat in the new hall in Caledra surrounded by the magicians, both Mystic and Dragon, who would be the tutors for the new magic. Halla held the baby seaqueen on her lap.

"I will speak in Landish," Klaris began, "because that is comfortable for most of us. This will be one of the first ways we begin the new millennium of magic."

"Humph," grumbled Professor Essen. "Ancient was always the language of Mystic."

Klaris did not respond to this comment and continued: "With my friend Halla Felstar, I have reviewed the councils and educational programs of Mystic and Dragon. While we respect these systems, we now have a different reality, and we are here to discuss a different approach."

She paused, letting Halla take the lead. "For starters, we have learned that Jezel is not habitable. Neither Dragonsholm nor Tropix survived the dragons. The remaining Jezellians have been invited to live on Farsouth."

Klaris leaned forward. "We regret the tremendous loss of Dragon magicians, which followed the loss of many Mystics when Castle Caledra fell to the earthquake last year."

She paused and thought again about the steps involved in taking an idea and making it reality. "The choices we make here will color how the Knownlands manages magic for the next millennium. I invite you to share with this circle your needs and the needs of the Mystic as you it see it, so we can develop a new plan for fulfilling all of our obligations."

Yuan Chen reached forward, his arms outstretched to the baby. "May I hold her?"

Professor Essen watched the child gurgle and smile. "I can't think any Weaver who had a such a young child," he said. "But some were parents. Many Weavers in the past spent winters in their home countries. The long winters here at Caledra are not to everyone's liking."

"Crossing the Barling Narrows to get here is not to my liking," said the Dock and Portal tutor, a woman from Ily. "Since the two magics are now one, there will be a lot more people at the acolyte and novice levels. Perhaps we could establish schools for them around the Knownlands, reserving Caledra for the Corridor Cadets and Tower Tested."

"The nyad magi have offered to host a learning center in the Verwood," Halla said. "Anyone would be welcome to study there."

Rhella was nodding. "Yuan and I have been discussing the idea of sharing the job of Tower Tutor, with just one of us here at a time."

"I volunteer to take the spring and summer sessions," Yuan said, smiling.

Baby Marith began to fuss and he handed her to Klaris, who gently rocked in her chair as the discussion continued, and the baby fell asleep.

Epilogue

Eight Years Later

"Sweet goddess, Corvyd, can't you just settle down and enjoy your life and privileges?" Lady Lannez snapped.

"I enjoy and appreciate them every day."

"I fail to see how establishing a council of merchants is enjoyable."

Corvyd took a steadying breath and remembered how he had once shared these prejudices. "Security is enjoyable, is it not? Our system, our governance will be more secure if the merchants have a voice."

"I don't care about their voice."

"You should," the baroness stated. She sat with her grandmotherly bulk comfortably settled in a soft chair by the window. Her eyes had been gazing out at the parkland, but her focus had been on the argument between her children.

Now finally, she turned her head to address her heir. "The world has changed, Lannez. The two magics are now one; the one deity is now two. If we don't adapt to these changes, we'll be obsolete."

Outside a group of children cantered down the parkland. One girl, riding more adroitly, led the others on a new smooth-gaited horse.

Lannez saw her daughter moving gracefully with her mount. "Couldn't you just have brought horses back from your visit to Kordon?" she grumbled at Corvyd. "Let's leave representative government to those beastly trolls."

"It's not representative government," Corvyd said gently, knowing he'd won. "And it's not coming from the trolls. Kordon and the Islish nations have all started increasing opportunities for the people to communicate with their lords and ladies."

"Communicate what?"

"Whatever they need to."

"Mam!" Doc rushed down the path and embraced his mother, who had appeared in the yard before the barrow with the royal group from Baria. "Mam." He squeezed her and she relaxed into his dear embrace.

Doc noted the impatience in the children, but first hugged Jax and then Klaris, before lifting eight-year-old Marith and swinging her in a wide circle. "Welcome to Hilsen Vale, your Majesty." She giggled with delight.

"Me too!"

"Me too!"

The twins, Rix and Flinys, were both missing their two front teeth. Doc lifted Rix and twirled him. "You want to fly, Prince Rix?"

"Higher!"

"My turn! My turn!" Flinys was risking her remaining teeth to get closer to Doc, despite her brother's flailing legs.

Adgar came down off the porch and hoisted Flinys so that both children flew in circles. Marith wanted her son again. "Doc, Adgar, put the twins down. Aren't there chicks at this time of year?"

"There are!" Doc smiled and moved to embrace his mother again.

"Yes!" Young Marith was off running, the twins close behind. Old Marith widened her hug to include Adgar.

"Hello, Weaver!" a voice neither old nor young, neither male nor female, wafted up the road. A small, gray-robed figure was skipping towards them through the midsummer sunshine, followed more sedately by Borrel, Lexyl, and a young troll, also in priestly gray.

"Hello, Oracle." Klaris and the others bowed. "You are full of potential today."

"Today, yes. For tomorrow."

The Weaver and her family had come to the Vale not just to visit their beloved friends, but for the Oracle's Ninething, which fell on the Summer Solstice this year.

Hilsen Vale was decorated with colorful streamers. Musicians played, jugglers danced, everyone ate and drank. Finally, as the sun dipped toward Daylor Peak, the people took small boats to the island in the lake and gathered in the stone circle.

The Oracle knelt in front of Sven Narbonne, high priest to this Oracle and the previous one. Standing next to Borrel, Lexyl heard the words of invocation, but her thoughts were focused on her memories. Only she thought of Tristan by their given name anymore. Only she, it seemed, felt the weight of that name.

She'd watched them grow, watched priests and priestesses come to them from across the Knownlands. Many had come to the Vale from the old Oracle's temple on Baria. Only young Gilbrick Vloggan was Vale-born.

It should have been eerie to see a child with tousled hair address adults with such clarity, but it wasn't. They ran and played with dogs, fairies, or other children, who never seemed worried by the opalescent eyes or the uncanny ability to speak to one's thoughts before one had heard them oneself. It was never scary; just heartbreaking.

The high priest drizzled some holy oil on to Tristan's head. The child grew very still; Klaris gasped and fell to her knees. Borrel, Jax, Flinys, and others who shared the new Mystic held each other. Lexyl, too, felt the Mystic bend and bow.

Jax took the golden chain from around his neck. He looked down at the gleaming medallion remembering a different Oracle. He thought of his dead brother and how Klaris had sat in a marooned boat without magic and translated the runes. He remembered the pull of chains as he'd waited in the now-ruined prison at Castle Kree where King Kodill had taken up the medallion and finally trusted him.

Jax stepped forward and handed the golden medallion to the child. "This is yours, Oracle. For another Paradox in another time."

A huge grin spread across the child's face as peace radiated through the crowd and spread out across the Knownlands. "We will remember," they said.

People around solstice fires broke into joyful song, and the fairy queen in the midst of an ecstatic ceremony trembled with a deeper release as the Oracle finally came into their own power, their own undeniable connection to the Holy Mother.

"By the cat god!" Lexyl shouted, her heart breaking. "Don't take them away from me!"

"We are always with you," the Oracle answered, but it was a voice Lexyl did not recognize.

"You are not my baby."

"Always."

The crowd left the henge, ferried on small boats, to dance around the Vale's bonfires. Children chased each other dangerously with burning branches; adults drank Aric's special golden solstice ale and moved with the insistent drums. The Oracle climbed to the standing stone that had been Lad Yob. Perched there, they felt held in a great love. They watched the alpenglow on the highest peaks and let the power of solstice fires and rites across the Knownlands flow through their multifaceted soul.

Embraced by Borrel, Lexyl sobbed in the shadows.

Late the next morning, Lexyl found Jax extracting a hypothermic Flinys from the icy waters of Daylor's Lake, where the girl had gone for a swim. The Eldar didn't understand the Islish they spoke, but the gist of the conversation was quite clear.

"I am not c-c-cold!" Flinys shuddered through blue lips. "And did you see the little beasties at the bottom, Daddy?" She held out her hand to show an orange salamander and some soft mud that she'd dredged from the bottom of the lake.

"Put it back, Flinys. It can't live out here."

"It's my pet."

"You will kill it. Put it back."

"I don't want to kill it. I'll keep it safe! I'll keep it in my bed!"

"Flinys."

The girl heard the command. She frowned at her father, placed a large kiss on the wriggling creature, getting mud all over her face, and then let the salamander go back into the clear water.

"Good. Now go back to Doc's burrow and get yourself warmed up."

She trudged off sulkily. Jax watched her go.

"Parenting is a challenge," Lexyl said dryly.

Jax bent to rinse the mud off his own hands. He watched the salamander calmly move into the deeper water as if unaware of its narrow escape. "It's an exercise in paradox."

Lexyl almost grinned. "Thank you for not spouting the usual bit about children being a blessing."

They walked in silence back to the druids' burrow, under the pines pungent in the warm summer sun. Young Rix was mitigating an argument that had developed between his sisters, one of them still wet and shivering, over some accommodation for the chicks.

Jax noted once again his son's growing ability to soothe feathers of many sorts. He lifted Jelly off one of the porch chairs and sat down, resettling the cat on his lap. Lexyl sat next to him. Jelly purred loudly.

Lexyl was notably not purring. Jax tried some soothing of his own. "Have you been back to Arandy?"

"No."

"I'm not much for the desert, you know," he said. "But I love the spicy food."

"Corn cakes and salsa!" Lexyl smiled. "Cactus nectar, oh and keffa! There's nothing but tea here, and that thick black beer they drink."

"The Vale Ale is an acquired taste."

"I haven't acquired it."

In the silence between them, they heard Jax's children laughing together over the baby chicks. Lexyl turned her eyes away. "I feel like a traitor to Tristan to say it, but I want a normal baby."

"What's normal?" Jax stretched his legs into the sun. "You're not, and your children aren't likely to be either."

"Speak for yourself."

"Speaker," Jelly agreed quite clearly, her golden eyes on Lexyl. "Speaker for All Eldars."

Three Years More

"I heard from Lexyl this morning," Klaris told Jax as they strolled through the gardens at Twistford. "She and Borrel now have a daughter."

Jax squeezed Klaris's hand. "Good. What did they name her?"

"Patience."

"Patience? That's an interesting name for the Speaker's heir." They walked in silence for a few more moments, until Jax continued softly, "At least she has an heir."

Klaris did not answer him. Like everyone else in Kordon, they were aware that Crown Princess Tallyn remained childless. Jax had spoken at length with Tallyn about this. He knew she was happy to exercise her life without the encumbrance of parenthood, but she still had a responsibility to secure the secession of the Kordish throne. Tallyn was thoughtful and long-sighted, but even she was running out of patience.

A summer later, Lord Admiral Jax Sharkin stood at the big stern windows of his flag ship. The Barian Fleet sailed calm summer seas south of Sageham, preparing for the yacht races later that afternoon. Both of his daughters would be outfitting their boats and crews, but his money was on the younger. Marith was adept, but she was not the gifted sailor Flinys was.

Now, however, he was thinking of Kordon. He remembered how he had struggled to measure up as a young would-be knight; how it had felt to be thrown from a horse, or patronized by a younger, right-handed noble child. He smiled at the view. There was some tragedy in what he was about to do today, but it wasn't his tragedy.

He turned back to face ten-year-old Rix, who stood impatiently waiting.

"You're enjoying fostering in Kree?" Jax asked the boy in Landish.

"Yep."

Jax didn't smile at the fluent slang, but it comforted him a bit. Klaris, Tallyn, Seaqueen Marith, and the great nobles of both Baria and Kordon had been apprised of this plan, but today he would finally inform his son.

"Rix, you are old enough to understand some things about your future." He paused and considered Rix's sun-streaked brown curls and dark skin. Despite the pale color of his islish eyes, he didn't look Kordish at all, but the sigil of his birthright had included so many lines of power that no one dared to challenge his rights. Jax had watched the easy way he rode both horses and the politics of fostering with deceptive nonchalance.

"When I sign these papers here, I will make you my heir to Darkwood. You'll assume the title of Viscount Norbay immediately, and you'll be the earl when I'm gone."

"Oh." The boy blinked, not liking to think of his dad being gone, but then he smiled. "If I'm the viscount, can I be excused from music lessons?"

"No. There's more. I'm removing you from the Barian succession."

"But that's Marith's anyway."

"Yes. And Flinys will be the lady admiral."

"She'll be good at it."

"Yes."

"Alright."

Jax dipped a quill in the pot of Barian Blue ink, but paused, his pen poised. He considered the lad standing before him. He seemed unconcerned that he would no longer be second in line for the Helm of Baria. Would a ten-year-old understand all the ramifications this change could mean? Did the boy conceive where his blood might yet lead?

A familiar smile opened on the boy's face. It was a crafty, slightly feral smile. "Sign it, Dad. The races are about to start."

Yes. The pen scratched across the paper. Yes, he understood.

Two More Years Later

Mother Marith watched the knighthood trials with increasing discomfort. The Kordish summer was just too hot, despite the canopy and expensive imported ice in a variety of festive drinks. The fifteen-year-old seaqueen performed the required horseback acrobatics along with the rest of her foster class to the general applause of the Kordish nobility. Her younger brother Rix, however, was the star of the event, riding better than the children three and four years his senior. Flinys barely kept her seat.

When the trials were over, the party moved to the gardens. With relief, the old druid found a shaded bench, well away from the musicians and the dancing. She relished the calm rustle of the breeze in the leaves and gurgle of the stream.

A cat leapt onto the bench and pushed against her wrinkled hand until Marith picked it up and settled it onto her lap.

"I miss old Jelly," Marith said. "Though she's long gone."

The cat purred.

"No human words for us?" Marith asked a little wistfully.

The cat collected itself into a comfortable ball. The old druid opened herself to the cat's contentment and realized she didn't need words to understand.

Even after living mostly among islish people for the last fifteen years, Marith struggled to understand the Islish voices intruding into her peace.

"The Weaver says I can go to the Acolyte Academy when I can levitate."

"I'm not letting you experiment on me anymore, Vigo."

Marith recognized Rix's voice as he came into view, walking with a nearly grown man. The young Viscount of Norbay saw her sitting on the bench and ran to embrace her. "Hello, Mam," he said in aristocratic, Kordish Landish. He nestled himself under her arm, waking the cat. "You remember Vigo Axian? He studies Mystic with Flinys and Wexalay."

Marith smiled at the other boy. "And how is your Landish coming along, Vigo?"

"That I must practice also, the Weaver says."

"Perhaps Prince Rix will let you practice languages with him, if not levitation."

"Maybe," Rix said in a stiff and stilted voice. "You know how it injures us Kordish to hear the king's Landish mispronounced."

Marith noted the impudent gleam in the pale blue eyes and tickled his ribs.

"No!" He giggled. "Mercy!" Horns blared across the park.

"What is happening?" Vigo asked in careful Landish.

"Cake!" Rix leapt away from the bench and dashed across the broad lawns. Vigo maintained his mature dignity just long enough to bow to the old druid before following.

Marith watched them go, thinking it was time for her return to the Vale for the last time. Doc had written that another of her old friends had died. It was time for her to sit on the Vale's Crone Council, which was the true power in the little community, despite what the magistrate said. She longed to hear Landish spoken by Hantish voices, and smell lilacs and pine, and taste Vale Ale.

The cat closed its eyes, and Marith distinctly understood its purr to mean *home.*

Jax was bent double with laughter and Tallyn wiped tears from her eyes, as Klaris dryly related the ongoing challenges of melding magical academic systems. Kodill saw them laughing and smiled. He turned to put his arm around his mother, who was watching the Viscount Prince Rix run across the grass.

"The council will ratify his status as heir tomorrow," Kodill said, a smile in his voice.

Hunched with age and bitterness, the dowager sneered. "The council might not."

"Tallyn already has all the votes she needs, and his performance in today's trials will make the choice obvious and easy." The king took his mother's withered arm and turned her back to the light of the party. "He's Valla's grandson. I like to think of her living through him."

"I'm damned if I'll ever see the spawn of Rax Sharkin sitting on the throne of Kordon," the dowager announced from her personal darkness.

The king patted her arm. "You probably won't," he said mildly. "You'll probably be long gone to the Isle of the Apples. As I will be." He felt oddly relieved. "Think of that, mother. You and I, staunch landish folks, at rest on an island while an islish person sits on the landish Kordish Throne."

"What a mess." The dowager said.

The king laughed. "What a paradox."

THE END

June 28, 2025

Character Names, Titles: Relationships

Allynor of Caer Keff, Duchess of Keffex

Alpeth: Florin and Borrel's aunt

Ansyn Bil, Queen of Kordon: wife of King Kodill

Al-Sefir Hewish, Priest to Vitrus

Aric: inn keeper in Hilsen Vale

Aychex: Duke Frinz Ellswyth

Blanx, Captain of the *Sharkin*

Bolo Powluna, Jax's steward in Baria

Borrel Starrish: Mystic, Florin's twin

Boss Taint: Director Hanter Iron Mines

Bryx Jorvan Sharkin, Sealord: Jax's older brother

Carden Yemmel, Lord of Traik: betrothed to Tallyn of Kordon

Carte Serge, Royal Mystic: Kordon

Cheshir Griffyn, Lady of Deepford: foster sister to Tallyn, Jax and Foby

Chevvain: Duchess Patrice Gracevine

Clairo: Duke Von Houghlow

Corvyd Cale, Lord of Cale: slave from Ily

Dayne Kora, heir to Rippsmarch: siblings - Koby and Thesally

"Doc", Mrac Appendel: child of Marith/spouse to Adgar

Dowager Stylla, Dowager Queen, Grandmother of Jax

Dury Axian: Troublemaker

Dylith: friend in Hilsen Vale

Earla Stona Swansee, Earla Tarron March

Eleeza St. Clare, Eldar Chieftess: Lexy's sister

Elmore Aethelyn, Earl of Vobury

Esmee Choles, Lady of Callisto

Essa of Farsouth, dec Queen of Farsouth: Klaris's grandmother

Estyl Pexborn, Duchess of Midipex: Spouse of Thorag Addle

Fairy Queen: rules the Fae

Father Mallix, Priest to Sageham

Fellix of Port Jorel, Barian Consort: Spouse of Seaqueen Pyrriv

Florin Starrish: Borrel's twin

Foby Kora, Lord of Rippsfell: Jax's foster brother

Frinz Ellswyth, Duke of Aychex: fostered with Dayne and Bryx

Gilbrick Vloggan: child of Magistrate Vloggan

Grisham: Ambassador of Baria

Grobber Vloggan, Magistrate Hilsen Vale

Halla Felstar, Red Dragon: Partner of Highlord Raggar

Hix Sharkin, Lord Admiral: second cousin to Sealord Rax

Janil Embay, Lord Admiral: Lord of Phlyx

Jax: see Javix Sharkin, below

Jeress of Farsouth, Queen of Farsouth

Jolira: slave from Ohe

Juna, Oracular Priestess

Karric: Captain of King's Guard/Tutor

Keffex: Duke Kevlor Brondon

Kevlor Brondon, Duke of Keffex: cousin to King Kodill

King Kodill, Kodill Brondon: see Kodill Brondon

Klaris de Farsouth, Princess of Farsouth: Weaver

Kodill Brondon, King of Kordon: Jax's uncle (mother's brother)

Koralixa Windish, Lady of Jeff

Lad Yob: Saghamite servant to Klaris

Lady Mollish, Priestess to Kree: druid

Lexyl St. Clare, Speaker's Heir: Mystic, sister to Eleeza St. Clare

Lord of Traik: see Carden Yemmel

Logil Lowax: Friend of Dury Axian

Marith Appendel, druid in Hilsen Vale: Doc's mother

Master Illat, Captain of the Flagship *Drixa*

Midipex: Duke Thorag Addle

Mother Ayslic, Priestess to Baria

Neben de Rillt, Lord of Rillt: Spouse to Shallyx of Callysto

Oblek, overmaster

Oklan Kora, Earl of Rippsmarch: kids: Dayne, Foby, Thessaly

Oracle, Speaks for the Goddess

Patrice Gracevine, Duchess of Chevvain

Prina: Eleeza's wife

Professor Essen, Bricks and Mortar Tutor

Professor Hiddicot, Dock & Portal Tutor

Professor Lellyn, Tower Tutor

Pyrriv Shakin, Seaqueen: Mother of Sealord Rax

Raef Raegis: Searan Royal Dragon Magic

Raggar, Dragon Highlord

Raisha Allanaugh: Kordish courtier

Rax Sharkin VII, Sealord of Baria: Bryx and Jax's father

Rippsmarch: Earl Oklan Kora

Rhella: Tower-Tested Mystic

Ryxa, First Lieutenant on *Drixa*

Shallix of Callisto: preeminent Barian sailor

Shaloh: Foby Kora's favorite dog

Shaman Ashande, Shaman in Arandy

Slave Wrangler: Hanter Iron Mines

Stona Swansea, Earla Tarron March

Stylla Aethelyn, Dowager Queen: grandmother to Jax, Tallyn and Bryx

Tallyn Brondon, Crown Princess: Jax's cousin and foster sibling

Thessaly Kora: Foby's younger sister, druid

Thorag Addle, Duke of Midipex: Chancellor of Kordon

Thyl Axian: wife of Dury

Trajan, Consort of Farsouth: husband of Queen Jeress

Valla Brondon, dec., Consort of Baria: child of Stylla; mother of Jax

Vigo Axian: child of Thyl and Dury Axian

Vobury: Earl Elmore Aethelyn

Von Houghlow, Duke of Clairo

Widow Keffex: Allynor of Caer Keff

Yan Chuan: Tower-Tested Mystic

Expanded biographical information:

Javix Brondon Fellix Sharkin: Prince of Baria, Prince of Kordon, Viscount Norbay. Nephew of King Kodill of Kordon; Son of Sealord Rax Sharkin & Valla Brondon of Kordon; foster siblings, Koby Fora of Rippsfell, Cheshire Griffyn of Deepford & Tallyn Bondon of Kordon. He dislikes the name Javix, especially because it's usually mispronounced in Landish.

Titles and Names:

Thorag Addle, Duke of Midipex, Lord Chancellor:

> Referred to as the Duke of Midipex, Lord Thorag, or simply by his territorial name: Midipex.

> He would be addressed formally as: Lord Thorag, Duke Thorag, or Your Grace

> Less Formal: my lord. His peers might call him Thorag, as could his wife, but she doesn't (this is explained in book two)

Crown Princess Tallyn Brondon:

> Referred to as Princess Tallyn

> Addressed formally as your royal highness (because she's heir to the throne), then Ma'am or my lady.

Prince Javix Sharkin

> Referred to as Prince Javix or Prince Jax

> Addressed formally as your highness, my lord, or sir.

> Might be referred to as Norbay (his territorial name) but since it's less important than being a Prince of the Blood, he'd more likely be called prince.

Kordish Royal Council:
> King Kodill
> Dowager Stylla (non voting)
> Crown Princess Tallyn
> Lord Chancellor, Duke of Midipex, Thorag Addle
> Duke of Keffex, Kevlor Brondon
> Duchess of Chevvain, Patrice Gracevine
> Duke of Aychex, Allister Ellswyth
> Duke of Clairo, Von Houghlow
> Earl of Vobury, Elmore Aethelyn
> Earla of Tarron March, Stona Sweansea
> Earla of Rippsmarch, Oklan Kora

Floating Islands:
> Helm, Bryx Sharkin
> Jeff: Koralixa Windish
> Rillt: Neben de Rillt
> Callisto: Esmee Choles
> Phlyx: Janil Embay
> Ayx: Villar d'Ayx

Mystic Studies at Caledra:
> Dock and Portal Acolytes, Professor Hiddicot
> Bricks and Mortar Novices, Professor Essen
> Foundation Firsts, Professor Visidor
> Corridor Cadets, Professor Ancellin
> Tower Tested, Professor Lellyn

Acknowledgements

I'm grateful to the many friends and family who have read this story, sometimes more than once, and made it so much better: Cathy Calhoun Damon, Warren Fox, Robbie Fox, Norma Staley, Kristen Gould Case, Mark Menlove, Andy Cier, Joe Totten, Lisa Cilva Ward, Karri Dell Hayes, Asha Rehnberg, Evan Gregory, Gloria Rice, Ellen Sherk, Alix Railton, Willoughby Staley and David Staley. I am deeply indebted to my cousin Valerie for introducing me to Starhawk and non-patriarchal religion. Starhawk continues to work in this space and can be found on Instagram. Adrian Fox Staley manages my online presence at Paradox Trilogy. Check it out for information on the backstory. I wouldn't be able to share the story without the amazing support and talent of Katie Mullaly at Surrogate Press and Michelle Rayner of Cosmic Design. Any errors in the text are entirely my own.

About the Author

C.A. Fox has taught skiing, sold books, encouraged critical thinking among college students, and raised two free thinking kids, not always with appreciation for their independent thoughts. Home is a place that requires high-elevation modifications for baking and the expectation that it may snow on any day of the year. Like the fictional poet, Featherfetch, Fox casts nets of words to catch the downy bits out of the wind. Visit *CAFoxBooks.com* for more information and follow on Facebook, *@Paradox Trilogy*.

www.ingramcontent.com/pod-product-compliance
Lightning Source LLC
Chambersburg PA
CBHW070201310726
48976CB00001B/169